# Count Brass

## By the same author

### The Tale of the Eternal Champion
*New Omnibus Editions, revised and with new introductions by the author.*

1 Von Bek
2 The Eternal Champion
3 Hawkmoon
4 Corum
5 Sailing to Utopia
6 A Nomad of the Time Streams
7 The Dancers at the End of Time
8 Elric of Melnibone
9 The New Nature of the Catastrophe
10 The Prince with the Silver Hand
11 Legends from the End of Time
12 Stormbringer
13 Earl Aubec
14 Count Brass

Also: A Warrior of Mars

*Science Fiction*

The Sundered Worlds
The Shores of Death
The Winds of Limbo
The Wrecks of Time

*Omnibuses*

A Cornelius Quartet
A Cornelius Calendar
Three Love Stories
*(Behold the Man,
Breakfast in the Ruins,
Constant Fire)* *
Comic Capers
*(The Jerry Cornell
Stories,* w. Jack
Trevor Story) *

*Colonel Pyat*

Byzantium Endures
The Laughter of Carthage
Jerusalem Commands
The Vengeance of Rome †

*Other novels*

Gloriana; or, The Unfulfill'd Queen
The Brothel in Rosenstrasse
Mother London

*Short stories and graphic novels*
Casablanca
Sojan (juvenile)
My Experiences in the Third World War
Lunching with the Antichrist*
The Swords of Heaven, The Flowers of
    Hell (with Howard Chaykin)
The Crystal and the Amulet
    (with James Cawthorn)
etc.

*Non-fiction*

The Retreat from Liberty
Letters from Hollywood
    (illus. M. Foreman)
Wizardry and Wild Romance
Death is No Obstacle
    (with Colin Greenland)

*Editor*

*New Worlds*
The Traps of Time
The Best of *New Worlds*
Best SF Stories from *New Worlds*
*New Worlds*: An Anthology
Before Armageddon
England Invaded
The Inner Landscape

*Records*

With *The Deep Fix*:
The New Worlds Fair
Dodgem Dude
The Brothel in Rosenstrasse etc.

With *Hawkwind*:
Warriors at the Edge of Time
Choose Your Masques
Zones
Sonic Attack etc.
Also work with *Blue Oyster Cult*,
    Robert Calvert etc.

For further information about Michael
Moorcock and his work please send SAE
to Nomads of the Time Streams,
18 Laurel Bank, Truss Hill Road,
South Ascot, Berks, UK. or PO Box
451048, Atlanta, Georgia, 30345–1048,
USA.

* In preparation (Orion Books)   † In preparation (Cape)

# Michael Moorcock

---

# COUNT BRASS

---

MILLENNIUM
AN ORION BOOK
LONDON

*Count Brass* © Michael Moorcock 1973
*The Champion of Garathorn* © Michael Moorcock 1973
*The Quest for Tanelorn* © Michael Moorcock 1975

This collected edition © Michael Moorcock 1993

Map by Jim Cawthorn

This edition first published
in Great Britain in 1993 by
Millennium
An imprint of Orion Books Ltd
Orion House, 5 Upper St Martin's Lane
London WC2H 9EA

A CIP catalogue record for this book is available
from the British Library

ISBN:(Csd) 1 85798 049 2
(Ppr) 1 85798 050 6

Millennium
Book Thirty One

Printed and bound in Great Britain by Clays Ltd, St Ives plc

Dear Reader,

Here we are at an ending to the Tale of the Eternal Champion. It isn't the first ending and it probably won't be the last but it is probably the nearest we shall ever come to resolution.

I wrote this sequence fairly rapidly under difficult circumstances with mounting debts and publishers who were willing to give me anything but money. I was feeling rather self-pitying. Reflecting how profligacy, recognized by saner ages as a social virtue, no longer received its proper respect, I dedicated the first part to Harrods of Knightsbridge and to William Butler, my friend and publisher.

Bill Butler was the proprietor of Unicorn Books, first of Brighton and later of Wales. A poet and writer, Bill found himself in trouble with the authorities when he published a famous story by J. G. Ballard about Ronald Reagan. This was years before Reagan had managed to do to the entire country what at that time he was only doing to California and is another example of the oracular power of the very writers who, ironically, had turned their backs on the predictive aspects of science fiction.

At his trial, Butler was supported by various people anxious to establish a genuinely free press in the UK. He won his case and it seemed another blow had been struck against the nonsense of the Obscene Publications Act, which fails to control what it is supposed to control and prosecutes those who were never meant to be its targets. Butler was not the only publisher whose literary work was seized and prosecuted under the OPA and similar cases continue to this day, with enormous amounts of time and public money spent in pursuit of 'crimes' which in most other Western democracies do not exist!

Bill had just completed his *Myth of the Hero* and was so exhausted he could not sleep. He took a barbiturate and washed it down with half a can of lager. A few hours later he was dead. His new book of poetry was due to be published by another friend of mine, Michael Dempsey. Dempsey died as a result of a freak accident and Bill's work became an archive. The 1960s and 70s were terrible years for losing friends, many of them through drug-related accidents and overdoses, but they were characteristically years of optimism and a willingness to take risks, to try new ideas – a spirit which was successfully quashed through the course of the Thatcher Age when our best resources, human and otherwise, were either sold off or ignored so that an illusion of wealth, based on short-term profits, could be created. Not so much a financial policy as a nursery fantasy.

Bill Butler died just before the beginning of the Thatcher years. I don't think he would have enjoyed them much. He was homosexual, associated with the alternative press and with the typical lifestyle of those days. He was familiar with most of the techniques used by repressive and prejudiced authority to keep people silent and without a franchise. He believed that you should judge society by the way it treats its weaker elements and he came to England from America in the early 60s because he thought the United Kingdom was a more tolerant and just society than his own. Gradually he discovered that the individual frequently has fewer rights and less power here and that what they think they have can sometimes easily be taken away.

It seems to me that since this sequence started to appear in 1973 we have witnessed an extraordinary erosion of liberty and hope in Britain. We have a generation that grew up knowing nothing better of government than the cheerless greed and jolly bullying of not very bright people terminally addicted to power. This was the atmosphere in the Russian empire twenty years ago.

I am not so pessimistic to believe that Granbretan is actually being conjured into existence but many old sf writers have the uneasy feeling today that when they thought they were exaggerating they were actually being too cautious. I really do believe that if we don't want a Dark Empire we have to be active in ensuring that our democracy is protected, which is why I support Charter 88 and continue to resist censorship. I also believe that investment in our best resource – our scientific and artistic genius – will produce genuine change for the better. It was that, after all, which gave us our industrial wealth in the first place.

The climate of the last decade and a half has made it harder for new writers to find a public. Ambitious writers of fantasy, for instance, have suffered from the creation of monolithic entertainment corporations whose logic, while frighteningly simplistic and ultimately doomed to failure, loves only common denominators. As we have seen in the popular music industry, originality is actively suppressed because it is not predictable and something which is not predictable can't be a safe element in a financial projection. Companies which accept the need for R&D in electronics set up no equivalents when they develop a publishing arm. There is a desperate need in modern society for new ethics, a new understanding of what self-interest and survival really are in a world which becomes increasingly centralized, inextricably multinational and, ironically, hugely dependent on its creative elements. Our democratic political systems have to grow increasingly flexible and responsive if they are to survive.

Bill Butler's death was to a degree symptomatic of what went wrong with the idealism of the 60s. People somehow thought that if everyone *felt* good then everything would get good. There was an assumption that we were all going to live forever – the flower children would smile and the miners would be perpetually employed. There were some dodgy bits of logic in all this and Wells's Eloi and Morlocks spring immediately to mind. What links the Golden Sixties to the Thatcher years is that both were to a large extent founded on illusions, a simple-minded notion that if you made things look right then they would therefore *be* right. It could be that illusion or style is an important element in modern society especially as the illusions get more and more realistic and the realities become increasingly illusory, but if that is the case we still need to develop ethical systems which take account of it.

This particular sequence has something to do with memory and our perceptions of reality but it was primarily planned to entertain and requires no interpretation. There are many sophisticated writers who are these days exploring the moral interface between reality and illusion – Storm Constantine, Mary Gentle, M. John Harrison, Jonathan Carroll, Robert Holdstock – and those who are currently publishing in NEW WORLDS. It is such writers, especially the new ones, that I would like to salute in this final sequence – all those of you who are discovering and creating new territory and carrying your own bold, distinctive banners into the very heart of Chaos!

Yours,
*Michael Moorcock*

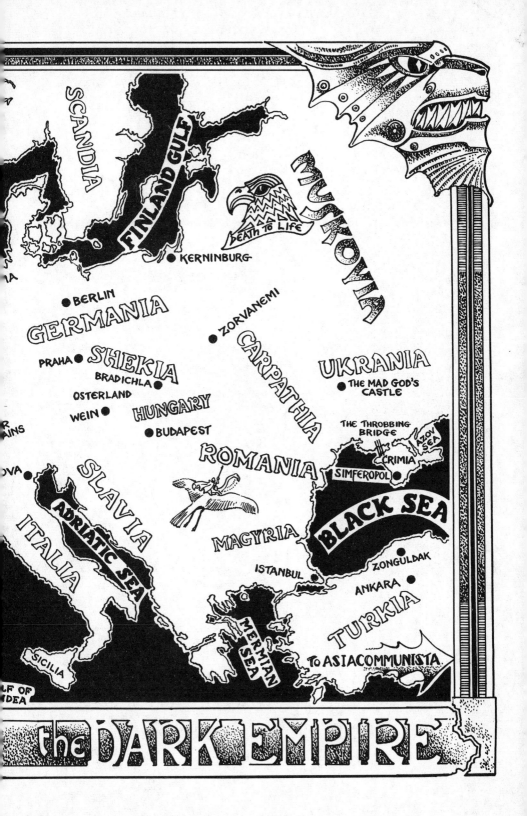

SCANDIA

FINLAND GULF

MUSKOVA

DEATH TO LIFE

KERNINBURG

BERLIN

GERMANIA

ZORVANEMI

CARPATHIA

UKRANIA

THE MAD GOD'S
CASTLE

PRAHA  SHEKIA
BRADICHLA

OSTERLAND

WEIN  HUNGARY

BUDAPEST

THE THROBBING
BRIDGE

AZOV
SEA

CRIMIA

ROMANIA

SIMFEROPOL

SLAVIA

ADRIATIC SEA

ITALIA

BLACK SEA

MAGYRIA

ZONGULDAK

ISTANBUL

ANKARA

SICILIA

MERMIAN
SEA

TURKIA

TO ASIACOMMUNISTA

LF OF
DEA

the DARK EMPIRE

# COUNT BRASS

To all those Nomads, especially Ian, Dave, John and Maureen, and, of course, Shane, Paul, Ed and Moe – for all their good friendship, support and enthusiasm over the years

*Then the earth grew old, its landscapes mellowing and showing signs of age, its ways becoming whimsical and strange in the manner of a man in his last years.*

– The High History of the Runestaff

*And when this History was done there followed it another. A romance involving the same participants in experiences perhaps even more bizarre and awesome than the last. And again the ancient Castle of Brass in the marshy Kamarg was the centre for much of this action . . .*

– The Chronicles of Castle Brass

# BOOK ONE
# OLD FRIENDS

## CHAPTER ONE

## The Haunting of Dorian Hawkmoon

It had taken all these five years to restore the land of Kamarg, to repopulate its marshes with the giant scarlet flamingoes, the wild white bulls and the horned great horses which had once teemed here before the coming of the Dark Empire's bestial armies. It had taken all these five years to rebuild the watchtowers of the borders, to put up the towns and to erect tall Castle Brass in all its massive, masculine beauty. And, if anything, in these five years of peace, the walls were built stronger, the watchtowers taller, for, as Dorian Hawkmoon had said once to Queen Flana of Granbretan, the world was still wild and there was still little justice in it.

Dorian Hawkmoon, the Duke of Köln, and his bride, Yisselda, Countess of Brass, old, dead Count Brass's daughter, were the only two who remained of that group of heroes who had served the Runestaff against the Dark Empire and finally defeated Granbretan in the great Battle of Londra, putting Queen Flana, sad Queen Flana, upon the throne so that she might guide her cruel and decadent nation towards humanity and vitality.

Count Brass had died slaying three barons (Adaz Promp, Mygel Holst and Saka Gerden) and in turn was slain by a Spearman of the Order of the Goat.

Oladahn of the Bulgar Mountains, beastman and loyal friend of Hawkmoon, had been hacked to pieces by the war axes of the Order of the Pig.

Bowgentle, the unwarlike, the philosophical, had been savaged and decapitated by Pigs, Goats and Hounds to the number of twelve.

Huillam D'Averc, mocker of everything, whose only faith had seemed to be in his own lack of good health, who had loved and been loved by Queen Flana, had died most ironically, riding to his love and being slain by one of her soldiers who thought D'Averc attacked her.

Four heroes died. Thousands of other heroes, unnamed in the histories, but brave, also died in the service of the Runestaff, in the destruction of the Dark Empire tyranny.

And a great villain died. Baron Meliadus of Kroiden, most ambitious, most ambivalent, most awful of all the aristocrats of

Granbretan, died upon the sword of Hawkmoon, died beneath the edge of the mystical Sword of the Dawn.

And the ruined world seemed free.

But that had been five years hence. Much had passed since then. Two children had been born to Hawkmoon and the Countess of Brass. They were called Manfred, who had red hair and his grandfather's voice and health and stood to be his grandfather's size and strength, and Yarmila, who had golden hair and her mother's gentle toughness of will, as well as her beauty. They were Brass stock, there was little in them of the Dukes of Köln, and perhaps that was why Dorian Hawkmoon loved his children so fiercely and so well.

And beyond the walls of Castle Brass stood four statues to the four dead heroes, to remind the inhabitants of the castle of what they had fought for and at what cost. And Dorian Hawkmoon would often take his children to those statues and tell them of the Dark Empire and its deeds. And they were pleased to listen. And Manfred assured his father that when he grew up his deeds would be as great as those of old Count Brass, whom he so resembled.

And Hawkmoon would say that he hoped they would have no need of heroes when Manfred was grown.

Then, seeing disappointment in his son's face, he would laugh and say there were many kinds of heroes and if Manfred had his grandfather's wisdom and diplomacy, his strong sense of justice, that would make him the best kind of hero – a justice-maker. And Manfred would only be somewhat consoled, for there is little that is romantic about a judge and much that is attractive to a four-year-old boy about a warrior.

And sometimes Hawkmoon and Yisselda would take their children riding through the wild marshlands of the Kamarg, beneath wide skies of pastel colours, of faded reds and yellows, where the reeds were brown and dark green and orange and, in the appropriate season, bent before the mistral. And they would see a herd of white bulls thunder by, or a herd of horned horses. And they might see a flock of huge scarlet flamingoes suddenly take to the air and drift on broad wings over the heads of the invading human beings, not knowing that it was Dorian Hawkmoon's responsibility, as it had been that of Count Brass, to protect the wildlife of the Kamarg and never to kill it, and only sometimes to tame it to provide riding beasts for land and sky. Originally this had been why the great watchtowers had been built and why the men who occupied those watchtowers were called Guardians. But now they guarded the human populace as well as the beasts, guarded them from any threat from beyond the Kamarg's borders (for no native-bred Kamargian would consider harming the animals which were found nowhere else in the world). The only beasts that were hunted (save for food) in the marshes were the baragoon, the marsh gibberers, the things which had once been men themselves before becoming the victims of sorcerous experiments conducted by an evil Lord Guardian who had been done away with by old Count Brass. But there were only one or two baragoons left in the Kamarg lands now for hunters had little difficulty identifying them – they were over eight feet tall, five feet broad, bile-coloured and they slithered on their bellies through the swamps, occasionally rising to rush upon whatever prey they could now find in the marshlands. None the less, on their rides, Yisselda and Dorian Hawkmoon would take care to avoid the places still thought to be inhabited by the baragoon.

Hawkmoon had come to love the Kamarg more than his own ancestral lands in far-off Germany, had even renounced his title to those lands now ruled well by an elected council as indeed were many of the European lands who had lost their hereditary rulers and chosen, since the defeat of the Dark Empire, to become republics.

Yet, for all that Hawkmoon was loved and respected by the people of the Kamarg, he was aware that he did not replace old Count Brass in their eyes. He could never do that. They sought Countess Yisselda's advice as often as they sought his and they looked with great favour on young Manfred, seeing him almost as a reincarnation of their old Lord Guardian.

Another man might have resented all this, but Hawkmoon, who had loved Count Brass as well as had they, accepted it with good grace. He had had enough of command, of heroics. He preferred to live the life of a simple country gentleman and wherever possible let the people have control of their own affairs. His ambitions were simple, too – to love his beautiful wife Yisselda and to ensure the happiness of his children. His days of history-making were over. All that he had left to remind him of his struggles against Granbretan was an oddly shaped scar in the centre of his forehead – where once had reposed the dreadful Black Jewel, the Braineater implanted there by Baron Kalan of Vitall when, years before, Hawkmoon had been recruited against his will to serve the Dark Empire against Count Brass. Now the jewel was gone and so was Baron Kalan, who had committed suicide after the Battle of Londra. A brilliant scientist, but perhaps the most warped of all the barons of Granbretan, Kalan had been unable to conceive of continuing to exist under the new and, in his view, soft order imposed by Queen Flana, who had succeeded the King Emperor Huon after Baron Meliadus had slain him in a desperate effort to make himself controller of Granbretan's policies.

Hawkmoon sometimes wondered what would have happened to Baron Kalan, or, for that matter, Taragorm, Master of the Palace of Time, who had perished when one of Kalan's fiendish weapons had exploded during the Battle of Londra, if they had lived on. Could they have been put into the service of Queen Flana and their talents used to rebuild the world they had helped destroy? Probably not, he thought. They were insane. Their characters had been wholly shaped by the perverted and insane philosophies which had led Granbretan to make war upon the world and come close to conquering it all.

After one of their marshland rides, the family would return to Aigues-Mortes, the walled and ancient town which was the principal city of the Kamarg, and to Castle Brass which stood on a hill in the very centre. Built of the same white stone as the majority of the town's houses, Castle Brass was a mixture of architectural styles which, somehow, did not seem to clash with each other. Over the centuries there had been additions and renovations; at the whim of different owners parts had been torn down and other parts built. Most of the windows were of intricately detailed stained glass, though the window frames themselves were as often round as they were square and as often square as they were oblong or oval. Turrets and towers sprang up from the main mass of stone in all kinds of surprising places; there were even one or two minarets in the manner of Arabian palaces. And Dorian Hawkmoon, following the fashion of his own German folk, had had many flagstaffs erected and upon these staffs floated beautiful coloured banners, including those of the Counts of Brass and the Dukes of Köln. Gargoyles festooned the gutters of the castle and many a gable was carved in stone in the likeness of a Kamargian beast – the bull, the flamingo, the horned horse and the marsh bear.

There was about Castle Brass, as there had been in the days of Count Brass himself, something at once impressive and comfortable. The castle had not been built to impress anyone with either the taste or the power of its inhabitants. It had hardly been built for strength (though it had already proven its strength) and aesthetic considerations, too, had not been made when rebuilding it. It had been built for comfort and this was a rare thing in a castle. It could be that it was the only castle in the world that had been built with such considerations in mind! Even the terraced gardens outside the castle walls had a homely appearance, growing vegetables and flowers of every sort, supplying not only the castle but much of the town with its basic requirements.

When they returned from their rides the family would sit down to a good, plain meal which would be shared with many of its retainers, then the children would be taken to bed by Yisselda and she would tell them a story. Sometimes the story would be an ancient one, from the time before the Tragic Millennium, sometimes it would be one she would make up herself and sometimes, at the insistence of Manfred and Yarmila, Dorian Hawkmoon would be called for and he would tell them of some of his adventures in distant lands when he served the Runestaff. He would tell them of how he had met little Oladahn, whose body and face had been covered in fine, reddish hair, and who had claimed to be the kin of Mountain Giants. He would tell them of Amarehk beyond the great sea to the north and the magical city of Dnark where he had first seen the Runestaff itself. Admittedly, Hawkmoon had to modify these tales, for the truth was darker and more terrible than most adult minds could conceive. He spoke most often of his dead friends and their noblest deeds, keeping alive the memories of Count Brass, Bowgentle, D'Averc and Oladahn. Already these deeds were legendary throughout Europe.

And when the stories were done, Yisselda and Dorian Hawkmoon would sit in deep armchairs on either side of the great fireplace over which hung Count Brass's armour of brass and his broadsword, and they would talk or they would read.

From time to time they would receive letters from Londra, from Queen Flana telling how her policies progressed. Londra, that insane roofed city, had been almost entirely dismantled and fine, open buildings put up instead on both sides of the River Tayme, which no longer ran blood red. The wearing of masks had been abolished and most of the people of Granbretan had, after a while, become used to revealing their naked faces, though some die-hards had had to receive mild punishment for their insistence on clinging to the old, mad ways of the Dark Empire. The Orders of the Beasts had also been outlawed and people had been encouraged to leave the darkness of their cities and return to the all but deserted and overgrown countryside of Granbretan, where vast forests of oak, elm or pine stretched for miles. For centuries Granbretan had lived on plunder and now she had to feed herself. Therefore, the soldiers who had belonged to the beast orders were put to farming, to clearing the forests, to raising herds and planting crops. Local councils were set up to represent the interests of the people. Queen Flana had called a parliament and this parliament now advised her and helped her rule justly. It was strange

9

how swiftly a warlike nation, a nation of military castes, had been encouraged to become a nation of farmers and foresters. The majority of the people of Granbretan had taken to their new lives with relief once it dawned on them that they were now free of the madness that had once infected the whole land – and sought, indeed, to infect the world.

And so the quiet days passed at Castle Brass.

And so they would have passed for always (until Manfred and Yarmila grew up and Hawkmoon and Yisselda became middle-aged and, eventually, old in their contentment, dying peacefully and cheerfully, knowing that the Kamarg was secure and that the days of the Dark Empire could never return) but for something strange that began to happen towards the close of the sixth summer since the Battle of Londra when, to his astonishment, Dorian Hawkmoon found that the people of Aigues-Mortes were beginning to offer him peculiar looks when he hailed them in the streets – some refusing to acknowledge him at all and others scowling and muttering and turning aside as he approached.

It was Dorian Hawkmoon's habit, as it had been Count Brass's, to attend the great celebrations marking the end of the summer's work. Then Aigues-Mortes would be decorated with flowers and banners and the citizens would put on their most elaborate finery, young white bulls would be allowed to charge at will through the streets and the guardians of the watchtowers would ride about in their polished armour and silk surcoats, their flame-lances on their hips. And there would be bull contests in the immeasurably ancient amphitheatre on the outskirts of the town. Here was where Count Brass had once saved the life of the great toreador Mahtan Just when he was being gored to death by a gigantic bull. Count Brass had leaped into the ring and wrestled the bull with his bare hands, bringing the beast to its knees and winning the acclaim of the crowd, for Count Brass had then been well into middle age.

But nowadays the festival was not a purely local affair. Ambassadors from all over Europe would come to honour the surviving hero and heroine of Londra and Queen Flana herself had visited Castle Brass on two previous occasions. This year, however, Queen Flana had been kept at home by affairs of state and one of her nobles attended in her name. Hawkmoon was pleased to note that Count Brass's dream of a unified Europe was beginning to become reality. The wars with Granbretan had helped break down the old boundaries and had brought the survivors together in a common cause. Europe still consisted of about a thousand small provinces, each independent of any other, but they worked in concert on many projects concerning the general good.

The ambassadors came from Scandia, from Muscovy, from Arabia, from the lands of the Greeks and the Bulgars, from Ukrainia, from Nürnberg and Catalania. They came in carriages, on horseback or in ornithopters whose design was borrowed from Granbretan. And they brought gifts and they brought speeches (some long and some short) and they spoke of Dorian Hawkmoon as if he were a demigod.

In past years their praise had found enthusiastic response in the people of the Kamarg. But for some reason this year their speeches did not get quite the same quality of applause as they once had. Few, however, noticed. Only Hawkmoon and Yisselda noticed and, without being resentful, they were deeply puzzled.

The most fulsome of all the speeches made in the ancient bullring of Aigues-Mortes came from Lonson, Prince of Shkarlan, cousin to Queen Flana, ambassador from Granbretan. Lonson was young and an enthusiastic supporter of the queen's policies. He had been barely seventeen when the Battle of Londra had robbed his nation of its evil power and thus he bore no great resentment of Dorian Hawkmoon von Köln – indeed, he saw Hawkmoon as a saviour, who had brought peace and sanity to his island kingdom. Prince Lonson's speech was rich with admiration for the new Lord Protector of the Kamarg. He recalled great deeds of battle, great achievements of will and self-discipline, great cunning in the arts of strategy and diplomacy by which, he said, future generations would remember Dorian Hawkmoon. Not only had Hawkmoon saved continental Europe – he had saved the Dark Empire from itself.

Seated in his traditional box with all his foreign guests about him, Dorian Hawkmoon listened to the speech with embarrassment and hoped it would soon end. He was dressed in ceremonial armour which was as ornate as it was uncomfortable and the back of his neck itched horribly. While Prince Lonson spoke it would not be polite to remove the helmet and scratch. He looked at the crowd seated on the granite benches of the amphitheatre and seated on the ground of the ring itself. Whereas most of the people were listening with approval to Prince Lonson's speech, others were muttering to each other, scowling. One old man, whom Hawkmoon recognized as an ex-guardian who had fought beside Count Brass in many of his battles, even spat into the dust of the arena when Prince Lonson spoke of Dorian Hawkmoon's unswerving loyalty to his comrades.

Yisselda also noticed this and she frowned, glancing at Hawkmoon to see if he had noticed. Their eyes met. Dorian Hawkmoon shrugged and gave her a little smile. She smiled back, but the frown did not altogether leave her brow.

And at last the speech was over and applauded and the people began to leave the arena so that the first of the bulls might be driven in and the first toreador attempt to remove the colourful ribbons which were tied to the beast's horns (for it was not the custom of the folk of the Kamarg to exhibit their courage by slaying animals – instead skill alone was pitted against the snorting savagery of the very fiercest bulls).

But when the crowd had departed there was one who remained. Now Hawkmoon recalled his name. It was Czernik, originally a Bulgar mercenary who had thrown in his lot with Count Brass and ridden with him through a dozen campaigns. Czernik's face was flushed, as if he had been drinking, and his stance was unsteady as he pointed a finger up at Hawkmoon's box and spat again.

'Loyalty!' the old man croaked. 'I know otherwise. I know who is Count Brass's murderer – who betrayed him to his enemies! Coward! Play-actor! False hero!'

Hawkmoon was stunned as he listened to Czernik rant. What could the old man mean?

Stewards ran into the ring to grasp Czernik's arms and attempt to hurry him off. But he struggled with them.

'Thus your master tries to silence the truth!' screamed Czernik. 'But it cannot be silenced! He has been accused by the only one whose word can be trusted!'

If it had only been Czernik who had shown such animosity, Hawkmoon would have dismissed his ravings as senile. But Czernik was not the only one. Czernik had expressed what Hawkmoon had seen on more than a score of faces that day – and on previous days.

'Let him be!' Hawkmoon called, standing up and leaning forward over the balustrade. 'Let him speak!'

For a moment the stewards were at a loss to know what to do. Then, reluctantly, they released the old man. Czernik stood there trembling, glaring into Hawkmoon's eyes.

'Now,' Hawkmoon called. 'Tell me of what you accuse me, Czernik. I will listen.'

The attention of the whole populace of Aigues-Mortes was upon Hawkmoon and Czernik now. There was a stillness, a silence in the air.

Yisselda tugged at her husband's surcoat. 'Do not listen to him, Dorian. He is drunk. He is mad.'

'Tell me!' Hawkmoon demanded.

Czernik scratched his head of grey, thinning hair. He stared around him at the crowd. He mumbled something.

'Speak more clearly!' Hawkmoon said. 'I am eager to hear, Czernik.'

'I called you murderer and murderer you be!' Czernik said.

'Who told you that I am a murderer?'

Again Czernik's mumble was inaudible.

'Who told you?'

'The one you murdered!' Czernik screamed. 'The one you betrayed.'

'A dead man? Whom did I betray?'

'The one we all love. The one I followed across a hundred provinces. The one who saved my life twice. The one to whom, living or dead, I would ever give my loyalty.'

Yisselda's whisper from behind Hawkmoon was incredulous. 'He can speak of none other but my father . . . '

'Do you mean Count Brass?' Hawkmoon called.

'Aye!' cried Czernik defiantly. 'Count Brass, who came to the Kamarg all those years ago and saved it from tyranny. Who fought the Dark Empire and saved the whole world! His deeds are well known. What was not known was that at Londra he was betrayed by one who not only coveted his daughter but coveted his castle, too. And killed him for them!'

'You lie,' said Hawkmoon evenly. 'If you were younger, Czernik, I would challenge you to defend your foul words with a sword. How could you believe such lies?'

'Many believe them!' Czernik gestured to indicate the crowd. 'Many here have heard what I have heard.'

'*Where* have you heard this?' Yisselda joined her husband at the balustrade.

'In the marshlands beyond the town. At night. Some, like me, journeying home from another town – they have heard it.'

'And from whose lying lips?' Hawkmoon was trembling with anger. He and Count Brass had fought side by side, each had been prepared to die for the other – and now this dreadful lie was being told – a lie which insulted Count Brass's memory. And that was why Hawkmoon was angry.

'From his own! From Count Brass's lips.'

'Drunken fool! Count Brass is dead. You said as much yourself.'

'Aye – but his ghost has returned to the Kamarg. Riding upon the back of his great horned horse in all his armour of gleaming brass, with his hair and his moustache all red as brass and his eyes like

13

burnished brass: He is out there, treacherous Hawkmoon, in the marsh. He haunts you. And those who meet him are told of your treachery, how you deserted him when his enemies beset him, how you let him die in Londra.'

'It *is* a lie!' shouted Yisselda. 'I was there. I fought at Londra. Nothing could save my father.'

'And,' continued Czernik, his voice deepening but still loud. 'I heard from Count Brass how you joined with your lover to deceive him.'

'Oh!' Yisselda clapped her hands to her ears. 'This is obscene! Obscene!'

'Be silent now, Czernik,' warned Hawkmoon hollowly. 'Still your tongue, for you go too far!'

'He awaits you in the marshes. He will take his vengeance upon you out there at night when next you travel beyond the walls of Aigues-Mortes – if you dare. And his ghost is still more of a hero, more of a man than are you, turncoat. Aye – turncoat you be. First you served Köln, then you served the Empire, then you turned against the Empire, then you aided the Empire in its plot against Count Brass, then once again you betrayed the Empire. Your history speaks for the truth of what I say. I am not mad. I am not drunk. There are others who have seen and heard what I have seen and heard.'

'Then you have been deceived,' said Yisselda firmly.

'It is you who have been deceived, my lady!' Czernik growled.

And then the stewards came forward again and Hawkmoon did not try to stop them as they dragged the old man from the amphitheatre.

The rest of the proceedings did not go well, after that. Hawkmoon's guests were too embarrassed to comment on the incident and the crowd's interest was not on the bulls or the toreadors who leaped so skilfully the ring, plucking the ribbons from the horns.

A banquet followed at Castle Brass. To the banquet had been invited all the local dignitaries of the Kamarg, as well as the ambassadors, and it was noticeable that four or five of the local people had not come. Hawkmoon ate little and drank more than was normal for him. He tried hard to rid himself of the gloomy mood into which Czernik's peculiar declarations had put him, but he found it difficult to smile even when his own children came down to greet him and be introduced to his guests. Every sentence he spoke required an effort and there was no flow of conversation, even among the guests. Many of the ambassadors made excuses and went early to their beds. And soon only Hawkmoon and Yisselda were left in the banqueting hall, still seated in their places at the head of the table, watching the servants clear away the remains of the meal.

'What could he have seen?' said Yisselda as, at last, the servants, too, left. 'What could he have heard Dorian?'

Hawkmoon shrugged. 'He told us. Your father's ghost . . . '

'A baragoon more articulate than most?'

'He described your father. His horse. His armour. His face.'

'But he was drunk even today.'

'He said that others saw Count Brass and heard the same story from his lips.'

'Then it is a plot. Some enemy of yours – one of the Dark Empire lords who survived unrepentant – dressed up with false whiskers and his face painted to resemble my father's.'

'That could be,' said Hawkmoon. 'But would not Czernik of all people have seen through such a deception? He knew Count Brass for years.'

'Aye. And knew him well,' Yisselda admitted.

Hawkmoon rose slowly from his chair and walked heavily towards the fireplace where Count Brass's wargear hung. He looked up at it, reached out to finger it. He shook his head. 'I must discover for myself what this "ghost" is. Why should anyone seek to discredit me in this way? Who could my enemy be?'

'Czernik himself? Could he resent your presence at Castle Brass?'

'Czernik is old – near senile. He could not have invented such an elaborate deception.'

'Has he not wondered why Count Brass should remain in the marshes complaining about me? That is not like Count Brass. He would come to his own castle if he were here. If he had a grudge he would tax me with it.'

'You speak as if you believe Czernik now.'

Hawkmoon sighed. 'I must know more. I must find Czernik and question him . . . '

'I will send one of our retainers into the town.'

'No. I will go into the town and search him out.'

'Are you sure . . . ?'

'It is what I must do.' He kissed her. 'I'll put an end to this tonight. Why should we be plagued by phantoms we have not even seen?'

He wrapped a thick cloak of dark blue silk about his shoulders and kissed Yisselda once more before going out into the courtyard and ordering his horned horse saddled and harnessed. Some minutes later he rode out from the castle and down the winding road to the town. Few lights burned in Aigues-Mortes, for all that there was supposed to be a festival in the town. Evidently the townspeople had been as affected by the scene in the bullring as had Hawkmoon and his guests. The wind was beginning to blow as Hawkmoon reached the streets; the harsh mistral wind of the Kamarg, which the people hereabouts called the Life Wind, for it was supposed to have saved their land during the Tragic Millennium.

If Czernik was to be found anywhere it was in one of the taverns on the north side of town. Hawkmoon rode to the district, letting his horse make its own speed, for in many ways he was reluctant to repeat the earlier scene. He did not want to hear Czernik's lies again; they were lies which dishonoured all, even Count Brass, whom Czernik claimed to love.

The old taverns on the north side were primarily of wood, with only their foundations being made of the white stone of the Kamarg. The wood was painted in many different colours and some of the most ambitious of the taverns had even painted whole scenes across the frontages – several of the scenes commemorating the deeds of Hawkmoon himself and others recalling earlier exploits of Count Brass before he came to save the Kamarg, for Count Brass had fought (and often been a prime mover) in almost every famous battle of his day. Indeed, not a few of the taverns were named for Count Brass's battles, as well as those of the four heroes who had served the Rune-staff. One tavern was called The Magyarian Campaign while another proclaimed itself The Battle of Cannes. Here were The Fort at Balancia, Nine Left Standing and The Banner Dipped in Blood – all recalling Count Brass's exploits. Czernik, if he had not fallen on his face in some gutter by now, would be bound to be in one of them.

Hawkmoon entered the nearest door, that of The Red Amulet (named for that mystic jewel he had once worn around his own neck), and found the place packed with old soldiers, many of whom he recognized. They were all pretty drunk, with big mugs of wine and ale in their hands. There was hardly a man among them who did not have scars on his face or limbs. Their laughter was harsh but not noisy – only their singing was loud. Hawkmoon felt pleased to be in such company and greeted many whom he knew. He went up to a one-armed Slavian – another of Count Brass's men – and greeted him with genuine pleasure.

'Josef Vedla! Good evening, Captain. How goes it with you?'

Vedla blinked and tried to smile. 'A good evening to you, my lord. We have not seen you in our taverns for many a month.' He lowered his eyes and took an interest in the contents of his wine-cup.

'Will you join me in a skin of the new wine?' Hawkmoon asked. 'I hear it is singularly good this year. Perhaps some of our other old friends will— ?'

'No thanks, my lord.' Vedla rose. 'I've had too much as it is.' Awkwardly he pulled his cloak around him with his single hand.

Hawkmoon spoke directly. 'Josef Vedla. Do you believe Czernik's tale of meeting Count Brass in the marsh?'

'I must go.' Vedla walked towards the low doorway.

'Captain Vedla. Stop.'

Reluctantly, Vedla stopped and slowly he turned to look at Hawkmoon.

'Do you believe that Count Brass told him I betrayed our cause? That I led Count Brass himself into a trap?'

Vedla scowled. 'Czernik alone I would not believe. He grows old and remembers only his youth when he rode with Count Brass. Maybe I wouldn't believe any veteran, no matter what he told me – for we all still mourn for Count Brass and would have him come back to us.'

'As would I.'

Vedla sighed. 'I believe you, my lord. Though few would, these days. At least – most are simply not sure . . . '

'Who else has seen this ghost?'

'Several merchants, journeying back late at night through the marsh roads. A young bull-catcher. Even one guardian on duty in an eastern tower claims to have seen the figure in the distance. A figure that was unmistakably Count Brass.'

'Do you know where Czernik is now?'

'Probably in The Dnieper Crossing at the end of this alley. That's where he spends his pension these days.'

They went out into the cobbled street.

Hawkmoon said: 'Captain Vedla, can you believe that I would betray Count Brass?'

Vedla rubbed his pitted nose. 'No. Nor can most. It is hard to think of you as a traitor, Duke of Köln. But the stories are so consistent. Everyone who has met this – this ghost – tells the same tale.'

'But Count Brass – alive or dead – is not one to hover on the edges of town complaining. If he wanted – if he wanted vengeance on me, do you not think he would come and claim it?'

'Aye. Count Brass was not a man to be indecisive. Yet,' Captain Vedla smiled wanly, 'we also know that ghosts are supposed to act according to the customs of ghosts.'

'You believe in ghosts, then?'

'I believe in nothing. I believe in everything. This world has taught me that lesson. What of the events concerning the Runestaff – would an ordinary man believe that they really took place?'

Hawkmoon could not help but return Vedla's smile. 'I take your point. Well, good night to you, Captain.'

'Good night, my lord.'

Josef Vedla strode off in the opposite direction while Hawkmoon led his horse down the street to where he could see the sign of the tavern called The Dnieper Crossing. The paint was peeling on the sign and the tavern itself sagged as if one of its central beams had been removed. It looked an unsavoury place and the smell which came out of it was a mixture of sour wine, animal dung, grease and vomit. It was evident why a drunkard would choose it, for more oblivion could be bought here at the cheapest price.

The place was almost empty as Hawkmoon ducked his head through the door and went inside. A few brands and candles illuminated the room. The unclean floor and the filthy benches and tables, the cracked leather of the wine-skins strewn here and there, the chipped wooden and clay beakers, the ill-clothed men and women who sat hunched or lay sprawled in corners, all gave credence to Hawkmoon's original impression. People did not come to The Dnieper Crossing for social reasons. They came here to get drunk as quickly as was possible.

A small, dirty man with a fringe of black, greasy hair around his bald pate, slid from a patch of darkness and smiled up at Hawkmoon. 'Ale, my lord? Good wine?'

'Czernik,' said Hawkmoon. 'Is he here?'

'Aye.' The small man jerked a thumb towards the corner and a door marked Privy. 'He's in there making space for more. He'll be out shortly. Shall I call him?'

'No.' Hawkmoon looked around and then sat down on a bench he judged to be somewhat cleaner than the rest. 'I'll wait for him.'

'And a cup of wine while you wait?'

'Very well.'

Hawkmoon left the wine untouched as he waited for Czernik to emerge. At last the old veteran came stumbling out and went straight to the bar. 'Another flagon,' he mumbled. He patted at his clothes, looking for his purse. He had not seen Hawkmoon.

Hawkmoon rose. 'Czernik.'

Czernik whirled around and almost fell over. He fumbled for a sword he had long since pawned to buy more drink. 'Have you come to kill me, traitor?' His bleary eyes slowly sharpened with hatred and fear. 'Must I die for telling the truth? If Count Brass were here . . .

You know what this place is called?'

'The Dnieper Crossing.'

'Aye. We fought side by side, Count Brass and I, at The Dnieper Crossing. Against Prince Ruchtof's armies, against his Cossaki. And the river was dammed with their bodies so that its course was changed for all time. And at the end of it all Prince Ruchtof's armies were dead and Count Brass and I were the only two of our side left alive.'

'I know the tale.'

'Then know that I am brave. That I do not fear you. Kill me, if you wish. But you shall not silence Count Brass himself.'

'I did not come to silence you, Czernik, but to listen. Tell me again what you saw and what you heard.'

Czernik glared suspiciously at Hawkmoon, 'I told you this afternoon.'

'I wish to hear it once more. Without any of your own accusations. Tell me, as you remember them, Count Brass's words to you.'

Czernik shrugged. 'He said that you had coveted his lands and his daughter ever since you first came to the Kamarg. He said that you had proved yourself a traitor several times over before you ever met him. He said that you fought the Dark Empire at Köln, then joined with the Beast Lords, even though they had slain your own father. Then you turned against the Empire when you thought you were strong enough, but they defeated you and took you back in chains of gilded iron to Londra where, in exchange for our own life you agreed to help them in a plot to betray Count Brass. Once out of their hands you came to the Kamarg and thought it easier to betray your Empire masters once again. This you did. Then you used your friends – Count Brass, Oladahn, Bowgentle and D'Averc – to beat the Empire and when they were no longer useful to you, you arranged things so that they should die in the Battle of Londra.'

'A convincing story,' said Hawkmoon grimly. 'It fits the facts well enough, though it leaves out details which would vindicate my actions. A clever fabrication, indeed.'

'You say Count Brass lies?'

'I say that what you saw in the marshes – the ghost or mortal – is not Count Brass. I know I speak the truth, Czernik, for I have no betrayals on my conscience. Count Brass knew the truth. Why should he lie after death?'

'I know Count Brass and I know you. I know that Count Brass would not tell such a lie. In diplomacy he was cunning – we all know that. But to his friends he spoke only the truth.'

19

'Then what you saw was not Count Brass.'

'What I saw was Count Brass. His ghost. Count Brass as he was when I rode at his side holding his banner for him when we went against the League of Eight to Italia, two years before we came to the Kamarg. I know Count Brass . . . '

Hawkmoon frowned. 'And what was his message?'

'He waits for you in the marshes every night, there to take his vengeance upon you.'

Hawkmoon drew a deep breath. He adjusted his swordbelt on his hip. 'Then I will go to him tonight.'

Czernik looked curiously at Hawkmoon. 'You are not afraid?'

'I am not. I know that whoever you saw cannot be Count Brass. Why should I fear a fraud?'

'Perhaps you do not remember betraying him?' Czernik suggested vaguely. 'Perhaps it was all done by the jewel you once wore in your forehead? Could it be the jewel which forced you to such actions, so that when it was removed you forgot all that you had planned?'

Hawkmoon offered Czernik a bleak smile. 'I thank you for that, Czernik. But I doubt if the jewel controlled me to that extent. Its nature was somewhat different.' He frowned. For a moment he had begun to wonder if Czernik were right. It would be horrifying if it were true . . . But no, it could not be true. Yisselda would have known the truth, however much he might have tried to hide it. Yisselda knew he was no traitor.

Yet something was haunting the marshlands and trying to turn the folk of the Kamarg against him and therefore he must get to grips with it once and for all – lay the ghost and prove to people like Czernik that he had betrayed no one.

He said nothing more to Czernik but turned and strode from the tavern, mounting his heavy black stallion and turning its head towards the town gates.

Through the gates he went and out into the moonlit marsh, hearing the first distant, keening notes of the mistral, feeling its cold breath on his cheek, seeing the surface of the lagoons ripple and the reeds perform an agitated dance in anticipation of the wind's full force which would come a few days later.

Again he let his horse find its own route, for it knew the marsh better than did he. And meanwhile he peered through the gloom, looking this way and that; looking for a ghost.

CHAPTER TWO

The Meeting in the Marsh

The marsh was full of small sounds — scuttlings and slitherings, coughs, barks and hoots as the night animals went about their business. Sometimes a larger beast would emerge from the darkness and blunder past Hawkmoon. Sometimes there would be a heavy splash from a lagoon as a large fish-eating owl plunged upon its prey. But no human figure — ghost or mortal — was seen by the Duke of Köln as he rode deeper and deeper into the darkness.

Dorian Hawkmoon was confused. He was bitter. He had looked forward to a life of rural tranquillity. The only problems he had anticipated were the problems of breeding and planting, of the ordinary business of raising children.

And now this damned mystery had emerged. Not even a threat of war would have disturbed him half as much. War, albeit with the Dark Empire, was clean compared to this. If he had seen the brazen ornithopters of Granbretan in the skies, if he had seen beast-masked armies and grotesque carriages and all the other bizarre paraphernalia of the Dark Empire in the distance, he would have known how to deal with it. Or if the Runestaff had called him, he would have known how to respond.

But this was insidious. How could he cope with rumours, with ghosts, with old friends being turned against him?

Still the horned stallion plodded on through the marsh paths. Still there was no sign that the marsh was occupied by anyone other than Hawkmoon himself. He began to feel tired, for he had risen much earlier than usual in order to prepare himself for the festival. He began to suspect that there was nothing out here, that Czernik and the others had imagined it all, after all. He smiled to himself. He had been a fool to take a drunkard's ravings seriously.

And, of course, it was at that moment that it appeared to him. It was seated on a hornless chestnut warhorse and the warhorse was draped with a canopy of russet silk. The armour shone in the moonlight and it was all of heavy brass. Burnished brass helmet, very plain and practical; burnished brass breastplate and greaves. From head to foot the figure was clad in brass. The gloves and the boots were of

21

brass links stitched upon leather. The belt was of brass chain brought together by a huge brass buckle and the belt supported a brass scabbard. In the scabbard rested something which was not of brass but of good steel. A broadsword. And then there was the face – the golden brown eyes, steady and stern, the heavy red moustache, the red eyebrows, the bronze tan.

It could be no other.

'Count Brass!' gasped Hawkmoon. And then he closed his mouth and studied the figure, for he had seen Count Brass dead on the battlefield.

There was something different about this man and it did not take Hawkmoon more than a moment to realize that Czernik had spoken the literal truth when he said it was the same Count Brass beside whom he had fought at the Dnieper Crossing. This Count Brass was at least twenty years younger than the one whom Hawkmoon had first met when he visited the Kamarg seven or eight years previously.

The eyes flickered and the great head, seemingly all of brazen metal, turned slightly so that those eyes now peered directly into Hawkmoon's.

'Are you the one?' said the deep voice of Count Brass. 'My nemesis?'

'Nemesis?' Hawkmoon uttered a sharp laugh. 'I thought you had to be mine, Count Brass!'

'I am confused.' The voice was definitely the voice of Count Brass, but it had a slightly dreamy quality to it. And Count Brass's eyes did not focus with their old, familiar clarity upon Hawkmoon's.

'What are you?' Hawkmoon demanded. 'What brings you to the Kamarg?'

'My death. I am dead, am I not?'

'The Count Brass whom I knew is dead. He died at Londra more than five years since. I hear that I have been accused of that death.'

'You are the one called Hawkmoon of Köln?'

'I am Dorian Hawkmoon, Duke of Köln, aye.'

'Then I must slay you, it seems.' This Count Brass spoke with some reluctance.

For all that his head whirled, Hawkmoon could see that Count Brass (or whatever the creature was) was quite as uncertain of himself as was Hawkmoon at that moment. For one thing, while Hawkmoon had recognized Count Brass, this man had not recognized Hawkmoon.

'Why must you slay me? Who told you to slay me?'

'The oracle. Though I am dead now, I may live again. But if I live again I must ensure that I do not die at the Battle of Londra. Therefore I must kill the one who would lead me to that battle and betray me to those against whom I fight. That one is Dorian Hawkmoon of Köln, who covets my land.'

'I have lands of my own. Your daughter was betrothed to me before the Battle of Londra. Someone deceives you, friend ghost.'

'A daughter? I have no daughter. Why should the oracle deceive me?'

'Because there are such things as false oracles. Does the name "Yisselda" mean nothing to you?'

A look of bewilderment passed briefly across the Count's features. 'I do not know anyone of that name.'

Hawkmoon gazed into the familiar brown eyes. 'Where do you come from?'

'From? Why, from Earth'

'Where do you believe this place to be, in that case?'

'The netherworld, of course. A place from which few escape. But I can escape. Only I must slay you first, Dorian Hawkmoon.'

'Something seeks to destroy me through you, Count Brass – if Count Brass you be. I cannot begin to explain this mystery, but I believe that you think you really are Count Brass and that I am your enemy. Perhaps all is a lie – perhaps only part.'

A frown passed across the Count's brazen brow. 'You confuse me. I do not understand. I was not warned of this.'

Hawkmoon's lips were dry. He was so bewildered that he could barely think. So many emotions moved in him at the same time. There was grief for the memory of his dead friend. There was hatred for whoever it was sought to mock that memory. There was fear in case this should be a ghost. There was sympathy, should this really be Count Brass raised from the dead and turned into an automaton.

He began to suspect not the Runestaff now, but the science of the Dark Empire. The whole affair had the stamp of the perverse genius of the scientists of Granbretan. But how could they have effected it? The two great sorcerer-scientists of the Dark Empire, Taragorm and Kalan, were dead. There had been none to equal them while they lived, and none to replace them when they died.

And why did Count Brass look so much younger? Why did he seem unaware that he possessed a daughter?

'Not warned by whom?' said Hawkmoon insistently. If it came to a fight he knew that Count Brass could easily defeat him. Count Brass had ever been the best fighter in Europe. Even in late middle-age there had been no one who could begin to match him in a man-to-man sword engagement.

'By the oracle. And another thing puzzles me, my enemy to be; why, if you still live, do you, too, dwell in the netherworld?'

'This is not the netherworld. It is the land of the Kamarg. Do you not recognize it, then – you, who were its Lord Guardian for so many years – who helped defend it against the Dark Empire? I do not think you can be Count Brass.'

The figure raised a gauntleted hand to its brow in a gesture of puzzlement. 'Think you that? Yet we have never met . . . '

'Not met? We have fought together in many battles. We have saved each other's lives. I think that you are a man who bears a resemblance to Count Brass, who has been trapped by some sorcery or other and taught to think that he *is* Count Brass – then despatched to kill me. Perhaps some remnants of the old Dark Empire still survive. Perhaps some of Queen Flana's subjects still hate me. Does that idea mean anything to you?'

'No. But I know that I am Count Brass. Do not confuse me further, Duke of Köln.'

'How do you know you are Count Brass? Because you resemble him?'

'Because I *am* him!' The man roared. 'Dead or alive – *I am Count Brass*!'

'How can you be, when you do not recognize me? When you did not even know you had a daughter? When you confuse this land of the Duke of Köln for some supernatural netherworld? When you recall nothing of what we went through together in the service of the Runestaff? When you believe that I, of all people, who loved you, whose life and dignity both were saved by you, should have betrayed you?'

'I know nothing of the events of which you speak. But I know of my travellings and of my battles in the service of a score of princes – in Magyaria, Arabia, Scandia, Slavia and the lands of the Greeks and Bulgars. I know of my dream, which is to bring unity to the squabbling princedoms of Europe. I know of my successes – aye, and of my failures, too. I know of the women I have loved, of the friends I have had – and of the enemies I have fought. And I know, too, that you are neither friend nor foe as yet, but will become my most treacherous enemy. On Earth I lie dying. Here I travel in search of the one who will finally take all I possess, including my very life.'

'And say again who has granted you this boon?'

'Gods – supernatural beings – the oracle itself – I know not.'

'You believe in such things?'

'I did not. Now I must, for the evidence is here.'

'I think not. I am not dead. I do not inhabit a netherworld. I am flesh and blood and so, by the looks of it, are you, my friend. I hated you when I first rode out to seek you. Now I see that you are as much a victim as am I. Return to your masters. Tell them that it is Hawkmoon who shall be avenged – upon them!'

'By Narsha's garter, I'll not be given orders!' roared the man in brass. His gloved right hand fell upon the hilt of his sword. It was a gesture typical of Count Brass. The expressions were Count Brass's too. Was this some terrible simulacrum of the Count, invented by Dark Empire science?

Hawkmoon was by now almost hysterical with bewilderment and grief.

'Very well, then,' he cried, 'let us go to it, you and I. If you are truly Count Brass you'll have little difficulty in slaying me. Then you will be content. And so will I, for I could not live with people suspecting that I had betrayed you!'

But then the man's expression changed and became thoughtful. 'I am Count Brass, be certain of that, Duke of Köln. But, as for the rest, it is possible that we are both victims of a plot. I have not merely been a soldier in my life, but a politician, too. I know of those who delight in turning friend against friend for their own ends. There is a slight possibility that you speak truth . . . '

'Well, then,' said Dorian Hawkmoon in relief, 'return with me to Castle Brass and we will discuss what we both know.'

The man shook his head. 'No, I cannot. I have seen the lights of your walled city and your castle above it. I would visit it – but there is something that stops me from so doing – a barrier. I cannot explain what its properties are. That is why I have been forced to wait for you in this damned marsh. I had hoped to get this business over with swiftly, but now . . . ' The man frowned again. 'For all that I am a practical man, Duke of Köln, I have always prided myself on being a just one. I would not slay you to fulfil some other's end – not unless I knew what that end was, at any rate. I must consider all that you have said. Then if I decide that you are lying to save your skin, I will kill you.'

'Or,' said Hawkmoon grimly, 'if you are not Count Brass, there is a good chance that I shall kill you.'

The man smiled a familiar smile – Count Brass's smile. 'Aye – if I am not Count Brass,' he said.

'I shall come back to the marsh at noon tomorrow,' said Hawkmoon. 'Where shall we meet?'

'Noon? There is no noon here. No sun at all!'

'In this you do lie,' Hawkmoon laughed. 'In a few hours it will be morning here.'

Again the man passed a gauntleted hand across his frowning brow. 'Not for me,' he said. 'Not for me.'

This puzzled Hawkmoon all the more. 'But you have been here for days, I heard.'

'A night – a long, perpetual night.'

'Does this fact, too, not make you believe you are the victim of a deception?'

'It might,' said the man. He gave a deep sigh. 'Well, come when you think. Do you see yonder ruin – on the hillock?' He pointed with a finger of brass.

In the moonlight Hawkmoon could just make out the shape of an old ruined building which Bowgentle had described as being that of a Gothic church of immense age. It had been one of Count Brass's favourite places. He had often ridden there when he felt the need to be alone.

'I know the ruin,' said Hawkmoon.

'Then meet me there. I shall wait as long as my patience lasts.'

'Very well.'

'And come armed,' said the man, 'for we shall probably need to fight.'

'You are not convinced of what I have said?'

'You have said nothing very much, friend Hawkmoon. Vague suppositions. References to people I do not know. You think the Dark Empire is bothered with us? It has more important matters to consider, I should think.'

'The Dark Empire is destroyed. You helped destroy it.'

And again the man grinned a familiar grin. 'That is where you are deceived, Duke of Köln.' He turned his horse and began to ride back into the night.

'Wait!' called Hawkmoon. 'What do you mean?'

But the man had begun to gallop now.

Wildly, Hawkmoon spurred his horse in pursuit. 'What do you mean?'

The horse was reluctant to go at such a pace. It snorted and tried to pull back, but Hawkmoon spurred the beast harder. 'Wait!'

He could just see the rider ahead, but his outline was becoming less well-defined. Surely he could not truly be a ghost?

'Wait!'

Hawkmoon's horse slipped in the slime. It whinnied in fear, as if trying to warn Hawkmoon of their mutual danger. Hawkmoon spurred the horse again. It reared. Its hind-legs began to slip in the mud.

Hawkmoon tried to control his steed, but it was falling and taking him with it.

And then they had both plunged off the narrow marsh road, broken through the reeds at the edge and fallen heavily into mud which gulped greedily and tugged them to itself. Hawkmoon tried to struggle back to the bank, but his feet were still in his stirrups and one of his legs was trapped beneath the bulk of his horse's floundering body.

He stretched out and grabbed at a bunch of reeds, trying to drag himself to safety; he moved a few inches towards the path and then the reeds were wrenched free and he fell back.

He became calm as he realized he was being pulled deeper and deeper into the swamp with every panicky movement.

He reflected that if he did have enemies who wished to see him dead he had, in his own stupidity, granted their wish, after all.

## CHAPTER THREE

## A Letter from Queen Flana

He could not see his horse, but he could hear it.

The poor beast was snorting as the mud filled its mouth. Its struggles had grown much weaker.

Hawkmoon had managed to free his feet from the stirrups and his leg was no longer trapped, but now only his arms, his head and his shoulders were above the surface. Little by little he was slipping to his death.

He had had some notion of climbing on to the horse's back and from there leaping to the path, but his efforts in that direction had been entirely unsuccessful. All he had done was push the animal a little further under. Now the horse's breathing was ugly, muffled, painful. Hawkmoon knew that his own breathing would soon sound the same.

He felt completely impotent. By his own foolishness he had got himself into this position. Far from solving anything, he had created a further problem. And, if he died, he knew, too, that many would say that he had been slain by Count Brass's ghost. This would give credence to the accusations of Czernik and others. It would mean that Yisselda herself would be suspected of helping him betray her own father. At best she could leave Castle Brass, perhaps going to live with Queen Flana, perhaps going to Köln. It would mean that his son Manfred would not inherit his birthright as Lord Guardian of the Kamarg. It would mean that his daughter Yarmila would be ashamed to speak his name.

'I am a fool,' he said aloud. 'And a murderer. For I have slain a good horse besides myself. Perhaps Czernik was right – perhaps the Black Jewel made me do acts of treachery I cannot now remember. Perhaps I deserve to die.'

And then he thought he heard Count Brass ride by, mocking him with ghostly laughter. But it was probably only a marsh goose whose slumber had been disturbed by a fox.

Now his left arm was being sucked down. Carefully he raised it. Even the reeds were out of reach now.

He heard his horse give one last sigh as its head sank beneath the mud. He saw its body heave as it sought to draw breath. And then it was still. He watched as its torso slipped from sight.

Now there were more ghostly voices to mock him. Was that Yisselda's voice? The cry of a gull. And the deeper voices of his soldiers? The bark of foxes and marsh bears.

This deception seemed, at that moment, to be the cruellest of all – for his own brain deceived him.

Again he was filled with a sense of irony. To have fought for so long and so hard against the Dark Empire. To have survived terrifying adventures on two continents – only to die in ignominy, alone, in a swamp. None would know where or how he had died. His grave would be unmarked. There would be no statue erected to him outside the walls of Castle Brass. Well, he thought, it was a quiet way to die, at least.

'Dorian!'

This time the bird's cry seemed to call his name. He called back at it, echoing it. 'Dorian!'

'Dorian!'

'My Lord of Köln,' said the voice of a marsh bear.

'My Lord of Köln,' said Hawkmoon in the same tone. Now it was completely impossible to free his left arm. He felt the mud burying his chin. The constricting mud against his chest made it that much harder for him to breathe. He felt dizzy. He hoped that he might become unconscious before the mud filled his mouth.

Perhaps if he died he would find that he dwelled in some netherworld. Perhaps he would meet Count Brass again. And Oladahn of the Bulgar Mountains. And Huillam D'Averc. And Bowgentle, the philosopher, the poet.

'Ah,' he said to himself, 'If I could be sure, then I would welcome this death a little more readily. Yet, there is still the question of my honour – and that of Yisselda. Yisselda!'

'Dorian!' Again the bird's cry bore an uncanny resemblance to his wife's voice. He had heard that dying men entertained such fancies. Perhaps for some it made death easier, but for him it made it that much harder.

'Dorian! I thought I heard you speak. Are you near by? What has happened?'

Hawkmoon called back to the bird. 'I am in the marsh, my love, and I am dying. Tell them that Hawkmoon was not a traitor. Tell them he was not a coward. Tell them, instead, that he was a fool!'

The reeds near the bank began to rustle. Hawkmoon looked towards them, expecting to see a fox. That would be terrible, to be attacked even as the mud dragged him under. He shuddered.

And then there was a human face peering at him through the reeds. And it was a face he recognized.

'Captain?'

'My Lord,' said Captain Josef Vedla. Then his face turned away as he spoke to someone behind him. 'You were right, my lady. He is here. And almost completely under.' A brand flared as Vedla extended it out as far as he could stretch, peering at Hawkmoon to see just how far he was buried. 'Quickly, men – the rope.'

'I am pleased to see you, Captain Vedla. Is my lady Yisselda with you, too?'

'I am, Dorian.' Her voice was tense. 'I found Captain Vedla and he took me to the tavern where Czernik was. It was Czernik who told us that you had ventured into the marsh. So we gathered what men we could and came to find you.'

'I am grateful, ' said Hawkmoon, 'though I should not have been if I had not acted so foolishly – ugh!' The mud had reached his mouth.

A rope was flung towards him. With his free right hand he just managed to grasp it and stick his wrist through the loop.

'Pull away,' he said, and groaned as the noose tightened on his wrist and he felt as if his arm were being dragged from its socket.

Slowly his body emerged from the mud, which was reluctant to give up its feast, until he was able to sit gasping on the bank while Yisselda, careless that he was covered in the slimy, stinking stuff from head to toe, embraced him, sobbing. 'We thought you dead.'

'I thought myself dead,' he said. 'Instead I have killed one of my best horses. I deserve to die.'

Captain Vedla was looking nervously about him. Unlike the guardians who were Kamarg bred, he had never been much attracted to the marsh, even in daylight.

'I saw the fellow who calls himself Count Brass.' Hawkmoon addressed Captain Vedla.

'And you killed him, my lord?'

Hawkmoon shook his head. 'I think he's some play-actor who bears a strong resemblance to Count Brass. But he is not Count Brass – living or dead – of that I'm almost certain. He's too young, for one thing. And he had not been properly educated in his part. He does not know the name of his daughter. He knows nothing of the Kamarg. Yet, I think, there is no malice in the fellow. He might be mad, but more likely he's been mesmerized into believing that he is Count Brass. Some Dark Empire trouble-makers, I'd guess, out to discredit me and avenge themselves at the same time.'

Vedla looked relieved. 'At least I will have something to tell the gossip-mongers,' he said. 'But this fellow must have had a startling resemblance to the old Count if he deceived Czernik.'

'Aye – he was everything – expressions, gestures and so on. But there is something a little vague about his manner – as if he is in a dream. That is what led me to suspect that he is not, himself, acting maliciously but had been put up to this by others.' Hawkmoon got up.

'Where is this imposter now?' Yisselda asked.

'He disappeared into the marsh. I was following him – at too great a speed – when this happened to me.' Hawkmoon laughed. 'I had become so worried, you know, that I thought for a moment he really had disappeared – like a ghost.'

Yisselda smiled. 'You can have my horse,' she said. 'I will ride on your lap, as I have done more than once before.'

And in a much relaxed mood the small party returned to Castle Brass.

By the next morning the story of Dorian Hawkmoon's encounter with the 'play-actor' had spread throughout the town and among the ambassadorial guests in the castle. It had become a joke. Everyone was relieved to be able to laugh, to mention it without danger of giving offence to Hawkmoon. And the festivities went on, growing wilder as the wind blew stronger. Hawkmoon, now that he had no-thing to fear for his honour, decided to make the false Count Brass wait for a day or two and this he did, throwing himself completely into the merry-making.

But then, one morning at breakfast, while Hawkmoon and his guests decided on their plans for that day, young Lonson of Shkarlan came down with a letter in his hand. The letter bore many seals and looked most impressive. 'I received this today, my lord,' said Lonson. 'It came by ornithopter from Londra. It is from the queen herself.'

'News from Londra. Splendid.' Hawkmoon accepted the letter and began to break the seals. 'Now, Prince Lonson, sit and break your fast while I read.'

Prince Lonson smiled and, at Yisselda's suggestion sat beside the lady of the castle, helping himself to a steak from the platter before him.

Hawkmoon began to read Queen Flana's letter. There was general news of the progress of her schemes for farming large areas of her nation. These seemed to be going well. Indeed, in some cases they had surpluses which they were able to trade with Normandia and

Hanoveria, whose own farming was going well, too. But it was towards the end of the letter that Hawkmoon began to give it more attention.

'And so we come to the only unpleasant detail of this letter, my dear Dorian. It seems that my efforts to rid my country of reminders of its dark past have not been entirely successful. Mask-wearing has sprung up again. There has been some attempt, I gather, to re-form some of the old Beast Orders – particularly the Order of the Wolf of which, you will recall, Baron Meliadus was Grand Master. Some of my own agents have, upon occasions, been able to disguise themselves as members of the cult and gain entry to meetings. An oath is sworn which might amuse you (I hope, indeed, that it will not disturb you!) – as well as swearing to bring back the Dark Empire in all its glory, to oust me from my throne and to destroy all those loyal to me, they also swear vengeance upon you and your family. Those who survived the Battle of Londra, they say, must all be wiped out. In your secure Kamarg, I doubt if you are in much danger from a few Granbretanian dissidents, so I advise you to continue to sleep well! I know for certain that these secret cults are not much popular and only flourish in those parts of Londra not yet rebuilt. The great majority of the people – aristocrats and commoners alike – have taken happily to rural life and to parliamentary government. It was our old way to rule thus, when Granbretan was sane. I hope that we are sane again and that, soon, even those few pockets of insanity will be cleansed from our society. One other peculiar rumour, which my agents have been unable to verify, is that some of the worst Dark Empire lords are still alive somewhere and waiting to resume their "rightful place as rulers of Granbretan". I cannot believe this – it seems to be a typical legend invented by the disinherited. There must be a thousand heroes sleeping in caves all over Granbretan alone, waiting to spring to somebody's assistance when the time is ripe (why is it never ripe, I wonder!). To be on the safe side, my agents are trying to find the source of these rumours, but several, I regret to say, have already died as the cultists discover their true identities. It should take several months, but I think we shall soon be completely rid of the mask-wearers, particularly since the dark places they prefer to inhabit are being torn down very rapidly indeed.'

'Is there disturbing news in Flana's letter?' Yisselda asked her husband as he folded the parchment.

He shook his head. 'Not really. It just fits with something that I heard recently. She says that mask-wearing has sprung up again in Londra.'

'But that is bound to happen for a while, surely? Is it widespread?'

'Apparently not.'

Prince Lonson laughed. 'There is surprisingly little of it, my lady, I assure you. Most of the ordinary people were only too pleased to rid themselves of uncomfortable masks and heavy clothes. This is true, too, of the nobility – save for the few who were members of warrior-castes and still survived (happily there were not many).'

'Flana says that there are rumours of some of the prime movers among them still being alive,' said Hawkmoon quietly.

'Impossible. You slew Baron Meliadus himself – *split*, Duke of Köln, from shoulder to groin!'

One or two of the other guests looked rather put out by Prince Lonson's remark. He apologized profusely. 'Count Brass,' he continued, 'despatched Adaz Promp and several more. Shenegar Trott you also slew, in Dnark; before the Runestaff. And the others – Mikosevaar, Nankenseen and the rest – all are dead. Taragorm died in an explosion and Kalan killed himself. What others are left?'

Hawkmoon frowned. 'All I can think of are Taragorm and Kalan,' he said. 'They are the only two whose deaths were unwitnessed.'

'But Taragorm died in an explosion of Kalan's battle-machine. None could have survived it.'

'You are right.' Hawkmoon smiled. 'It is silly to speculate like this. There are better things to do.'

And again he turned his attention to the day's festivities.

But that night, he knew, he would ride out to the ruin and confront the one who called himself Count Brass.

## CHAPTER FOUR

A Company of the Dead

Thus it was at sunset that Dorian Hawkmoon, Duke of Köln, Lord Guardian of the Kamarg, rode out again upon the winding marsh roads, deep into his domain, watching the scarlet flamingoes wheel, seeing the herds of white bulls and horned horses in the distance, like clouds of fast-flowing smoke passing through the green and tawny reeds, seeing the lagoons turned to pools of blood by the red and sinking sun. Breathing the sharp air borne by the mistral, and coming at last to a small hill on which stood a ruin of immense age – a ruin around which ivy, purple and amber, climbed. And there, as the last rays of the sun died, Dorian Hawkmoon dismounted from his horned horse and waited for a ghost to come.

The wind tugged at his high-collared cloak. It blew at his face and froze his lips. It made the hairs of his horse's coat ripple like water. It keened across the wide, flat marshlands. And, as the day animals began to compose themselves for slumber, and before the night animals began to emerge, there fell upon the great Kamarg a terrible stillness.

Even the wind dropped. The reeds no longer rustled. Nothing moved.

And Hawkmoon waited on.

Much later he heard the sound of a horse's hooves on the damp marshland ground. A muffled sound. He reached over to his left hip and loosened his broadsword in its scabbard. He was in armour now. Steel armour which had been made to fit every contour of his body. He brushed hair from his eyes and adjusted his plain helm – as plain as Count Brass's own. He threw back the cloak from his shoulders so that it should not encumber his movements.

But there was more than one horseman approaching. He listened carefully. The moon was full tonight but the riders came from the other side of the ruin and he could see nothing of them. He counted. Four horsemen, by the sound of it. So – the imposter had brought allies. It had been a trap, after all. Hawkmoon sought cover. The only cover was in the ruin itself. Cautiously he moved towards it, clambering over the old, worn stones until he was certain that he was hidden from anyone who came from either side of the hill. Only the horse betrayed his presence.

The riders came up the hill. He could see them now, in silhouette. They rode their horses straight-backed. There was a pride in their stance. Who could they be?

Hawkmoon saw a glint of brass and knew that one of them was the false Count. But the other three wore no distinctive armour. They reached the top of the hill and saw his horse.

He heard the voice of Count Brass calling:

'Duke of Köln?'

Hawkmoon did not reply.

He heard another voice. A languid voice. 'Perhaps he has gone to relieve himself in yonder ruin?'

And, with a shock, Hawkmoon recognized that voice too.

It was the voice of Huillam D'Averc. Dead D'Averc, who had died so ironically in Londra.

He saw the figure approach, a handkerchief in one hand, and he recognized the face, too. It was D'Averc's. Then Hawkmoon knew, terrifyingly, who the other two riders were.

'Wait for him. He said he'd come, did he not, Count Brass?' Bowgentle was speaking now.

'Aye. He said so.'

'Then I hope he hurries, for this wind bites even through *my* thick pelt.' Oladahn's voice.

And Hawkmoon knew then that this was a nightmare, whether he slept or whether he was awake. It was the most painful experience of his life to see those who so closely resembled his dead friends walking and talking as they had walked and talked in each other's company some five years since. Hawkmoon would have given his own life if it would have brought them back, but he knew that it was impossible. No kind of resurrection drug could revive one who, like Oladahn of the Bulgar Mountains, had been torn to pieces and those pieces scattered. And there were no signs of wounds on the others, either.

'I shall catch a chill, that's certain – and die a second time, perhaps.' This was D'Averc, typically thoughtful for his own health, which was as robust as anyone's. Were these ghosts?

'What has brought us together, I wonder,' mused Bowgentle. 'And to such a bleak and sunless world? We met once, I believe, Count Brass – at Rouen, was it not? At the Court of Hanal the White?'

'I believe so.'

'By the sound of him, this Duke of Köln is worse than Hanal for indiscriminate bloodletting. The only thing we have in common, as

far as I can tell, is that we shall all die by his hand if we do not kill
him now. Yet, it is hard to believe . . . '

'He suggested that we were the victims of a plot, as I told you,' said
Count Brass. 'It could be true.'

'We are victims of something, that's certain,' said D'Averc, blowing
his nose delicately upon his lacy handkerchief. 'But I agree that it
would be best to discuss the matter with our murderer before we
despatch him. What if we kill him and nothing comes of it – we
remain in this dreadful, gloomy place for eternity – with him as a
companion, for he'll be dead, too.'

'How did you come to die?' Oladahn asked almost conversationally.

'A sordid death – a mixture of greed and jealousy was my undoing.
The greed was mine. The jealousy another's.'

'You intrigue us all,' laughed Bowgentle.

'A mistress of mine was, it happened, married to another gentleman. She was a splendid cook – her range of recipes was incredible,
my friends, both at the stove and in the bed, if you follow me. Well, I
was staying with her for a week while her husband was away at
Court – this was in Hanoveria where I myself had business at the
time. The week was splendid, but it came to an end, for her husband
was due to return that night. To console me, my mistress cooked a
splendid supper. A triumph! She never cooked a better. There were
snails and soups and goulashes and little birds in exquisite sauces and
soufflés – well, I see I discomfort you and I apologize . . . The meal, in
short, was superb. I had more than is good for one of my delicate
health and then I begged my mistress while there was still time to
favour me with her company in bed for just one short hour, since her
husband was not due back for two. With some reluctance she agreed.
We fell into bed. We rounded off the meal in ecstasy. We fell asleep.
So fast asleep, I might add, that we were only awakened by her
husband shaking us awake!'

'And he killed you, eh?' said Oladahn.

'In a manner of speaking. I leapt up. I had no sword. I had no
cause to kill him, either, of course, since he was the injured party (and
I've a strong sense of justice). Up I jumped and out of the window I
dashed. No clothes. Lots of rain. Five miles back to my own lodgings.
Result, of course, pneumonia.'

Oladahn laughed and the sound of his merriment was agonizing to
Hawkmoon. 'Of which you died?'

'Of which, to be accurate, if that peculiar oracle is correct, I am
dying, while my spirit sits on a windy hill and is no better off, it

seems!' D'Averc went to shelter beside the ruin and was not five feet from where Hawkmoon crouched. 'How did you come to die, my friend?'

'I fell off a rock.'

'A high one?'

'No – about ten feet.'

'And it killed you?'

'No, it was the bear that killed me. It was waiting below.'

Again Oladahn laughed.

And again Hawkmoon felt a pang of pain.

'I died of the Scandian plague,' said Bowgentle. 'Or am to die of it.'

'And I in battle against King Orson's elephants in Tarkia,' put in the one who believed himself to be Count Brass.

And Hawkmoon was reminded most strongly of actors preparing themselves for their parts. He would have believed they were actors, too, had it not been for their speech inflections, their gestures, their ways of expressing themselves. There were slight differences, but none to make Hawkmoon suspect these were not his friends. Yet, just as Count Brass had not known him, so these did not know each other.

Some idea of the possible truth was beginning to dawn on Hawkmoon as he emerged from hiding and confronted them.

'Good evening, gentlemen.' He bowed. 'I am Dorian Hawkmoon von Köln. I know you Oladahn – and you Bowgentle – and you D'Averc – and we've met already Count Brass. Are you here to slay me?'

'To discuss if we should,' said Count Brass, seating himself upon a flat rock. 'Now I regard myself as a reasonable judge of men. In fact I'm an exceptionally good judge, or I should not have survived this long. And I do not believe, Dorian Hawkmoon, that you have much treachery in you. Even in a situation which might justify such treachery – or which you would consider as justifying treachery – I doubt if you would be a traitor. And that is what disturbs me about this situation. Secondly, all four of us are known to you but we do not know you. Thirdly we appear to be the only four sent to this particular netherworld and that is a coincidence I mistrust. Fourthly we were each told a similar story – that you would betray us at some future date. Now, assuming that this, itself, is a future date where all five of us have met and become friends, what does that suggest to you?'

'That you are all from my past!' said Hawkmoon. 'That is why you look younger to me, Count Brass – and you, Bowgentle – and you,

Oladahn – and you, too, D'Averc . . . '

'Thank you,' said D'Averc sardonically.

'Which means that none of us died in the way we think we died – in battle at Tarkia, in my case – of sickness in the castle of Bowgentle and D'Averc – attacked by a bear in the case of Oladahn, here . . . '

'Exactly,' said Hawkmoon, 'for I met you all later and you were all very much alive. But I remember you telling me, Oladahn, how once you were nearly killed by a bear – and you told me how close you came to death in Tarkia, Count Brass – and, Bowgentle, I remember some mention of the Scandian plague.'

'And I?' asked D'Averc with interest.

'I forget, D'Averc – for your illnesses tended to run into each other and I never saw you in anything but the best of health . . . '

'Ah! Am I to be cured, then?'

Hawkmoon ignored D'Averc and continued. 'So this means you are not going to die – though you, yourselves, think that you might. Whoever is deceiving us wants you to think that it is by their efforts that you'll survive.'

'Much what I worked out.' Count Brass nodded.

'But that's as far as my logic leads me,' said Hawkmoon, 'for a paradox is involved here – why, when we *did* (or do) meet, did we not remember this particular meeting?'

'We must find our villains and ask them that question, I think,' said Bowgentle. 'Of course, I have studied something of the nature of time. Such paradoxes, according to one school of thought, would necessarily resolve themselves – memories would be wiped clean of anything which contradicted the normal experience of time. The brain, in short, would sponge out anything which was apparently inconsistent. However, there are certain aspects of that line of reasoning with which I am not wholly happy . . . '

'Perhaps we could discuss the philosophical implications at some other time, Sir Bowgentle,' said Count Brass gruffly.

'Time and philosophy are but one subject, Count Brass. And only philosophy may easily discuss the nature of time.'

'Perhaps. But there is the other matter – the possibility that we are being manipulated by malicious men who are somehow able to control time. How do we reach them and what do we do when we do reach them?'

'I remember something concerning crystals,' mused Hawkmoon, 'which transported men through alternate dimensions of the Earth. I wonder if these crystals, or something like them, are being used again?'

38

'I know nothing of crystals,' said Count Brass, and the other three agreed that they knew nothing, either.

'There are other dimensions, you see,' Hawkmoon went on. 'And it could be that there are dimensions where live men almost identical to men living in this dimension. We found a Kamarg that was not dissimilar to this. I wonder if that is the answer. Yet, still not quite the answer.'

'I barely follow you,' growled Count Brass. 'You begin to sound like this sorcerer fellow . . . '

'Philosopher,' corrected Bowgentle, 'and poet.'

'Aye, it's complicated thinking that's involved if we're to get closer to the truth,' said Hawkmoon. He told them the story of Elvereza Tozer and the Crystal Rings of Mygan – how they had been used to transport himself and D'Averc through the dimensions, across seas – perhaps through time itself. And since they all had played parts in this drama, Hawkmoon felt the strangeness of the situation – for he spoke familiarly of them as his friends – and he referrred to events which were to take place in their future. And when he was finished they seemed convinced that he had produced a likely explanation for their present situation. Hawkmoon remembered, too, the Wraith-folk, those gentle people who had given him a machine which had helped lift Castle Brass from its own space-time into another, safer space-time when Baron Meliadus attacked them. Perhaps if he were to travel to Soryandum in the Syranian Desert he might again enlist the help of the Wraith-folk. He put this to his friends.

'Aye, an idea worth trying,' said Count Brass. 'But in the meantime we're still in the grip of whomever put us here in the first place – and we've no explanation of how they've accomplished that or, for that matter, exactly why they have done it.'

'This oracle you spoke of,' said Hawkmoon. 'Where is it? Can you tell me exactly what happened to you – after you "died"?'

'I found myself in this land, with all my wounds healed and my armour repaired . . . '

The others agreed that this was what happened to them.

'With a horse and with food to last me for a good while – though unpalatable stuff it is.'

'And the oracle?'

'A sort of speaking pyramid about the height of a man – glowing – diamond-like – hovering above the ground. It appears and vanishes at will, it seems. It told me all that I told you when we first met. I assumed it to be supernatural in origin – though it went against all my previous beliefs . . . '

'It is probably of mortal origin', said Hawkmoon. 'Either the work of some sorcerer-scientist such as those who once worked for the Dark Empire – or else something which our ancestors invented before the Tragic Millennium.'

'I've heard of such,' agreed Count Brass. 'And I prefer that explanation. It suits my temperament more, I must admit.'

'Did it offer to restore you to life once I was slain?' Hawkmoon asked.

'Aye – that's it, in short.'

'That's what it told me,' said D'Averc, and the others nodded.

'Well, perhaps we should confront this machine, if machine it be, and see what happens?' Bowgentle suggested.

'There is another mystery, however,' Hawkmoon said. 'Why is it that you are in perpetual night in the Kamarg, whereas, for me, the days pass normally?'

'A splendid conundrum,' said D'Averc in some delight. 'Perhaps we should ask it. After all, if this is Dark Empire work, they would hardly seek to harm me – I am a friend of Granbretan!'

And Hawkmoon smiled a private smile.

'You are at present, Huillam D'Averc.'

'Let's make a plan,' said Count Brass practically. 'Shall we set off now to see if we can find the diamond pyramid?'

'Wait for me here,' said Hawkmoon. 'I must return home first. I will be back before dawn – that is, in a few hours. Will you trust me?'

'I'd rather trust a man than a crystal pyramid,' smiled Count Brass.

Hawkmoon walked to where his horse grazed. He lifted himself into his saddle.

As he rode away from the little hill, leaving the four men behind him, he forced himself to think as clearly as was possible, trying to avoid considering the paradoxical implications of what he had learned this night and to concentrate on what was likely to have created the situation. There were two possibilities, in his experience, as to what was at work here – the Runestaff on the one hand and the Dark Empire on the other. But it could be neither – some other force. Yet the only other people with great scientific resources were the Wraith-folk of Soryandum and it seemed unlikely that they would concern themselves with the affairs of others. Besides, only the Dark Empire would want him destroyed – by one or all of his now-dead friends. It was an irony which would have suited their perverse minds. Yet – the fact came back to him – all the great leaders of the old Dark Empire were dead. But then so were Count Brass, Oladahn, Bowgentle and D'Averc dead.

Hawkmoon drew a deep breath of cold air into his lungs as the town of Aigues-Mortes came in sight. The thought had already come to him that perhaps even this was a complicated trap and that soon he, too, might be dead.

And that was why he rode back to Castle Brass, to take his leave of his wife, to kiss his children and to write a letter which should be opened if he did not return.

# BOOK TWO
# OLD ENEMIES

## CHAPTER ONE

## A Speaking Pyramid

Hawkmoon's heart was heavy as he rode away from Castle Brass for the third time. The pleasure he felt at seeing his old friends again was mixed with the painful knowledge that, in one sense, they *were* ghosts. He had seen them dead, all of them. Also these men were strangers. Whereas he recalled conversations, adventures and events they had shared, they knew nothing of these things; they did not know each other, even. Hanging over everything was the knowledge that they would die, in their own futures, and that his being reunited with them might last only a few more hours, whereupon they might be snatched away again by whomever or whatever was manipulating them. It was even possible that when he returned to the ruin on the hill they would already be gone.

That was why he had told Yisselda as little of the night's occurrences as possible, merely letting her know that he must go away, to seek the source of whatever it was that threatened him. The rest he had put in the letter so that, if he did not return, she would learn all of the truth that he knew at this stage. He had not mentioned Bowgentle, D'Averc and Oladahn and had made it plain to her that he considered Count Brass an imposter. He did not want her to share the burden which now lay upon his shoulders.

There were still several hours to go before dawn when he at last reached the hill and saw that four men and four horses waited for him there. He reached the ruin and dismounted. The four came towards him out of the shadows and for an instant he believed that he was really in a netherworld, in the company of the dead, but he dismissed this morbid thought and said, instead:

'Count Brass, something puzzles me.'

The Count all clad in brass inclined his brazen head. 'And what is that?'

'When we parted – at our first meeting – I told you that the Dark Empire was destroyed. You told me that it was not. This puzzled me so much that I attempted to follow you but, instead, stumbled into the marsh. What did you mean? Do you know more than you have told me?'

'I spoke only the simple truth. The Dark Empire grows in strength. It extends its boundaries.'

And then something became clear to Hawkmoon and he laughed. 'In what year was the battle of which you spoke – in Tarkia?'

'Why, this year. The sixty-seventh Year of the Bull.'

'No, you are wrong,' said Bowgentle. 'This is the eighty-first Year of the Rat . . . '

'The ninetieth Year of the Frog,' said D'Averc.

'The seventy-fifth Year of the Goat,' Oladahn contradicted.

'You are all wrong,' said Hawkmoon. 'This year – the year in which we are now as we stand upon this hillock – is the eighty-ninth Year of the Rat. Therefore, to you all the Dark Empire still thrives, has not even begun to show her full strength. But to me, the Empire is over – pulled down primarily by we four. Now do you see why I suspect that we are the objects of Dark Empire vengeance? Either some Dark Empire sorcerer has looked into the future and seen what we did, or else some sorcerer has escaped the doom we brought to the Beast Lords and is now trying to repay us for the injury we did to them. The five of us came together some six years ago, to serve the Runestaff, of which you have all doubtless heard, against the Dark Empire. We were successful in our mission, but four died to achieve that success – you four. Save for the Wraith-folk of Soryandum, who take no interest in human affairs, the only ones capable of manipulating Time are the Dark Empire sorcerers.'

'I have often thought that I should like to know how I was to die,' said Count Brass, 'but now I am not so sure.'

'We have only your word, friend Hawkmoon,' said D'Averc. 'There are still many mysteries unsolved – among them the fact that if all this is taking place in our future, why did we not recall having met you before when we *did* meet?' He raised his eyebrows and then began to cough into his handkerchief.

Bowgentle smiled. 'I have already explained the theory concerning this seeming paradox. Time does not necessarily flow in a linear motion. It is our minds which perceive it flowing in this way. *Pure Time* might even have a random nature . . . '

'Yes, yes,' said Oladahn. 'Somehow, good Sir Bowgentle, you have a way of confusing me further with your explanations.'

'Then let us just say that Time might not be what we think it to be,' said Count Brass. 'And we've some proof of that, after all, for we do not need to believe Duke Dorian – we have certain knowledge that we were all wrenched from different years and stand together now. Whether we're in the future or the past, it's clear we are in different time-periods to those we left behind. And, of course, this does help to support Duke Dorian's suggestions and to contradict what the pyramid told us.'

'I support that logic, Count Brass,' Bowgentle agreed. 'Both intellectually and emotionally I am inclined to throw in my lot, for the moment, with Duke Dorian. I am not sure what I would have done, anyway, had I planned to kill him, for it goes against all my beliefs to take the life of another being.'

'Well, if you two are convinced,' said D'Averc yawning, 'I am prepared to be. I never was a judge of character. I rarely knew where my real interests lay. As an architect my work, grandly ambitious and minutely paid, was always done for some princeling who was promptly dethroned. His successor never seemed to favour my work – and I had usually insulted the fellow, anyway. As a painter I chose patrons who were inclined to die before they could begin seriously to support me. That is why I became a freelance diplomat – to learn more of the ways of politics before I returned to my old professions. As yet I do not feel I have learned anything like enough . . . '

'Perhaps that is because you prefer to listen to your own voice,' said Oladahn gently. 'Had not we better set off to seek the pyramid, gentlemen?' He hefted his quiver of arrows on his back and unstrung his bow to loop it over his shoulder. 'After all, we do not know how much time we have left.'

'You are right. When dawn comes I might see you all vanish,' Hawkmoon said. 'I should like to know how the days pass normally for me, in their proper cycle, while for you it is eternal night.' He returned to his horse and climbed into the saddle. He had saddle-panniers now, full of food. And there were two lances in a scabbard slung at the back of his saddle. The tall horned stallion he rode was the best horse in the stables of Castle Brass. It was called Brand because its eyes flashed like fire.

The others went to their own horses and mounted. Count Brass pointed down the hillock to the south. 'There's a hellish sea yonder – uncrossable I was told. It is to its shore we must go and on that shore we shall see the oracle.'

'The sea is only the sea into which flows the Rhône,' said Hawkmoon mildly. 'Called by some the Middle Sea.'

Count Brass laughed. 'A sea I have crossed a hundred times. I hope you are right, friend Hawkmoon – and I suspect that you are. Oh, I look forward to matching swords with the ones who deceive us!'

'Let us hope that they give us the opportunity,' drily said D'Averc. 'For I've a feeling – and, of course, I'm not the judge of men that you are, Count Brass – that we shall have little opportunity for swordplay when dealing with our foes. Their weapons are likely to be a little more sophisticated.'

Hawkmoon indicated the tall lances protruding from the rear of his saddle. 'I have two flame-lances here, for I anticipated the same situation.'

'Well, flame-lances are better than nothing,' agreed D'Averc, but he still looked sceptical.

'I have never much favoured sorcerous weapons,' said Oladahn with a suspicious glance at the lances. 'They are inclined to bring stronger forces against those who wield them.'

'You are superstitious, Oladahn. Flame-lances are not the products of supernatural sorcery, but of the science which flourished before the coming of the Tragic Millennium.' Bowgentle spoke kindly.

'Aye,' said Oladahn. 'I think that proves my point, Master Bowgentle.

Soon the dark sea could be seen glinting ahead.

Hawkmoon felt his stomach muscles tighten as he anticipated the encounter with the mysterious pyramid which had tried to get his friends to kill him.

But the shore, when they reached it, was empty save for a few clumps of seaweed, some tufts of grass growing on sandhills, the surf which lapped the beach. Count Brass took them to where he had erected an awning of his cloak behind a sandhill. Here was his food and some of the equipment he had left behind when he set out to meet Hawkmoon. On the way the four had told Hawkmoon how they had come to meet, each, at first, mistaking another for Hawkmoon and challenging him.

'This is where it appears, when it appears,' Count Brass said. 'I suggest you hide in yonder patch of reeds, Duke Dorian. Then I'll tell the pyramid that we have killed you and we'll see what happens.'

'Very well.' Hawkmoon unshipped the flame-lances and led his horse into the cover of the tall reeds. From a distance he saw the four men talking for a while and then he heard Count Brass's great voice calling out:

'Oracle! Where are you? You may release me now. The deed is done! Hawkmoon is dead.'

Hawkmoon wondered if the pyramid, or those who manipulated it, had any means of testing the truth of Count Brass's words. Did they peer into the whole of this world or merely a part of it? Did they have human spies working for them?

'Oracle!' called Count Brass again. 'Hawkmoon is dead by my

hand!'

It seemed to Hawkmoon then that they had entirely failed to deceive the so-called oracle. The mistral continued to howl across the lagoons and the marshes. The sea whipped at the shore. Grass and reeds waved. Dawn was fast approaching. Soon the first grey light would begin to appear and then his friends might vanish altogether.

'Oracle! Where are you?'

Something flickered, but it was probably only a wind-borne firefly. Then it flickered again, in the same place, in the air just above Count Brass's head.

Hawkmoon slipped a flame-lance into his hand and felt for the stud which, when pressed, would discharge ruby fire.

'Oracle!'

An outline appeared, white and tenuous. This was the source of the flickering light. It was the outline of a pyramid. And within the pyramid was a fainter shadow which was gradually obscured as the outline began to fill in.

And then a diamond-like pyramid about the height of a man was hovering above Count Brass's head and to his right.

Hawkmoon strained both ears and eyes as the pyramid began to speak.

'You have done well, Count Brass. For this we will send you and your companions back to the world of the living. Where is Hawkmoon's corpse?'

Hawkmoon was astonished. He had recognized the voice from the pyramid but he could hardly believe it.

'Corpse?' Count Brass was non-plussed: 'You did not speak of his corpse. Why should you? You work in my interest, not I in yours. That is what you told me.'

'But the corpse . . . ' The voice was almost pettish now.

'Here is the corpse, Kalan of Vitall!' And Hawkmoon rose from the reeds and strode towards the pyramid. 'Show yourself to me, coward. So you did not kill yourself, after all. Well, let me help you now . . . '

And, in his anger, he pressed the stud of the flame-lance and the red fire leapt out from the ruby tip and splashed against the pulsing pyramid so that it howled and then it whined and then it whimpered and became transparent so that the cringing creature within could be seen by all of the five who watched.

'Kalan!' Hawkmoon recognized the Dark Empire scientist. 'I guessed it must be you. None saw you die. All thought that the pool of matter left on the floor of your laboratory must be your remains. But you deceived us!'

49

'It is too hot!' screamed Kalan. 'This machine is a delicate thing. You'll destroy it.'

'Should I care?'

'Aye – the consequences . . . They would be terrible.'

But Hawkmoon continued to play the ruby fire over the pyramid and Kalan continued to cringe and to scream.

'How did you make these poor fellows think it was a netherworld they inhabited? How did you make it perpetual night for them?'

Kalan wailed: 'How do you think? I merely made a split-second of their days so that they did not even notice the sun's passing. I speeded up their days and I slowed down their nights.'

'And how did you make the barrier which meant they could not reach Castle Brass or the town?'

'Just as easy. Ah! Ah! Every time they reached the walls of the city, I shifted them back a few minutes so that they might never quite reach the walls. These were crude skills – but I warn you, Hawkmoon, the machine is not crude – it is hyperdelicate. It could go out of control and destroy us all.'

'As long as I could be sure of your destruction, Kalan, I would not care!'

'You are cruel, Hawkmoon!'

And Hawkmoon laughed at the note of accusation in Kalan's voice. Kalan – who had implanted the Black Jewel in his skull – who had helped Taragorm destroy the crystal machine which had protected Castle Brass – who had been the greatest and most evil of the geniuses who had supplied the Dark Empire with its scientific power – accusing Hawkmoon of cruelty!

And the ruby fire continued to play over the pyramid.

'You are wrecking my controls!' Kalan screamed. 'If I leave now I shan't be able to return until I have made repairs. I will not be able to release these friends of yours . . . '

'I think we can do without your help, little man!' Count Brass laughed. 'Though I thank you for your concern. You sought to deceive us and now you are paying the price.'

'I spoke the truth – Hawkmoon will lead you to your deaths.'

'Aye – but they'll be noble deaths and not the fault of Hawkmoon.'

Kalan's face twisted. He was sweating as the pyramid grew hotter and hotter. 'Very well. I retreat. But I'll take my vengeance on all four of you yet – alive or dead, I'll still reach you all. Now I return . . . '

'To Londra?' Hawkmoon cried. 'Are you hidden in Londra?'

Kalan laughed wildly. 'Londra? Aye – but no Londra that you know. Farewell, horrid Hawkmoon.'

And the pyramid faded and then vanished and left the five standing on the shore in silence, for there seemed nothing to say at that stage.

A little while later Hawkmoon pointed to the horizon.

'Look,' he said.

The sun was beginning to rise.

## CHAPTER TWO

## The Return of the Pyramid

For a while, as they breakfasted on the unpalatable food Kalan of Vitall had left for Count Brass and the others, they debated what they must do.

It had become obvious that the four were stranded, for the present, in Hawkmoon's time-period. How long they could remain there none knew.

'I spoke of Soryandum and the Wraith-folk,' Hawkmoon told his friends. 'It is our only hope of getting help, for the Runestaff is unlikely to give us aid, even if we could find it to ask for such aid.' He had told them much of the events which were to occur in their futures and had taken place in his past.

'Then we should make haste,' said Count Brass, 'lest Kalan returns – as return, I'm sure, he will. How shall we reach Soryandum?'

'I do not know,' Hawkmoon said honestly. 'They shifted their city out of our dimensions when the Dark Empire threatened them. I can only hope that they have moved it back to its old location now that the threat has passed.'

'And where is Soryandum – or where was it?' Oladahn asked.

'In the Syranian Desert.'

Count Brass raised his red eyebrows. 'A wide desert, friend Hawkmoon. A vast desert. And harsh.'

'Aye. All of those things. That is why so few travellers ever came upon Soryandum.'

'And you expect us to cross such a desert in search of a city which *might* be there?' D'Averc smiled sourly.

'Aye. It is our only hope, Sir Huillam.'

D'Averc shrugged and turned away. 'Perhaps the dry air would be good for my chest.'

'So we must cross the Middle Sea, then?' said Bowgentle. 'We need a boat.'

'There is a port not far from here,' said Hawkmoon. 'There we should find a boat to take us on the long journey to the coasts of Syrania – to the port of Hornus, if possible. After that we journey inland, on camels if we can hire them, beyond the Euphrates.'

'A journey of many weeks,' said Bowgentle thoughtfully. 'Is there no quicker route?'

'This is the quickest. Ornithopters would fly faster, but they are notoriously capricious and have not the range we need. The riding flamingoes of the Kamarg would have offered us an alternative but, I fear, I do not want to draw attention to us in the Kamarg – it would cause too much confusion and pain to those we all love – or will love. Therefore we must go in disguise to Marshais, the largest port hereabouts, and take passage as ordinary travelers aboard the first available ship.'

'I see that you have considered this carefully.' Count Brass rose and began to pack his gear into his saddlebags. 'We'll follow your plan, my lord of Köln, and hope that we are not traced by Kalan before we reach Soryandum.'

Two days later they came, cloaked and cautious, into the bustling city of Marshais, perhaps the greatest seaport on this coast. In the harbour were over a hundred ships – far-going, tall-masted trading vessels, used to plying all kinds of seas in all kinds of weather. And the men, too, were fit to sail in such ships – bronzed by wind, sun and sea, tough, hard-eyed, harsh-voiced seamen for the most part, who kept their own counsel. Many were stripped to the waist, wearing only divided kilts of silk or cotton, dyed in dozens of different shades, with anklets and wristlets often of precious metal studded with gem-stones. And around their necks and heads were tied long scarves, as brightly coloured as their britches. Many wore weapons at their belts – knives and cutlasses for the most part. And most of these men were worth only what they wore – but what they wore, in the way of bracelets and earrings and the like, was worth a small fortune and might be gambled away in a few hours ashore in any of the scores of taverns, inns, gaming houses and whorehouses which lined all the streets leading down to the quays of Marshais.

Into all this noise and bustle and colour came the five weary men, their hoods about their faces, for they wanted none to recognize them. And Hawkmoon knew, best of all, that they would be recognized – five heroes whose portraits hung on many an inn-sign, whose statues filled many a square, whose names were used for the swearing of oaths and for the telling of yarns which could never be as incredible as the truth. There was only one danger that Hawkmoon could see – that in their unwillingness to show their faces they might be mistaken for Dark Empire men, unrepentant and still desiring to hide their heads in masks. They found an inn, quieter than most, in the backstreets and asked for a large room in which they might all stay for a night while one of them went down to the quayside to enquire about a ship.

It was Hawkmoon, who had been growing a beard as they travelled, who elected to make the necessary enquiries and soon after they had eaten he left for the waterfront and returned quite quickly with good news. There was a trader leaving by the first tide of the morning. He was willing to take passengers and charged a reasonable fee. He was not going to Hornus but to Behruk a little further up the coast. This was almost as good and Hawkmoon had decided on the spot to book passages for them all aboard his ship. They all lay down to sleep as soon as this was settled, but none slept well, for there was ever the thought to plague them that the pyramid with Kalan in it would return.

Hawkmoon realized of what the pyramid had reminded him. It was something like the Throne-Globe of the King-Emperor Huon – the thing which had supported the life of that incredibly ancient homunculus before he had been slain by Baron Meliadus. Perhaps the same science had created both? It was more than likely. Or had Kalan found a cache of old machines, such as were buried in many places upon the planet, and used them? And where was Kalan of Vitall hiding? Not in Londra but in some other Londra? Is that what he meant?

Hawkmoon slept poorest of all that night as these thoughts and a thousand others sped through his head. And his sword lay, un-scabbarded, in his hand when he did sleep.

On a clear autumn day they set sail in a tall, fast ship called *The Romanian Queen* (Her home port was on the Black Sea) whose sails and decks gleamed white and clean and who seemed to speed without effort over the water.

The sailing was good for the first two days, but on the third day the wind dropped and they were becalmed. The captain was reluctant to unship his vessel's oars, for he had a small crew and did not want to overwork them, so he decided to risk a day's wait and hope that the wind would come up. The coast of Kyprus, an island kingdom which, like so many, had once been a vassal state of the Dark Empire, could just be seen off to the east and it was frustrating for the five friends to have to peer through the narrow porthole of their cabin and see it. All five had remained below decks for the whole voyage. Hawkmoon had explained this strange behaviour by saying that they were members of a religious cult making a pilgrimage and according to their vows,

54

must spend their whole waking time in prayer. The captain, a decent sailor who wanted only a fair price for the passage and no trouble from his passengers, accepted this explanation without question.

It was about noon on the next day, when a wind had still not materialized, that Hawkmoon and the others heard a commotion above their heads – shouts and oaths and running of booted and bare feet to and fro.

'What can it be?' Hawkmoon said. 'Pirates? We have met with pirates before in near-by waters, have we not Oladahn?'

But Oladahn merely looked astonished. 'Eh? This is my first sea voyage, Duke Dorian!'

And Hawkmoon, not for the first time, remembered that Oladahn was still to experience the adventure of the Mad God's ship, and he apologized to the little mountain man.

The commotion grew louder and more confused. Staring through the porthole, they could see no sign of an attacking ship and there were no sounds of battle. Perhaps some seamonster, some creature left over from the Tragic Millennium, had risen from the waters outside their field of vision?

Hawkmoon rose and put on his cloak, drawing the cowl over his head. 'I'll investigate,' he said.

He opened the door of the cabin and climbed the short stairway to the deck. And there, near the stern, was the object of the crew's terror, and from it came the voice of Kalan of Vitall exhorting the men to fall upon their passengers and slay them immediately or the whole ship would go down.

The pyramid was glowing a brilliant, blinding white and stood out sharply against the blue of the sky and the sea.

At once Hawkmoon dashed back into the cabin and picked up a flame-lance.

'The pyramid has come back!' he told them. 'Wait here while I deal with it.'

He climbed the companionway and rushed across the deck towards the pyramid, his passage encumbered by the frightened crewmen who were backing away rapidly.

Again a beam of red light darted from the ruby tip of the flame-lance and splashed against the white of the pyramid, like blood mingling with milk. But this time there were no screams from within the pyramid, only laughter.

'I have taken precautions, Dorian Hawkmoon, against your crude weapons. I have strengthened my machine.'

'Let us see to what degree,' Hawkmoon said grimly. He had

guessed that Kalan was nervous of using his machine's power to manipulate time, that perhaps Kalan was unsure of the results he would achieve.

And now Oladahn of the Bulgar Mountains was beside him, a sword in his furry hand, a scowl on his face.

'Begone, false oracle!' shouted Oladahn. 'We do not fear you now.'

'You should have cause to fear me,' said Kalan, his face now just visible through the semi-transparent material of the pyramid. He was sweating. Plainly the flame-lance was having at least some effect. 'For I have the means of controlling all events in this world – and in others!'

'Then control them!' Hawkmoon challenged, and he turned the beam of his flame-lance to full strength.

'Aaah! Fools – destroy my machine and you disrupt the fabric of time itself. All will be thrown into flux – chaos will rage throughout the universe. All intelligence shall die!'

And then Oladahn was running at the pyramid, his sword whirling, trying to cut through the peculiar substance which protected Kalan from the powers of the flame-lance.

'Get back, Oladahn!' Hawkmoon cried. 'You can do nothing with a sword!'

But Oladahn hacked twice at the pyramid and he stabbed through it, it seemed, and almost ran Kalan of Vitall through before the sorcerer turned and saw him and adjusted a small pyramid he held in his hand, grinning at Oladahn with horrible malice.

'Oladahn! Beware!' Hawkmoon yelled, sensing some new danger.

Again Oladahn drew back his arm for another blow at Kalan.

Oladahn screamed.

He looked about him in bewilderment as if he saw something other than the pyramid and the deck of the ship. 'The bear!' he wailed. 'It has me!'

And then, with a chilling shout, he vanished.

Hawkmoon dropped the flame-lance and ran forward, but he had only a glimpse of Kalan's chuckling features before the pyramid, too, had disappeared.

There was nothing of Oladahn to be seen. And Hawkmoon knew that, initially at least, the little man had been thrown back to the moment he had first left his own time. But would he be allowed to remain there?

Hawkmoon would not have cared so much – for he knew that Oladahn had survived the fight with the bear – if he had not become suddenly aware of the great power which Kalan wielded.

In spite of himself, Hawkmoon shuddered. He turned and saw that both captain and crew were offering him strange suspicious looks.

Without speaking to them he went straight back to his cabin.

Now it had become more urgent than ever that they should find Soryandum and the Wraith-folk.

## CHAPTER THREE

The Journey to Soryandum

Soon after the incident on deck the wind sprang up with great force so that it seemed that a storm might be in the offing and the captain ordered all sails on so that he could run before the storm and get into Behruk with all possible speed.

Hawkmoon suspected that the captain's haste had more to do with his wish to unload his passengers than his cargo, but he sympathized with the man. Another captain, after such an incident, might have been justified in throwing the remaining four overboard.

Hawkmoon's hatred for Kalan of Vitall grew more intense. This was the second time that he had been robbed of his friend by a Dark Empire lord and, if anything, he felt this second loss more painfully than he did the first, for all that he had been, in some ways, more prepared for it. He became determined, no matter what befell, to seek out Kalan and destroy him.

Disembarking on the white quayside of Behruk, the four took fewer precautions to hide their identities here. Their legends were familiar to the folk who dwelt along the Arabian Sea but their descriptions were not so well-known. None the less they lost no time in going speedily to the market-place and there purchasing four sturdy camels for their expedition into the hinterland.

Four days riding saw them used to the lolloping beasts and most of their aches gone. Four days riding also saw them on the edge of the Syranian desert, following the Euphrates as it wound through great sanddunes, while Hawkmoon looked often at the map and wished that Oladahn, the Oladahn who had fought at his side against D'Averc in Soryandum, when they were still enemies, was here to help him recall their route.

The huge, hot sun had turned Count Brass's armour into glaring gold. He dazzled the eyes of his companions almost as much as the pyramid of Kalan of Vitall had dazzled them. And Dorian Hawkmoon's steel armour shone, in contrast, like silver. Bowgentle and Huillam D'Averc, who wore no armour at all, made one or two acid comments about this effect, though they stopped when it became evident that the armoured men were suffering considerably more discomfort in the heat and, while waterholes and the river were close, took to pouring whole helmets-full of water through the necks of their breastplates.

The fifth day's riding saw them passed beyond the river and into the desert proper. Dull yellow sand stretched in all directions. It rippled sometimes, when a faint breeze blew across the desert, reminding them, intolerably, of the water they had left behind.

The sixth day's riding saw them leaning wearily over the pommels of their high saddles, their eyes glazed and their lips cracked as they preserved their water, not knowing when next they might find a waterhole.

The seventh day's riding saw Bowgentle fall from his saddle and lie spreadeagled upon the sand and it took half their remaining water to revive him. After he had fallen they sought the scant shade of a dune and remained there through the night until the next morning when Hawkmoon dragged himself to his feet and said he would continue alone.

'Alone? Why is that?' Count Brass got up, the straps of his brass armour were creaking. 'For what reason, Duke of Köln?'

'I will scout while you rest. I could swear that Soryandum was near here. I will circle about until I find it – or find the site on which it stood. Whatever else, there is bound to be a source of water there.'

'I can see sense in that,' Count Brass agreed. 'And if you grow weary, then one of us can relieve you, and so on. Are you certain that we are close to Soryandum?'

'I am. I shall look for the hills which mark the end of the desert. They should be near. If only these dunes were not so high, I am sure we should see the hills by now.'

'Very well,' said Count Brass. 'We shall wait.'

And Hawkmoon goaded his camel to its feet and rode away from where his friends still sat.

But it was not until the afternoon that he climbed the twentieth dune of the day and saw at last the green foothills of the mountains at the foot of which had lain Soryandum.

But he could not see the ruined city of the Wraith-folk. He had marked his way carefully on his map and now he retraced his journey.

He was almost back at the spot where he had left his friends when he saw the pyramid again. Foolishly he had decided to leave his encumbering flame-lances behind and he was not sure if any of the others knew how to work the lances, or whether they would care to, after what had happened to Oladahn.

He dismounted from the camel and proceeded as cautiously as he could, using the little cover available to him. Automatically he had drawn his sword.

Now words reached him from the pyramid. Kalan of Vitall was once again trying to convince his three friends that they should kill him when he returned.

'He is your enemy. Whatever else I might have told you, I spoke truth when I said that he will lead you to your deaths. You know Huillam D'Averc that you are a friend of Granbretan – Hawkmoon will turn you against the Dark Empire. And you, Bowgentle, you hate violence – Hawkmoon will make you a man of violence. And you, Count Brass, who has always been neutral where the affairs of Granbretan are concerned, he will set you upon a course which will make you fight against that very force which now you regard as a unifying factor in the future of Europe. And, as well as being deceived into acting against your better interests, you will be slain. Kill Hawkmoon now and . . . '

'Kill me, then!' Hawkmoon stood up, impatient with Kalan's cunning. 'Kill me yourself, Kalan. Why can't you?'

The pyramid continued to hover over the heads of the three men as Hawkmoon looked down upon it from the dune.

'And why would killing me now make all that has gone before different, Kalan? Your logic is either very bad, or else you have not told us all that you should!'

'You grow boring, besides,' said Huillam D'Averc. He drew his slim sword from its scabbard. 'And I am very thirsty and tired, Baron Kalan. I think I will try my luck against you, for there's precious little else to do in this desert!'

And suddenly he had leaped forward, stabbing and stabbing again with his foil, the steel passing into the white material of the pyramid.

Kalan screamed as if wounded. 'Look to your own interest, D'Averc – it lies with me!'

D'Averc laughed and passed his sword again into the pyramid.

And again Kalan shouted. 'I warn you, D'Averc – if you make me, I shall rid this world of you!'

'This world has nothing to offer. And it does not want me haunting it, either. I think I'll find your heart, Baron Kalan, if I continue

60

to search.'

He stabbed once more.

Kalan shouted once more.

Hawkmoon cried: 'D'Averc, be careful!' He began to run and slide down the dune, trying to reach the flame-lance. But D'Averc had vanished, silently, before he had got halfway to the weapon.

'D'Averc!' Hawkmoon's voice had a baying quality, a mournful quality. 'D'Averc!'

'Be silent, Hawkmoon,' said Kalan's voice from the glowing pyramid. 'Listen to me, you others. Kill him now – or D'Averc's fate shall be yours.'

'It does not seem a particularly terrible fate.' Count Brass smiled.

Hawkmoon picked up the flame-lance. Kalan could obviously see through the pyramid for he screamed. 'Oh, you are crude, Hawkmoon. But you shall die yet.'

And the pyramid faded and was gone.

Count Brass looked about him, a sardonic expression on his bronzed face. 'Should we find Soryandum,' he said, 'it could come to pass that there'll be nothing of us to find in Soryandum. Our ranks are reducing swiftly, friend Hawkmoon.'

Hawkmoon gave a deep sigh. 'To lose good friends twice over is hard to bear. You cannot understand that. Oladahn and D'Averc were strangers to you as was I a stranger to them. But they were old, dear friends to me.'

Bowgentle put a hand on Hawkmoon's shoulder. 'I can understand,' he said. 'This business is harder on you than it is on us, Duke Dorian. For all that we are bewildered – tugged from our times, given omens of death on all sides, discovering peculiar machines which order us to kill strangers – you are sad. And grief could be called the most weakening of all the emotions. It robs you of will when you most need your will.'

'Aye,' Hawkmoon sighed again. He flung down the flame-lance. 'Well,' he said. 'I have found Soryandum – or, at least, the hills in which Soryandum lies. We can get there by nightfall, I'd guess.'

'Then let us hurry on to Soryandum,' said Count Brass. He brushed sand from his face and his moustache. 'With luck we shall not see Baron Kalan and his damned pyramid for a few days yet. And by that time we might have gone a stage or two further towards solving this mystery.' He slapped Hawkmoon on the back. 'Come, lad. Mount up. You never know – perhaps this will all end well. Perhaps you'll see your other friends again.'

Hawkmoon smiled bitterly. 'I have the feeling I'll be lucky if I ever see my wife and children again, Count Brass.'

CHAPTER FOUR

A Further Encounter with
another Old Enemy

But there was no Soryandum in the green foothills bordering the Syranian desert. They found water. They found the outline which marked the area of the city, but the city had gone. Hawkmoon had seen it go, when threatened by the Dark Empire. Plainly the people of Soryandum had been wise, judging that the threat was not yet over. Wiser, Hawkmoon thought sardonically, than he. So, after all, their journey had been for nothing. There was only one other faint hope – that the cave of machines from which, years before, he had taken the crystal machines, was still intact. Miserably he led his two companions deep into the hills until Soryandum was several miles behind them.

'It seems that I have led you on a useless quest, my friends,' Hawkmoon told Bowgentle and Count Brass. 'And, moreover, offered you a false hope.'

'Perhaps not,' said Bowgentle thoughtfully. 'It could be that the machines remain intact and that I, who have some slight experience of such things, might be able to see a use for them.'

Count Brass was ahead of the other two, striding in his armour of brass, up the steep hill to stand on the brow and peer into the valley below.

'Is this your cave?' he called.

Hawkmoon and Bowgentle joined him. 'Aye – that's the cliff,' said Hawkmoon. A cliff which looked as if a giant sword had sheared a hill in two. And there, some distance to the south, he saw the cairn of granite, made from the stone sliced from the hill to make the cave in which the weapons were stored. And there was the cave opening, a narrow slit in the cliff face. It looked undisturbed. Hawkmoon's spirits began to rise a little.

He went faster down the hill. 'Come, then,' he called, 'let's hope the treasures are intact!'

But there was something that Hawkmoon had forgotten in his confusion of thoughts and emotions. He had forgotten that the ancient technology of the Wraith-folk had had a guardian. A

63

guardian that he and Oladahn had fought once before and had failed to destroy. A guardian that D'Averc had only just managed to escape from. A guardian that could not be reasoned with. And Hawkmoon wished that they had not left their camels resting at the sight of Soryandum, for all he wished for now was a chance to flee swiftly.

'What is that sound?' asked Count Brass as a peculiar, muted wailing came from the crack in the cliff. 'Do you recognize it, Hawkmoon?'

'Aye,' said Hawkmoon miserably. 'I recognize it. It is the cry of the machine-beast – the mechanical creature which guards the caves. I had assumed it destroyed but now it will destroy us, I fear.'

'We have swords,' said Count Brass.

Hawkmoon laughed wildly. 'We have swords, aye!'

'And there are three of us,' Bowgentle pointed out. 'All cunning men.'

'Aye.'

The wailing increased as the beast scented them.

'We have only one advantage, however,' said Hawkmoon softly. 'The beast is blind. Our only chance is to scatter and run, making for Soryandum and our camels. There my flame-lance might prove effective for a short while.'

'Run?' Count Brass looked disgruntled. He drew his great sword and stroked his red moustache. 'I have never fought a mechanical beast before. I do not care to run, Hawkmoon.'

'Then die – perhaps for the third time!' Hawkmoon shouted in frustration. 'Listen to me Count Brass – you know I am not a coward – if we are to survive, we must get back to our camels before the beast catches us. Look!'

And the blind machine-beast emerged from the opening in the cliff, its huge head casting about for the source of the sounds and the scents it hated.

'Nion!' hissed Count Brass. 'It is a large beast.'

It was at least twice the size of Count Brass. Down the length of its back was a row of razor-sharp horns. Its metal scales were multicoloured and half-blinded them as it began to hop towards them. It had short hind-legs and long fore-legs which ended in metal talons. Roughly of the proportions of a large gorilla, it had multi-faceted eyes which had been broken in a previous fight with Hawkmoon and Oladahn. As it moved, it clashed. Its voice was metallic and made their teeth ache. Its smell, coming to them even from that distance, was also metallic.

Hawkmoon tugged at Count Brass's arm. 'Please, Count Brass, I beg you. This is not the right ground on which to choose to make a stand.'

This logic appealed to Count Brass. 'Aye,' he said, 'I can see that. Very well, we'll make for the flat ground again. Will it follow us?'

'Oh, of that you can be certain!'

And then, in three slightly different directions, the companions began to run back towards the site of Soryandum as fast as they could before the beast decided which of them it would follow.

Their camels could smell the machine-beast, that was evident as they came panting back to where they had tethered their animals. The camels were tugging at the ropes which had been pegged to the ground. Their ugly heads reared, their mouths and nostrils twisted, their eyes rolled and their hooves thumped nervously at the barren ground.

Again the wailing shriek of the machine-beast echoed through the hills behind them.

Hawkmoon handed a flame-lance to Count Brass, 'I doubt if these will have much effect, but we must try them.'

Count Brass grumbled. 'I'd have preferred a hand-to-hand engagement with the thing.'

'That could still happen,' Hawkmoon told him with grim humour.

Hopping, waddling, running on all fours, the mighty metal beast emerged over the nearest hill, pausing as, again, it sought their scent – perhaps it even heard the sound of their heartbeats.

Bowgentle positioned himself behind his friends, for he had no flame-lance. 'I am beginning to become tired of dying,' he said with a smile. 'Is that the fate of the dead, then? To die again and again through uncountable incarnations? It is not an appealing conception.'

'Now!' Hawkmoon said, and pressed the stud of his flame-lance. At the same time Count Brass activated his lance.

Ruby fire struck the mechanical beast and it snorted. Its scales glowed and in places became white hot, but the heat did not seem to have any effect upon the beast at all. It did not notice the flame-lances. Shaking his head, Hawkmoon switched off his lance and Count Brass did the same. It would be stupid to use up the lances' power.

'There is only one way to deal with such a monster,' said Count Brass.

'And what is that?'

'It would have to be lured into a pit . . . '

'But we do not have a pit,' Bowgentle pointed out, nervously eyeing the creature as it began to hop nearer.

'Or a cliff,' said Count Brass. 'If it could be tricked to fall over a cliff . . . '

'There is no cliff near by,' Bowgentle said patiently.

'Then we shall perish, I suppose,' said Count Brass with a shrug of his brazen shoulders. And then, before they could guess at what he planned, he had drawn his great broadsword and with a wild battle-yell was rushing upon the machine-beast – seemingly a man of metal attacking a monster of metal.

The monster roared. It stopped and it reared upon its hindquarters, its taloned paws slashing here and there at random, making the very air whistle.

Count Brass ducked beneath the claws and aimed a blow at the thing's midriff. His sword clanged on its scales and clanged again. Then Count Brass had jumped back, out of the reach of those slashing talons, bringing his sword down upon the great wrist as it passed him.

Hawkmoon joined him now, battering at one of the creature's legs with his own sword. And Bowgentle, able to forget his dislike of killing where this mechanical thing was concerned, tried to drive his blade up into the machine-beast's face, only to have the metal jaws close on the sword and snap it off cleanly.

'Get back, Bowgentle,' Hawkmoon said. 'You can do nothing now.'

And the beast's head turned at the sound and the talons slashed again so that, in avoiding them, Hawkmoon stumbled and fell.

In again came Count Brass, roaring almost as loudly as his adversary. Again the blade clanged on the scales. And again the beast turned to seek the source of this new irritation.

But all three were tiring. Their journeys across the desert had weakened them. Their run from the hills had tired them further. Hawkmoon knew that it was inevitable that they should perish here in the desert and that none should know the manner of their passing.

He saw Count Brass shout as he was flung backwards several feet by a sideswipe of the beast's paw. The Count, encumbered by his heavy armour, fell helplessly upon the barren ground, winded and, for the moment, unable to rise.

The metal beast sensed its opponent's weakness and lumbered forward to crush Count Brass beneath its huge feet.

Hawkmoon shouted wordlessly and ran at the thing, bringing his sword down upon its back. But it did not pause. Closer and closer it came to where Count Brass lay.

Hawkmoon darted around to put himself between the creature and his friend. He struck at its whirling talons, at its torso. His bones ached horribly as his sword shuddered with every blow he struck.

And still the beast refused to alter its course, its blind eyes staring ahead of it.

Then Hawkmoon, too, was flung aside and lay bruised and dazed, watching in horror as Count Brass struggled to rise. He saw one of the monstrous feet rise up above Count Brass's head, saw Count Brass raise an arm as if it would protect him from being crushed. Somehow he managed to get to his feet and began to stumble forward, knowing that he would be too late to save Count Brass, even if he could get to the machine-beast in time. And as he moved, so did Bowgentle – Bowgentle who had no weapon save the stump of a sword – rushing at the beast as if he thought he could turn it aside with his bare hands.

And Hawkmoon thought: 'I have brought my friends to yet another death. It is true what Kalan told them. I am their nemesis, it seems.'

## CHAPTER FIVE

# Some Other Londra

And then the metal beast hesitated.

It whined almost plaintively.

Count Brass was not one to miss such an opportunity. Swiftly he rolled from under the great foot. He still did not have the strength to rise to his feet, but he began to crawl away, his sword still in his hand.

Both Bowgentle and Hawkmoon paused, wondering what had caused the beast to stop.

The machine-creature cringed. Its whine became placatory, fearful. It turned its head on one side as if it heard a voice which none of the others could hear.

Count Brass rose, at last, to his feet and wearily prepared himself again to fight the monster.

Then, with an enormous crash which made the earth shake, the beast fell and the bright colours of its scales became dull as if suddenly rusted. It did not move.

'What?' Count Brass's deep voice was puzzled. 'Did we *will* it to death?'

Hawkmoon began to laugh as he noticed the faintest of outlines begin to appear against the clear, desert sky. 'Someone might have done,' he said.

Bowgentle gasped as he, too, noticed the outlines. 'What is it? The ghost of a city?'

'Almost.'

Count Brass growled. He sniffed and hefted his sword. 'I like this new danger no better.'

'It should not be a danger – to us,' said Hawkmoon. 'Soryandum is returning.'

Slowly they saw the outlines grow firmer until soon a whole city lay spread across the desert. An ancient city. A ruined city.

Count Brass cursed and stroked his red moustache, his stance still that of one prepared for an attack.

'Sheath your sword, Count Brass,' Hawkmoon said. 'This is Soryandum that we sought. The Wraith-folk, those ancient immortals of whom I told you, have come to our rescue. This is lovely Soryandum. Look.'

And Soryandum was lovely, for all that she lay in ruins. Her moss-grown walls, her fountains, her tall, broken towers, her blossoms of ochre, orange and purple, her cracked, marble pavements, her columns of granite and obsidian – all were beautiful. And there was an air of tranquillity about the city, even about the birds which nested in her time-worn houses, the dust which blew through her deserted streets.

'This is Soryandum,' said Hawkmoon again, almost in a whisper.

They stood in a square, beside the dead beast of metal.

Count Brass was the first to move, crossing the weed-grown pavement and touching a column. 'It is solid enough,' he grunted. 'How can this be?'

'I have ever rejected the more sensational claims of those who believe in the supernatural,' said Bowgentle. 'But now I begin to wonder . . . '

'This is science that has brought Soryandum here,' Hawkmoon said. 'And it is science that took her away. I know. I supplied the machine the Wraith-folk needed, for it is impossible for them to leave their city now. These folk were like us once, but over the centuries, according to a process I cannot begin to understand, they have rid themselves of physical form and have become creatures of mind alone. They can take physical shape when they desire it and they have greater strength than most mortals. They are a peaceful people – and as beautiful as this city of theirs.'

'You are most flattering, old friend,' said a voice from the air.

'Rinal?' said Hawkmoon, recognizing the voice. 'Is that you?'

'It is I. But who are your companions? Our instruments are confused by them. It is for this reason that we were reluctant to reveal either ourselves or our city, in case they should have deceived you in some way into leading them to Soryandum when they had evil designs against our city.'

'They are good friends,' said Hawkmoon, 'but not of this time. Is that what confuses your instruments, Rinal?'

'It could be. Well, I shall trust you Hawkmoon, for I have reason to. You are a welcome guest in Soryandum, for it is thanks to you that we still survive.'

'And it is thanks to you that I survive.' Hawkmoon smiled. 'Where are you Rinal?'

The figure of Rinal, tall, ethereal, appeared suddenly beside him. His body was naked and without ornament and it had a kind of milky opaque quality. His face was thin and his eyes seemed blind – as blind as those of the machine-beast – yet looked clearly at Hawkmoon.

'Ghosts of cities, ghosts of men,' said Count Brass sheathing his sword. 'Still, if you saved our lives from that thing,' he pointed at the dead machine-beast, 'I must thank you.' He recovered his grace and bowed. 'I thank you most humbly, Sir Ghost.'

'I regret that our beast caused you so much trouble,' said Rinal of Soryandum. 'We created it to protect our treasures, many centuries ago. We would have destroyed it, save that we feared the Dark Empire folk would return to take our machines and put them to evil use – and also, we could do nothing until it came into the environs of our city, for, as you know, Dorian Hawkmoon, we have no power beyond Soryandum now. Our existence is completely linked with the existence of the city. It was an easy matter to tell the beast to die, however, once it was here.'

'It was as well for us, Duke Dorian, that you advised us to flee back here,' said Bowgentle feelingly. 'Otherwise we should all three be dead by now.'

'Where is your other friend,' said Rinal. 'The one who came with you first to Soryandum!'

'Oladahn is twice-dead,' said Hawkmoon in a low voice.

'Twice?'

'Aye – just as these other friends of mine came close to dying for at least a second time.'

'You intrigue me,' said Rinal. 'Come, we'll find you something with which to sustain yourselves as you explain all these mysteries to myself and the few others of my folk who remain.'

Rinal led the three companions through the broken streets of Soryandum until they came to a three-storied house which had no entrance at ground level. Hawkmoon had visited the house before. Although superficially no different to the other ruins of Soryandum, this was where the Wraith-folk lived when they needed to take material form.

And now two others emerged from above, drifting down towards Hawkmoon, Count Brass and Bowgentle and lifting them effortlessly, bearing them upward to the second level and a wide window which was the entrance to the house.

In a bare, clean room food was brought to them, though Rinal's folk had no need of food themselves. The food was delicious, though unfamiliar. Count Brass attacked it with vigour, speaking hardly at all as he listened to Hawkmoon tell Rinal of why they sought the assistance of the Wraith-folk of Soryandum.

And when Hawkmoon had finished his tale, Count Brass continued to eat, to Bowgentle's quiet amusement. Bowgentle himself was more interested in learning more about Soryandum, and its inhabitants, its history and its science and Rinal told him much, between listening to Hawkmoon. He told Bowgentle how, during the Tragic Millennium, most of the great cities and nations had concentrated their energies on producing more and more powerful weapons of war. But Soryandum had been able to remain neutral, thanks to her remote geographical position. She had concentrated on understanding more of the nature of space, of matter and of time. Thus she had survived the Tragic Millennium and remembered all her knowledge while elsewhere knowledge died and superstition replaced it, as was ever the case in such situations.

'And that is why we now seek your help,' said Hawkmoon. 'We wish to find out how Baron Kalan escaped and to where he fled. We wish to discover how he manages to manipulate the stuff of time, to bring Count Brass and Bowgentle – and the others I mentioned – from one age to another and still not create a paradox in our minds at least.'

'That sounds the simplest of the problems,' said Rinal. 'This Kalan seems to have got control of enormous power. Is he the one who destroyed your crystal machine – the one we gave you which allowed you to shift your own castle and city out of this space-time?'

'No, that was Taragorm I believe,' Hawkmoon told Rinal. 'But Kalan is just as clever as the old Master of the Palace of Time. However, I suspect that he is unsure of the nature of his power. He is reluctant to test it to its fullest extent. And, also, he seems to think that my death *now* might change *past* history. Is that possible?'

Rinal looked thoughtful. 'It could be,' he said. 'This Baron Kalan must have a very subtle understanding of time. Objectively, of course, there is no such thing as past, present or future. Yet Baron Kalan's plot seems unnecessarily complicated. If he can manipulate time to that extent, could he not merely seek to destroy you *before* – subjectively speaking – you could be of service to the Runestaff?'

'That would change all the events concerning our defeat of the Dark Empire?'

'That is one of the paradoxes. Events are events. They occur. They are truth. But truth varies in different dimensions. It is just possible that there is some dimension of Earth so like your own that similar events are about to take place in it . . . ' Rinal smiled. Count Brass's bronzed forehead had furrowed and he was plucking at his

71

moustache and shaking his head from side to side as if he thought Rinal mad.

'You have another suggestion, Count Brass?'

'Politics are my interest,' said Count Brass. 'I've never cared over-much for the more abstract areas of philosophy. My mind is not trained to follow your reasoning.'

Hawkmoon laughed. 'Mine, neither. Only Bowgentle appears to know of what Rinal speaks.'

'Something,' Bowgentle admitted. 'Something. You think that Kalan might be in some other dimension of the Earth where a Count Brass, say, exists who is not quite the same as the Count Brass who sits beside me now?'

'What?' Count Brass growled. 'Have I a doppelganger?'

Hawkmoon laughed again. But Bowgentle's face was serious as he said: 'Not quite, Count Brass. It occurs to me that, in this world, you would be the doppelganger – and I, for that matter. I believe that this is not our world – that the past we recall would not be quite the same in detail, as that which friend Hawkmoon recalls. We are interlopers, through no fault of our own. Brought here to kill Duke Dorian. Yet, save for reasons of perverse vengeance, why could not Baron Kalan kill Duke Dorian himself? Why must he use us?'

'Because of the repercussions – if your theory is correct – ' put in Rinal. 'His action must conflict with some other action which is against his interests. If he slays Hawkmoon, something will happen to him – a chain of events will come to pass which would be just that much different to the chain of events which will take place if one of you kills him.'

'Yet he must have allowed for the possibility that we would not be deceived into killing Hawkmoon?'

'I think not,' said Rinal. 'I think things have gone awry for Baron Kalan. That is why he continued to try to force you to kill Hawkmoon even when it became obvious that you were suspicious of the situation. He must have based some plan on the expectation of Hawkmoon's being slain in the Kamarg. That is why he grows more and more hysterical. Doubtless he has other schemes afoot and sees them all endangered by Hawkmoon's continuing to live. That, too, is why he has only dispatched those of you who have directly attacked him. He is somehow vulnerable. You would be well advised to dis-cover the nature of that vulnerability.'

Hawkmoon shrugged. 'What chance have we of making such a discovery, when we do not even know where Baron Kalan is hiding?'

'It might be possible to find him,' mused Rinal. 'There are certain devices we invented when we were learning to shift our city through the dimensions – sensors and the like which can probe the various layers of the multiverse. We shall have to prepare them. We have used only one probe, to watch this area of our own Earth while we remained hidden in the other dimension. To activate the others will take a short while. Would this be helpful to you?'

'It would,' said Hawkmoon.

'Does it mean we'll be given a chance to get our hands on Kalan?' growled Count Brass.

Bowgentle placed a hand on the shoulder of the man who would become, in later years, his closest friend. 'You are impetuous, Count. Rinal's machines can only see into these dimensions. It will be another matter altogether, I am sure, to travel into them.'

Rinal inclined his thin-skulled head. 'That is true. However, let us see if we *can* find Baron Kalan of the Dark Empire. There is a good chance that we shall fail – for there are an infinity of dimensions, of this Earth alone.'

Through most of the following day, while Rinal and his people worked on their machines, Hawkmoon, Bowgentle and Count Brass slept, recouping the strength they had expended in travelling to Soryandum and fighting the metal beast.

And then, in the evening, Rinal floated through the window so that the rays of the setting sun seemed to radiate from his opaque body.

'They are ready, the devices,' he said. 'Will you come now? We are beginning to scan the dimensions.'

Count Brass leapt up. 'Aye, we'll come.'

The others rose as two of Rinal's fellows entered the room and, in strong arms, lifted them up, through the window and to the floor above where were assembled an array of machines unlike any machines they had ever seen before. Like the crystal device which had shifted Castle Brass through the dimensions, these were more like jewels than machines – some of the jewels nearly the height of a man. At each of the machines floated one of the Wraith-folk, manipulating smaller jewels, not dissimilar to that small pyramid which Hawkmoon had seen in the hands of Baron Kalan.

A thousand pictures flashed upon the screens as the probes delved the dimensions of the multiverse, showing peculiar, alien scenes, many of which seemed to bear little relation to any Earth Hawkmoon knew.

And then, hours later, Hawkmoon cried: 'There! A beast-mask! I saw it.'

The operator stroked a series of crystals, trying to fix on the image which had flashed on to the screen so briefly. But it was gone.

Again the probes began their search. Twice more Hawkmoon thought he saw scenes providing evidence of Kalan's whereabouts, but twice more they lost the scene.

And then, at last, by the purest chance, they saw a white, glowing pyramid and it was unmistakably the pyramid in which Baron Kalan travelled.

The sensors received a particularly strong signal, for the pyramid was in the process of completing a journey of its own, returning, Hawkmoon hoped, to its base.

'We can follow it easily enough. Watch.'

Hawkmoon, Count Brass and Bowgentle gathered round the screen as it shadowed the milky pyramid until at last it came to a stop and began to turn transparent, revealing the hateful face of Baron Kalan of Vitall. Unaware that he was being observed by those he sought to destroy, he climbed from his pyramid into a large, dark, untidy room that might have been a copy of his old laboratory in Londra. He was frowning, consulting notes he had made. Another figure appeared and spoke to him, though the three friends heard no sound. The figure was clad in the old manner of the folk of the Dark Empire – a huge, cumbersome mask was on his head, completely covering it. The mask was of metal, enamelled in a score of colours, and had been fashioned to resemble the head of a hissing serpent.

Hawkmoon recognized it as the mask of the Order of the Snake – the order to which all sorcerers and scientists of old Granbretan had had to belong. Even as they watched, the snake-masked one handed another mask to Kalan who donned it hurriedly, for no Granbretanian of his kind could bear to be seen unmasked by any of his fellows.

Kalan's mask was also in the form of a serpent's head, but more ornate than his servant's.

Hawkmoon rubbed at his jaw, wondering why he felt something was wrong about the scene. He wished that D'Averc, more familiar with the intimate ways of the Dark Empire, was with him now, for D'Averc would have noticed.

And then it dawned on Hawkmoon that these masks were cruder than any he had seen in Londra, even those worn by the humblest servants. The finish of the masks, their design, was not of the same quality. But why should this be?

Now the probes followed Kalan from his laboratory and through winding passages very like those which had once connected buildings in Londra. Superficially this place could have been Londra. But, again, these passages were subtly different. The stone was poorly faced, the carvings and murals were by inferior artists. None of this would have been tolerated in Londra where, for all their perverse tastes, the Lords of the Dark Empire had demanded the highest standards of craftsmanship, down to the smallest detail.

Here, detail was lacking. The whole thing resembled a bad copy of a painting.

The scene flickered as Kalan entered another chamber where more masked ones met. This chamber also looked familiar, but crude, like everything else.

Count Brass was fuming. 'When can we get there? That's our enemy. Let's deal with him at once!'

'It is not easy to travel through the dimensions,' Rinal said mildly. 'Moreover, we have not yet traced exactly where it is that we were watching.'

Hawkmoon smiled at Count Brass. 'Have patience, sir.'

This Count Brass was more impetuous than the man Hawkmoon had known. Doubtless it was because he was some twenty years younger. Or perhaps, as Rinal had suggested, he was not the same man – only a man very nearly the same, from another dimension. Still, Hawkmoon thought, he was satisfied with this Count Brass, wherever he came from.

'Our probe falters,' said the Wraith-man operating the screen. 'The dimension we study must be many layers away.'

Rinal nodded. 'Aye, many. Somewhere even our old adventuring ancestors never explored. It will be hard to find a doorway through.'

'Kalan found one,' Hawkmoon pointed out.

Rinal smiled faintly. 'By accident or by design, friend Hawkmoon?'

'By design, surely? Where else would he have discovered some other Londra?'

'New cities can be built,' said Rinal.

'Aye,' said Bowgentle. 'And so can new realities.'

## CHAPTER SIX

## Another Victim

The three men waited anxiously while Rinal and his people considered the possibility of journeying into the dimension where Baron Kalan of Vitall was hiding.

'Since this new cult has grown up in the real Londra, I would assume that Kalan is visiting his supporters secretly. That explains the rumour that some of the Dark Empire Lords are still alive in Londra,' Hawkmoon mused. 'Our only other chance would be to go to Londra and seek Kalan out there, when he makes his next visit. But would we have the time?'

Count Brass shook his head. 'That Kalan – he is desperate to accomplish his scheme. Why he should be so hysterical, with all the dimensions of space and time to play with, I cannot guess. Yet, though he can presumably manipulate us at will, he does not. I wonder why we should be so crucial to his plans?'

Hawkmoon shrugged. 'Perhaps we are not. He would not be the first Dark Empire Lord to let a thirst for vengeance get in the way of his own self-interest.' He told them the story of Baron Meliadus.

Bowgentle had been pacing among the crystalline instruments, trying to understand the principles by which they worked, but they defeated him. Now they were all dormant as the Wraith-folk busied themselves in another part of the building with the problem of designing a machine which could shift through the dimensions. They would adapt the crystal engine which moved their city, but the actual engine they must retain, in case further danger threatened them.

'Well,' said Bowgentle, scratching his head, 'I can make nothing of the things. All I can say for certain is that they work!'

Count Brass stirred in his armour. He went to the window and looked out into cool night. 'I'm becoming impatient with being cooped up here,' he said. 'I could do with some fresh air. What about you two?'

Hawkmoon shook his head. 'I'll rest.'

'I'll come with you,' said Bowgentle to Count Brass. 'But how do we leave?'

'Call Rinal,' Hawkmoon said. 'He'll hear you.'

And this they did, looking slightly uncomfortable as the Wraith-folk, seemingly so frail, bore them through the window and down to the earth. Hawkmoon settled himself in a corner of the room and slept.

But strange, disquieting dreams, in which his friends changed into enemies and his enemies into friends, the living became the dead and the dead became the living, while some became the unborn, disturbed him and he forced himself awake, sweating, to find Rinal standing over him.

'The machine is ready,' said the Wraith-man. 'But it is not perfect, I fear. All it can do is pursue your pyramid. Once the pyramid materializes in this world again, our sphere will follow it, wherever it goes – but it has no navigating power of its own – it can *only* follow the pyramid. Therefore there is a strong danger of your being trapped in some other dimension for all time.'

'It is a risk I'm prepared to take, for one,' Hawkmoon said. 'It will be better than the nightmares I experience, awake or dreaming. Where are Count Brass and Bowgentle?'

'Somewhere near by, walking and talking through the streets of Soryandum. Shall I tell them you wish to see them?'

'Aye,' said Hawkmoon, rubbing sleep from his eyes. 'We had best make our plans as soon as possible. I have a feeling we shall see Kalan again before long.' He stretched and yawned. The sleep had not really helped him. Rather it appeared to have made him feel wearier than before.

He changed his mind. 'No, perhaps I had better speak with them myself. The air might refresh me.'

'As you will. I'll take you down.' Rinal floated towards Hawkmoon.

As Rinal began to lift him towards the window, Hawkmoon asked: 'Where is the machine you mentioned?'

'The dimension-travelling sphere? Below in our laboratory. Would you like to see it tonight?'

'I think I had better. I have a feeling Kalan could reappear at any time.'

'Very well. I shall bring it to you shortly. The controls are simple – indeed they are scarcely controls at all since the purpose of the sphere is to make itself the slave of another machine. However, I understand your eagerness to see it. Go now and speak with your friends.'

The Wraith-man, virtually invisible in the moonlit street, drifted away, leaving Hawkmoon to find Bowgentle and Count Brass by himself.

He walked through overgrown streets, between ruined buildings through which the moonlight glared, enjoying the peace of the night and feeling his head begin to clear. The air was very sweet and cool.

At length he heard voices ahead of him and was about to call out when he realized that he heard the tones of three voices, not two. He began to run softly towards the source of the voices, keeping to the shadows, until he stood in the cover of a ruined colonnade and looked into a small square where stood Count Brass and Bowgentle. Count Brass stood frozen, as if mesmerized, and Bowgentle was remonstrating in a low voice with a man who sat cross-legged in the air above him, the outline of the pyramid glowing only very faintly, as if Kalan had deliberately tried to escape attention. Kalan was glaring at Bowgentle.

'What do you know of such matters?' Baron Kalan demanded. 'Why – you are barely real yourself!'

'That's as may be. I suspect that your own reality is also at stake, is it not? Why can you not kill Hawkmoon yourself? Because of the repercussions, eh? Have you plotted the possibilities following such an action? Are they not very palatable?'

'Be silent, puppet!' Baron Kalan demanded. 'Or you, too, will return to limbo. I offer you full life if you destroy Hawkmoon – or can convince Count Brass to do it!'

'Why did you not send Count Brass to limbo just now when he attacked you? Is it because you must have Hawkmoon killed by one of us and now there are only two left who can do your work?'

'I told you to be silent!' Kalan snarled. 'You should have worked with the Dark Empire, Sir Bowgentle. Such wit as yours is wasted among the barbarians.'

Bowgentle smiled. 'Barbarians? I have heard something of what, in my future, the Dark Empire will do to its enemies. Your choice of words is poor, Baron Kalan.'

'I warned you,' Kalan said menacingly. 'You go too far. I am still a Lord of Granbretan. I cannot tolerate such familiarity!'

'Your lack of tolerance has been your downfall once – or will be. We are beginning to understand what it is you try to do in your imitation Londra . . . '

'You know?' Kalan looked almost frightened. His lips pursed and his brows drew together. 'You know, eh? I think we made a mistake in bringing a pawn of your perception on to the board, Sir Bowgentle.'

'Aye, perhaps you did.'

Kalan began to fiddle with the small pyramid he held in his hand.

'Then it would be wise to sacrifice that pawn now,' he muttered.

Bowgentle seemed to realize what was in Kalan's mind. He took a step backward. 'Is that really wise? Are you not manipulating forces you barely understand?'

'Perhaps.' Baron Kalan chuckled. 'But that is no comfort to you, eh?'

Bowgentle grew pale.

Hawkmoon made to move forward, wondering at the manner in which Count Brass still remained frozen, seemingly unaware of what was taking place. Then he felt a light touch on his shoulder and he started, turning and reaching for his sword. But it was the almost invisible Wraith-man, Rinal, who stood before him. Rinal whispered:

'The sphere comes. This is your chance to follow the pyramid.'

'But Bowgentle is in danger . . . ' Hawkmoon murmured. 'I must try to save him.'

'You will not be able to save him. It is unlikely that he will be harmed, that he will retain anything but the dimmest memory of these events – as you recall a fading dream.'

'But he is my friend . . . '

'You will serve him better if you can find a way of stopping Kalan's activities for ever.' Rinal pointed. Several of his folk were drifting down the street towards them. They were carrying a large sphere of glowing yellow. 'There will be a few moments after the pyramid has gone when you'll be able to follow it.'

'But Count Brass – he has been mesmerized by Kalan.'

'The power will fade when Kalan leaves.'

Bowgentle was speaking hurriedly. 'Why should you fear my knowledge, Baron Kalan? You are strong. I am weak. It is you who manipulates me!'

'The more you know the less I can predict,' said Kalan. 'It is simple, Sir Bowgentle. Farewell.'

And Bowgentle cried out, whirled as if trying to escape. He began to run and as he ran he faded, faded until he had disappeared altogether.

Hawkmoon heard Baron Kalan laugh. It was a familiar laugh. A laugh he had grown to hate. Only Rinal's hand on his shoulder stopped him from attacking Kalan who, still unaware that he was observed, addressed Count Brass:

'You will gain much, Count Brass, by serving my purpose – and gain nothing if you do not. Why should it be Hawkmoon who plagues me always? I had thought it a simple matter to eliminate him and yet in every probability I investigate he emerges again. He is eternal, I sometimes think – perhaps immortal. Only if he is slain by another hero, another champion of that damned Runestaff, can events progress along the course I choose. So slay him, Count Brass. Earn life for yourself and for me!'

Count Brass moved his head. He blinked. He looked around him as if he did not see the pyramid, or its occupant.

The pyramid began to glow with a milky whiteness. The whiteness became brilliant, blinding. Count Brass cursed and threw his arm up to protect his eyes.

And then the brilliance faded and there was only a dim outline against the night.

'Quickly,' said Rinal. 'Into the sphere.'

As Hawkmoon passed through an entrance that was like a flimsy curtain which instantly reformed behind him, he saw Rinal drift over to Count Brass, seize him and bear him to the sphere, flinging him in after Hawkmoon so that he sprawled, sword still in hand, at Hawkmoon's feet.

'The sapphire,' Rinal said urgently. 'Touch the sapphire. It is all you must do. And I wish you success, Dorian Hawkmoon, in that other Londra!'

Hawkmoon reached out and touched the sapphire stone suspended in the air before him.

At once the sphere seemed to spin around them, while he and Count Brass remained motionless. They were in complete blackness now and the white pyramid could be seen through the walls of the sphere.

Suddenly there was sunshine and a landscape of green rocks. This faded almost as quickly as it had appeared. More images followed rapidly.

Megaliths of light, lakes of boiling metal, cities of glass and steel, battlefields on which thousands fought, forests through which strode shadowy giants, frozen seas – and always the pyramid was ahead of them as it shifted through plane after plane of the Earth, through worlds which seemed totally alien and worlds which seemed absolutely identical to Hawkmoon's.

Once before had Hawkmoon travelled through the dimensions. But then he had been escaping from danger. Now he went towards it.

Count Brass spoke for the first time. 'What happened back there? I remember trying to attack Baron Kalan, deciding that even if he sent me to limbo I should have his life first. Next I was in this – this chariot. Where is Bowgentle?'

'Bowgentle had begun to understand Kalan's plot,' Hawkmoon

said grimly, keeping his eyes fixed on the pyramid ahead. 'And so Kalan banished him back to wherever it was he came from. But Kalan also gave something away. He said that, for some reason, I could only be slain by a friend – by some other who had served the Runestaff. And that, he said, would ensure the friend's life.'

Count Brass shrugged. 'It still has the smell of a perverse plot to me. Why should it matter who slays you?'

'Well, Count Brass,' said Hawkmoon soberly. 'I have often said that I would give anything for you not to have died on the battlefield at Londra. I would give my life, even. So, if the time ever comes when you wish to be done with all this – you can always kill me.'

Count Brass laughed. 'If you want to die, Dorian Hawkmoon, I am sure you can find one more used to cold-blooded assassination in Londra, or wherever it is we journey to now.' He sheathed his great brass-hilted sword. 'I'll save my own strength for dealing with Baron Kalan and his servants when we get there!'

'If they are not prepared for us,' said Hawkmoon, as wild scenes continued to come and go at even greater speed. He felt dizzy and he closed his eyes. 'This journey through infinity appears to take an infinity! Once I cursed the Runestaff for meddling in my affairs, but now I wish greatly that Orland Fank was here to advise me. Still, it is plain by now that the Runestaff plays no part in this.'

'Just as well,' growled Count Brass. 'There is already too much sorcery and science involved for my taste! I'll be happier when all this is finished, even should it mean my own death!'

Hawkmoon nodded his agreement. He was remembering Yisselda and his children, Manfred and Yarmila. He was remembering the quiet life of the Kamarg and the satisfactions he had got from seeing the marshlands restocked, the harvests brought in. And he was regretting bitterly that he had ever allowed himself to fall into the trap Baron Kalan had evidently set for him when he had sent Count Brass through time to haunt the Kamarg.

And at that, another thought occurred to him. Had *all* this been a trap?

Did Baron Kalan actually *want* to be followed? Were they being lured, even now, to their doom?

# BOOK THREE

# OLD DREAMS
# AND NEW

## CHAPTER ONE

## The World Half-Made

Count Brass, lying uncomfortably along the curve of the sphere's
interior, groaned and shifted his brass-clad bulk again. He peered
through the misty yellow wall and watched the landscape outside
change forty times in as many seconds. The pyramid was still ahead
of them. Sometimes the outline of Baron Kalan could be seen within.
Sometimes the vessel's surface turned to that familiar, blinding white.

'Ah, my eyes ache!' grumbled Count Brass. 'They grow weary of so
many variegated sights. And my head aches when I strive to consider
exactly what is happening to us. If I should ever tell of this adventure
I shall never have my word believed again!'

And then Hawkmoon cautioned him to silence, for the scenes came
and went much more slowly until at last they ceased to change. They
hung in darkness. All they could see beyond the sphere was the white
pyramid.

Light came from somewhere.

Hawkmoon recognized Baron Kalan's laboratory. He acted swiftly,
instinctively. 'Quickly, Count Brass, we must leave the sphere.'

They dived through the curtain and onto the dirty flagstones of the
floor. By chance they were behind several large and crazily shaped
machines at the back of the laboratory.

Hawkmoon saw the sphere shudder and vanish. Now only Kalan's
pyramid offered an escape from this dimension. Familiar smells and
sounds came to Hawkmoon. He remembered when he had first visited Kalan's laboratories, as a prisoner of Baron Meliadus, to have
the Black Jewel implanted in his skull. He felt a strange coldness in
his bones. Their arrival had been unnoticed it seemed, for Kalan's
serpent-masked servants had their attention on the pyramid, standing
ready to hand their master his own mask when he emerged. The
pyramid sank slowly to the ground and Kalan stepped out of it,
accepting the mask without a word and donning it. There was something hasty about his movements. He said something to his servants
and they all followed him as he left the laboratory.

Cautiously Hawkmoon and Count Brass emerged. Both had un-
sheathed their swords.

Assured that the laboratory was, indeed, completely deserted, they debated their next action.

'Perhaps we should wait until Kalan returns and slay him on the spot,' Count Brass suggested, 'using his own machine for our escape.'

'We do not know how to operate the machine,' Hawkmoon reminded his friend. 'No, I think we should learn more of this world and Kalan's plans before we consider killing him. For all we know he has other allies, more powerful than himself, who would continue to put his schemes into effect.'

'That's fair enough,' Count Brass agreed. 'But this place makes me nervous. I've never been one to enjoy being underground. I prefer the open spaces. That's why I could never remain in one city for long.'

Hawkmoon began to inspect Baron Kalan's machines. Many of them were familiar to him in appearance, but he could make out little of their functions. He wondered if he should destroy the machines first, but then he decided it would be wiser to learn for what purpose they were intended. They could produce a disaster by tampering with the kind of forces with which Kalan was experimenting.

'With the right masks and clothes,' Hawkmoon said, as they both padded towards the door, 'we would have an improved chance of exploring this place undiscovered. I think we should make that objective our first priority.'

Count Brass agreed.

They opened the door of the laboratory and found themselves in a low-ceilinged passage. The smell was musty, the air stale. Once the whole of Londra had reeked of the same stink. But, now that he was able to inspect the murals and carvings on the walls more closely, Hawkmoon was certain this was not Londra. The absence of detail was most noticeable. Paintings were done in outline and then filled in with solid colours, not the subtle shades of the clever Granbretanian artists. And whereas colours had been clashed in old Londra with the intention of making an effect, these colours were merely poorly selected. It was as if someone who had only seen Londra for half-an-hour or so had tried to recreate it.

Even Count Brass, who had only visited Granbretan once, on some diplomatic errand, noticed the contrast. On they crept, without encountering anyone, trying to determine which way Baron Kalan had gone, when all at once they had turned a corner in the passage and come face to face with two soldiers of the Mantis Order – King Huon's old Order – armed with long pikes and swords.

Immediately, Count Brass and Hawkmoon took up a fighting stance, expecting the two soldiers to attack. The mantis-masks nodded on the men's shoulders, but they only stared at Count Brass and his companion, as if puzzled.

One of the soldiers spoke in a vague, muffled voice from within his mantis-helm. 'Why do you go unmasked?' he said. 'Should this be?'

His voice had a distant, dreamlike quality, not unlike that of Count Brass when Hawkmoon had first encountered him in the Kamarg.

'Aye. It is correct,' said Hawkmoon. 'You are to give us your masks.'

'But unmasking is forbidden in the passages!' said the second soldier in horror. His gauntleted hands went to his great-insect helm as if to protect it. Mantis eyes seemed to stare sardonically into Hawkmoon's.

'Then we must fight you for them,' growled Count Brass. 'Draw your swords.'

Slowly the two drew their swords. Slowly they assumed defensive positions.

It was horrible work, killing those two, for they did not make any more than a token effort to defend themselves. They went down in the space of half-a-minute and Hawkmoon and Count Brass began immediately to strip them of their masks and their outer clothes of green silk and green velvet.

They stripped the pair just in time. Hawkmoon was wondering what to do with the bodies when, suddenly, they vanished.

Count Brass snorted suspiciously. 'More sorcery?'

'Or an explanation of why they behaved so strangely,' said Hawkmoon thoughtfully. 'They vanished as Bowgentle, Oladahn and D'Averc vanished. The Mantis Order was ever the fiercest in Granbretan and those who belonged to it were arrogant, proud and quick to strike. Either those fellows were not really of Granbretan, but playing parts for Baron Kalan's benefit – or else they *were* from Granbretan, but in some kind of trance.'

'They seemed to be in a dream, right enough,' agreed Count Brass.

Hawkmoon adjusted his stolen mask upon his head. 'Best behave the same, if challenged,' he said. 'That, too, will be to our advantage.'

Together they continued to make their way through the passages, moving at a measured pace, like that of patrolling soldiers.

'At least,' said Count Brass in a low voice, 'we shall have little trouble with corpses if all those we slay disappear with such fortunate alacrity!'

They paused at several doors and tried them, but all were secured. They passed many other masked men, from all the main orders – Pig, Vulture, Dragon, Wolf and the like – but saw no other members of the Order of the Snake. Members of this Order, they were sure, would lead them eventually to Kalan. It would also be useful to exchange mantis-masks for serpent masks at some stage. Finally they found themselves at a door larger than the others and this was guarded by two men who wore the same masks now worn by Hawkmoon and Count Brass. A guarded door was an important door, thought Hawkmoon. Behind it might lie something which would help answer the questions he had followed Kalan to solve. He thought quickly, saying in as dreamy a voice as he could manage:

'We have orders to relieve you. You may return to your quarters now.'

One of the guards spoke. 'Relieve us? Have we been here for a full period of duty, then? I thought it was but an hour. But then time . . . ' He paused. 'It is all so strange.'

'You are relieved,' said Count Brass, guessing Hawkmoon's plan. 'That is all we know.'

Sluggishly the two guards saluted and marched away, leaving Hawkmoon and Count Brass to take up their positions.

As soon as the guards were gone, Hawkmoon turned and tried the latch of the door. It was locked.

Count Brass glanced around him, shuddering. 'This seems more of a true netherworld than the one I first found myself in,' he said.

'I think you could be close to the truth,' Hawkmoon told him as he bent to inspect the lock. Like so many of the other artefacts here it was crude. He took out the emerald-pommelled poignard which he had got from the mantis-warrior. He inserted the point in the lock and shifted it about for several seconds before twisting it sharply. There was a click and the door swung open.

The two companions stepped through.

And both gasped in unison at what they saw.

## CHAPTER TWO

A Museum of the Living and the Dead

'King Huon!' Hawkmoon murmured. Quickly he closed the door behind him, looking up at the great globe suspended above his head. In the globe swam the wizened figure of the ancient king who had once spoken with the voice of a golden youth. 'I thought you slain by Meliadus!'

A tiny whisper escaped the globe. It was almost a thought, so tenuous was it. 'Meliadus,' it said 'Meliadus.'

'The king dreams,' said the voice of Flana, Queen of Granbretan.

And there she was, in her heron-mask, made up of fragments of a thousand jewels, in her lush brocade gown, coming slowly towards them.

'Flana?'

Hawkmoon moved towards her. 'How did you come to be here?'

'I was born in Londra. Who are you? Though you be of the King-Emperor's own Order, you speak insolently to Flana, Countess of Kanbery.'

'Queen Flana now,' said Hawkmoon.

'Queen . . . queen . . . queen . . . ' said the distant voice of King Huon from behind them.

'King . . . ' Another figure moved blindly past them. 'King Meliadus . . . '

And Hawkmoon knew that if he tore off that wolf-helm from the figure he would see the face of Baron Meliadus, his old foe. And he knew that the eyes would be glazed, as Flana's eyes would be glazed. There were others in this room – all Dark Empire folk. Flana's old husband, Assrovak Mikosevaar; Shenegar Trott in his silver mask; Pra Flenn, Duke of Lakasdeh, in his grinning dragon-helm, who had died before his nineteenth birthday and had personally slain over a hundred men and women before his eighteenth. Yet, for all that this was an assembly of the fiercest of the Granbretanian warlords, none attacked. They hardly lived at all. Only Flana – who still lived in Hawkmoon's world – seemed to be able to frame a coherent sentence. The rest were like sleep-walkers, mumbling one or two words, but no more. And Hawkmoon's and Count Brass's entrance into this weird museum of the living and the dead had set them to babbling, like birds in an aviary.

It was unnerving, particularly to Dorian Hawkmoon, who had slain many of these people himself. He seized upon Flana, ripping off his own mask so that she could see his face.

'Flana! Do you not recognize me? Hawkmoon? How came you here?'

'Remove your hand from me, warrior!' she said automatically, though it was plain she did not really care. Flana had never understood much concerning protocol. 'I do not know you. Put your mask back on!'

'Then you, too, must have been drawn from a time before we met – or else from some other world altogether,' Hawkmoon said.

'Meliadus... Meliadus... ' said the whispering voice of King Huon in the Throne Globe above their heads.

'King... king... ' said wolf-masked Meliadus.

And: 'The Runestaff... ' murmured fat Shenegar Trott, who had died trying to possess that mystic wand... 'The Runestaff... '

It was all they could speak of – their fears or their ambitions. The chief fears or ambitions which had driven them through their lives and brought about their ruin.

'You are right,' said Hawkmoon to Count Brass. 'This is the world of the dead. But who keeps these poor creatures here? For what purposes have they been resurrected? It is like an obscene treasure-house – human loot – the loot of time – all crowded together!'

'Aye,' sniffed Count Brass. 'I wonder if, until recently, I was part of this collection. Could that not be possible, Dorian Hawkmoon?'

'These are all Dark Empire folk,' said Hawkmoon. 'No, I think you were seized from a time before all these died. Your youth speaks for that – and your own recollection of the Battle of Tarkia.'

'I thank you for that reassurance,' said Count Brass.

Hawkmoon put a finger to his lips. 'Do you hear something? In the passage?'

'Aye.'

'Into the shadows,' said Hawkmoon. 'I think someone approaches. They might notice the guard gone.'

Not one of the people in the room, even Flana, tried to stop them as they squeezed through the company and hid in the darkest corner, sheltered by the bulk of Adaz Promp and Jherek Nankenseen, who had ever enjoyed each other's company, even in life.

The door opened and there was Baron Kalan of Vitall, Grand Master of the Order of the Serpent, all rage and bewilderment.

'The door open and the guards gone!' he raved. He glared at the company of living-dead. 'Which of you did this? Is there one who does more than dream – who plots to rob me of my power? Who seeks that power for himself – You, Meliadus – do you wake?' He pulled the wolf-helm free, but Meliadus's face was blank.

Kalan slapped the face, but Meliadus did not react. He grunted.

'You, Huon? Even you are no longer as powerful as am I. Do you resent that?'

But Huon merely whispered the name of the one who would kill him. 'Meliadus . . . ' he whispered. 'Meliadus . . . '

'Shenegar Trott? You, cunning one?' Kalan shook the unresponsive shoulder of the Count of Sussex. 'Did you unlock the door and dismiss the guards. And why?' He frowned. 'No, it could only be Flana . . . ' He searched for the heron mask of Flana Mikosevaar, Countess of Kanbery, among those many masks (whose workmanship was noticeably superior to Kalan's). 'Flana is the only one who suspects . . . '

'What do you want with me now, Baron Kalan?' said Flana, drifting forward. 'I am tired. You must not disturb me.'

'You cannot deceive me, traitress-to-be. If I have an enemy here, it is you. Who else could it be? It is in everyone's interest, save yours, for the old Empire to be restored.'

'As usual, I fail to understand you, Kalan.'

'Aye, it's true that you *should* not understand – but I wonder . . . '

'Your guards came in here,' Flana went on. 'They were impolite fellows, but one was handsome enough.'

'Handsome? They removed their masks?'

'One did, aye.'

Kalan's eyes darted this way and that as he considered the implications of her remark. 'How . . . ?' he muttered. 'How . . . ?' He looked hard at Flana. 'I still think this is your doing!'

'I do not know of what you accuse me, Kalan, and I do not care, for this nightmare will end soon, as nightmares must.'

Kalan's eyes glinted sardonically in his snake mask. 'Think you Madam?' He turned away to inspect the lock. 'My plans go constantly awry. Every action I take leads to further complications. There must be a single action which will wipe out the complexities at a stroke. Oh, Hawkmoon, Hawkmoon, I wish you would die.'

At this Hawkmoon stepped out swiftly and tapped Kalan upon the shoulder with the flat of his sword. Kalan turned and the tip of the sword slipped under the mask and rested against the throat.

'If the request had been couched more politely, in the first place,'

Hawkmoon said with grim humour, 'I might have complied. But now you have offended me, Baron Kalan. Too often have you shown yourself unfriendly to me.'

'Hawkmoon . . . ' Kalan's voice sounded like those of the living-dead around him. 'Hawkmoon . . . ' He took a deep breath. 'How did you come here?'

'Don't you know, Kalan?' Count Brass emerged, drawing off his own mask. He was grinning a big, wide grin – the first Hawkmoon had seen on his face since they had met in the Kamarg.

'Is this a counterplot – did *he* bring you – ? No . . . He would not betray me. We have too much at stake.'

'Who is that?'

But Kalan had become cautious. 'Killing me at this point could easily bring disaster upon us all,' he said.

'Aye – and not killing you, that could produce a similar effect!' Count Brass laughed. 'Have we anything to lose, Baron Kalan?'

'You have your life to lose, Count Brass,' Kalan said savagely. 'At best you could become like these others. Is that an attractive thought?'

'No.' Count Brass began to strip off the mantis-clothing which had covered his brass armour.

'Then do not be a fool!' Kalan hissed. 'Kill Hawkmoon now!'

'What did you try to do, Kalan?' Hawkmoon interrupted. 'Re-surrect the whole Dark Empire? Did you hope to restore it here to its former glory – in a world where Count Brass and myself and the others never existed? But you found when you went back into the past and brought them here to rebuild Londra, that their memories were poor. It was as if they all dreamed. They had too many conflicting experiences in their minds and this confused them – made their brains dormant. They could not remember details – that is why all your murals and your artefacts are so crude, is it not? Why your guards are so ineffectual, why they do not fight. And when they are killed here, they vanish – for even you cannot control time to the extent that it tolerates the paradox of the twice-dead. You began to realize that if you altered history – even if you were successful in re-establishing the Dark Empire – all would suffer from this mental confusion. Everything would break down as swiftly as you built it. Any triumph you had would turn to ashes. You would rule over unreal creatures in an unreal world.'

Kalan shrugged. 'But we have taken steps to adjust matters. There are solutions, Hawkmoon. Perhaps our ambitions have become a little less grandiose, but the result could be much the same.'

'What do you intend to do?' Count Brass growled.

Kalan gave a humourless laugh. 'Ah, that now depends on what you do to me. Surely you can see that? Already there are eddies of confusion in the time-streams. One dimension becomes clogged with the constituents of another. Originally my scheme was simply to get vengeance on Hawkmoon by having him killed by one of his friends. I'll admit I was foolish to think it could be so simple. And also, instead of remaining in your dreamlike state, you began to wake, to reason, to refuse to listen to what I told you. That is not what should have happened and I do not know why.'

'By bringing my friends out of a time before any of us had met, you created an entirely new stream of possibilities,' said Hawkmoon. 'And from these sprang dozens more – half-worlds which you can't control, which become confused with the one from which we all originally came . . . '

'Aye.' Kalan nodded his great mask. 'But there is still hope, if you, Count Brass, slay this Hawkmoon. Surely you realize that your friendship with him led directly to your own death – or will lead to it in your future . . . '

'So Oladahn and the others were merely returned to their own time, believing themselves to have dreamed what happened here?' said Hawkmoon.

'Even that dream will fade,' said Kalan. 'They will never know that I tried to help them save their own lives.'

'And why do you not kill me, Kalan? You have had the opportunity. Is it, as I suspect, that if you do, then the logic resulting from such an action leads inexorably to your own destruction?'

Kalan was silent. But his silence confirmed the truth of what Hawkmoon had said.

'And only if I am killed by one of my already dead friends will it be possible to remove my unwanted presence from all those possible worlds you have explored, those half-worlds your instruments have detected, where you hope to restore the Dark Empire? Is that why you are so insistent on Count Brass killing me? And do you intend, once he had done that, to restore the Dark Empire, unchallenged, to its original world – with yourselves ruling behind these puppets of yours?' Hawkmoon spread his hand to indicate the living-dead. Even Queen Flana was quiescent now as her brain shut off the information which might easily turn it insane. 'These shadows will appear to be the great warlords come back from the dead, to hold sway over Granbretan again. You will even have a new Queen Flana to re-nounce the throne in favour of this Shadow Huon.'

'You are an intelligent young man, for a savage.' A languid voice came from the doorway. Hawkmoon kept the tip of his sword against Kalan's throat as he looked towards the source of the voice.

A bizarre figure stood there, between two mantis-masked guards who bore flame-lances and looked anything but indecisive. There were, it now seemed, others in this world who were more than shadows. Hawkmoon recognized the figure, clad in a gigantic mask which was also a working clock and was, even as its wearer spoke, chiming the first eight bars of Sheneven's *Temporal Antipathies*, all of gilded and enamelled brass, with numerals of inlaid mother-of-pearl and hands of filigree silver, balanced by a golden pendulum in a box worn upon his chest.

'I thought you might be here, too, My Lord Taragorm,' said Hawkmoon. He lowered his sword as the flame-lances nudged his midriff.

Taragorm of the Palace of Time voiced his golden laughter.

'Greetings, Duke Dorian. You will note, I hope, that these two guards are not of the company of the Dreaming Ones. These escaped with me at the Siege of Londra, when it became obvious to Kalan and myself that the battle was lost to us. Even then we could probe a little way into the future. My sad accident was arranged – an explosion produced to cause my apparent death. And Kalan's suicide, as you already know, was in reality the occasion of his first jump through the dimensions. We have worked so well together, since then. But there have been a few complications, as you've guessed.'

Kalan moved forward and took the swords of Count Brass and Hawkmoon. Count Brass was scowling but seemed too astonished to resist at that moment. He had never seen Taragorm, Master of the Palace of Time, before.

Taragorm continued, his voice full of amusement. 'Now that you have been gracious enough to visit us, I hope those complications can be dispensed with, at long last. I had not hoped for such a stroke of luck! You were ever headstrong, Hawkmoon.'

'And how will you achieve it – freeing yourselves of the complications you have created?' Hawkmoon folded his arms on his chest.

The clock face inclined itself slightly to one side, the pendulum beneath continued to swing, balanced as it was by complicated machinery, allowing for every movement of Taragorm's body.

'You will know when we return to Londra shortly. I speak, of course, of the true Londra, where we are soon expected, not this poor imitation. Kalan's idea, not mine.'

'You supported me!' said Kalan in an aggrieved tone. 'And it is I who take all the risks, travelling back and forth through a thousand dimensions . . . '

'Let us not have our guests think us petty, Baron Kalan,' Taragorm chided. There had always been something of a rivalry between the two of them. He bowed slightly to Count Brass and Hawkmoon. 'Please come with us while we make the final preparations for our journey back to our old home.'

Hawkmoon stood his ground. 'If we refuse?'

'You will be stranded here forever. You know we cannot, ourselves, kill you. You bank on that, do you? Well, alive in this place or dead in another, it's all much of a muchness, friend Hawkmoon. And now, please cover up your naked face. I know it might seem rude, but I am dreadfully old-fashioned about such things.'

'I regret that, in this too, I must give offence,' said Hawkmoon with a small bow. He let the guards lead him through the door. He saluted the dull-eyed Flana and the others, who had even stopped breathing, it seemed. 'Farewell, sad shades. I hope I shall, at length, be the cause of your release.'

'I hope so, also,' said Taragorm. And the hands on the face of his mask moved a fraction and its bell began to strike the hour.

CHAPTER THREE

Count Brass Chooses to Live

They were back in Baron Kalan's laboratory.

Hawkmoon considered the two guards who now had their swords. He could tell that Count Brass was also wondering whether it would be possible to rush the flame-lances.

Kalan was already in the white pyramid, making adjustments to the smaller pyramids which were suspended before him. Because he was still wearing his serpent-mask, he had greater difficulty in manipulating the objects and arranging them to his satisfaction. It seemed to Hawkmoon, as he watched, that somehow this scene symbolized a salient aspect of the Dark Empire culture.

For some reason Hawkmoon felt singularly calm as he considered his situation. Instinct told him to bide his time, that the crucial moment of action would come quite soon. And for this reason he relaxed his body and took no notice of the guards with their flame-lances, concentrating on what Kalan and Taragorm were saying.

'The pyramid is almost ready,' Kalan told Taragorm. 'But we must leave swiftly.'

'Are we all to crowd into that thing?' Count Brass said, and he laughed. Hawkmoon realized that Count Brass, too, was biding his time.

'Aye,' said Taragorm. 'All.'

And, as they watched, the pyramid began to expand until it was twice its size, then three times, then four and at last it filled the entire cleared space in the centre of the laboratory and suddenly Count Brass, Hawkmoon, Taragorm and the two mantis-masked guards were engulfed by the pyramid and stood within it while Kalan, suspended above their heads, continued to play with his odd controls.

'You see,' said Taragorm. His voice was amused. 'Kalan's talents always lay in his understanding of the nature of space. Whereas mine, of course, lie in my understanding of time. That is why together we can produce such whimsicalities as this pyramid!'

And now the pyramid was travelling again, shunting through the myriad dimensions of Earth. Once more Hawkmoon saw bizarre scenery and peculiar mirror-images of his own world and many of them

96

were not the same as those he had witnessed on his journey to Kalan's and Taragorm's half-world.

And then it seemed they were in the darkness of limbo again. Beyond the flickering walls of the pyramid Hawkmoon could see nothing but solid blackness.

'We are there,' said Kalan, and he turned a crystal control. The vessel began to shrink again, growing smaller and smaller until it could barely contain Kalan's body. The sides of the pyramid clouded and turned to the familiar brilliant white. Hanging in the blackness over their heads it seemed to provide no illumination beyond its immediate area. Hawkmoon could see nothing of his own body, let alone those of the others. He knew only that his feet stood upon smooth and solid ground and that his nostrils picked up a damp, stale smell. He stamped his foot upon the ground and the sound echoed and echoed. It seemed that they were in a cavern of some kind.

Now Kalan's voice boomed from the pyramid.

'The moment has come. The resurrection of our great Empire is at hand. We, who can bring life to the dead and death to the living, who have remained faithful to the old ways of Granbretan, who are pledged to restore her greatness and her domination over the whole world, bring the faithful ones the creature they most desire to see. Behold!'

And suddenly Hawkmoon was engulfed in light. The source was a mystery, but the light blinded him and made him cover his eyes. He cursed as he turned this way and that, trying to avoid it.

'See how he wriggles,' said Kalan of Vitall. 'See how he cringes, this, our arch-enemy!'

Hawkmoon forced himself to stand still and open his eyes to the terrible light.

A dreadful whispering was coming from all around him now, and a slithering, and a hissing. He peered about him, but could still see nothing beyond the light. The whispering grew to a murmur and the murmur to a muttering and the muttering to a roar and the roar became a single word, voiced by what must have been a thousand throats.

'Granbretan! Granbretan! Granbretan!'

And then there was silence.

'Enough of this!' came the voice of Count Brass. 'Have done with – aah!'

And now Count Brass, too, was surrounded with the same strange radiance.

'And here is the other,' said Kalan's voice. 'Faithful, look upon him and hate him, for this is Count Brass. Without his help, Hawkmoon would never have been able to destroy that which we love. By treachery, by stealth, by cowardice, by begging the assistance of those more powerful than themselves, they thought they could destroy the Dark Empire. But the Dark Empire is not destroyed. She will grow stronger and greater still! Behold, Count Brass!'

And Hawkmoon saw the white light surrounding Count Brass grow a peculiar blue colour and Count Brass's armour of brass glowed blue, too, and Count Brass clapped his gauntleted hands to his helmeted head and he opened his mouth and let out a scream of pain.

'Stop!' cried Hawkmoon. 'Why torture him?'

Lord Taragorm's voice came from near by, soft and pleased. 'Surely you know why, Hawkmoon?'

And now brands flared and Hawkmoon saw that, indeed, they stood in a great cavern. And the five of them – Count Brass, Lord Taragorm, the two guards and himself – stood upon the top of a ziggurat raised in the centre of the cavern, while Baron Kalan in his pyramid hovered above their heads.

And below there were at least a thousand masked figures, travesties of beasts, with heads of Pig and Wolf and Bear and Vulture, swarming below and screaming out now as Count Brass screamed and fell to his knees, still surrounded by the awful blue flame.

And the leaping light of the brands showed murals and carvings and bas-reliefs which were, in the details of their obscenity, evidently of true Dark Empire workmanship. And Hawkmoon knew that they must be in Londra proper, probably in some cavern beneath a cavern, far below the foundations of the city.

He tried to reach Count Brass, but the light around his own body stopped him.

'Torture me!' cried Hawkmoon. 'Leave Count Brass and torture me!'

And again came Taragorm's soft, sardonic voice. 'But we *do* torture you, Hawkmoon, do we not?'

'Here is the one who brought us to the edge of annihilation!' came Kalan's voice from above. 'Here is the one who, in his pride, thought he had destroyed us. But we shall destroy him. And with his destruction will come an end to all restraint upon us. We shall emerge, we shall conquer. The dead shall return and lead us – King Huon . . . '

'King Huon!' roared the masked crowd.

'Baron Meliadus!' cried Kalan.

'Baron Meliadus!' roared the crowd.

'Shenegar Trott, Count of Sussex!'

'Shenegar Trott!'

'And all the great heroes and demigods of Granbretan shall return!'

'All! All!'

'Aye – all shall return. And they shall have vengeance upon this world!'

'Vengeance!'

'The Beasts shall have vengeance!'

And again, quite suddenly, the crowd fell silent.

And again Count Brass screamed and tried to rise on his knees and beat at his body as the blue flame brought pain.

Hawkmoon saw that Count Brass was sweating, that his eyes burned as if with fever, that his lips writhed.

'Stop!' he cried. He tried to break through the light which held him, but again without success. 'Stop!'

But now the beasts were laughing: Pigs giggled, dogs cackled, wolves barked and insects hissed. They laughed to see Count Brass in such pain and his friend in such helpless misery.

And Hawkmoon realized they were trapped in a ritual – a ritual which had been promised these mask-wearers in return for their loyalty to the unregenerate lords of the Dark Empire.

And what would the ritual lead to?

He began to guess.

Count Brass rolled upon the floor now, nearly falling over the edge of the ziggurat. And, every time he came close to the edge, something rolled him back to the centre. The blue flame ate at his nerves and his screams came louder and louder. He had lost all dignity, all identity, in that pain.

Hawkmoon wept as he begged Kalan and Taragorm to desist.

At last it stopped. Count Brass got shakily to his feet. The blue light faded to white and then the white light faded, too. Count Brass's face was taut. His lips were all bloody. His eyes had horror in them.

'Would you kill yourself, Hawkmoon, to end your friend's agony?' Taragorm's taunting voice came from beside the Duke of Köln. 'Would you do that?'

'So that is the alternative. Did your prognosis show you that your cause would triumph if I slew myself?'

'It improves our chances. It would be best if Count Brass could be prevailed upon to kill you but, if he will not . . . ' Taragorm shrugged. 'This is the next best thing.'

Hawkmoon looked towards Count Brass. For an instant their eyes met and he stared into yellow orbs that were full of agony. Hawkmoon nodded. 'I will do it. But first you must release Count Brass.'

Your own death will release Count Brass,' said Kalan from above. 'Be sure of that.'

'I do not trust you,' Hawkmoon said.

The beasts below watched on with bated breath as they waited for their enemy to die.

'Will this be sufficient evidence of our faith?' The white light faded from around Hawkmoon, too. Taragorm took Hawkmoon's sword from the soldier who still held it. He handed it to Hawkmoon. 'There. Now you can kill me or kill yourself. Only be assured that if you kill me, Count Brass's torture will continue. If you kill yourself, it will cease.'

Hawkmoon licked his dry lips. He looked from Count Brass to Taragorm to Kalan and to the blood-hungry crowd. To kill himself for the pleasure of these degenerates was loathsome. And yet, it was the only way to save Count Brass. But what of the rest of the world? He was too dazed to think of anything more, to consider any further possibilities.

Slowly he shifted his sword in his hand until the pommel was upon the flagstones and the tip under his breastplate, resting against his flesh.

'You will still perish,' Hawkmoon said. His smile was bitter as he contemplated the frightful crowd. 'Whether I live or die. You will perish because of the rot that is in your souls. You perished before because you turned inward upon each other as a response to the great danger which threatened you. You squabbled, beast against beast, as we attacked Londra. Could we have succeeded without your help? I think not.'

'Be silent!' Kalan cried from his pyramid. 'Do what you have agreed to do, Hawkmoon, or Count Brass begins to dance again!'

But then Count Brass's voice, deep and huge and weary, came from behind Hawkmoon.

Count Brass said:

'No!'

'If Hawkmoon goes back on his word, Count Brass, then back comes flame and pain . . . ' said Taragorm, as one might address a child.

'No,' said Count Brass, 'I'll suffer no more.'

'You wish to kill yourself, too?'

'My life means very little at this moment. It was because of Hawkmoon that I have suffered so. If he is to die, at least give me the pleasure of despatching him! I'll do what you wanted me to do in the first place. I see now that I have borne many ordeals for the sake of one who is, indeed, my enemy. Aye – let me kill him. Then I shall die. And I shall have died avenged.'

The pain had plainly turned Count Brass mad. His yellow eyes rolled. His lips twisted back to reveal ivory teeth. 'I shall have died avenged!'

Taragorm was surprised. 'This is more than I hoped for. Our faith in you, Count Brass, was justified, after all.' Taragorm's voice was gleeful as he took the brass-hilted broadsword from the mantis-guard and handed it to Count Brass.

Count Brass took his sword in both his great hands. His eyes narrowed as he turned to look at Hawkmoon.

'I shall feel better, taking an enemy with me,' said Count Brass.

And he raised the long sword above his head. And his brass armour picked up the light from the brands and made his whole head and his whole body shine as if with fire.

And Hawkmoon peered into those yellow eyes and knew that he saw death there.

## CHAPTER FOUR

A Great Wind Blowing

But it was not his own death that Hawkmoon saw.

It was Taragorm's death.

In an instant Count Brass had shifted his stance, shouted to Hawkmoon to take the guards, and brought the massive sword down upon the ornate clock-mask.

There came a howl from below as the crowd understood what was happening. Beast-masks tossed from side to side as the Dark Empire creatures began to climb the steps of the ziggurat.

Kalan cried out from above. Hawkmoon, reversing his sword swiftly, swept it round to knock the flame-lances from the hands of the guards. They fell back. Kalan's voice continued to wail hysterically from the pyramid. 'Fools! Fools!'

Taragorm was staggering. It was evidently Taragorm who controlled the white fire, for it flickered around Count Brass as he raised his sword for a second blow. Taragorm's clock was split, the hands buckled, but the head beneath was evidently still intact.

The sword smashed into the ruined mask and the two sides fell away.

And there was revealed a head far smaller, in proportion, than the body on which it sat. A round, ugly head – the head of something which might have thrived during the Tragic Millennium.

And then that tiny, round, white thing was lopped from its stalk by a sideswipe of Count Brass's sword. Taragorm was now most certainly dead.

Beasts began to clamber onto the platform from all sides.

Count Brass roared with battle-joy as his sword took lives, as blood splashed in the flame-light, as men screamed and fell.

Hawkmoon was still engaged on the far side of the ziggurat with the two mantis-guards who had drawn their own swords.

And now a great wind seemed to be blowing through the cavern, a whistling wind, a wailing wind.

Hawkmoon drove his sword point first through the eyeslit of the nearest mantis-warrior. He tugged the sword free and slashed at the other, driving the edge into the neck so hard that it smashed through the metal and severed the jugular. Now he could try to reach Count Brass.

'Count Brass!' he called. 'Count Brass!'

Kalan was cackling in panic above. 'The wind!' he cried. 'The time-wind!'

But Hawkmoon ignored him. He was bent on reaching his friend's side and dying with his friend if need be.

But the wind blew still more strongly. It buffeted Hawkmoon. He found that he could barely move against it. And now beast-masked warriors of Granbretan were falling back, plunging over the sides of the ziggurat as the wind blew them, too.

Hawkmoon saw Count Brass swinging his broad-sword two-handed. The count's armour still shone like the sun itself. He had planted his feet upon a pile of those he had already slain and he was roaring with gigantic good humour as beasts came at him, slashing with swords and pikes and spears, his own blade moving with the regularity with which Taragorm's pendulum had once moved.

And Hawkmoon laughed, too. This would be the way to die, if die they must. Again he fought against the wind, wondering from where it came as he struggled to reach Count Brass.

But then he was picked up by it. He struggled as the ziggurat fell away below him and the scene became smaller and smaller, the figure of Count Brass himself so tiny that he could barely be seen now – and Kalan's white pyramid seemed to shatter as he passed it and Kalan screamed as he went tumbling down towards the fight.

Hawkmoon tried to see what held him. But nothing visible held him at all. Only the wind.

What had he heard Kalan call it? The time-wind?

Had they, then, in slaying Taragorm, released other forces of space and time – perhaps created the chaos which Kalan's and Taragorm's experiments had brought so close?

Chaos. Would he be blown forever upon this wind of time?

But no – he had left the cavern and was in Londra itself. Yet this was not the reformed Londra. This was the Londra of the old, bad days – the crazy towers and minarets, the jewelled domes, built upon both sides of the blood-red River Thayme. The wind had blown him into the past. Metal wings clashed as ornate ornithopters flew by. There seemed to be much activity in this Londra. For what did they prepare?

And again the scene shifted.

Again Hawkmoon looked down upon Londra. But now a battle raged. Explosions. Flame. The shouts of the dying. He recognized it.

This was the Battle of Londra.

Down he began to tumble. Down and down until he could barely think and hardly knew who he was.

And then he was Dorian Hawkmoon, Duke von Köln, a flashing mirror-helm upon his head, the Sword of the Dawn in his hand, the Red Amulet about his throat and a Black Jewel embedded in his skull.

Again he was at the Battle of Londra.

And he thought his new thoughts and his old together as he spurred his horse into the fray. And there was a great pain in his head and he knew the Black Jewel gnawed at his brain.

All about him men were fighting. The strange Legion of the Dawn, emitting its rosy aura, was driving through warriors who wore fierce wolf and vulture helms. All was confusion. Through his pain-glazed eyes Hawkmoon could hardly see what was happening. He glimpsed one or two of his Kamargian warriors. He saw two or three other mirror-helms flashing in the thick of the battle. He realized that his own sword arm was rising and falling, rising and falling as he beat off the Dark Empire warriors who were on all sides of him.

'Count Brass,' he murmured. 'Count Brass.' He remembered that he sought to be at the side of his old friend, though he hardly knew why. He saw the barbaric Warriors of the Dawn, with their painted bodies, their spiked clubs and their barbed lances decorated with tufts of dyed hair, slicing through the massed ranks of the Dark Empire warriors. He looked about him, trying to see which of those who wore the mirror-helms was Count Brass.

And still the pain in his skull grew and grew. And he gasped and wished that he could tear the mirror-helm free from his own head. But his hands were already occupied with fending off those warriors who pressed about him.

And then he saw something flash like gold and he knew it was the brazen hilt of Count Brass's sword and he spurred his horse through the throng.

The man in the mirror-helm and the armour of brass was fighting three great Dark Empire lords. Hawkmoon saw him standing there in the mud, horseless and brave, while the three – Hound, Goat and Bull – rode down on him. He saw Count Brass swing his broad-sword and cut at the legs of his opponents' horses so that Adaz Promp was thrown forward to land at Count Brass's feet and be swiftly slain. He saw Mygel Holst trying to get to his feet, his arms widespread as he begged for mercy. He saw Mygel Holst's head fly from its shoulders. Now only one of the lords remained alive, Saka Gerden in his massive bull-helm, rising to his feet and shaking his head as the mirror-mask blinded him.

Hawkmoon ploughed on, still crying out: 'Count Brass! Count Brass!'

Though he knew this was a dream, a distorted memory of the Battle of Londra, he still felt that he must reach his old friend's side. But before he could reach Count Brass, he saw the count wrench off his mirror-mask and face Saka Gerden bareheaded. Then the two closed.

Hawkmoon was nearly there by now, fighting wildly with his only object being to reach Count Brass.

And then Hawkmoon saw a rider of the Order of the Goat, a spear poised in his hand, riding down on Count Brass from behind. Hawkmoon yelled, spurred his horse forward and drove the Sword of the Dawn deep into the throat of the Goat rider just as Count Brass split the skull of Saka Gerden.

Hawkmoon kicked the corpse of the Goat Rider free from its saddle and called:

'A horse for you, Count Brass.'

Count Brass offered Hawkmoon a quick grin of thanks and swung up into the saddle, his mirror-helm forgotten on the ground.

'Thanks!' shouted Count Brass above the din of the battle. 'Now we'd best try to re-group our forces for the final assault.'

His voice had a peculiar echo to it. Hawkmoon swayed in his saddle as the pain from the Black Jewel grew still more intense. He tried to reply, but he could not. He looked for Yisselda in the ranks of his own forces, but could not see her.

The horse seemed to gallop faster and faster as the battle-noise began to fade. Then he was no longer astride a horse at all. A wind blew him on. A strong, cold wind, like the wind that blew across the Kamarg.

The sky was darkening. The battle was behind him. He began to fall through the night. He saw swaying reeds where he had seen fighting men. He saw glistening lagoons and marshes. He heard the lonely bark of a marsh fox and he mistook it for Count Brass's voice.

And suddenly the wind no longer blew.

He tried to move of his own accord, but something tugged at his body. He no longer wore the mirror-helm. His sword was no longer in his hand. His vision cleared as the terrible pain fled from his skull.

He lay immersed in marsh mud. It was night-time. He was sinking slowly into the greedy earth. He saw part of the body of a horse just in front of him. He reached towards it, but only one arm was free from the mud now. He heard his name being called and he mistook it for the cry of a bird.

'Yisselda,' he murmured. 'Oh, Yisselda!'

## CHAPTER FIVE

Something of a Dream

He felt as if he had already died. Fantasies and memories became confused as he waited for the marsh to swallow him. Faces appeared before him. He saw the face of Count Brass which shifted from relative youth to relative age even as he watched. He saw the face of Oladahn of the Bulgar Mountains. He saw Bowgentle and he saw D'Averc. He saw Yisselda. He saw Kalan of Vitall and Taragorm of the Palace of Time. Beast faces loomed on all sides. He saw Rinal of the Wraith-folk, Orland Fank of the Runestaff and his brother The Warrior in Jet and Gold. He saw Yisselda again. But weren't there other faces, too? Children's faces. Why did he not see them. And why did he confuse them with the face of Count Brass? Count Brass as a child? He had not known him then. He had not been born then.

Count Brass's face was concerned. It opened its lips. It spoke.

'Is that you, young Hawkmoon?'

'Aye, Count Brass. It is Hawkmoon. Shall we die together?'

He smiled at the vision.

'He still raves,' said a sad voice which was not that of Count Brass. 'I am sorry, my lord. I should have tried to stop him.'

Hawkmoon recognized the voice of Captain Josef Vedla.

'Captain Vedla? Have you come to pull me from the marsh for a second time?'

A rope fell near Hawkmoon's free hand. Automatically he passed his wrist through the loop. Someone began to pull at the rope. Slowly he was tugged free of the marsh.

His head was still aching, as if the Black Jewel had never been removed. But the ache was fading now and his brain was clearing. Why should he be reliving what was, after all, a fairly mundane incident in his life? – though he had come very close to death.

'Yisselda?' He looked for her face among those bending over him. But his fantasy remained. He still saw Count Brass, surrounded by his old Kamargian soldiers. There was no woman here at all.

'Yisselda?' he said again.

Count Brass said softly. 'Come, lad, we'll take you back to Castle Brass.'

Hawkmoon felt himself lifted in the count's massive arms and carried to a waiting horse.

'Can you ride yourself?' Count Brass asked.

'Aye.' Hawkmoon clambered into the saddle of the horned stallion and straightened his back, swaying slightly as his feet sought the stirrups. He smiled. 'Are you a ghost still, Count Brass? Or have you truly been restored to life? I said I would give anything for you to be brought back to us.'

'Restored to life? You should know that I am not dead!' Count Brass laughed. 'Are these fresh terrors come to haunt you, Hawkmoon?'

'You did not die at Londra?'

'Thanks to you, aye. You saved my life. If that Goat rider had got his spear into me, the chances are I'd be dead now.'

Hawkmoon smiled to himself. 'So events can be changed. And without repercussion, it seems. But where are Kalan and Taragorm now? And the others . . .' He turned to Count Brass as they rode together along the familiar marsh trails. 'And Bowgentle, and Oladahn, and D'Averc?'

Count Brass frowned. 'Dead these five years. Do you not remember? Poor lad, we all suffered after the Battle of Londra.' He cleared his throat. 'We lost much in our service of the Runestaff. And you lost your sanity.'

'My sanity?'

The lights of Aigues-Mortes were coming in sight. Hawkmoon could see the outline of Castle Brass on the hill.

Again Count Brass cleared his throat. Hawkmoon stared at him, 'My sanity, Count Brass?'

'I should not have mentioned it. We'll soon be home.' Count Brass would not meet his gaze.

They rode through the gates of the town and began to ascend the winding streets. Some of the soldiers rode their horses in other directions as they neared the castle, for they had quarters in the town itself.

'Good night to you!' called Captain Vedla.

Soon only Count Brass and Hawkmoon were left. They entered the courtyard of the castle and dismounted.

The hall of the castle looked little different from when Hawkmoon had last seen it. Yet it had an empty feel to it.

'Is Yisselda sleeping?' Hawkmoon asked.

'Aye,' said Count Brass wearily. 'Sleeping.'

Hawkmoon looked down at his mud-caked clothes. He no longer wore armour. 'I'd best bathe and get to bed myself,' he said. He looked hard at Count Brass and then he smiled. 'I thought you slain, you know, at the Battle of Londra.'

'Aye,' said Count Brass in the same troubled voice. 'I know. But now you know I'm no ghost, eh?'

'Just so!' Hawkmoon laughed with joy. 'Kalan's schemes served us much better than they served him, eh?'

Count Brass frowned. 'I suppose so,' he said uncertainly, as if he was not sure what Hawkmoon meant.

'Yet he escaped,' Hawkmoon went on. 'We could have trouble from him again.'

'Escaped? No. He committed suicide after taking that jewel from your head. That is what disturbed your brain so much.'

Hawkmoon began to feel afraid.

'You remember nothing of our most recent adventures then?' He moved to where Count Brass warmed himself at the fire.

'Adventures? You mean the marsh? You rode off in a trance, mumbling something of having seen me out there. Vedla saw you leave and came to warn me. That is why we went in search of you and just managed to find you before you died . . .'

Hawkmoon stared hard at Count Brass and then he turned away. Had he dreamed all the rest. Had he truly been mad?

'How long have I – have I been in this trance you mention, Count Brass?'

'Why, since Londra. You seemed rational enough for a little while after the jewel was removed. But then you began to speak of Yisselda as if she still lived. And there were other references to some you thought dead – such as myself. It is not surprising that you should have suffered such strain, for the jewel was . . .'

'Yisselda!' Hawkmoon cried out in sudden grief. 'You say she is dead?'

'Aye – at the Battle of Londra, fighting as well as any other warrior – she went down . . .'

'But the children – the children . . .' Hawkmoon struggled to remember the names of his children. 'What were they called? I cannot quite recall . . .'

Count Brass sighed a deep sigh and put his gauntleted hand on Hawkmoon's shoulder. 'You spoke of children, too. But there were no children. How could there be?'

'No children.'

Hawkmoon felt strangely empty. He strove to remind himself of something he had said quite recently. '*I would give anything if Count Brass could live again . . .*'

And now Count Brass lived again and his love, his beautiful Yisselda, his children, they were gone to limbo – they had never existed in all those five years since the Battle of Londra.

'You seem more rational,' said Count Brass. 'I had begun to hope that your brain was healing. Now, perhaps, it has healed.'

'Healed?' The word was a mockery. Hawkmoon turned again to confront his old friend. 'Have all in Castle Brass – in the whole Kamarg – thought me mad?'

'Madness might be too strong a word,' said Count Brass gruffly. 'You were in a kind of trance, as if you dreamed of events slightly different to those which were actually taking place . . . that is the best way I can describe it. If Bowgentle were here, perhaps he could have explained it better. Perhaps he could have helped you more than we could.' The count in brass shook his heavy, red head. 'I do not know, Hawkmoon.'

'And now I am sane,' said Hawkmoon bitterly.

'Aye, it seems so.'

'Then perhaps my madness was preferable to this reality.' Hawkmoon walked heavily towards the stairs. 'Oh, this is so hard to bear.'

Surely it could not all have been a graphic dream. Surely Yisselda had lived and the children had lived?

But already the memories were fading, as a dream fades. At the foot of the stairs he turned again to where Count Brass still stood, looking into the fire, his old head heavy and sad.

'We live – you and I? And our friends are dead. Your daughter is dead. You were right, Count Brass – much was lost at the Battle of Londra. Your grandchildren were lost, also.'

'Aye,' said Count Brass almost inaudibly. 'The future was lost, you could say.'

EPILOGUE

Nearly seven years had passed since the great Battle of Londra, when the power of the Dark Empire had been broken. And much had taken place in those seven years. For five of them Dorian Hawkmoon, Duke of Köln, had suffered the tragedy of madness. Even now, two years since he had recovered, he was not the same man who had ridden so bravely on the Runestaff's business. He had become grim, withdrawn and lonely. Even his old friend, Count Brass, the only other survivor of the conflict, hardly knew him now.

'It is the loss of his companions – the loss of his Yisselda,' whispered the sympathetic townspeople of the restored Aigues-Mortes. And they would pity Dorian Hawkmoon as he rode, alone, through the town and out of the gates and across the wide Kamarg, across the marshlands where the giant scarlet flamingoes wheeled and the white bulls galloped.

And Dorian Hawkmoon would ride to a small hill which rose from the middle of the marsh and he would dismount and lead his horse up to the top where stood the ruin of an ancient church, built before the onset of the Tragic Milleniun.

And he would look out across the waving reeds and the rippling lagoons as the mistral keened and its melancholy voice would echo the misery in his eyes.

And he would try to recall a dream.

A dream of Yisselda and two children whose names he could not remember. Had they ever had names in his dream?

A foolish dream, of what might have been, if Yisselda had survived the Battle of Londra.

And sometimes, when the sun began to set across the broad marshlands and the rain began to fall, perhaps, into the lagoons, he would stand upon the highest part of the ruin and raise his arms out to the ragged clouds which raced across the darkening sky and call her name into the wind.

'Yisselda! Yisselda!'

And his cry would be taken up by the birds which sailed upon that wind.

'Yisselda!'

And later Hawkmoon would lower his head and he would weep and he would wonder why he still felt, in spite of all the evident truth, that he might one day find his lost love again.

Why did he wonder if there were still some place – some other Earth perhaps – where the dead still lived? Surely such an obsession showed that there was a trace of madness left in his skull?

Then he would sigh and arrange his features so that none who saw him would know that he had mourned and he would climb upon his horse and, as the dusk fell, ride back to Castle Brass where his old friend waited for him.

Where Count Brass waited for him.

*This ends the first of the Chronicles of Castle Brass.*

# THE CHAMPION OF GARATHORM

## The Second Book of
## The Chronicles of Castle Brass

To all those nomads who travel the roads of England,

and enrich the world with their variety and

sense of community . . .

# BOOK ONE
## DEPARTURES

## CHAPTER ONE

Representations and Possibilities

Dorian Hawkmoon was no longer mad, yet neither was he healthy. Some said that it was the Black Jewel which had ruined him when it had been torn from his forehead. Others said that the war against the Dark Empire had exhausted him of all the energy he would normally need for a full lifetime and that now there was no more energy left. And some would have it that Hawkmoon mourned for the love of Yisselda, Count Brass's daughter, who had died at the Battle of Londra. In the five years of his madness Hawkmoon had insisted that she was still alive, that she lived with him at Castle Brass and bore him a son and a daughter.

But while causes might be the subject of debate in the inns and taverns of Aigues-Mortes, the town which sheltered beneath the great Castle of Brass, the effects themselves were plain to all.

Hawkmoon brooded.

Hawkmoon pined and shunned human company, even that of his good friend Count Brass. Hawkmoon sat alone in a small room at the top of the castle's highest tower and, with chin on fist, stared out over the marshes, the fields of reeds, the lagoons, his eyes fixed not on the wild white bulls, the horned horses or the giant scarlet flamingoes of the Kamarg, but upon a distance, profound and numinous.

Hawkmoon tried to recall a dream or an insane fantasy. He tried to remember Yisselda. He tried to remember the names of the children he had imagined while he had been mad. But Yisselda was a shadow and he could see nothing of the children at all. Why did he yearn? Why was he full of such a deep and lasting sense of loss? Why did he sometimes nurse the thought that this, which he experienced now, was madness and that the dream – that of Yisselda and the children – had been the reality?

Hawkmoon no longer knew himself and had lost the inclination, as a result, to communicate with others. He was a ghost. He haunted his own apartments. A sad ghost who could only sob and groan and sigh.

At least he had been proud in his madness, said the townsfolk. At least he had been complete in his delusions.

'He was happier mad.'

Hawkmoon would have agreed with such sentiments, had they been expressed to him.

When not in the tower he haunted the room where he had set up his War Tables – high benches on which rested models of cities and castles occupied by thousands of other models of soldiers. In his madness he had commissioned this huge array from Vaiyonn, the local craftsman. To celebrate, he had told Vaiyonn, their victories over the Lords of Granbretan. And represented in painted metal were the Duke of Köln himself, Count Brass, Yisselda, Bowgentle, Huillam D'Averc and Oladahn of the Bulgar Mountains – the heroes of the Kamarg, most of whom had perished at Londra. And here too were models of their old enemies, the Beast Lords – Baron Meliadus in his wolf helm, King Huon in his Throne Globe, Shenegar Trott, Adaz Promp, Asrovak Mikosevaar and his wife, Flana (now the gentle Queen of Granbretan). Dark Empire infantry, cavalry and flyers were ranged against the Guardians of the Kamarg, against the Warriors of Dawn, against the soldiers of a hundred small nations.

And Dorian Hawkmoon would move all these pieces about his vast boards, going through one permutation after another; fighting a thousand versions of the same battle in order to see how a battle which followed it might have changed. And his heavy fingers were often upon the models of his dead friends, and most of all they were upon Yisselda. How could she have been saved? What set of circumstances would have guaranteed her continuing to live?

Sometimes Count Brass would enter the room, his eyes troubled. He would run his fingers through his greying red hair and watch as Hawkmoon, absorbed in his miniature world, brought forward a squadron of cavalry here, drew back a line of infantry there. Hawkmoon either did not notice the presence of Count Brass on these occasions or else he preferred to ignore his old friend until Count Brass would clear his throat or otherwise make it evident that he had come in. Then Hawkmoon would look up, eyes introspective, bleak, unwelcoming, and Count Brass would ask softly after Hawkmoon's health.

Hawkmoon would reply curtly that he was well.

Count Brass would nod and say that he was glad.

Hawkmoon would wait impatiently, anxious to get back to his manoeuvrings on his tables, while Count Brass looked around the room, inspected a battle-line or pretended to admire the way Hawkmoon had worked out a particular tactic.

Then Count Brass would say:

'I'm riding to inspect the towers this morning. It's a fine day. Why don't you come with me, Dorian?'

Dorian Hawkmoon would shake his head. 'There are things I have to do here.'

'This?' Count Brass would indicate the wide trestles with a sweep of his hand. 'What point is there? They are dead. It is over. Will your speculation bring them back? You are like some mystic – some warlock – thinking that the facsimile can manipulate that which it imitates. You torture yourself. How can you change the past? Forget. Forget, Duke Dorian.'

But the Duke of Köln would purse his lips as if Count Brass had made a particularly offensive remark, and would turn his attention back to his toys. Count Brass would sigh, try to think of something to add, then he would leave the room.

Hawkmoon's gloom coloured the atmosphere of the whole Castle Brass and there were some who had begun to voice the opinion that, for all that he was a Hero of Londra, the duke should return to Germany and his traditional lands, which he had not visited since his capture, at the Battle of Köln, by the Dark Empire lords. A distant relative now reigned as Chief Citizen there, presiding over a form of elected government which had replaced the monarchy of which Hawkmoon was the last living direct descendant. But it had never entered Hawkmoon's mind that he had any home other than his apartments in Castle Brass.

Even Count Brass would sometimes think, privately, that it would have been better for Hawkmoon if he had been killed at the Battle of Londra. Killed at the same time that Yisselda had been killed.

And so the sad months passed, all heavy with sorrow and useless speculation, as Hawkmoon's mind closed still more firmly around its single obsession until he hardly remembered to take sustenance or to sleep.

Count Brass and his old companion, Captain Josef Vedla, debated the problem between themselves, but could arrive at no solution.

For hours they would sit in comfortable chairs on either side of the great fireplace in the main hall of Castle Brass, drinking the local wine and discussing Hawkmoon's melancholia. Both were soldiers and Count Brass had been a statesman, but neither had the vocabulary to cope with such matters as sickness of the soul.

'More exercise would help,' said Captain Josef Vedla one evening. 'The mind will rot in a body which does nothing. It is well known.'

'Aye – a healthy mind knows as much. But how do you convince a sick mind of the virtues of such action?' Count Brass replied. 'The longer he remains in his apartments, playing with those damned models, the worse he gets. And the worse he gets, the harder it is for us to approach him on a rational level. The seasons mean nothing to him. Night is no different from day for him. I shudder when I think what must be happening in his head!'

Captain Vedla nodded. 'He was never one for over-much intro-spection before. He was a man. A soldier. Intelligent without being, as it were, *too* intelligent. He was practical. Sometimes it seems to me that he is a different man entirely now. As if the old Hawkmoon's soul was driven from its body by the terrors of the Black Jewel and a new soul entered to fill the place!'

Count Brass smiled at this. 'You're becoming fanciful, captain, in your old age. You praise the old Hawkmoon for being practical – and then make a suggestion like that!'

Captain Vedla was also forced to smile. 'Fair enough, Count Brass! Yet when one considers the powers of the old Dark Empire lords and remembers the powers of those who helped us in our struggle, per-haps the idea could have some foundation in terms of our own experience?'

'Perhaps. And if there were not more obvious answers to explain Hawkmoon's condition, I might agree with your theory.'

Captain Vedla became embarrassed, murmuring: 'It *was* merely a theory.' He raised his glass to catch the firelight, studying the rich, red wine within. 'And this stuff is doubtless what encourages me to voice such theories!'

'Speaking of Granbretan,' said Count Brass later, 'I wonder how Queen Flana is coping with the problem of the unregenerates who still, from what she has said in her letters, inhabit some of the darker, less accessible parts of underground Londra? I have had little news from her in recent months. I wonder if the situation has worsened, so that she devotes more time to it.'

'You have had a letter from her recently, surely?'

'By messenger. Two days ago. Aye. The letter was much briefer, however, than those she used to send. It was almost formal. Merely extending the usual invitation to visit her whenever I desired.'

'Could it be that, of late, she has become offended that you have not taken her up on her offer of hospitality?' Vedla suggested. 'Per-haps she thinks you do not feel friendship for her.'

'On the contrary, she is the nearest thing to my heart save for the memory of my own dead daughter.'

'But you have not indicated as much?' Vedla poured himself more wine. 'Women require these affirmations, you know. Even queens.'

'Flana is above such feelings. She is too intelligent. Too sensible.

Too kind.'

'Possibly,' said Captain Vedla, as if he doubted Count Brass's words.

Count Brass understood the implication. 'You think I should write to her in more – more flowery terms?'

'Well . . .' Captain Vedla grinned.

'I was never capable of these literary flourishes.'

'Your style at its best (and on whatever subject) usually resembles communiques issued in the field during the heat of a battle,' Captain Vedla admitted. 'Though I do not mean that as an insult. On the contrary.'

Count Brass shrugged. 'I would not like Flana to think I did not remember her with anything but the greatest affection. Yet I cannot write. I suppose I should go to Londra – accept her offer.' He stared around his shadowed hall. 'It might be a change. This place has become almost overpoweringly gloomy of late.'

'You could take Hawkmoon with you. He was fond of Flana. It might be the only thing likely to attract him away from his toy soldiers.' Captain Vedla caught himself speaking sardonically and regretted it. He had every sympathy for Hawkmoon, every respect for him even in his present state of mind. But Hawkmoon's brooding was a strain on all who had been even remotely connected with him in the past.

'I'll suggest it to him,' said Count Brass. Count Brass understood his own feelings. Much of him wanted to get away from Hawkmoon for a while. Yet his conscience would not let him go alone at least until he had put the idea to his old friend. And Vedla was right. A trip to Londra might force Hawkmoon out of his brooding mood. The chances were, however, that it would not. In which case, Count Brass anticipated a journey and a visit involving more emotional strain on himself and the rest of his party than that which they now experienced within the confines of Castle Brass.

'I'll speak to him in the morning,' Count Brass said after a pause. 'Perhaps by returning to Londra itself, rather than by involving himself with models of the place, the melancholy in him will be exorcized . . .'

Captain Vedla agreed. 'It is something we should have considered earlier, maybe?'

Count Brass was, withour rancour, thinking that Captain Vedla was expressing a certain amount of self-interest when he suggested that Hawkmoon go with him to Londra.

'And would you journey with us, Captain Vedla?' he asked with a faint smile.

'Someone would be needed here to act on your behalf . . .' Vedla said. 'However, if the Duke of Köln declined to go then, of course, I would be glad to accompany you.'

'I understand you, captain.' Count Brass leaned back in his chair, sipping his wine and regarding his old friend with a certain amount of humour.

After Captain Josef Vedla had left, Count Brass remained in his chair. He was still smiling. He cherished his amusement, for it had been a long while since he had felt any at all. And now that the idea was in his mind, he began to look forward to his visit to Londra, for he only realized at this moment to what extent the atmosphere had become oppressive in Castle Brass, once so famous for its peace.

He stared up at the smoke-darkened beams of the roof, thinking sadly of Hawkmoon and what he had become. He wondered if it was altogether a good thing that the defeat of the Dark Empire had brought tranquillity to the world. It was possible that Hawkmoon, even more than himself, was a man who only came alive when conflict threatened. If, for instance, there was trouble again in Granbretan – if the unregenerate remnants of the defeated warriors were seriously troubling Queen Flana – perhaps it would be a good notion to ask Hawkmoon to make it his business to find them and destroy them.

Count Brass sensed that a task of that nature would be the only thing which could save his friend. Instinctively he guessed that Hawkmoon was not made for peace. There were such men – men fashioned by fate to make war, either for good or for evil (if there was a difference between the two qualities) – and Hawkmoon might well be one of them.

Count Brass sighed and returned his attention to his new plan. He would write to Flana in the morning, sending news ahead of his intended visit. It would be interesting to see what had become of that strange city since he had last visited it, as a conqueror.

## CHAPTER TWO

Count Brass goes a-Journeying

'Give Queen Flana my kindest compliments,' said Dorian Hawkmoon distantly. He held a tiny representation of Flana in his pale fingers, turning the model this way and that as he spoke. Count Brass was not entirely sure that Hawkmoon realized he had picked the model up. 'Tell her that I do not feel fit enough to make the journey.'

'You would feel fitter once you had begun to travel,' Count Brass pointed out. He noticed that Hawkmoon had covered the windows with dark tapestries. The room was lit now by lamps, though it neared noon. And the place smelled dank, unhealthy, full of festering memories.

Hawkmoon rubbed at the scar on his forehead, where the Black Jewel had once been imbedded. His skin was waxy. His eyes burned with a dreadful, feverish light. He had become so thin that his clothes draped his body like drowned flags. He stood looking down at the table bearing the intricate model of old Londra, with its thousands of crazy towers, interconnected by a maze of tunnels so that no in-habitant need ever see daylight.

Suddenly it occurred to Count Brass that Hawkmoon had caught the disease of those he had defeated. It would not have surprised the Count to discover that Hawkmoon had taken to wearing an ornate and complicated mask.

'Londra has changed,' said Count Brass, 'since last you saw it. I hear that the towers have been torn down – that flowers grow in wide streets – that there are parks and avenues in place of the tunnels.'

'So I believe,' said Hawkmoon without interest. He turned away from Count Brass and began to move a division of Dark Empire cavalry out from beyond Londra's walls. He seemed to be working on a battle situation where the Dark Empire had defeated Count Brass and the other Companions of the Runestaff. 'It must be exceptionally – pretty. But for my own purposes I prefer to remember Londra as it was.' His voice became sharp, unwholesome. 'When Yisselda died there,' he said.

Count Brass wondered if Hawkmoon was blaming him – accusing him of cohabiting with those whose compatriots had slain Yisselda.

He ignored the inference. He said: 'But the journey itself. Would that not be exhilarating? The last you saw of the outside world it was wasted, ruined. Now it flourishes again.'

'I have important things to do here,' Hawkmoon said.

'What things?' Count Brass spoke almost sharply. 'You have not left your apartments for months.'

'There is an answer,' Hawkmoon told him curtly, 'in all this. There is a way to find Yisselda.'

Count Brass shuddered.

'She is dead,' he said softly.

'She is alive,' Hawkmoon murmured. 'She is alive. Somewhere. In another place.'

'We once agreed, you and I, that there was no life after death,' Count Brass reminded his friend. 'Besides – would you resurrect a ghost. Would that please you – to raise Yisselda's shade?'

'If that were all I could resurrect, aye.'

'You love a dead woman,' Count Brass said in a quiet, disturbed voice. 'And in loving her you have fallen in love with death itself.'

'What is there in life to love?'

'Much. You would discover it again if you came with me to Londra.'

'I have no wish to see Londra. I hate the city.'

'Then just travel part of the distance with me.'

'No. I am dreaming again. And in my dreams I come closer to Yisselda – and our two children.'

'There never were children. You invented them. In your madness you invented them.'

'No. Last night I dreamed I had another name, but that I was still the same man. A strange, archaic name. A name from before the Tragic Millenium. John Daker. That was the name. And John Daker found Yisselda.'

Count Brass was close to weeping at his friend's insane mutterings. 'This reasoning – this dreaming – will bring you much more pain, Dorian. It will heighten the tragedy, not decrease it. Believe me. I speak the truth.'

'I know that you mean well, Count Brass. I respect your view and I understand that you believe that you are helping me. But I ask you to accept that you are not helping me. I must continue to follow this path. I know that it will lead me to Yisselda.'

'Aye,' said Count Brass sorrowfully. 'I agree. It will lead you to your death.'

'If that is the case, the prospect does not alarm me.' Hawkmoon turned again to regard Count Brass. The count felt a chill go through him as he looked at the gaunt, white face, the hot eyes which burned in deep sockets.

'Ah, Hawkmoon,' he said. 'Ah, Hawkmoon.'

And he walked towards the door and he said nothing else before he left the room.

And he heard Hawkmoon shout after him in a high, hysterical voice:

'I *will* find her, Count Brass!'

Next day Hawkmoon drew back the tapestry to peer through his window down into the courtyard below. Count Brass was leaving. His retinue was already mounted on good, big horses, caparisoned in the Count's red colours. Ribbons and pennants waved on holstered flame-lances, surcoats curled in the breeze, bright armour shone in the early morning sunlight. The horses snorted and stamped their feet. Servants moved about, making last minute preparations, handing warming drinks up to the horsemen. And then the Count Brass himself emerged and mounted his chestnut stallion, his brazen armour flickering as if fashioned from flame. The count looked up at the window, his face thoughtful for a moment. Then his expression changed as he turned to give an order to one of his men. Hawkmoon continued to watch.

While looking down upon the courtyard, he had been unable to rid himself of the sensation of observing particularly detailed models; models which moved and talked, yet were models nonetheless. He felt he could reach down and move a horseman to the other side of the courtyard, or pick up Count Brass himself and send him off away from Londra in another direction altogether. He had vague feelings of resentment towards his old friend which he could not understand. Sometimes it occurred to him, in dreams, that Count Brass had bought his own life with that of his daughter. Yet how could that be? And neither was it a thing which Count Brass could possibly conceive of doing. On the contrary, the brave old warrior would have given his life for a loved one without a second thought. Still, Hawkmoon could not drive the thought from his skull.

For a moment he felt a pang of regret, wondering if he should, after all, have agreed to accompany Count Brass to Londra. He watched as Captain Josef Vedla rode forward and ordered the portcullis raised in the gateway. Count Brass had left Hawkmoon to rule in his place; but really the stewards and the veteran Guardians of the Kamarg could run things perfectly well and would make no demands on Hawkmoon for a decision.

But no, thought Hawkmoon. This was not a time for action, but a time for thought. He was determined to find a way through to those ideas which he could feel in the back of his own mind and yet which he could not, as yet, reach. For all his old friends might disdain his 'playing with toy soldiers' he knew that by putting the models through a thousand permutations it might release, at some point, those thoughts, those elusive notions which would lead him to the truth involving his own situation. And once he understood the truth, he was sure he would find Yisselda alive. He was almost sure, too, that he would find two children — perhaps a boy and a girl. They had all judged him mad for five years, yet he was convinced that he had not been mad. He believed that he knew himself too well — that if he ever did go mad it would not be in the way his friends had described.

Now Count Brass and his retinue were waving to the castle's retainers as they rode through the gates on the first stage of the long journey to Londra.

Contrary to Count Brass's suspicions, Dorian Hawkmoon still held his old friend in great esteem. It caused him a pang of sorrow to see Count Brass leaving. Hawkmoon's problem was that he could no longer express any of the sentiments he felt. He had become too single-minded in his considerations, too absorbed in the problems which he attempted to solve in his obsessive manipulation of the tiny figures on his boards.

Hawkmoon continued to watch as Count Brass and his men rode down through the winding streets of Aigues-Mortes. The streets were lined with townsfolk, bidding Count Brass farewell. At last the party reached the walls of the town and rode out across the broad road through the marshes. Hawkmoon looked after them until they were out of sight, then he turned his attention back to his models.

Currently he was working out a situation in which the Black Jewel had not been set in his forehead, but in that of Oladahn of the Bulgar Mountains, and where the Legion of the Dawn could not be summoned. Would the Dark Empire have been defeated then? And if it could have been defeated, how might that have been accomplished? He had reached the point he had reached a hundred times before, of re-enacting the Battle of Londra. But this time it struck him that he, himself, might have been killed. Would this have saved Yisselda's life?

If he hoped, by going through these permutations of past events, to find a means of releasing the truth he believed to be hidden in his mind, he failed again. He completed the tactics involved, he noted the fresh possibilities involved, he considered his next development. He wished that Bowgentle had not died at Londra. Bowgentle had known much and might have helped him in this line of reasoning.

There again, the messengers of the Runestaff – The Warrior in Jet and Gold, Orland Fank or even the mysterious Jehamia Cohnalias, who had not claimed to be human – might have helped him. He had called to them for their help in the darkness of the nights, but they had not come. The Runestaff was safe now and they had no need of Hawkmoon's help. He had felt abandoned, though he knew they owed him nothing.

Yet could the Runestaff be involved in what had happened to him, was happening to him now? Was that strange artefact under some new threat? Had it set into motion a fresh series of events, a new pattern of destiny? Hawkmoon had a sense that there was more to his situation than anything which the ordinary, observed facts might suggest. He had been manipulated by the Runestaff and its servants just as he now manipulated his model soldiers. Was he being manipulated again? And was that why he turned to the models, deceiving himself that he controlled something when, in fact, he was controlled?

He pushed such thoughts aside. He must devote himself to his original speculations.

And thus it was that he avoided confronting the truth.

By pretending to search for the truth, by pretending that he was single-minded in that quest, he was able to escape it. For the truth of his situation might have been intolerable to him.

And that was ever the way of mankind.

## CHAPTER THREE

A Lady all in Armour

A month went by.

Twenty alternative destinies were played out on Hawkmoon's wargame boards. And Yisselda came no closer to him, even in his dreams.

Unshaven, red-eyed, acned, his skin flaking with eczema, weak from lack of food, flabby from lack of exercise, Dorian Hawkmoon had nothing of the hero left in him, either in his mind, his character or his body. He looked thirty years older than his real age. His clothes, stained, torn, ill-smelling, were the clothes of a beggar. His unwashed hair hung in greasy strands about his face. His beard contained flecks of distasteful substances. He had taken to wheezing, to muttering to himself, to coughing. His servants avoided him as much as they could. He had little cause to call on them and so he did not notice their absence.

He had changed beyond recognition, this man who had been the Hero of Köln, the Champion of the Runestaff, the great warrior who had led the oppressed to victory over the Dark Empire.

And his life was fading from him, though he did not realize it.

In his obsession with alternative destinies he had come close to fixing his own; he was destroying himself.

And his dreams were changing. And because they were changing he slept even less frequently than before. In his dreams he had four names. One of them was John Daker, but much more often now did he sense the other names – Erekosë and Urlik. Only the fourth name escaped him though he knew it was there. On waking, he could never recall the fourth name. He began to wonder if there was such a thing as reincarnation. Was he remembering earlier lives? That was his instinctive conclusion. Yet his common sense could not accept the idea.

In his dreams he sometimes met Yisselda. In his dreams he was always anxious, always weighed down by a sense of heavy responsibility, of guilt. He always felt that it was his duty to perform some action, but could never recall what that action was. Had he lived other lives that had been just as tragic as this one? The thought of an eternity of tragedy was too much for him. He drove it off, almost before it had formed.

And yet these ideas were half-familiar. Where had he heard them before? In other, earlier dreams? In conversation with someone? With Bowgentle? In Danark, the distant city of the Runestaff?

He began to feel threatened. He began to know terror. Even the models on his tables were half-forgotten. He began to see shadows moving at the corners of his eyes.

What was causing the fear?

He thought that possibly he was close to understanding the truth concerning Yisselda and that there were certain forces pledged to stop him; forces which might kill him just as he was on the point of discovering how to reach her.

The only thing which Hawkmoon did not consider – the only answer which did not come to mind – was that his fear was, in fact, fear of himself, fear of facing an unpleasant truth. It was the lie which was threatened, the protecting lie and, as most men will, he fought to defend that lie, to stave off its attackers.

It was at this time that he began to suspect his servants of being in league with his enemies. He was sure that they had made attempts to poison him. He took to locking his doors and refusing to open them when servants came to perform some necessary function. He ate the barest amount necessary to keep alive. He collected rain water from the cups he set out on the sills out of his windows and he drank only that water. Yet still fatigue would overwhelm his weakened body and then the little dreams would come to the man who dwelt in darkness. Dreams which in themselves were not unpleasant – gentle landscapes, strange cities, battles which Hawkmoon had never taken part in, peculiar, alien folk whom Hawkmoon had never encountered even in the strangest of his adventures in the service of the Runestaff. And yet they terrified him. Women appeared in those dreams, also, and some might have been Yisselda, yet he experienced no pleasure when he dreamed of these women, only a sense of deep disquiet. And once, fleetingly, he dreamed that he looked in a mirror and saw a woman there in place of his own reflection.

One morning he awoke from such a slumber and instead of rising, as was his habit, and going directly to his tables, he remained where he lay, looking up at the rafters of his room. In the dim light filtering through the tapestries across the window he could, quite plainly, see the head and shoulders of a man who bore a strong resemblance to the dead Oladahn. The resemblance was mostly in the way the head was held, in the expression, in the eyes. There was a wide-brimmed hat on the long, black hair and a small black and white cat sat on the shoulder. Hawkmoon noticed, without surprise, that the cat had a pair of wings folded neatly on its back.

'Oladahn?' Hawkmoon said, though he knew it was not Oladahn.

The face smiled and made as if to speak.

Then it had vanished.

Hawkmoon pulled dirty silk sheets over his head and lay there trembling. It began to dawn on him that he was going mad again, that perhaps Count Brass had been right, after all, and that he had experienced hallucinations for five years.

Later Hawkmoon got up and uncovered his mirror. Some weeks before he had thrown a robe over the mirror, for he had not wished to see himself.

He looked at the wretch who peered back at him through the dusty glass.

'I see a madman,' Hawkmoon murmured. 'A dying madman.'

The reflection aped the movement of the lips. The eyes were frightened. Above them, in the centre of the forehead, was a pale scar, perfectly circular, where once a black jewel had burned, a jewel which could eat a man's brain.

'There are other things which eat at a man's brain,' muttered the Duke of Köln. 'Subtler things than jewels. Worse things than jewels. How cleverly, after they are dead, do the Dark Empire lords reach out to take vengeance on me. By slaying Yisselda they brought slow death to me.'

He covered the mirror again and sighed a thin sigh. Painfully he walked back to his couch and sat down again, not daring to look up at the ceiling where he had seen the man who so much resembled Oladahn.

He was reconciled to the fact of his own wretchedness, his own death, his own madness. Weakly, he shrugged.

'I was a soldier,' he said to himself. 'I became a fool. I deceived myself. I thought I could achieve what great scientists and sorcerers achieve, what philosophers achieve. And I was never capable of it. Instead, I turned myself from a man of skill and reason into this diseased thing which I have become. And listen. Listen, Hawkmoon. You are talking to yourself. You mutter. You rave. You whine. Dorian Hawkmoon, Duke von Köln, it is too late for you to redeem yourself. You rot.'

A small smile crossed his sick lips.

'Your destiny was to fight, to carry a sword, to perform the rituals of war. And now tables have become your battle-fields and you have lost the strength to bear a dirk, let alone a sword. You could not sit a horse if you wished to.'

He let himself drop back onto his soiled pillow. He covered his face with his arms. 'Let the creatures come,' he said. 'Let them torment me. It is true. I am mad.'

He started, believing he heard someone groaning beside him. He forced himself to look.

It was the door which groaned. A servant had pushed it open. The servant stood nervously in the opening.

'My lord?'

'Do they all say I am mad. Voisin?'

'My lord?'

The servant was an old man, one of the few who still regularly attended Hawkmoon. He had served Hawkmoon ever since the Duke of Köln had first come to Castle Brass. Yet there was a nervous look in his eyes as he replied.

'Do they, Voisin?'

Voisin spread his hands. 'Some do, my lord. Others say you are unwell – a physical disease. I have felt for sometime that perhaps a doctor could be called . . .'

Hawkmoon felt a return of his old suspicions. 'Doctors? Poisoners?'

'Oh, no, my lord!'

Hawkmoon controlled himself. 'No, of course not. I appreciate your concern, Voisin. What have you brought me?'

'Nothing, my lord, save news.'

'Of Count Brass? How fares Count Brass in Londra?'

'Not of Count Brass. Of a visitor to Castle Brass. An old friend of the count's, I understand, who, on hearing that Count Brass was absent and that you were undertaking his responsibilities, asked to be received by you.'

'By me?' Hawkmoon smiled grimly. 'Do they know what I have become, in the outside world?'

'I think not, my lord.'

'What did you tell them?'

'That you were not well but that I would convey the message.'

'And that you have done.'

'Aye, my lord, I have.' Voisin hesitated. 'Shall I say that you are indisposed . . .?'

Hawkmoon began to nod assent but then changed his mind, push-

131

ing himself from the bed and standing up. 'No. I will receive them. In the hall. I will come down.'

'Would you wish to – to prepare yourself, my lord? Toilet things – some hot water?'

'No. I will join our guest in a few minutes.'

'I will take your decision to them.' Rather hastily Voisin departed from Hawkmoon's apartments, plainly disturbed by Hawkmoon's decision.

Deliberately, maliciously, Hawkmoon made no attempt to improve his appearance. Let his visitor see him as he was.

Besides, he was almost certainly mad. Even this could be one of his fantasies. He could be anywhere – in bed, at his tables, even riding through the marshes – and only believing that these events were taking place. As he left his bed-chamber and passed through the room in which his model tables had been set up, he brushed at ranks of soldiers with his dirty sleeves, he knocked over buildings, he kicked at a leg so that an earthquake took place in the city of Köln.

He blinked as he came out onto the landing, lit by huge, tinted windows at both ends. The light hurt his eyes.

He walked towards the stairs which wound down to the great hall. He clutched a rail, feeling dizzy. His own infirmity amused him. He looked forward to his visitor's shock when he appeared.

A servant hurried up to help him and he leaned heavily on the young man's arm as, slowly, they descended.

And at last he reached the hall.

An armoured figure stood admiring one of Count Brass's battle trophies – a lance and a dented shield which he had won off Orson Kach during the Rhine Cities Wars, many years before.

Hawkmoon did not recognize the figure at all. It was fairly short, stocky and had a somewhat belligerent stance. Some old fighting companion of the count's, when he was a mercenary general, almost certainly.

'Greetings,' wheezed Hawkmoon. 'I am the present custodian of Castle Brass.'

The figure turned. Cool, grey eyes looked Hawkmoon up and down. There was no shock in the eyes, no expression at all as the figure stepped forward, hand extended.

Indeed, it was likely that Hawkmoon's own face betrayed surprise, at very least.

For his visitor, dressed all in battered armour, was a middle-aged woman.

'Duke Dorian?' she said. 'I am Katinka van Bak. I've been travelling many nights.'

## CHAPTER FOUR

## News from Beyond the Bulgar Mountains

'I was born in sea-drowned Hollandia,' said Katinka van Bak, 'though my mother's parents were traders from Muskovia. In the battles between our country and the Belgic States, my kin were slain and I became a captive. For a while I served – in a manner you can imagine – in the retinue of Prinz Lobkowitz of Berlin. He had aided the Belgics in their war and I was part of his spoil.' She paused to take another slice of cold beef from the plate before her. Her armour was discarded and she wore a simple silk shirt and a pair of blue cotton breks. For all she leaned her arms on the table and spoke in blunt, unladylike tones, she was not unfeminine and Hawkmoon found himself liking her very much.

'Well, I spent much time in the company of warriors and it became my ambition to learn their skills. It amused them to teach me to use sword and bow and I continued to affect an awkwardness with weapons long after I had mastered their use. In this means I succeeded in not arousing any suspicion as to my plans.'

'You planned to escape?'

'A little more than that.' Katinka van Bak smiled and wiped her lips. 'There came a time when Prinz Lobkowitz himself heard of my eccentricity. I remember his laughter when he was taken to the quadrangle outside the dormitories where we girls lived. The soldier who had made me his special protégé gave me a sword and we duelled, he and I, for a while, to demonstrate to the prince the charming artlessness with which I thrust and parried. This was fine amusement indeed and Prinz Lobkowitz said that as he was entertaining guests that evening it would be a novel idea to show me off to them, something to make a change from the usual jongleurs and such who normally performed at such functions. This suited me well. I fluttered my lashes and smiled shyly and pretended to be pleased that I had been granted such an honour – pretended that I did not realize they were all laughing at me.'

Hawkmoon tried to imagine Katinka van Bak fluttering her lashes and playing the ingenue, but the effort defeated his imagination. 'And what happened?' He was genuinely curious. For the first time in months something was happening to take his attention away from his own problems. He rested an unshaven chin on a scabrous hand as Katinka van Bak continued.

'Well, that evening I was presented to the delighted guests who watched me girlishly duelling with several of Prinz Lobkowitz's warriors. They ate much as they watched, but they drank more. Several of the prince's guests – men and women – offered to buy me for large sums and this, of course, increased Prinz Lobkowitz's pride that he owned me. Naturally, he refused to sell. I remember his calling out to me:

'"And now, little Katinka, how many other martial arts do you pursue? What will you show us next?"

'Judging my moment to be the right one, I curtseyed prettily and, as if with naive boldness, said:

'"I have heard that you are a great swordsman, Your Grace. The best in all the province of Berlin."

'"So it is said," replied Lobkowitz.

'"Would you do me the honour of crossing swords with me, my lord? So that I may test my skill against the finest blade in this hall?"

'Prince Lobkowitz was taken aback by this at first, but then he laughed. It was hard for him to refuse in front of his guests, as I'd known. He decided to indulge me, but said gravely:

'"In Berlin there are different stakes for different forms of duelling. We fight for a first body-cut, for a first cut on the left cheek, for a first cut on the right cheek and so on – up to duelling to the death. I would not like to spoil your beauty, little Katinka."

'"Then let us fight to the death, Your Grace!" I said, as if carried away by the reception I had received.

'Laughter filled the hall, then. But I saw many an eager eye looking from me to the prince. None doubted that the prince would win any duel, of course, but they would be gratified at seeing my blood spilled.

'Lobkowitz was nonplussed, too drunk to think clearly, to work out the implications of my suggestion. But he did not wish to lose face in front of his guests.

'"I would not kill such a talented slave," he said jovially. "I think we should consider some other stake, little Katinka."

'"My freedom, then?" I suggested.

'"Neither would I lose so entertaining a girl ..." he began. But then the crowd was roaring at him to take more sporting an attitude. After all, they all knew he would play with me for a while before delivering a token cut or disarming me.

'"Very well!" He smiled and shrugged and accepted a blade from one of his guards, stepping from his table to the floor and taking up a fighting stance before me. "Let's begin." I could see that he intended to display his own skill in the manner in which he would prolong the duel.

'The fight began clumsily enough. Awkwardly I thrust and insouciantly he parried. The crowd of guests cheered me on and some even began to make wagers on how long the duel would last – though none wagered that I would win, of course.' Katinka van Bak poured a cup of apple juice for herself and swallowed it down before going on with her story.

'As you have guessed, Duke Dorian, I had become a swordswoman of no mean ability. Slowly I began to reveal my talent and slowly it dawned on Prinz Lobkowitz that he was having to use more and more of his skill to defend himself. I could see that he was beginning to realize that he fought an opponent who might well be his match. The idea of being beaten by a slave – and a slave-girl, at that – was not a pleasant one. He began to fight seriously. He wounded me twice. Once in the left shoulder and once in the thigh. But I fought on. And now, I recall, there was absolute silence in the hall, save for the sound of our steel and of Prinz Lobkowitz's heavy breathing. We fought for an hour. He would have killed me if he could.'

'I remember,' said Hawkmoon, 'a tale I heard when I ruled in Köln. So you are the woman who . . .?'

'Who slew the Prince of Berlin? Aye. I killed him in his own hall, before his own guests, in the presence of his own bodyguards. I took him in his heart with a single clean thrust. He was the first I killed. And before they could believe what they had seen I had raised my sword and reminded them all of the prince's bargain – that if I won the duel I should have my freedom. I doubt if any of the prince's close retainers would have kept that bargain. They would have slain me there and then if it had not been for Lobkowitz's friends and those who had had ambitions upon his territories. Several of them gathered round me to offer me positions in their households – as a novelty, you understand, rather than for my battle-skill. I accepted a post in the guard of Guy O'Pointte, Archduke of Bavaria. On the spot. The archduke's guard was the largest there, you understand, since he was the most powerful of the nobles assembled. After that, the dead prince's men decided to honour their master's bargain.'

'And that is how you became a soldier?'

'Aye. Eventually I became Guy O'Pointte's chief general. When the archduke was murdered by his uncle's family, I left the service of

Bavaria and went to find a new position. And that, of course, is when I met Count Brass. We've served as mercenaries together in half the armies of Europe – and often on the same side! At about the time your count settled here in the Kamarg, I went east and joined the permanent service of the Prince of Ukrainia, where I advised him on the reconstruction of his army. We put a good defence against the legions of the Dark Empire.'

'You were captured by the Beast Lords?'

Katinka van Bak shook her head. 'I escaped to the Bulgar Mountains, where I remained until after you and your comrades had turned the tables on them at the Battle of Londra. It fell upon me to help restore Ukrainia, the prince's youngest niece being the only surviving member of the family. I became Regent of Ukrainia, through no particular wish of my own.'

'You have renounced that position, then? Or are you merely visiting us incognito?'

'I did not renounce the position and I am not visiting you incognito,' said Katinka van Bak firmly, as if chiding Hawkmoon for trying to hurry her in her story. 'Ukrainia was invaded.'

'What? By whom? I thought the world at relative peace!'

'So it is. Or was until a short time ago when we who dwell to the east of the Bulgar Mountains began to hear of an army which had gathered in those mountains.'

'The Dark Empire resurgents!'

Katinka van Bak held up a chiding hand to silence him.

'It was a rabble army,' she went on. 'Certainly it was that. But I do not think it was the remains of the Dark Empire army. Though it was vast and had powerful weapons at its disposal, no individual comprising it resembled another. They wore different styles of clothing, carried different kinds of weapons, belonged to different races – some of which were by no means human. Do you follow me – each one looked as if he belonged to a *different* army!'

'A band composed of soldiers who survived the conquerings of the Dark Empire?'

'I think not. I do not know where these came from. All I do know is that every time they ventured from their mountains – which they had made their own and turned them into an impregnable fortress – almost – no expedition ever sent against this army was ever successful. Each force was wiped out. They kill whole populations – to the last new-born baby – and strip villages, cities, whole nations of everything of value. In that respect they are like bandits, rather than an organized army with some ultimate purpose. These seem to attack countries for loot alone. And as a result they extend their activities further and further, returning always with their booty, their stolen food and – very occasionally – women, to their mountain stronghold.'

'Who leads them?'

'I know not, though I've fought them when they came against the Ukraine. Either several lead them or none does. There is no-one to reason with, to parley with. They seem moved only by greed and a lust to kill. They are like locusts. There is no other description which fits them better. Even the Dark Empire allowed survivors, for it planned to rule the world and needed people to serve it. But these – these are worse.'

'It's hard to conceive of an aggressor worse than the Dark Empire,' said Hawkmoon feelingly. 'But,' he added quickly, 'I believe you, of course, Katinka van Bak.'

'Aye, believe me, for I'm the sole survivor. I thank the life I've led. It has given me the experience to know when a situation is lost and how to escape the consequences of such a loss. No other creature remains alive in Ukrainia or many other lands beyond the Bulgar Mountains.'

'So you fled to warn the lands this side of the mountains? To raise an army, perhaps, against this powerful rabble?'

'I fled. That is all. I have told my story to anyone who will listen, but I do not expect much will be done as a result. Most will not care what has happened to folk dwelling in such distant parts, even if they believed me in the first place. Therefore, to try to raise an army would be fruitless. And, I'll add, any human army which went against those who now occupy the Bulgar Mountains would be utterly destroyed.'

'Will you go on to Londra? Count Brass will be there by now.'

Katinka van Bak sighed and stretched. 'Not immediately, I think. If at all. I am weary. I have been riding almost without pause since leaving Ukrainia. If you do not object, I'll remain at Castle Brass until my old friend returns. Unless I have a whim to continue on to Londra. At the moment, however, I have no inclination to move beyond these walls.'

'You are, of course, fully welcome,' said Hawkmoon eagerly. 'It is an honour for me. You must tell me more of your tales of the old days. And you must give me your theories about this rabble army – where it might have come from, and so on.'

'I have no ideas on that subject,' said Katinka van Bak. 'There is no logical explanation. They appeared overnight and have been there ever since. Discourse with them is impossible. It is like attempting to talk reasonably to a hurricane. There is a sense of desperation about them, a wild contempt for their own lives as well as yours. And the clothing and forms of the soldiers, as I have said, is so disparate. Not two alike. And yet, you know, I thought I recognized one or two familiar faces in the throng which swept over us. Soldiers I'd known who had been dead these many years since. And I'll swear I saw Count Brass's old friend, Bowgentle, riding with them. Yet I heard Bowgentle was killed at Londra . . .'

'He was. He was. I saw his remains.' Hawkmoon, whose interest up until now had been relatively faint, now became eager to hear all Katinka van Bak could tell him. He felt he was on the verge of solving the problem he had been working on all this time. Perhaps he had not been so insane, after all. 'Bowgentle, you say. And others who were familiar – yet dead?'

'Aye.'

'Did any women ride in the army?'

'Yes. Several.'

'Any you recognized . . .?' Hawkmoon leaned across the table, staring intensely at Katinka van Bak.

She frowned, trying to recall, then she shook her head so that her grey braids swung. 'No.'

'Not Yisselda, perhaps? Yisselda of Brass?'

'She who died at Londra, too?'

'So it's said.'

'No. Besides I should not have recognized her. She was a small child when last I saw her.'

'Ah,' said Hawkmoon, resuming his chair. 'Yes. I forgot.'

'That is not to say she could not have been there,' went on the warrior woman. 'There were so many. I did not see half the army which conquered me.'

'Well, if you recognized Bowgentle, perhaps all the others were there – all those who died at Londra?'

'I said I thought the man I saw resembled Bowgentle. But why should Bowgentle or anyone else who was a friend of yours ride in such an army?'

'True.' Hawkmoon drew his brows together in thought. His eyes had lost their dullness. His movements had become somewhat more energetic. 'Say that he and the others were charmed, perhaps. In trances. Forced to do the will of an enemy. The Dark Empire had powers which could make such a thing possible.'

'It is fanciful, Duke Dorian . . .'

'As would sound the History of the Runestaff, if we did not know it to be true.'

'I agree, but . . .'

'I have long cherished an instinct, you see,' Hawkmoon told her, 'that Yisselda did not die at Londra, for all there were many witnesses to her death and burial. It is also possible that none of our other friends died at Londra – that all were victims of some secret Dark Empire counterplan. Could not the Dark Empire have substituted bodies for Yisselda and the rest, then borne the real people away to the Bulgar Mountains – captured others, too? Could you not have fought an army of Dark Empire slaves, controlled by those who escaped our vengeance?'

'But so few did escape. And none of the Lords lived after the Battle of Londra. So who could be making such plans, even if they were likely? Which they most decidedly are not, Duke Dorian.' Katinka van Bak pursed her lips. 'I thought you a man of sense. A practical soldier, like myself.'

'I thought so once – until this idea came into my mind – that Yisselda still lives. Somewhere.'

'I had heard that you were not wholly your old self . . .'

'You mean that you had heard I was mad. Well, madam, I do believe I am mad. Perhaps I have indulged in mad follies, of late, but only because the idea – the central idea – has truth in it.'

'I accept what you say,' said Katinka van Bak evenly. 'But I would need considerable proof of such a theory. *I* do not have an instinct that the dead live . . .'

'I think Count Brass has,' Hawkmoon told her. 'Though he would not admit it. I think it is something he refuses to consider for he fears that he would go as mad as he thought me to be.'

'And that could also be,' agreed Katinka van Bak, 'but again I have no evidence that Count Brass thinks as you say. I should have to meet him again and talk with him in order to test your words.'

Hawkmoon nodded. He thought for a moment and then said:

'But suppose I have a means of defeating this army? What would you say? If my theories led me to the truth concerning the army and its origins and that they, in turn, led me to an understanding of its weaknesses.'

'Then your theories would be a practical direction,' Katinka van Bak said. 'But unfortunately there is only one way to test them and that involves losing one's life if one is wrong. Eh?'

'I would willingly take that risk. When I fought the Dark Empire I soon realized there was no way to overcome it by direct confrontation, but if one sought weaknesses in the leaders, and made use of those weaknesses, then they could be defeated. That is what I learned in the service of the Runestaff.'

'You think you know how to defeat that rabble?' Katinka van Bak was by now half-convinced.

'Obviously I do not know the exact nature of the weakness. But I could discover it probably better than anyone else in the world!'

'I think you could!' exclaimed Katinka van Bak, grinning. 'I'm with you there. But I think it is too late to look for weaknesses.'

'If I could observe them. If I could find a hiding place, perhaps in the mountains themselves, and watch them, then perhaps I could think of a way of defeating them.' Hawkmoon was thinking of another thing he might gain from observing the rabble army, but he kept that idea to himself. 'You hid in those same mountains for a long while, Katinka van Bak. You, better than anyone save Oladahn himself, could find me a lair from which I might spy on the locusts!'

'I could, but I have just fled from those parts. I have no wish to lose my life, young man, as I told you. Why should I take you into the Bulgar Mountains, the very stronghold of my enemies?'

'Had you not nursed at least a little hope that your Ukrainia might be avenged? Did you not think to yourself, even secretly, that you might enlist the help of Count Brass and his Kamargians against your foes?'

Katinka van Bak smiled. 'Well, I knew the hope to be foolish, but . . .'

'And now I offer you a chance of taking that vengeance. All you need do is lead me into the mountains, find me a place that is relatively safe, and then you could even depart if you wished.'

'Are your motives selfless, Duke Dorian?'

Hawkmoon hesitated. Then he admitted: 'Perhaps not wholly selfless. I wish to test my theory that Yisselda still lives and that I can save her.'

'Then I think I'll take you to the Bulgar Montains,' said Katinka van Bak. 'I do not trust a man who tells me that anything he does is completely selfless. But I think I can trust you.'

'I think you can,' said Hawkmoon.

'The only problem that I can see,' added the warrior woman frankly, 'is whether you'll survive the journey. You are in extremely poor condition, you know.' She reached forward and fingered his garments just as if she were a peasant woman buying a goose in the market. 'You need fattening up for a start. Let a week pass first. Get some food into your belly. Exercise. Ride. We'll have a mock duel or two together . . .'

Hawkmoon smiled. 'I am glad that you hold no grudge against me, my lady, or I should think twice about accepting that last suggestion at face value!'

And Katinka van Bak flung back her head and laughed.

Reluctantly – A Quest

Hawkmoon ached in every limb. He made a sorry sight as he stumbled out into the courtyard where Katinka van Bak already waited, mounted on a frisky stallion whose hot breath clouded the early morning air. Hawkmoon's mount was a less nervous beast, but known for his reliability and stamina, yet Hawkmoon did not relish the prospect of climbing into the animal's saddle. His stomach was griping him, his head swam, his legs shook, for all that he had spent more than a week exercising and eating a good diet. His appearance had improved a little, and he was cleaner, but he was not the Runestaff Hero who had ridden out against Londra only seven years earlier. He shivered, for winter was beginning to touch the Kamarg. He wrapped his heavy leather cloak about him. The cloak was lined with wool and was almost too warm when closed. So heavy was the cloak that it almost bore him to the ground as he walked. He carried no weapons. His sword and flame-lance were in saddle scabbards. He wore, as well as the cloak, a thick quilted jerkin of dark red, doeskin leggings stitched with complicated designs by Yisselda, when she lived, and plain knee-boots of good, gleaming leather. Upon his head was a simple helmet. Aside from this, he wore no armour. He was not strong enough to wear armour.

Hawkmoon was still not healthy, either in mind or body. What had driven him to improve his physical condition to this degree had not been disgust with what he had become but his insane belief that he might find Yisselda alive in the Bulgar Mountains.

With some difficulty, he mounted his horse. Then he was bidding farewell to his stewards, completely forgetful that Count Brass had left the responsibility of running the province in his hands, and following Katinka van Bak through the gate and down through the empty streets of Aigues-Mortes. No citizens lined these streets. None, save the servants at the castle, knew that he was leaving Castle Brass, heading east where Count Brass had headed west.

By noon the two figures had passed through the reed-fields, passed the marshes and lagoons, and were following a hard white road past one of the great stone towers which marked the borders of the land of which Count Brass was Lord Protector.

Weary of riding even this comparatively short distance, Hawkmoon was beginning to regret his decision. His arms ached from clinging to his saddle pommel, his thighs gave him agonizing pain and his legs had gone completely numb. Katinka van Bak, on the other hand, seemed tireless. She kept stopping her own horse to allow Hawkmoon to catch up, yet was deaf to his suggestions that they stop and rest for a while. Hawkmoon wondered if he would last the journey, if he would not die on the way to the Bulgar Mountains. He wondered, from time to time, how he could ever have conceived a liking for this fierce, heartless woman.

They were hailed by a Guardian who saw them from his post at the top of the tower. His riding flamingo stood beside him and his scarlet cloak waved in the breeze so that for a moment Hawkmoon saw man and bird as one creature. The Guardian raised his long flame-lance in salute as he recognized Hawkmoon. Hawkmoon managed to wave a feeble hand in return, but was unable to call back in reply to the Guardian's greeting.

Then the tower had dwindled behind them as they took the road to Lyonesse, with a view to skirting the Switzer Mountains which were said to be tainted still with the poisons of the Tragic Millenium and which were, besides, all but impassable. Also, in Lyonesse Katinka van Bak had acquaintances who would give them provisions for the remainder of their journey.

They camped on the road that night and in the morning Hawkmoon had become fully convinced of his own imminent death. The pain of the previous day was as nothing with the agony he felt now. Katinka van Bak, however, continued to show no mercy, heaving him peremptorily upon his patient horse before climbing into her own saddle. Then she grasped his bridle and led horse and swaying rider after her.

Thus they progressed for three more days, hardly resting at all, until Hawkmoon collapsed altogether, falling from his saddle in a faint. He no longer cared whether he found Yisselda or not. He neither blamed nor condoned Katinka van Bak for her ruthless treatment of his person. His pain had faded to a perpetual ache. He moved when the horse moved. He stopped when the horse stopped. He ate the food which Katinka van Bak would occasionally put in front of him. He slept for the few hours she allowed him. And then he fainted.

He woke once and opened his eyes to receive a view of his own swaying feet on the other side of his horse's belly, and he knew that

Katinka van Bak continued her journey, having slung him over the saddle of his own steed.

It was in this manner, some time later, that Dorian Hawkmoon, Duke von Köln, Champion of the Runestaff, Hero of Londra, entered the old city of Lyon, capital of Lyonesse, his horse led by an old woman in dusty armour.

And the next time Dorian Hawkmoon woke he lay in a soft bed and there were young maidens bending over him, smiling at him, offering him food. He refused to accept their existence for some moments.

But they were real and the food was good and the rest revived him.

Two days later the reluctant Hawkmoon, in considerably better condition now, left with Katinka van Bak to continue their quest for the rabble army of the Bulgar Mountains.

'You're filling out at last, lad,' said Katinka van Bak one morning as they rode into the sun which was turning to a glowing green the rolling, gentle hills of the land through which they travelled. She rode beside him now, no longer finding it necessary to lead his horse. She slapped him on the shoulder. 'You've good bones. There was nothing wrong with you that couldn't be put right, as you see.'

'Health achieved through such an ordeal as that, madam,' said Hawkmoon feelingly, 'is scarcely worth attaining.'

'You'll feel grateful to me yet.'

'I tell you honestly, Katinka van Bak, I am not sure I shall!'

And at this Katinka van Bak, Regent of Ukrainia, laughed heartily and spurred her stallion along the narrow track through the grass.

Hawkmoon was forced to admit to himself that the worst of his aches had disappeared and he was much more capable of sustaining long horseback journeys now. He was still subject to occasional stomach gripes and he was by no means as strong as he had once been, yet he was almost at the stage where he could enjoy the sights and smells and sounds around him for their own sake. He was amazed at how little sleep Katinka van Bak seemed to need. Half the time they rode on through the best part of the night before she was ready to make camp. As a result they made excellent time, but Hawkmoon felt permanently weary.

They reached the second main stage of their journey when they entered the territories of Duke Mikael of Bazhel, a distant kinsman of Hawkmoon's and for whom Katinka van Bak had once fought during the duke's squabble with another of his relatives, the now long-dead Pretender of Strasbourg. During the occupation of his lands by the Dark Empire, Duke Mikael had been subject to the grossest humiliation and he had never quite recovered from it. He had become distinctly misanthropic and his wife performed most of his functions for him. She was called Julia of Padova, daughter of the Traitor of Italia, Enric, who had formed a pact with the Dark Empire against his fellows and had been slain by the Beast Lords for his pains. Perhaps because of the knowledge she had of her father's baseness, Julia of Padova ruled the province well and with considerable fairness. Hawkmoon remarked on the wealth which was evident everywhere about the countryside. Fat cattle grazed on good grass. The farmhouses were well kept and shone with fresh paint and polished stone, their gables carved in the intricate style favoured by the peasants of these parts.

But when they came to Bazhel, the capital city, they were received by Julia of Padova with only moderate politeness and her hospitality was not lavish. It seemed that she did not like to be reminded of the old, dark days when the Dark Empire had ruled the whole of Europe. Therefore she was not pleased to see Hawkmoon, for he had played such an important part against the Empire and thus she could not help but be reminded of it – of her husband's humiliation and of her father's treachery.

So it was that the pair did not remain long in Bazhel, but struck on for Munchenia, where the old Prince tried to smother them with gifts and begged them to stay longer and tell him of their adventures. Aside from warning him of what had happened in Ukrainia (he was sceptical) they told him nothing of their quest and reluctantly bade him farewell, armed with better weapons than those they had carried, and dressed in better clothes, though Hawkmoon had retained his big leather cloak, for the winter was making itself evident across the whole land now.

By the time Dorian Hawkmoon and Katinka van Bak reached Linz, now a Republic, the first snows had begun to fall in the streets of the little wooden city, rebuilt from that which had been completely razed by the armies of Granbretan.

'We must make better time,' Katinka van Bak told Hawkmoon as they sat in the tap-room of a good inn near the central square of the city. 'Else the passes in the Bulgar Mountains will be blocked and our whole journey will have no point.'

'I wonder if it does have a point,' Hawkmoon said, sipping a negus with some relish, holding the steaming winecup in his gloved hands. He had now changed beyond recognition from the creature he had become at Castle Brass, though all who had known him before that time would have recognized him immediately. His face had become strong again and muscles rippled beneath his silk shirt. His eyes were bright and healthy and his skin glowed. His long fair hair shone.

'You wonder if you'll find Yisselda there?'

'That, aye. And I wonder if the army is as strong as you thought. Perhaps they were lucky in the manner in which they overwhelmed your forces.'

'Why do you think this now?'

'Because we have heard no rumours. Not a single hint that anyone in these parts had received even an inkling of this force which occupies the Bulgar Mountains.'

'I have seen this army,' Katinka van Bak reminded him. 'And it is vast. Believe me in that. It is powerful. It could take over the whole world. Believe me in that also.'

Hawkmoon shrugged. 'Well, I do believe you, Katinka van Bak. But I still find it strange that no rumours have come to our ears. When we have spoken of this army there is never another who confirms what we say. It is no wonder that little attention is paid to us!'

'Your brain sharpens,' said Katinka van Bak approvingly, 'but as a result you are less able to believe the fantastical!' She smiled. 'Is that not often the case?'

'Often, aye.'

'Would you turn back?'

Hawkmoon studied the hot wine in his cup. 'It is a long journey home. But now I feel guilty, leaving my duties in the Kamarg to go upon this quest.'

'You were not performing those duties very well,' she reminded him softly. 'You were not in a position to do so – mentally or physically.'

Hawkmoon smiled grimly. 'That's true. I have benefited a great deal from this journey. Yet that does not change the fact that my responsibilities lie firstly in the Kamarg.'

'It is a longer journey to the Kamarg, now, than it is to the Bulgar Mountains,' she said.

'You were at first reluctant to go on this quest,' he said. 'But now you are the most anxious of us to complete it!'

She shrugged. 'Say that I like to finish what I begin. Is that unusual?'

'I would say it was typical of you, Katinka van Bak.' Hawkmoon sighed. 'Very well. Let's go to the Bulgar Mountains, then, as

147

quickly as our horses will take us. And let us make haste back to the Kamarg when our errand is done. With information and the strength of the Kamarg we shall find a way of defeating those who destroyed your land. We'll confer with Count Brass who, almost certainly, will have returned by then.'

'A sensible scheme, Hawkmoon.' Katinka van Bak seemed relieved. 'And now I'll to bed.'

'I'll finish my wine and copy your example,' said Hawkmoon. He laughed. 'You still manage to tire me out, even now.'

'Another month and our situation will be reversed,' she promised. 'Goodnight to you, Hawkmoon.'

Next morning their horses' hooves galloped through shallow snow and more snow was falling from an overcast sky. But by the early afternoon the clouds had cleared and the sky was blue and empty over their heads while the snow had begun to melt. It was not a serious fall, but it was an omen of what they might expect to find when they approached the Bulgar Mountains.

They rode through a hilly land which had once been part of the Kingdom of Wien, but so crushed had been that kingdom that its population had all but disappeared. Now grass had grown back on the burned ground and the many ruins were vine-covered and picturesque. Later travellers might come to marvel at such pretty relics, thought Hawkmoon, but he could never forget that they were the result of Granbretan's savage lust to rule the world.

They were passing the remains of a castle which looked down on them from a rise above the path they followed when Hawkmoon thought he heard a sound from the place.

He whispered to Katinka van Bak who was riding just ahead.

'Did you hear it? From the castle?'

'A human voice? Aye. I did. Could you hear the words?' She turned in her saddle to look back at him.

He shook his head. 'No. Should we investigate?'

'Our time runs short.' She pointed to the sky where more clouds were gathering.

But by now they had both pulled in their horses and were still, looking up at the castle.

'Good afternoon!'

The voice was strangely accented but cheerful.

'I had a feeling you would be passing this way, Champion.'

And from the ruins now stepped a slim young man wearing a hat with a huge brim, turned up at one side. There was a feather stuck in

the band. He wore a velvet jerkin, rather dusty, and blue velvet
pantaloons. On his feet were soft doeskin boots. He carried a small
sack over his back. At his hip was a plain, slender sword.

And it was with horror that Dorian Hawkmoon recognized him.

Hawkmoon found himself drawing his sword, though the stranger
had offered him no harm.

'What? You think me an enemy?' said the youth, smiling. 'I assure
you that I am not.'

'You have seen him before, Hawkmoon?' Katinka van Bak said
sharply. 'Who is he?'

He was the vision Hawkmoon had had when he lay upon his bed
in Castle Brass, before the coming of the warrior woman.

'I know not,' said Hawkmoon thickly. 'This has a terrible smell of
sorcery to it. Dark Empire work perhaps. He resembles – he looks
like an old friend of mine – yet there is nothing evidently the same
about them . . .'

'An old friend, eh?' said the stranger. 'Well I am that, Champion.
What do they call you in this world?'

'I do not understand you.' Reluctantly Hawkmoon sheathed his
sword.

'It is often the case when I recognize you. I am Jhary-a-Conel and
I should not be here at all. But such strange disruptions have been
taking place in the multiverse of late! I was wrenched from four
separate incarnations in as many minutes! And what do they call
you, then?'

'I still do not understand,' said Hawkmoon doggedly. 'Call me? I
am the Duke von Köln. I am Dorian Hawkmoon.'

'Then greetings again, Duke Dorian. I am your companion.
Though for how long I shall remain with you I know not. As I say,
strange disruptions are . . .'

'You babble a considerable amount of nonsense, Sir Jhary,' said
Katinka van Bak impatiently. 'How came you to these parts?'

'Through no volition of my own was I transported to this wasteland, madam.'

Suddenly the young man's bag began to jump and writhe and
Jhary-a-Conel lowered it gently to the ground, opening it and
drawing out a small, winged black and white cat. The same
Hawkmoon had seen in the vision.

Hawkmoon shuddered. While he could find nothing to dislike
about the young man himself, he had a terrible premonition that
a-Conel's appearance heralded some unpleasant doom for him. Just
as he could not see why he thought a-Conel resembled Oladahn,

149

neither could he work out why other things were familiar, too. Echoes. Echoes like those which had convinced him Yisselda still lived . . .

'Do you know Yisselda?' he said tentatively. 'Yisselda of Brass?'

Jhary-a-Conel frowned. 'I do not believe so. But then I know so many people and forget most of them, just as I might well forget you some day. That is my fate. As, of course, it is yours.'

'You speak familiarly of my fate. Why should you know more of it than do I?'

'Because I do, in this context. Another time neither shall recognize the other. Champion, what calls you now?'

As a Champion of the Runestaff, Hawkmoon was used to this form of address, though it was rare for most to use it. The rest of the sentence was a mystery to him.

'Nothing calls me. I am upon a quest with this lady here. An urgent quest.'

'Then we must not delay. A moment.'

Jhary-a-Conel raced back up the hill and into the ruined castle. A moment later he emerged leading an old yellow horse. It was the unloveliest nag Hawkmoon had ever seen.

'I doubt if you would be able to keep up with us mounted on that creature,' Hawkmoon said. 'Even if we had agreed that you should accompany us. And we have not agreed.'

'But you will.' Jhary-a-Conel put a foot into a stirrup and swung himself into his saddle. The horse seemed to sag under his weight. 'After all, it is our fate to ride together.'

'That may seem pre-ordained to you, my friend,' said Hawkmoon grimly, 'but I share no such belief.' And yet, he realized, he did. It seemed to him that it was perfectly natural that Jhary should ride with them. At the same time he resented both Jhary's assumption and his own.

Hawkmoon looked to Katinka van Bak to see what she thought. She merely shrugged. 'I've no objection to another sword riding with us,' she said.

She cast a disdainful look at Jhary's horse. 'Not,' she added, 'that I think you'll be riding with us for long.'

'We shall see,' Jhary told her cheerfully. 'Where do you ride?'

Hawkmoon became suspicious. Suddenly it occurred to him that this man might be a spy for those who now occupied the Bulgar Mountains.

'Why do you ask?'

Jhary shrugged. 'I wondered. I had heard of some trouble in the mountains to the east of here. A wild band who swoop down to destroy everything before returning to their retreat.'

'I have heard a story like that,' Hawkmoon admitted cautiously. 'Where did you hear it?'

'Oh, from a traveller I met on the road.'

At last Hawkmoon had heard confirmation of what Katinka van Bak had told him. He was relieved to find that she had not been lying to him. 'Well,' he said, 'we ride in that general direction. Perhaps we shall see for ourselves.'

'Indeed,' said Katinka van Bak with a crooked smile.

And now there were three riding for the Bulgar Mountains. A strange threesome, in truth. They rode for some days and Jhary's nag appeared to have no great trouble in keeping pace with the other horses.

One day Hawkmoon turned to their new companion and asked him: 'Did you ever have occasion to meet a man called Oladahn? He was quite short and covered all over in red hair. He claimed to be kin to the Bulgar Mountain Giants (whom none, to my knowledge, has ever seen). An expert archer.'

'I've met many expert archers, among them Rackhir the Red Archer who is perhaps the greatest in all the multiverse, but never one called Oladahn. Was he a good friend of yours?'

'My closest friend for a long while.'

'Perhaps I have borne that name,' Jhary-a-Conel said frowning. 'I have borne many, of course. It seems vaguely familiar. Just as the name Corum or Urlik would seem familiar to you.'

'Urlik?' Hawkmoon felt the blood leave his face. 'What know you of that name?'

'It is your name. Or one of them, at least. As is Corum. Though Corum was not a human manifestation and would therefore be a little harder for you to recall.'

'You speak so casually of incarnations! Do you really mean to claim you can recall past lives as easily as I can recall past adventures?'

'Some lives. By no means all. And that is just as well. In another incarnation I might not remember this one, for instance. Yet my name has not changed, in this case, I note.' Jhary laughed. 'My memories come and go. Just as yours do. It is what saves us.'

'You speak in riddles, friend Jhary.'

'So you often tell me.' Jhary shrugged. 'Yet this adventure does seem a little different, I'll admit. I am in the peculiar situation, at present, of being shifted willy-nilly through the dimensions. Disruptions on a large scale – brought about by the experiments of some foolish sorcerer, no doubt. And then, of course, there is always the interest that the Lords of Chaos show when such opportunities are offered. I would imagine they are playing some part in this.'

'The Lords of Chaos? Who are they?'

'Ah, it is something you must discover, if you do not know. Some say that they dwell at the end of time and their attempts to manipulate the universe according to their own desires are the result of their own world's dying. But that is a rather narrow theory. Others suggest that they do not exist at all, but are conjured up, periodically, by men's imaginations.'

'You are a sorcerer yourself, Master Jhary?' asked Katinka van Bak, falling back to join them.

'I think not.'

'A philosopher at least,' she said.

'My experience moulds my philosophy, that is all.'

And Jhary seemed to tire of the conversation and refused to be drawn further on that particular topic.

'My only experience of the sort you hint at,' said Hawkmoon, 'was with the Runestaff. Could the Runestaff be involved in what is happening in the Bulgar Mountains?'

'The Runestaff? Perhaps.'

Snow had fallen heavily on the great city of Pesht. Built of white, carved stone, the city had survived the Dark Empire sieges and now looked much as it had done before Granbretan had ridden out on her conquerings. Snow sparkled on every surface and its glare, as they approached at night under a full moon, made it seem that Pesht burned with white fire.

They arrived at the gates after midnight and had some difficulty rousing the guard who let them in with a considerable amount of grumbling and querying their business in the city. Down broad, deserted avenues they rode, seeking the palace of Prince Karl of Pesht. Prince Karl had once courted Katinka van Bak and asked her to be his wife. They had been lovers for three years, the warrior woman had told Hawkmoon, but she would never marry him. Now he had married a princess from Zagredia and was happy. They were friends. She had stayed with him during her flight from Ukrainia. He would be surprised to see her.

Prince Karl of Pesht was surprised. He arrived in his own ornate hall in a brocade dressing gown, his eyes still thick with sleep. But he was pleased to see Katinka van Bak.

'Katinka! I thought you planned to winter in the Kamarg!'

'That had been my plan.' She went forward and seized the tall old man's shoulders, kissing him swiftly on both cheeks in the military fashion, so that it seemed more as if she was presenting a soldier with a medal than greeting an ex-lover. 'But Duke Dorian here persuaded me to accompany him to the Bulgar Mountains.'

'Dorian? The Duke of Köln. I have heard much of you, young man. It is an honour to have you under my roof.' Prince Karl smiled as he shook Hawkmoon's hand. 'And this?'

'A companion of the road,' said Hawkmoon. 'His name is a strange one. Jhary-a-Conel.'

Jhary swept off his hat in an elaborate bow. 'An honour to meet the Prince of Pesht,' he said.

Prince Karl laughed. 'A privilege to entertain any companion of the great Hero of Londra. This is wonderful. You will stay for some time?'

'For the night only, I regret,' said Hawkmoon. 'Our business in the Bulgar Mountains is urgent.'

'What could possibly take you there? Even the legendary mountain giants are all dead now, I gather.'

'You have not told the prince?' said Hawkmoon in surprise, turning to Katinka van Bak. 'Of the raiders. I thought . . .'

'I did not wish to alarm him,' she said.

'But his city is not so distant from the Bulgar Mountains that it cannot be in danger of attack!' Hawkmoon said.

'Attack? What is this? An enemy from beyond the mountains?' Prince Karl's expression changed.

'Bandits,' said Katinka van Bak, darting a hard, meaning glance at Hawkmoon. 'A city of the size of Pesht has nothing to fear. A land so well defended as yours is under no threat.'

'But . . .' Hawkmoon restrained himself. Plainly Katinka van Bak had a reason for not telling the Prince of Pesht all she knew. But what could that reason possibly be? Did she suspect Prince Karl of being in league with her enemies? If so, she could have warned him earlier. Besides, it was inconceivable that this fine old man would ally himself with such a rabble. He had fought well and nobly against the Dark Empire and had been imprisoned for his pains, though he had not been subjected to the indignities normally visited upon captured enemy aristocrats by the Dark Empire.

'You will be weary from so much riding,' said Prince Karl tactfully. He had already ordered his servants to prepare rooms for his

153

guests. 'You will want to seek your beds. I have been selfish in thinking only of my own pleasure at seeing you again, Katinka, and meeting this hero here.' He smiled and put his arm around Hawkmoon's shoulders. 'But at breakfast, perhaps, we can talk a little. Before you leave?'

'It would please me greatly, sire,' said Hawkmoon.

And when Hawkmoon lay in a great bed in a well-appointed room in which a comfortable fire blazed, he watched the shadows playing on the rich tapestries which decorated the walls and he brooded for a few minutes on the reasons for Katinka van Bak's reticence before falling into a deep and dreamless sleep.

The big sleigh could have taken a dozen armoured men and could have been sold for a fortune, for it was inlaid with gold, platinum, ivory and ebony, as well as precious jewels. The carvings cut into the wood of its frame were the work of a master. Hawkmoon and Katinka van Bak had been reluctant to accept the gift from Prince Karl, but he was insistent. 'It is what you will need in this weather. Your riding beasts can follow and thus be fresh when you need them.' Eight black geldings pulled the sleigh and they were clad in harness of black leather and fine silver. Silver bells had been fixed to the harness, but these had been muffled for obvious reasons.

The snow was falling thickly and the roads which led to Pesht were all slippery with ice. It was logical to use a sleigh under such circumstances. The sleigh was piled with provisions, with furs, with a pavilion which could be quickly erected in even the worst weather. There were ancient devices, relatives to the flame-lances, on which food could be prepared. And there seemed enough food of all kinds to feed a small army. Prince Karl had not been expressing mere politeness when he had said he was delighted to receive them.

Jhary-a-Conel felt no reluctance in accepting the sleigh. He laughed with pleasure as he climbed in and seated himself amidst a profusion of expensive furs. 'Remember when you were Urlik,' he said, addressing Hawkmoon, 'Urlik Skarsol, Prince of the Southern Ice. Bears drew your carriage then!'

'I remember no such experience,' said Hawkmoon sharply. 'I wish I could understand your motives in continuing this pretence.'

'Ah, well,' replied Jhary philosophically, 'perhaps you will understand later.'

Prince Karl of Pesht bid them farewell personally, waving to them from Pesht's impressive walls until they were out of sight.

The great sleigh moved swiftly and Hawkmoon wondered why

the speed of its travelling filled him with a mixture of exhilaration and misgivings. Again Jhary had mentioned something which roused an echo of memory. And yet it was obvious to him that he could never have been this 'Urlik' – for all he seemed to remember dreaming once of such a name.

And now the going was speedy, for the weather had been turned to their advantage. The eight black geldings seemed tireless as they strained in their harness, dragging the sleigh closer and closer to the Bulgar Mountains.

But still Hawkmoon had a terrifying sense of familiarity. The image of a silver chariot, its four wheels fixed to skis, moving implacably over a great ice plain. Another image of a ship – but a ship which travelled upon another ice plain. And they were not the same worlds – of that he was sure. Neither was either one this world, his world. He drove the thoughts away as best he could, but they were persistent.

Perhaps he should put all his questions to Katinka van Bak and to Jhary-a-Conel, but he could not bring himself to ask them. He felt that the answers might not be to his taste.

So they drove on through the swirling snow and the ground rose steeply and the speed of their travelling decreased a little, but not very much.

From what he could see of the surrounding landscape, there was no evidence at all of recent raids. Sitting with his hands on the reins of the eight black geldings, Hawkmoon put this to Katinka van Bak.

Her answer was brief:

'Why should there be such signs? I told you that they raided only on the other side of the mountains.'

'Then there must be an explanation for that,' Hawkmoon said. 'And if we find the explanation we might also find their weakness.'

Finally the roads became too steep and the geldings' hooves slipped on the ice as they strove to haul the sleigh behind them. The snow had abated and it was late in the afternoon. Hawkmoon pointed to a mountain meadow below them. 'The horses may be pastured there. The grazing is reasonable and – look – a cave where they might stable themselves. It is the most we can do for them, I fear.'

'Very well,' agreed Katinka van Bak. With great difficulty they managed to turn the horses and lead them back down the path until they reached the snow-covered meadow. Hawkmoon cleared snow with his boot to indicate the grass below, but the geldings needed no help from him. They were used to such conditions and were soon using their hooves to clear the snow so that they might graze. And since it was almost sunset, the three decided to spend the night in the cave with the horses before continuing into the mountains.

'These conditions are an advantage,' said Hawkmoon. 'For our enemies have little chance of seeing us.'

'True enough,' said Katinka van Bak.

'And similarly,' Hawkmoon went on, 'we must be wary. For we shall not see them until they are upon us. Do you know this area, Katinka van Bak?'

'I know it fairly well,' she told him. She was lighting a fire inside the cave, for their cooking stoves, provided by the prince, did not give out enough heat to warm them.

'This is snug,' said Jhary-a-Conel. 'I would not mind spending the rest of the winter here. Then we could travel on when spring comes.'

Katinka offered him a glance of contempt. He grinned and kept silence for a while.

They led their horses now, beneath a cold, hard sky. Save for a little withered moss and some stunted grey and brown birches, nothing grew in these mountains. A sharp wind blew. A few carrion birds wheeled away amongst the jagged peaks. The sounds of their breathing, of their horses' hooves clicking on the rocks, of their own slippery progress, were the only sounds. The scenery viewed from these high mountain paths was beautiful in the extreme, yet it was also deadly. It was dead. It was cold. It was cruel. Many travellers must have died in these parts during the season of winter.

Hawkmoon wore a thick fur robe over his leather coat. Though he sweated, he did not dare take any of his clothing off for fear he would freeze to the spot when he stopped. The others, too, wore heavy furs – hoods, gloves and boots as well as coats. And the climbing was almost always upward. Only occasionally might a path take a downward turn, only to soar again around the next bend.

Yet the mountains, for all their deadly beauty, seemed peaceful. An immense sense of peace filled the valleys, and Hawkmoon could barely believe that a great force of bandits hid here. There was no atmosphere to indicate that the mountains had been invaded. He felt as if he were one of the first human beings ever to come this way. Although the going was difficult and very wearying, he felt more relaxed here than he had felt since he had been a child in Köln, when the old Duke, his father, had ruled. His responsibilities had become simple. To stay alive.

And at last they reached a slightly wider path where there was room enough for Hawkmoon to stretch to his full length had he so desired. And this path ended suddenly at a big, black cave entrance.

'What's this?' Hawkmoon asked Katinka. 'It seems a dead end. Is it a tunnel?'

'Aye,' replied Katinka van Bak. 'It's a tunnel.'

'And how much further do we journey when we reach the other end of the tunnel?'

Hawkmoon leaned against the rock wall, just at the entrance to the tunnel.

'That depends,' said Katinka van Bak mysteriously. And she would not say more.

Hawkmoon was too weary to ask her what she meant. Jerking his body forward, he plunged into the tunnel, leading his horse behind him, glad that snow no longer dragged at his boots once he had gone a few yards into the great cavern. Inside it was quite warm and there was a smell. It was almost like the smell of spring. Hawkmoon remarked on it, but neither of the others could smell the odour so that he wondered if perhaps some perfume clung to his big fur cloak. The floor of the cavern levelled out now and it became much easier to walk. 'It is hard to believe,' said Hawkmoon, 'that this place is natural. It is a wonder of the world.'

They had been walking for an hour, with no sight of the other end of the tunnel, when Hawkmoon began to feel nervous.

'It cannot be natural,' he repeated. He ran his gloved hands along the walls, but there were no signs of tools having been used to create them. He turned back to the others and thought, in the gloom, that he noticed peculiar expressions on both their faces. 'What do you think? You know this place, Katinka van Bak. Are there any mentions of it in the histories? In legends?'

'Some,' she admitted. 'Go on, Hawkmoon. We shall soon be at the other side.'

'But where does it lead?' He brought his body fully round to confront them. The fireglobe in his hand burned dully and turned his face to a demonic red. 'Directly to the Dark Empire camp? Do you two work for my old enemies? Is this a ruse? You have neither of you told me enough!'

'We are not in the pay of your enemies,' said Katinka van Bak. 'Continue, Hawkmoon, please. Or shall I lead?' She stepped forward.

Hawkmoon involuntarily put a hand to the hilt of his sword, pushing back his great fur cloak to do so. 'No. I trust you, Katinka

157

van Bak, yet everything in me warns me of a trap. How can this be?'

'You must go on, Sir Champion!' said Jhary-a-Conel quietly, stroking the fur of his small black and white cat, which had emerged from his jerkin. 'You must.'

'Champion? Champion of what?' Still Hawkmoon's hand gripped the sword hilt. 'Of what?'

'Champion Eternal,' said Jhary-a-Conel, softly still. 'Fate's soldier . . .'

'No!' Though the words were all but meaningless, Hawkmoon could not bear to hear them. 'No!'

His gloved hands flew to his ears.

And that was when his two friends rushed at him.

He was still not as strong as he had been before his madness. He was weary from the climb. He struggled against them until he felt Katinka van Bak's dagger pricking his eye and heard her urgent voice in his ear:

'Killing you is the easiest way to achieve our purpose, Hawkmoon,' she said. 'But it would not be the kindest. Besides, I am reluctant to cut you off from this body, should you desire to return to it. Thus I shall only kill you if you make it impossible for me to do ought else. Do you understand?'

'I understand treachery,' he said savagely, still testing his strength against their clutches, 'and I thought I smelled the spring. I smelled traitors, instead. Traitors who posed as friends.'

One of them extinguished the fireglobe. The three stood in blackness and Hawkmoon heard the echoes of his words.

'Where is this place?' He felt the dagger point prick his eye again. 'What are you doing to me?'

'It was the only way,' said Katinka van Bak. 'It was the only way, Champion.'

It was the first time she had called him that, though Jhary had used the term frequently.

'Where is this place?' he said again. 'Where?'

'I wish that I knew,' said Katinka van Bak. And her voice was almost sad.

Then she evidently struck him on the back of the head with her armoured gauntlet. He felt the blow and guessed what caused it. For a moment he thought that it had not succeeded in its intention of driving consciousness from him. Then he realized that he had sunk to his knees.

Then he felt that his body was falling away from him in the

blackness of the cave.

And then he knew that her blow had done what it had intended, after all.

BOOK TWO
# A HOMECOMING

# CHAPTER ONE

## Ilian of Garathorm

Hawkmoon listened to ghosts.

Each ghost spoke to him in his own voice.

In Hawkmoon's voice . . .

*. . . then I was Erekosë and I slew the human race. And Urlik Skarsol, Prince of the Southern Ice, who slew the Silver Queen from Moon. Who bore the Black Sword. Now I hang in limbo and await my next task. Perhaps through this I shall find a means of returning to my lost love Ermizhad. Perhaps I shall find Tanelorn.*

*(I have been Elric)*

*Fate's soldier . . . Time's tool . . . Champion Eternal . . . Doomed to perpetual strife.*

*(I have been Corum. In more than one life I have been Corum)*

*I know not how it began. Perhaps it will end in Tanelorn.*

*Rhalina, Yisselda, Cymoril, Zarozina . . .*

*So many women.*

*(I have been Arflane. Asquiol. Aubec.)*

*All die, save me.*

*(I have been Hawkmoon . . .)*

'No! I am Hawkmoon!'

*(We are all Hawkmoon. Hawkmoon is all of us)*

*All live, save me.*

*John Daker? Was he the first?*

*Or the last?*

*I have betrayed so many and been betrayed so much.*

Faces floated before him. Each face was different. Each face was his own face. He shouted and tried to push them away.

But he had no hands.

He tried to revive himself. Better to die under Katinka van Bak's knife than suffer this torment. It was what he had feared. It was what he had tried to avoid. It was the reason he had not pursued his argument with Jhary-a-Conel. But he was alone against a thousand – a thousand manifestations of himself.

*The struggle is eternal. The fight is endless.*

*And now we must become Ilian. Ilian, whose soul was driven out.*

*Is this not a strange task?*

*'I am Hawkmoon. Only Hawkmoon.'*

*And I am Hawkmoon. And I am Urlik Skarsol. And I am Ilian of Garathorm. Perhaps here I shall find Tanelorn. Farewell to the South Ice and the dying sun. Farewell to the Silver Queen and the Screaming Chalice. Farewell Count Brass. Farewell Urlik. Farewell Hawkmoon . . .*

And Hawkmoon began to feel his memories fading from him. In their place came crowding a million other memories. Memories of bizarre worlds and exotic landscapes, of creatures both human and inhuman. Memories that could not possibly belong to a single man, and yet they were like those dreams he had had at Castle Brass. Or had he experienced them at Castle Brass? Perhaps it had been elsewhere? In Melniboné? In Loos Ptokai? In Castle Erorn by the sea? Aboard that strange ship which travelled beyond the Earth? Where? Where had he dreamed those dreams?

And he knew that he had dreamed them in all of those places and that he would dream them again in all those places.

He knew that there was no such thing as Time.

Past, present and future were all the same. They existed all at the same moment – and they did not exist at any moment.

He was Urlik Skarsol, Prince of the Southern Ice, and his chariot was drawn by bears, moving across the ice beneath a dying sun. Moving towards a goal. Searching, as Hawkmoon searched for Yisselda, for a woman whom he could not reach. Ermizhad. And Ermizhad had not loved Urlik Skarsol. She had loved Erekosë. Yet Erekosë was Urlik Skarsol, too.

Tanelorn. That was Urlik's goal.

Tanelorn. Should it be Hawkmoon's?

The name was so familiar. Yet he had found Tanelorn many times. He had dwelled there once and each time Tanelorn had been different.

Which Tanelorn must he seek?

And there was a sword. A sword which had many manifestations. A black sword. Yet it was often disguised. A sword . . .

Ilian of Garathorm bore a good sword. Ilian felt for it, but it was not there. Ilian's hands ran over chain mail, over silk, over flesh. Ilian's hands touched cool turf and Ilian's nose smelled the richness of spring. Ilian's eyes opened. Two strangers stood there, a young man and a middle-aged woman. Yet their faces were familiar.

Hawkmoon said: 'Katinka van . . .' and then Ilian forgot the rest of the name. Hawkmoon felt his body and was astonished. 'What have you made me into . . .?' And Ilian wondered at those words, even though they came from Ilian's mouth.

'Greetings, Ilian of Garathorm, Champion Eternal,' said the young man with a smile. He had a small black and white cat on his shoulder. The cat had a pair of wings folded on its back.

'And Hawkmoon, farewell – for the moment, at least,' said the middle-aged woman who was dressed all in battered plate armour.

Ilian said vaguely: 'Hawkmoon? The name is familiar. Yet I thought for an instant I was called Urlik Skarsol, also. Who are you?'

The young man bowed, showing none of the patronizing mockery or condescension with which Ilian had become familiar, even when at court.

'I am Jhary-a-Conel. And this lady is Katinka van Bak, whom you may remember.'

Ilian frowned. 'Yes . . . Katinka van Bak. You are the one who saved me when Ymryl's pack pursued me . . .'

And then, for a moment, Ilian's memory faded.

Hawkmoon said, through Ilian's lips: 'What have you done to me, Katinka van Bak?' He felt at his body in horror. His skin was softer. His form was different. He had become shorter. 'You have made me into . . . into a woman!'

Jhary-a-Conel leaned forward, his eyes full of an abnormal intensity. 'It had to be done. You are Ilian of Garathorm. This world needs Ilian. Trust us. It will benefit Hawkmoon, too.'

'You plotted this together. There was no army in the Bulgar Mountains! That tunnel . . .'

'It led here. To Garathorm,' Katinka van Bak said. 'I discovered this passage between the dimensions when I hid from the Dark Empire. I was here when Ymryl and the others arrived. I saved your life, Ilian, but they were able, with their sorcery, to drive your spirit from you. I was in despair for Garathorm. Then I met Jhary here. He conceived a solution. Hawkmoon was close to the point of death. As a manifestation of the eternal Champion his spirit could substitute for Ilian's – for she is another manifestation of that Champion, you see. That story I told you. I knew it might bring you here – through the tunnel. The army I described does raid beyond the Bulgar Mountains. It raids Garathorm.'

Hawkmoon's brain was whirling. 'I don't understand. I occupy another's body? Is that what you are saying? This *can* only be Dark Empire work!'

'Believe us that it is not!' said Katinka van Bak seriously.

'Though the Dark Empire has played some part, I feel, in bringing this disaster about,' said Jhary-a-Conel. 'The exact part is yet to be discovered. But only as Ilian can you hope to oppose those who now rule this world. It is Ilian's fate, you see. Only Ilian's. Hawkmoon could not have succeeded.'

'So you have imprisoned me in this woman's body . . . But how? What sorcery accomplished it?'

Jhary looked at the grassy ground. 'I have some skill in this particular area. But you must forget that you are Hawkmoon. Hawkmoon has no place in Garathorm. You *must* be Ilian, or our work is wasted. Ilian – whom Ymryl desired. And because he could not possess her, he drove her spirit from her. Even Ymryl did not realize what he was doing – that Ilian's destiny is to wage war against him. Ymryl merely sees you, Ilian, as a desirable woman, albeit a fierce foe who led the remnants of her father's army against him.'

'Ymryl . . .' Hawkmoon strove to hang on to his own identity, but it was slipping away from him again. 'Ymryl, who serves Chaos. Ymryl, the Yellow Horn. They came from nowhere and Garathorm fell to them. Ah, I remember the fires. I remember my father, kindly Pyran. With all his reluctance to fight, he battled Ymryl long . . .'

'And then you took up Pyran's flaming banner. Remember, Ilian? You took up that burning flag, the fame of all Garathorm, and you rode against Ymryl's force . . .' Katinka van Bak said softly. 'I had taught you the use of sword, shield and axe, while I guested at Pyran's court, after I fled the Dark Empire. And you put all my learning to splendid use until only you and I remained alive upon the field.'

'I remember,' said Ilian. 'And we were only spared because they were amused to discover our feminine sex. Ah, the humiliation I felt when Ymryl tugged the helm from my head! "You shall rule beside me," he said. And he reached out a hand still covered in the blood of my people, and he touched my body! Oh, I remember.' Ilian's voice became hard and fierce. 'And I remember that it was then I swore to slay him. Yet there was only one way and I was unable to follow it. I could not. And, because I resisted him, he imprisoned me . . .'

'Which was when I was able to rescue you. We fled. His pack followed. We fought it and destroyed it. But Ymryl's sorcerers found us. In his rage he made them reach out and drive your spirit from you.'

'Ah, the sending. Yes. They attacked. I remember nothing more.'

'We were hiding in the cave. I had some idea to take you through, back to my own world where I thought you would be safe. But then, when your soul went out of you, there was no point to it. I met

166

Jhary-a-Conel, who had been drawn to Garathorm by the same forces which brought Ymryl. Between us we determined what we must try to do. Your memories were still within your skull. Only an – an *essence* – was lacking. So we had to find a new soul. And Hawkmoon's was not in use then, as he rotted in his tower at Castle Brass. With many misgivings we did what we had to do. And now you have a soul again.'

'And Ymryl?'

'He believes you – gone. He had doubtless forgotten you and thinks he rules all Garathorm with nothing to fear. His rabble army rides roughshod over all the land. Yet even those creatures have hardly been able to spoil Garathorm's beauty.'

'Garathorm is still lovely,' agreed Ilian. She looked from where she stood on the slopes of the hill, the cave mouth behind her, and saw her world with fresh eyes, as if for the first time.

Not far off was the edge of the great forest – the forest which covered this world's single continent. Save for Garathorm, all the rest was sea containing the occasional small island. And the trees were huge. Some stretched several hundred feet into the air.

The sky was wide and blue and in it burned a huge golden sun. The sun shone on flowers whose heads measured more than twelve feet across. It made their colours almost blinding in their intensity. Scarlets, purples and yellows predominated. Among the blooms flew butterflies whose propotions matched those of the flowers and whose colours were even richer. One particularly glorious insect had wings measuring nearly two feet long. And among the vine-hung boles of the trees fluttered great birds, their plumage glittering in the deep shadows of the forest. And Ilian knew that there was hardly a bird or a beast in that forest which a human had to fear. She breathed the thick air with relish and she smiled.

'Yes,' she said, 'I am Ilian of Garathorm. Who could wish to be anything else? Who would want to dwell anywhere but in Garathorm, even in these times?'

'Exactly,' said Jhary-a-Conel in some relief.

Katinka van Bak began to unwrap a big fur cloak which Ilian did not recall having seen before. In the cloak was a variety of stone pots. The lids of the pots were sealed with wax.

'Preserves,' explained Katinka van Bak. 'Meats, fruits and vegetables. These will sustain us for a while. Let's eat now.'

And while they ate, Ilian recalled the terrors of the past months.

Garathorm had become a united land some two centuries earlier, thanks to the diplomacy (not to mention the lust for power) of Ilian's ancestors. And for those two hundred years there had been peace and prosperity for all the inhabitants of the great arboreal continent. Learning flourished, as did the arts. Garathorm's capital, the ebony city of Virinthorm, had grown to great proportions. Its suburbs stretched for several miles from the old city, under the branches of the great, sheltering trees, which protected Garathorm from the heavy rains which, for a month every year, beat down upon the island continent. Once, it was said, there had been other continents and Garathorm had been a desert. Then some cataclysm had swept the earth, perhaps causing the melting of the polar ice, and when the cataclysm was past, only Garathorm remained. And Garathorm was changed, becoming a place where foliage grew to enormous proportions. The reason for this was still unknown. Garathorm's scholars had yet to find a clue to the answer. Perhaps it lay beneath the sea, in the drowned lands.

Twenty years earlier Ilian's father, Pyran, had come to the throne on the death of his uncle. Ilian had been born but two years before, almost to the day. And Pyran's rule began what many believed to be a Golden Age for Garathorm. Ilian had grown up in an atmosphere of humanity and happiness. Always an active girl, she had spent much time riding the ostrich-like *vayna* through the forests. The *vayna* could make considerable speed upon the ground, and almost as good speed when it ran along the thick branches of the trees, leaping from branch to branch with a rider clinging to its back. It was one of the most exhilarating pastimes in Garathorm. And when, several years ago, Katinka van Bak had suddenly arrived at the court of King Pyran, exhausted, confused and close to death from many wounds, Ilian took to her immediately. Katinka's story had been a strange one. Somehow she had been transported through time – either into the future or the past, she could not be sure – after fleeing from enemies who had defeated her in a great battle. The details of her passage through time were vague, but she had soon become a welcome guest at the court and, to occupy her own mind as much as to help Ilian, had agreed to teach Ilian the martial arts. In Garathorm there were no warriors. There was only a ceremonial guard and groups of others whose task it was to protect the remoter farmsteads against attacks from the few wild beasts which still remained in Garathorm. Yet Ilian took to the sword and the axe as if she was the cub of some ancient reaver. It was as if she had always pursued such arts. And she found a peculiar satisfaction in learning everything Katinka van Bak could teach her. For all that her childhood was happy, it had always seemed to lack something until that moment.

Her father had been amused by her enthusiasm for such archaic pursuits. And her enthusiasm had been infectious amongst many of the young people at court. Eventually there had been several hundred girls and boys who felt at ease with a sword and a buckler and elaborate mock tournaments became a feature of court festivals.

Perhaps it was not coincidence, then, but some working of Fate, that had prepared a small but highly skilled army to resist Ymryl when he came.

Ymryl had come suddenly to Virinthorm. A few rumours had arrived ahead of him and King Pyran had sent emissaries to investigate the disturbing reports coming from the remoter quarters of the continent. But before the emissaries could return, Ymryl had arrived. It emerged later that he was part of a larger army which had swept over the whole of Garathorm and taken all the main provincial cities within a matter of weeks. At first it was thought that they had come from some previously unknown land beyond the sea, but there was no evidence to suggest it. Like Katinka van Bak, Ymryl and his comrades had arrived mysteriously in Garathorm. They hardly seemed, themselves, to know how they had got there.

Speculation as to their origin became unimportant. All efforts were put into resisting them. Scholars were asked to invent weapons. Engineers, too, found that they were asked to put their skills to conceiving methods of destruction. They were not used to thinking in such terms and few weapons were produced. Katinka van Bak, Ilian and about two hundred others, harried Ymryl's rabble army, and scored a few victories in skirmishes, but when Ymryl was ready to march against the tree-sheltered city of Virinthorm, he marched. He could not be resisted. There were two battles fought in the great glade beyond the city. At the first battle King Pyran brought out the ancient war-flag of his ancestors – the burning flag, which blazed with a strange fire and which was made of a cloth which never perished. With that flag held in his own hand, he went against Ymryl, leading an army of poorly armed and untrained citizens. King Pyran was slaughtered with his folk and Ilian had barely managed to drag the burning banner from his dead hand before she escaped with the remains of her own professional fighters – those who had once shared her enthusiasm for military arts and who had swiftly become hardened veterans.

There had been one last battle in which Ilian and Katinka van Bak had led a few hundred survivors against Ymryl. They had put up a splendid fight and taken many of the invaders that day, but they were

169

eventually beaten. Ilian was not sure if any of her people had escaped, but there seemed to be no survivors, save herself and Katinka van Bak.

And they had been captured. And Ymryl had lusted for her and seen, too, that with her at his side he would have no difficulty in ruling those citizens who still hid in the forests beyond Virinthorm and crept out at night to slaughter his men.

When she had resisted him, he had given orders that she should be imprisoned, that she should be kept awake and fed only the minimum to keep her alive. He had known that she would eventually agree to what he wanted.

And now, as she ate, Ilian suddenly remembered what she had done. Something which Katinka van Bak had not mentioned. And Ilian could barely swallow the food in her mouth as she turned to look at Katinka van Bak.

'Why did you not remind me of that?' she said coldly. 'Of my brother.'

'You were not to blame for that,' said Katinka van Bak. The older woman lowered her eyes to the ground. 'I should have done what you did. Anyone would. They tortured you.'

'And I told them. I told them where he would be hiding. And they found him and they slew him.'

'They tortured you,' said Katinka van Bak harshly. 'They tore your body. They abused it. They did not let you sleep. They did not let you eat. They wanted two things from you. You only gave them one. That was a triumph!'

'You mean I gave them my brother instead of myself. Is that a triumph?'

'In the circumstances, yes. Forget it, Ilian. We may yet avenge your brother – and the rest.'

'I must do much to atone for that thing,' said Ilian. She knew there were tears in her eyes and she tried to force them back.

'There is much, anyway, that must be done,' said Jhary-a-Conel.

CHAPTER TWO

Outlaws of a Thousand Spheres

The small black and white cat drifted high above the forest on a warm upcurrent of air. The sun was setting. The cat waited, for it preferred to go about its business at night. From the ground, if it could be seen at all, the cat would have been mistaken for a hawk. It hovered, keeping its position by the slightest movements of its wings, close to a city but recently occupied by a huge and ferocious army.

Katinka van Bak had not lied when she had described the army which had defeated her. Her only lie concerned where she had engaged this army and what its intentions were. In a sense, of course, it had occupied the Bulgar Mountains, for did not this land, in some mysterious way, exist within that range?

As the sun sank, so the small black and white cat dropped lower and lower until at last it had settled upon a branch close to the top of one of the tallest trees. A breeze blew, rustling the leaves and making the trees, from where the cat sat, seem to move like the waves of a strange sea.

The cat jumped and landed on a lower branch, jumped again and this time spread its wings, soaring a few feet before finding another foothold.

Slowly it began to descend towards the city, whose lights could be seen far below. Not for the first time was the cat scouting for its master, Jhary-a-Conel; going somewhere where Jhary himself, or his friends, could not go.

At last the cat lay stretched on a branch directly over the centre of the city. Virinthorm had no walls, for it had been long since she had needed them, and all her main buildings were built of carved, polished ebony, inlaid with whale ivory bought from the coastal peoples to the south. Those people had once hunted whales, but now the few who were left were hunted by monsters themselves. The other buildings were all built of hardwood, for stone was a rarity in Garathorm, and all had a rich, mellow look to them – those which had been left untouched by the invaders' brands.

The cat dropped still lower, digging its claws into the smooth roof of a large building and climbing to the main beam.

171

A terrible smell filled the city. It was a smell of death and of decay. The cat found it at once unpleasant and interesting but it denied itself the instinct to explore the source of the odours. Instead it spread its wings and flew away from the building and then back again, losing height rapidly and then gliding gracefully through an open window.

The cat's unusual sixth sense had not betrayed it. It found itself in a bedroom. The room was strewn with rich brocades, silks and feather cloaks. The bed was unmade and in great disorder. Empty wine-cups were scattered everywhere and there was evidence that much wine had been spilled throughout the room over the course of weeks or months. On the bed lay a naked man. To one side of him, huddled in each other's arms and sleeping fitfully, lay two young girls. There were many minor cuts and bruises on their bodies. Both had black hair and pale skins. The man had bright yellow hair, which might have been dyed. The hair on his body was not the same colour, but a reddish brown. It was an extremely muscular body and it must have measured at least seven feet long. The head was large and tapered from the wide cheek-bones to the jaw, almost to a point. It was a brutish head and a powerful head, yet there was also a look of weakness in it. Something about that pointed jaw and that cruel mouth made the face not quite handsome (though some might have found it so) and instead it was oddly repulsive.

This was Ymryl.

Around his neck was slung by a cord a silver-dressed amber horn.

This was Ymryl, the Yellow Horn.

And his horn could be heard for miles, if he needed to summon his men. And it was said that the notes of that horn could be heard elsewhere, too. It was said that they could be heard in Hell, where Ymryl had comrades.

Ymryl stirred, as if he sensed the cat's presence. The cat swiftly flew to a ledge high up on the far wall. Trophies had once been kept there, but the gold shield, won by one of Ilian's ancestors, had been dragged from its place months before. Ymryl coughed and groaned and opened his eyes a fraction. He rolled over on the bed and leaning his elbows on the back of one of the girls poured hmself wine from the jug which rested on the nearby table. He drained the wine-cup, sniffed and sat up straighter on the bed.

'Garko!' growled Ymryl. 'Garko! Here!'

From another room a creature came scuttling. The creature had four short legs, a round torso into which was set a face, and long spindly arms ending in large hands.

'Master?' whispered Garko.

'What's the hour?'

'Just past sunset, master.'

'So I've slept through the day, have I?' Ymryl got up and dragged on a dirty robe, looted from the king's own chests. 'Doubtless it has been another dull day. No news from the west?'

'None. If they planned to attack, we should know by now, lord.'

'I suppose so. By Arioch! I grow bored, Garko. I begin to suspect that somehow we are all in this damned place as a punishment. I wish I knew how I had offended the Lords of Chaos, if that's the case. We thought at first that we had been given a paradise to loot. Few of the people knew the first thing about making war. It was so easy to take over their cities. And now we find ourselves with nothing to do. How go the sorcerer's experiments?'

'He remains frustrated in his attempts to get his dimension travelling machine to work for him. I have little faith in him, master.'

Ymryl sniffed. 'Well, he slew the maid for me – or the next best thing. And at some distance. That was clever. Perhaps he will yet find a way through for us.'

'Perhaps, master.'

'I cannot understand why even the most powerful amongst us is unable to summon word from the Lords of Chaos. If I were not Ymryl, the Yellow Horn, if I were a lesser man, I should feel abandoned. I ruled a great nation in my own world, Garko. I ruled it in the name of Chaos. I gave Arioch many sacrifices, Garko. Many.'

'So you have told me, master.'

'And there are others here who were kings in their own worlds. Some ruled empires. And barely one of us seems to have shared the same time or even the same plane. That is what puzzles me. Each creature – human or unhuman (like yourself) – came here at the identical moment, and came here from a different world. It could only be the work of Arioch. Or some other powerful Chaos Lord, for we are all – or most of us – servants of those great Lords of Entropy. And still Arioch does not tell us his reason for bringing us here.'

'It could be that he has none, master.'

Ymryl snorted. Without much anger, he cuffed Garko across the top of his head. 'Arioch always has reasons. Yet he is good to those who serve him without question – as I served him for many years in my own world. I thought at first that this must be a reward . . .'

Ymryl took his jug and his cup to the window and stared out at the city he had conquered while he poured himself more wine. He tilted back his yellow head and gulped the wine. 'I grow so bored. So bored. I thought those who took the westerly provinces would have become greedy by now and would have tried to attack us. But they, it seems, are as wary as I. They do not wish to anger Arioch by turning on the others. I am beginning to alter my thinking on that subject now. I think Arioch expects us to fight. He wishes to discover which is the strongest. That could be why we were brought here. A test, you see, Garko.'

'A test. I see, master.'

Ymryl sniffed. 'Summon the sorcerer. I would consult with him. It could be that he can help me understand what to do.'

Garko backed from the room. 'I will summon him, master.'

The small black and white cat watched as Ymryl strode about the room, his brows drawn in thought. There was an immense sense of physical power about the man and yet at the same time there was an indecisiveness which perhaps he had not always had. Perhaps, before he pledged himself to Chaos, he had been stronger. It was often said that Chaos warped those who served it – and not always physically.

Once Ymryl paused and stared about him, as if he again sensed the presence of the cat. But then he raised his head and murmured:

'Arioch! Arioch! Why do you not come? Why do you send no messenger to us?'

For a few moments Ymryl waited expectantly, then he shook his head and continued his pacing.

Some time later Garko returned.

'The sorcerer is here, master.'

'Let him enter.'

Then there came into the room a bent figure in a long green robe decorated with writhing black serpents. Upon his face was a mask moulded to resemble the head of a striking snake. The mask was made of engraved platinum and its details were picked out in precious stones.

'Why did you summon me, Yellow Horn?' The sorcerer's voice was faintly muffled, slightly querulous, yet deferential withal. 'I was in the middle of an experiment.'

'The experiment, if it is as successful as the rest, can wait a little, Baron Kalan.'

'I suppose you are right.' The serpent mask turned this way and that as its owner glanced about the brightly lit room. 'What did you wish to discuss with me, Ymryl?'

'I wanted your opinion of our situation. My own opinion you know – that we are here because of some scheme brewed by the Lord of Chaos . . .'

'Yes. And as you know, I have no experiences of these supernatural

174

beings. I am a scientist. If such beings exist, then they seem devious to the point of stupidity — '

'Silence!' Ymryl raised his hand. 'I tolerate your blasphemies, Baron Kalan, because I respect your talents. I have assured you that Duke Arioch of Chaos and the rest not only exist but take a great interest in the affairs of mankind, in every sphere of existence.'

'Very well, if I must accept that notion, then I am as much at a loss as yourself to understand why they do not manifest themselves. My own theory is linked to my own experience. In my experiments in the realm of time-manipulation I caused an immense disruption which resulted, among other things, in this particular phenomenon. Like you, I sense that I am stranded here. Certainly all the efforts I have made to send my pyramid through the dimensions have met with total failure. That in itself is a problem I find hard to answer. Some conjunction of the planes has doubtless taken place — but why so many folk from so many different planes should all find themselves suddenly in this world, as we found ourselves, I do not know.'

Ymryl yawned and fingered his yellow horn. 'And that is the sum of what you have said. You do not know.'

'I assure you, Ymryl, that I am working on the problem. But I must do so in my own way — '

'Oh, I'm not blaming you, sorcerer. It seems the most ironic thing of all that there are so many clever people here and none can solve the problem. The languages we speak sound the same, but they are all essentially different. Our terms are not the same. Our references are not the same. What I call sorcery, you call "science". I speak of gods and you speak of the principles of science. They are all the same thing. Yet the words themselves confuse us.'

'You are an intelligent man, Ymryl,' Kalan said. 'I'll grant you that. I wonder why you waste your time as you do. You seem to get little relish even from your butchery, your wenching, your drinking . . .'

'You begin to go too far, even for my tolerance,' Ymryl said softly. 'I must spend my time somehow. And I've little respect for scholarship, save where it's useful. Your knowledge has proved useful to me once. I live in the patient hope that it will prove useful a second time. I am damned, you see, Baron Kalan. I know that. I was damned the instant I accepted the gift of this horn I wear about my throat. The horn that helped me rise from being the leader of a brand of cattle-thieves to be ruler of Hythiak, the most powerful nation in my world.' Ymryl smiled bleakly. 'The horn was given me by Duke Arioch himself. It summoned aid from Hell whenever I needed it. It made me great. Yet it made me, also, a slave. Slave to the Lords of

Chaos. I can never relinquish their gift, just as I can never now refuse to serve them. And being damned, I see no point to life. I had ambition when I was a cattle-raider. Now I have only nostalgia for those simple days, when I spent my time drinking, killing and wenching.' And Ymryl's bleak smile widened and he laughed. 'I appear to have gained very little from my bargain.'

He put an arm around the stooped shoulders of the sorcerer and led him from the room.

'Come. I'll see how you progress with your experiments!'

The little cat crept further out onto the ledge and looked down. The two young girls still slept in each other's arms.

The cat heard Ymryl's laughter echoing back to the room. It launched itself from the ledge and flew over the bed and out through the window, heading back to where it had left Jhary-a-Conel.

## CHAPTER THREE

## A Meeting in the Forest

'So we can anticipate a falling out, soon, amongst the invaders,' said Jhary-a-Conel. By some mysterious means the cat had communicated to him all it had seen. He stroked its small round head and it purred.

It was dawn. From the cave Katinka van Bak led three horses. Two of the horses were good, strong stallions. The third horse was Jhary's yellow nag. By now Ilian had become used to the sense of familiarity she had when she saw things she was sure she could never have seen before. She mounted one of the stallions and settled herself in the saddle, inspecting the weapons she found in the saddle sheaths – the sword and the lance with the odd, ruby tip where its point should be.

Without thinking, she looked for a grip half-way down the shaft. The grip had a jewel set into it. She knew that if she pressed the jewel destroying flame would leap from the ruby tip of the lance. Philosophically, she shrugged, glad enough to have a weapon that was as powerful as those possessed by many of Ymryl's warriors. She noticed that Katinka van Bak had a similar weapon, though Jhary's arms were of the more conventional kind, an ordinary lance, a shield and a sword.

'What of these gods in whom Ymryl pins so much faith,' Katinka asked Jhary as they rode into the massive forest, 'do they have any reality at all, Jhary?'

'They had once – or will have. I suspect that they exist when men need them to exist. But I could be wrong. Rest assured, however, Katinka van Bak, that when they do exist they are extremely powerful.'

Katinka van Bak nodded. 'Then why do they not help Ymryl?'

'It is possible that they do,' Jhary said, 'without him realizing it.' he took a deep breath of the sweet air. He looked admiringly at the huge blooms, the variety of greens and browns of the trees. 'Though often these gods are unable to enter human worlds themselves and must work through agents like Ymryl. Only a powerful sorcery could bring Arioch through, I suspect.'

'And this Dark Empire lord – Baron Kalan, without a doubt – he has not sufficient skill?'

'I am sure his skill is sufficient, in his own sphere. But if he does not believe in Arioch — save, perhaps, intellectually — then he is useless to Ymryl. It is lucky for us.'

'The thought of more powerful beings than Ymryl and his pack invading Garathorm is not a pleasant one,' said Ilian. Though undisturbed by the strange half-memories which flitted through her head from time to time, she had become gloomier since she had remembered her screaming betrayal of her brother, Bradne. She had never seen his body, though she had heard there was little left of it when Ymryl's raiders brought it back to the city, for Katinka van Bak had appeared to rescue her before Ymryl could enjoy the sight of Ilian's horror.

Ymryl had guessed what would follow. She would have been so full of self-disgust that she would have agreed to any demands he made on her. She knew that she would have given herself up to him then, almost gratefully, as a means of atoning for her guilt. She drew a hissing breath as she recalled her feelings. Well, at least she had denied Ymryl the fulfilment of his scheme.

Small comfort, thought Ilian cynically. But she would have felt no better now if she had lain with Ymryl. It would not have absolved her, it would only have indulged her own sense of hysteria at the time. She could never satisfy her own conscience, for all her friends did not blame her for what she had done, but at least she could use the hatred she felt to good effect. She was determined to destroy Ymryl and all his fellows, even though she was sure such an action would result in her own destruction. That was what she wanted. She would not die before Ymryl was slain.

'We must accept the possibility that your countrymen will not reveal themselves to us,' Katinka van Bak said. 'Those who still fight Ymryl will have become wary, suspecting treachery from anyone.'

'And particularly from me,' said Ilian bitterly.

'They might not know of your brother's capture,' said Jhary. 'Or at least they might not know of the circumstances which led to his capture . . .' But the suggestion sounded weak in his own ears.

'Ymryl will have made sure all your folk will know what you did,' Katinka van Bak said. 'It would be what I would do in his position. And you can be certain that he would have had the worst interpretation put upon the facts. With the last of their hereditary rulers proven a traitress, their morale will decline and they will cause Ymryl far less trouble. I have taken cities in my time. And so, doubtless, has Ymryl taken others before Virinthorm. If he could not use you one way, Ilian, he would have used you another!'

'Any interpretation put upon my treachery could be no worse than the truth, Katinka van Bak,' said Ilian of Virinthorm.

The older woman said nothing to this. She merely pursed her lips and clapped her heels to the flanks of her horse, riding on ahead.

For the best part of the day they pressed through the tangled forest. And the deeper they went, the darker it became – a cool, green, restful darkness, full of heady scents. They were to the north east of Virinthorm and riding away from the city rather than towards it. Katinka van Bak had a feeling she knew where she might find some of the surviving Garathormians.

And at last they entered a warm, sunlit glade, blinking painfully in the bright light, and Katinka van Bak pointed to the other side of the glade.

Ilian saw dark shapes beneath the trees. Jagged shapes. And she remembered.

'Of course,' she said. 'Tikaxil! Ymryl knows nothing of the old city.'

Tikaxil had existed long before Virinthorm. It had once been a thriving trading city, home of Ilian's ancestors. A walled city. The walls had been made of huge blocks of hardwood, each block placed upon the other. Most of those blocks had disappeared now, or rotted into nothing, but a few fragments of the ramparts remained. And there were one or two ebony houses which, for all they were thickly wound about with creepers and low branches, were almost as good as when they had been built.

In the middle of the glade the three stopped and dismounted, looking warily around them. Overhead massive tree branches waved and mottled shadows skipped across the grass.

Ilian kept seeing the moving shadows as figures. It was possible that Ymryl's men and not her own folk were camped here – if anyone was camped here at all. She kept her hand near the oddly familiar flame-lance, ready to meet an attack.

Katinka van Bak spoke clearly.

'If you are friends of ours you will recognize us. You will know that we come to ally ourselves with you against Ymryl.'

'The place is deserted,' said Jhary-a-Conel, dismounted from his yellow nag and looking about him. 'But it will make a good place to camp tonight.'

'See – this is your queen, Ilian, Pyran's daughter. Remember how she bore the burning banner into battle with Ymryl's army? And I am Katinka van Bak, also known to you as Ymryl's enemy. This is Jhary-a-Conel. Without his help, your queen would not be here now.'

179

'You speak to birds and squirrels, Katinka van Bak,' said Jhary-a-Conel. 'There are none here from Garathorm.'

He had not finished this sentence before the nets swept and engulfed them. It was a tribute to the training of each of them that they did not struggle but calmly attempted to draw their swords, to cut their way free. But Katinka and Ilian were still mounted. Ilian tried to slash her way clear, but her horse kept rearing and whinnying in fear.

Only Jhary was unmounted and he managed to crawl under the edge of the net and be ready with his sword as a score of men and women, all armed, came rushing at them from behind the ruined ramparts.

Ilian's arms became increasingly entangled in the tough fibres of the net and, as she struggled, she found herself slipping from the saddle and falling to the ground.

She felt someone kick her in the stomach. She gasped in pain, hearing someone snarling insults at her, though she could not make out the words.

Katinka van Bak had misjudged the situation, obviously. These folk were not friends.

CHAPTER FOUR

A Pact is Made

'You are fools!' said Katinka van Bak contemptuously. 'You do not deserve the chance we offer. Ymryl's plans are well suited by your actions. Do you not realize that you are doing exactly what he would want you to do?'

'Silence!' The young man with the scar along his jaw glared at her.

Ilian raised her head, feebly shaking it to free the strands of hair which clung to the sweat on her face. 'Why reason with them, Katinka? They are right from their point of view.'

They had been hanging by their arms for the best part of three days, being released only to eat and relieve themselves. For all the pain involved, it was nothing compared with what Ilian had suffered in Ymryl's dungeons. She was hardly aware of the discomfort. And their captors had concentrated most of their spleen on her. She had received several kicks since the first. She had been spat upon, slapped, reviled. It meant nothing to her. It was her due, that was all.

'They'll destroy themselves if they destroy us,' said Jhary-a-Conel quietly. He, too, seemed hardly to notice the pain. He seemed to have been sleeping through most of their ordeal. His black and white cat had vanished.

The young man looked from Ilian to Katinka to Jhary. 'We are doomed anyway,' he said. 'It will not be long before Ymryl's hounds sniff us out.'

'That is my point,' said Katinka van Bak.

Ilian looked across the ruins of the old city. Attracted by the sound of voices the others were coming over to the tree where the three prisoners hung. Ilian recognized many of the faces. These were the young people with whom she had spent so much time in the old days. These were the trained fighters, those who had resisted Ymryl longest, as well as a few citizens who had either managed to escape from Virinthorm or who had not been near the city when Ymryl had captured it. And there was not one there who did not hate her with that hatred that only comes from those who have admired

181

someone and then discovered that person to be despicable.

'There is not one here who would not have given the information Ilian gave Ymryl,' said Katinka. 'You must know little of life if you do not understand that. You are still soft, you fighters. you are not realistic. We are the only chance you have of fighting Ymryl and winning. To misuse us so is to misuse your assets. Forget your hatred of Ilian – at least until we have fought Ymryl. You have insufficient resources, my friends, to discard the best!'

The young man with the scar was called Mysenal of Hinn and he was a distant relative of Ilian's. Once, Ilian knew, he had had an infatuation for her, as had many other young men of the court. Mysenal frowned. 'Your words are sensible, Katinka van Bak, and you have advised us well in the past. But how do we know that these sensible words are not being used to deceive us? For all we know you've made some bargain with Ymryl to deliver us into his hands.'

'You must remember that I am Katinka van Bak. I would not do such a thing.'

'Queen Ilian betrayed her own brother,' Mysenal reminded Katinka.

Ilian closed her eyes. Now there was pain, but not from the ropes which chafed her wrists.

'Under abominable torture,' Katinka pointed out impatiently. 'Just as, perhaps, I would have done. Have you any notion of Ymryl's skills in that quarter?'

'Some,' Mysenal admitted. 'Yet . . .'

'And why, if we were in league with Ymryl, would we come here alone? If we knew where you camped, we had merely to tell him. He could have sent a force to destroy you and caught you by surprise . . .'

'Not by surprise. There are guards in the high branches for more than a mile in all directions. We should have known and we should have fled. We knew you were coming and had time to prepare for you, had we not?'

'True. But my point is still valid.'

Mysenal of Hinn sighed. 'Some of us would rather have vengeance on this traitress than fight Ymryl. Some of us feel we should try to make a life for ourselves here, in the hope that Ymryl will forget us.'

'He will not. He is bored. It will please him, soon, to hunt you down himself. You are only tolerated at present because he thought that those who conquered the west were readying themselves to attack Virinthorm. Thus he kept most of his forces in the city. But now he knows that the west does not immediately prepare to march. He will be reminded of you.'

'The invaders quarrel amongst themselves?' Mysenal's voice became interested. 'They fight each other?'

'Not yet. But it is inevitable. I see you realize the implications of that. It is what we came to tell you, among other things.'

'If they fall upon each other, then we have a better chance of striking effectively at those who took Virinthorm!' Mysenal rubbed at his scar. 'Aye.' Then he frowned again. 'But this information could be part of your ruse to deceive us . . .'

'It is a complicated interpretation, I'll give you that,' said Jhary-a-Conel wearily. 'Why not accept that we came to join with you against Ymryl? It is the most likely explanation.'

'I believe them.' It was a girl who spoke. Ilian's old friend Lyfeth, who had been her brother's lover.

Lyfeth's words carried weight with the others. After all, Lyfeth had most to hate Ilian for.

'I think we should cut them down, for a while at least. We should listen to everything they have to say. Katinka van Bak is responsible for us being able to put up at least a little resistance to Ymryl, remember that. And we have no grudge against the other fellow, Jhary-a-Conel, at all. Also it could be that – that Ilian —' Lyfeth plainly found it hard even to speak Ilian's name – 'would make amends for her treachery. I cannot say that I would not have betrayed Bradne if subjected to the tortures Katinka van Bak has described. I knew her once as a friend. I thought highly of her, as did we all. She fought well in her father's stead. Yes, I think I am prepared to trust her, with a certain amount of caution.'

Lyfeth advanced to where Ilian hung.

Ilian dropped her head and closed her eyes again, unable to look into Lyfeth's face.

But Lyfeth streched out a hard hand and grasped Ilian under the chin, harshly forcing her head up.

Ilian opened her eyes and tried to stare back at Lyfeth. Lyfeth's own eyes were enigmatic. There was hatred there, but also sympathy.

'Hate me, Lyfeth of Ghant,' said Ilian, for Lyfeth's ears only. 'You need do no more. But listen to me, also, for I do not come to betray you.'

Lyfeth bit her lower lip. Once she had been beautiful – more beautiful than Ilian – but now her face had hardened and her skin was pale, rough. Her hair had been cut short, to the nape of her neck. She wore no ornament. Her patched smock was green, to blend with the foliage, and belted at the waist with a broad, woven belt, at which hung her sword and dagger. Her legs were bare and she wore tough-soled sandals on her feet. Her garb was no different from that worn by most here. With her chain-mail jerkin and leggings, Ilian felt almost overdressed.

'Whether you came to betray us or not this time, that's not important,' said Lyfeth. 'For there would still be every reason to punish you for Bradne's death. An uncivilized opinion, I know, Ilian. But I feel it strongly. However, if you have the means of defeating Ymryl, then we should listen to you. Katinka van Bak's reasoning is good.' Lyfeth turned away, letting Ilian's head drop again. 'Cut them down!'

'The Yellow Horn will soon make plans to attack the west,' said Jhary-a-Conel. His cat had returned to his shoulder and he stroked it absently as he told Mysenal and the others of all he had discovered through its help. 'Who rules in the west now, do you know?'

'One called Kagat Bearclaw had the cities of Bekthorm and Rivensz under his sway,' said Lyfeth, 'but more recent news suggests that he was murdered by a rival and that two or three rule there now, among them one called Arnald of Grovent, who has little resemblance to a man, but is blessed with the body of a lion and the face of an ape, though he walks on two legs.'

'A Chaos creature,' mused Jhary-a-Conel. 'There are so many here. It is as if Garathorm has become a world to which all those who serve Chaos are banished! An unpleasant thought.'

There had been two other large cities in the west, Ilian recalled. 'What of Poytarn and Masgha?' she asked.

Mysenal looked surprised. 'You have not heard. A vast explosion destroyed Masgha – and destroyed all those within it. It was nought to do with those who resist the conquerors, by all accounts. They destroyed themselves, by accident. Some sorcerous experiment, no doubt.'

'And Poytarn?'

'Looted, razed and abandoned. Those who did it rode to the coast, doubtless hoping to find other rich pickings. They'll be disappointed. The sea villages would be deserted. Those who lived on the coast were the luckiest of us. Many were able to put to sea and escape to distant islands before the invaders found them. The invaders have no ships and thus could not pursue them. I hope they fare well. We would attempt to follow them, if there were any ships

184

left.'

'They have made counter-attacks?'

'Not yet,' said Lyfeth. 'Soon, we hope.'

'Or not at all,' said someone else. 'They probably have enough sense to bide their time – or merely forget the problems of the mainland.'

'Still, they are potential allies,' said Katinka van Bak. 'I had not realized so many had escaped.'

'But we cannot contact them,' Lyfeth pointed out patiently. 'No ships.'

'There might be other means devised. But we must consider that later.'

Ilian said: 'It seems to me that Ymryl places much faith in that yellow horn he wears ever about his neck. If that could be stolen from him or destroyed by some means, it would weaken his confidence. Perhaps he even draws his power from the horn, as he believes. If so, there would be even more reason to part him from it.'

'A good thought,' said Mysenal. 'But hard to accomplish. Would you not say so, Katinka van Bak?'

Katinka nodded. 'However, it is an important factor, and something we must continue to consider.' She sniffed and rubbed at her nose. 'The first thing we need are some better weapons than these. Something a little more modern, in my terms. Flame-lances and the like. If each of us was armed with a flame-lance, we should immediately triple our striking power. How many are here, Lyfeth?'

'Fifty-three.'

'So we need fifty-four good weapons – the extra one being for Jhary here, who has weapons as primitive as yours. Weapons which depend upon a power source . . .'

'I follow your reasoning,' Jhary said. 'You see a certain expenditure of resources by Ymryl and the others, when they eventually do war on each other. If we are then in possession of weapons like flame-lances, we shall have a considerable advantage, no matter how small our numbers.'

'Exactly. But the problem is how to capture such a large supply, eh?'

'It could mean a visit to Garathorm itself,' said Ilian. She stood up, stretching her bruised muscles and wincing. She had stripped off her chain armour and was now dressed in a green smock like the others. She had made every effort to show her ex-friends that she wished to be accepted as one of them. 'For that is where we should find such weapons.'

'And death,' said Lyfeth. 'We should find death there, too.'

'We should have to disguise ourselves,' Katinka van Bak stroked her lips.

'Better,' said Jhary-a-Conel, 'we should bring the weapons to us.'

'What do you mean?' Ilian asked him.

# The Raid on Virinthorm

There were eight.

Ilian was in the fore. She was dressed again in her shining chain armour, with her helmet on her golden hair, a slender sword in her gauntleted hand.

She led the remaining seven along the wide branches of the trees, balancing expertly, for she had trodden the tree-roads since she was a child.

Virinthorm was ahead.

Slung on her back was one of their two flame-lances. The other was back at the camp, with Katinka van Bak.

Ilian paused as they reached the outskirts of Virinthorm and could see the city's conquerors moving about in the streets.

Virinthorm had, over the months, become a series of smaller townships. Each township attracted groups of races of men or other creatures to it, so that those from similar eras or similar worlds or those who resembled each other physically would band together.

The township on which Ilian and her small band now spied was one which they had selected specially. It was made up mainly of folk who resembled mankind in many ways and yet who were not men.

The features of these peole — who were drawn from many spheres and eras — were familiar to Ilian. Indeed, now that she looked upon them, she had a great reluctance to put her plan into action. They were tall and slender, with slanting, almond eyes, ears which came almost to points. While the eyes of some of them were like those of ordinary men, others had eyes that were purple and yellow, others had eyes that were flecks of blue and silver which sparkled constantly. They seemed a proud and intelligent people and were plainly given to avoiding most of their fellows. Yet Ilian also knew that these could be the cruellest of all the invaders.

'Call them Eldren, call them Vadhagh, call them Melniboneans,' Jhary-a-Conel had said to her, 'but remember that these are renegades all of some kind, else they would not league themselves with Ymryl. And doubtless they also serve Chaos as willingly as does Ymryl. Feel no regret for what you do.'

Ilian drew the flame-lance off her back, then began to work her way round to the far side of the unhumans' enclave. On this side dwelled a group of warriors who had all been born at the end of or immediately after the Tragic Millenium. As a group, they were one of the best armed. Each man had at least one flame-lance.

It was about an hour to dusk. Ilian judged her moment the right one. She picked out an unhuman warrior at random, pointed the flame-lance with a skill she had no right to possess and touched the jewelled stud. Immediately a beam of red light issued from the ruby tip and burned a clean hole through the breastplate of the warrior, through his torso and through the backplate on the other side. Ilian released the stud and moved back into the leafier branches to watch what would happen next.

Already a crowd had gathered around the corpse. Many of the eldritch-featured men pointed at once towards the neighbouring camp. Swords slipped from scabbards. Ilian heard oaths, a babble of rage. Her plan had worked so far. The unhumans had drawn the obvious conclusion that one of their number had been murdered by those to whom the flame-lance was their first weapon.

Leaving the corpse where it lay about thirty of the unhumans, all dressed in a variety of styles of clothing and armour, each looking faintly different to the other, began to run towards the neighbouring camp.

Ilian smiled as she watched them. Her old pleasure in fighting and tactics was returning.

She saw the unhumans gesticulating as they reached the other camp. She saw warriors come running out of their houses, buckling on swords. She knew that Ymryl had banned the use of power weapons within the confines of the camp and that this made the crime doubly treacherous. Yet she did not expect a fully-fledged fight to develop yet. She had noticed that the discipline of the camp though crude was effective and designed to stop such squabbles between different factions.

Now Tragic Millenium swords flashed in the dying light of the sun, but still they were not used. A man who was obviously the leader of the unhumans was deep in argument with the chief of the humans. Then both groups trooped back to the unhumans' camp to inspect the corpse. Again the Tragic Millenium leader was plainly denying that his men had anything to do with the murder. He indicated that they were all only armed with swords and knives. Still the unhuman leader was not mollified. The source of the beam seemed obvious to him. Then the human chief pointed in the direction of his own camp and again the warriors stalked across the space between their camps. Here the human pointed to a sturdily built house whose doors and windows were heavily padlocked. He sent one of his men away. The man returned with a bunch of keys. The keys were used to open one of the doors. By straining her eyes Ilian could just see inside. As she had hoped, this was the house where the flame-lances were stored. It was one of the necessary things she had to know before she could continue. Now, as the two factions separated, not without exchanging many scowls, she and her band settled down to wait for night.

They lay in the boughs overlooking the Tragic Millenium camp, almost directly over the flame-lance storehouse.

Ilian signed to the nearest youth who nodded and drew an exquisitely made dagger from his shirt. This was a captured dagger, belonging to the unhumans. Silently, the young man dropped down through the trees until he stood in the shadows of the street. He waited for nearly half-an-hour before a warrior came strolling by. Then he leapt from the dark. One arm went around the throat of the warrior. The dagger rose. The dagger fell. The warrior screamed. Again the dagger struck. Again the warrior screamed. The young man was not striking for the death, but to inflict pain, to force the warrior to yell out.

The third blow was the death blow. The dagger jutted through the man's throat as his corpse fell to the ground. The youth jumped up and began to climb up the side of a house, jumping into the lower branches of a tree and then disappearing as he climbed higher to rejoin his comrades.

This time the scene was enacted from the point of view of the Tragic Millenium soldiers who came running to discover the body with the unhuman dagger sticking in its throat.

It was obvious to them what had happened. In spite of their innocence. In spite of their protestations, the unhumans had taken a cowardly vengeance on them for a crime they could not possibly have committed.

As one man the Tragic Millenium soldiers raced towards the unhumans' camp.

And that was when Ilian dropped from her tree onto the roof of the armoury. Swiftly she slung her own flame-lance from her back and directed its beam close to her feet, cutting a circle large enough to admit her body. Meanwhile the others had joined her on the roof. One of them held her flame-lance as she lowered herself into the building.

She was in a loft. The lances were plainly stored in the rooms below. She found a trap-door and eased it open, dropping into deeper darkness. Slowly her eyes became used to the gloom. A little light came through chinks in the shutters on the windows. She had found some of the lances, at least. She went back the way she had come and signalled for all but one of her band to follow her. While they began to remove the lances, forming a human chain to take them out of the opening she had carved, she explored the lower rooms, finding more lances there, as well as a variety of edged weapons, including some fine throwing axes. These she had to ignore, and it would not be possible to steal more than sixty or so of the lances in the time they had, for there was also the question of carrying them back to their own camp. As she turned to go something came to mind. How did she know that the tips of the lances unscrewed from their shafts? She did not stop to wonder on this but crossed to where she had seen the lances stacked and began to unscrew the ruby tips. As she unscrewed them she picked up a well-balanced axe, placed the tip upon the floor and smashed the axe not on the ruby, which would not break, but upon the stem which screwed into the shaft, denting it so that they would have considerable difficulty in repairing their lances. It was the best she could do.

She heard voices outside. She crossed silently to the nearest window and looked down.

Other soldiers had appeared in the street. These looked like those Ymryl had made into his personal guard. They had doubtless been sent to quell the trouble. Ilian admired Ymryl's efficiency. He never seemed to care about such things, yet he always reacted swiftly when there was any danger of disruption in his camp. Already the soldiers were yelling at the embattled unhumans and Tragic Millenium humans, forcing them to lay down their weapons.

Ilian climbed back to where her band was getting the last of the flame-lances through the hole.

'Go,' she whispered. 'The danger increases. Leave now.'

'You, Queen Ilian?' said the youth who had killed the soldier.

'I'll follow. There is something I must try to finish here.'

She watched until the last of her band had disappeared and then she went back to unscrew the tips of the few remaining flame-lances. Smashing the axe down on the last, she heard a yell, a commotion. Again she peered through the crack in the shutter.

Men were pointing at the roof of the building. Ilian looked round for her own flame-lance and then realized that it had gone with her comrades. She had only her sword. She ran up the stairs, reached the loft, jumped and swung up through the hole she had herself made.

They had seen her.

And that was when an arrow whistled past her shoulder, so close that involuntarily she ducked back, lost her footing on the roof beam and fell down the sloping roof towards the ground on the other side of the house. But men were already running here. She managed to grasp a gable as she went over the edge. Her arms were almost pulled from her body as she swung there with arrows whistling on all sides. One or two arrows struck her helmet and mail, but did not penetrate. She got a foothold somewhere and pushed herself back up again, crouching behind the gable as she ran along, searching for a branch low enough to jump for. But there was no such branch. Now figures were appearing above her. They had found what had happened to their weapons and where she had entered. She could hear their angry shouts and she was glad she had gone back to destroy every one of the flame-lances. If they had had them now, she would be dead already. She reached the far end of the roof and prepared to jump to the next. It was her only means of escape.

She launched herself into space, hands clutching for the gable of that house. She grasped the carved wood and felt it give sickeningly beneath her weight. She hung there, thinking she would fall, but the gable held and she hauled herself up. They had realized where she was and more arrows sought her. She jumped from that roof to another, closer, realizing with despair that she was moving deeper and deeper into the city as they pursued her. She prayed that she would eventually come to a spot where a branch brushed the roofs. In the trees she had a much better chance of escape. She was consoled, at least, that her comrades were getting away in the other direction.

Three more roofs and they had lost her for the moment. She breathed in relief. But it was a matter of time before they caught her, she was sure.

If she could get into one of the houses and hide, then they would assume she had escaped. When the pursuit died down it would not be too difficult to leave at her leisure.

She saw an unlit house ahead.

That would do.

She jumped across the gap between the roofs, landed, swung over the edge of the roof and down to a window ledge. Crouching on the ledge she forced open the shutters and crept in, drawing the shutters to behind her.

She was tired. The chain-mail was heavy on her body. She wished she had time to remove it. Without it she could jump higher, climb faster. But it was too late to worry about such things now.

The room in which she found herself smelled musky as if the windows had not been opened for a long time. As she moved across it, she bumped her knee against something. A chest? A bed?

And then she heard a stifled moan.

Ilian peered into the gloom.

A figure lay upon the rumpled bed. It was the figure of a woman.

And she was bound.

Was this some fellow-citizen whom one of the invaders was keeping prisoner? Ilian bent forward to remove the gag which had been tightly drawn about the girl's mouth.

'Who are you?' Ilian whispered. 'Do not fear me. I'll save you if that's possible, though I'm in great danger myself.'

And then Ilian gasped as the gag came free.

She recognized the face.

It was the face of a ghost.

Ilian felt terror shiver through her body. It was a terror that she could not name. A terror which she had never felt before, for while she recognized the face, she could not name it.

Neither could she remember where, in all her life, she had seen it before.

She tried to stop her impulse to shrink away from the bound figure on the bed.

'Who are you?' said the woman.

## CHAPTER SIX

## The Wrong Champion

Ilian controlled herself. She found a lamp, found flint and tinder and lit the lamp while she took deep breaths and tried to rationalize what was happening to her. The shock of recognition had been strong – yet she could swear she had never seen the woman before.

Ilian turned. The woman was dressed in a filthy white gown. She had evidently been kept prisoner here for some time. She began to try to struggle into a sitting position on the bed. Her hands were locked in front of her, in a complicated leather harness which also bound her throat, her legs and her feet.

Ilian wondered if this were a madwoman. Perhaps it had been foolish to cut the gag without thinking. There was something wild about the woman's eyes, but again that could merely be because she had been captive so long.

'Are you of Garathorm?' Ilian asked, holding up the lamp to peer once more at the woman's pale features.

'Garathorm? This place? No.'

'You seem familiar.'

'You, also. Yet . . .'

'Aye,' said Ilian feelingly. 'You have never seen me before either.'

'My name is Yisselda of Brass. I am Baron Kalan's captive and have been since I came here.'

'Why are you his prisoner?'

'He is afraid I might escape and be seen. He wants me for himself. I seem to represent some sort of talisman for him. He has done me no great harm. Can you cut this harness, do you think?'

Reassured by Yisselda of Brass's level tones, Ilian bent and sliced through the straps. Yisselda gasped as feeling returned to her limbs. 'I thank you.'

'I am Ilian of Garathorm. Queen Ilian.'

'King Pyran's daughter!' Yisselda seemed astonished. 'But Kalan drew your soul from you, did he not?'

'So I gather. But I have a new soul now.'

'Indeed?'

Ilian smiled. 'Do not ask me to explain. So not all who came so suddenly to our world are evil.'

'Most are those whom we should call evil. Most are pledged to Chaos, Kalan tells me, and believe they cannot be slain. But he hardly believes that theory himself. It is what he is told.'

Ilian was trembling, wondering why she had the impulse to embrace this woman, to hold her in a way that was more than comradely. She had never felt such impulses before. Her knees shook. Without thinking, she sat down on the bed.

'Fate,' she murmured. 'They say I serve Fate. Do you know aught of that, Yisselda of Brass? I know your name so well – and that of Baron Kalan. It seems to me I have been searching for you – searching all my life – and yet it is not I who searched. Oh . . .' She was close to fainting. She put a hand to her brow. 'This is horrifying.'

'I understand you. Kalan thinks that his experiments in time distortion have created this situation. Our lives are mixed up so much. One possibility clashes with another. It must even be possible to meet oneself, under these conditions.'

'Kalan was responsible for letting Ymryl and the rest through?'

'So he believes. He spends his whole time trying to restore the balance which he himself disrupted. And I am important to him in his experiments. He has no wish to go with Ymryl on the morrow.'

'Tomorrow? Where does Ymryl ride?'

'Against the west. Against one called Arnald of Grovent, I understand.'

'So they fight at last!' Ilian forgot everything but that fact for a moment. She was exhilarated. Their opportunity was coming sooner than she had hoped.

'Baron Kalan is Ymryl's mascot,' said Yisselda. She had found a comb somewhere and was trying to comb out her tangled hair. 'Just as I am Kalan's. I survive thanks to a chain of superstition!'

'And where is Kalan now?'

'Doubtless in Ymryl's palace – your father's palace, is it not?'

'It is. What does he there?'

'Some of his experiments. Ymryl has set him up with a laboratory, though really Kalan prefers to work from here. He will take me with him when he works, sitting me down and talking to me as if I were a pet dog. It is the most attention he pays me. Needless to say I understand little of what he talks about. I was present, however, when he stole your soul. That was horrible. How did you recover it?'

Ilian did not answer. 'How did he – steal my soul?'

'With a jewel, similar to that which threatened to eat my Hawkmoon's brain when it was imbedded in his skull. A jewel of similar properties, at any rate . . .'

'Hawkmoon? That name . . .'

'Aye? You know Hawkmoon. How does he fare? Surely he is not in this world . . .?'

'No – no. I do not know him. I do not know why I should. Yet it sounded so familiar.'

'You are unwell, Ilian of Garathorm?'

'Aye. Aye. I could be.' Ilian felt faint. Doubtless the exertions she had had to make to escape Ymryl's soldiers had tired her more than she had at first realized. Again she made an effort to recover. 'This jewel, then? Kalan has it? And my soul, he believes, is in it?'

'Yes. But he is plainly wrong. Somehow your soul was released from the jewel.'

'Plainly,' Ilian smiled grimly. 'Well, we must consider a means of escaping. You do not look fit enough to climb rooftops and swing through trees with me.'

'I can try,' said Yisselda. 'I am stronger than I seem.'

'Then we must try, then. When do you expect Kalan's return?'

'He only recently left.'

'Then we have some time. I will use it in resting.' Ilian leaned back on the bed. 'My head aches so.'

Yisselda reached forward to massage Ilian's brow, but Ilian drew away with a gasp. 'No!' She licked dry lips. 'No. I thank you for your consideration.'

Yisselda went to the still shuttered window and cautiously opened it a little, breathing in the cooler night air.

'Kalan is to try to help Ymryl make contact with this black god of his, this Arioch.'

'Whom Ymryl believes responsible for placing him here?'

'Yes. Ymryl will blow that Yellow Horn he has and Kalan will try to concoct some form of spell. Kalan is cynical concerning their chances of raising the demon.'

'Ymryl's horn is dear to him. Does he never let it off his person?'

'Never, so Kalan says. The only one who could make Ymryl give up his horn is Arioch himself.'

The time passed with painful slowness. While Ilian tried to rest, Yisselda extinguished the lamp and watched the streets, noticing that patrols of soldiers still searched there for Ilian. Some were even on the rooftops at one stage. But eventually they seemed to have given up the search and Yisselda went to rouse Ilian, who was by now sleeping fitfully.

195

Yisselda shook Ilian's shoulder and Ilian shuddered, waking with a start.

'They are gone,' said Yisselda. 'I think we can risk leaving. How shall we go? Into the street?'

'No. But a coil of rope would help. Is there one in the house, do you think?'

'I will see.'

Yisselda returned in a few minutes with a length of rope coiled over her shoulder. 'It is the longest I could find. Is it strong enough?'

'It will have to be.' Ilian smiled. She opened the window wide and looked up. The nearest large branch was some ten feet overhead. Ilian took the rope and made a noose at one end, coiling the rope so that it was the same circumference as the noose. Then she began to swing the coil round and round before releasing it suddenly.

The noose settled over a branch, held, and Ilian tightened the knot.

'You'll have to climb onto my back,' Ilian told Yisselda, 'curling your legs around my waist and hanging on as hard as you can. Do you think you'll be able to?'

'I must,' said Yisselda simply. She did as she was ordered and then Ilian pulled herself onto the window sill, took a good grip on the rope, turning it round her hand once or twice, and then flung herself out over the rooftops, narrowly missing the spire of one of the old trading halls. Her feet struck another branch and she dug in her heels, straining with all her might to get a better grip on the branch above her. She was about to slip when Yisselda reached up and pulled herself onto the branch, leaning down to help Ilian after her. They lay panting on the great branch.

Ilian sprang up. 'Follow me,' she said. 'Keep your arms spread for balance. And keep moving.'

She began to run along the bole.

And Yisselda, somewhat shakily, followed her.

They were back at the camp by morning and they were jubilant.

Katinka van Bak came out of the shack she had built for herself from old planks and she was delighted to see Ilian. 'We feared for you,' she said. 'Even those who profess to hate you so. The others came back with the flame-lances. A good haul.'

'Excellent. And I have more information.'

'Good. Good. You'll want to breakfast – and rest, too, I should think. Who is this?' Katinka van Bak seemed to notice the woman in the white, soiled dress for the first time.

'She is called Yisselda of Brass. She, like you, is not of

Garathorm . . .'

Ilian noticed the look of astonishment which appeared on Katinka's face then. 'Yisselda? Count Brass's daughter?'

'Aye,' said Yisselda in some delight. 'Though Count Brass is dead – slain at the Battle of Londra.'

'Not so! Not so! He dwells still at Castle Brass! So Hawkmoon was right. You are alive! This is the strangest thing I have yet to experience – but by far the most pleasurable.'

'You have seen Dorian? How is he?'

'Ah —' Katinka van Bak seemed to become evasive. 'He is well. He is well. He has been ill, but now all the portents are that he will recover.'

'I wish it was possible to see him again. He is not in this plane?'

'Unfortunately he could not be.'

'How came you here? In the same manner as myself?'

'Pretty much the same, aye.' Katinka van Bak turned to see that Jhary-a-Conel had emerged from one of the ebony houses still standing. He was rubbing sleep from his eyes and looked barely awake. 'Jhary. This is Yisselda of Brass. Hawkmoon was right.'

'She is alive!' Jhary slapped his thigh, looking with some irony from Ilian to Yisselda and back again. 'Ha! This is the best I've ever known! Oh, dear!' And he burst into laughter which Ilian and Yisselda found inexplicable.

Ilian felt anger rise in her. 'I become bored with your mysteries and your hints, Sir Jhary! I become bored with them!'

'Aye!' Jhary continued to laugh. I think it is the best way to respond to it all, madam!'

# BOOK THREE
# A LEAVETAKING

## CHAPTER ONE

## Sweet Battle, Triumphant Vengeance

There were nearly a hundred of them now and most of them had flame-lances. They had been hastily trained in the use of the lances by Katinka van Bak and some of the lances were inclined to be faulty, for they were very old, but the weapons gave confidence to all who bore them.

Ilian turned in her saddle to look back at her troops. Each man and woman was mounted, mostly on striding *vayna* birds. Each hailed the burning banner as she turned. The fiery thing, which burned without consuming the cloth, fluttered over her armoured head. It was their pride. And they were going to Virinthorm.

Beneath the great, green trees of Garathorm they rode: Ilian, Katinka van Bak, Jhary-a-Conel, Yisselda of Brass, Lyfeth of Ghant, Mysenal of Hinn and the rest. All, save Katinka van Bak, were youthful.

It seemed to Ilian that, while her own crimes had not been forgotten by those she led, she and her people were united again. But much would depend on how they fared in the battles which lay ahead.

They rode through the morning and by the afternoon they had come in sight of Virinthorm.

Spies had already reported the departure of Ymryl with his main force. He had left less than a quarter of his men behind to defend Virinthorm, not expecting any kind of full scale attack. Yet still those defenders were some five hundred strong and would have been more than sufficient to defeat Ilian's force, had they not been armed with flame-lances.

Yet even the flame-lances only improved the chances of the Garathormians. It was by no means certain that they would defeat Ymryl's men. This, however, was the only chance they might have to try.

And they sang as they rode. They sang the old songs of their land. Gay songs, full of their love for their rich, arboreal world. They hardly paused as they reached the suburbs of Virinthorm and spread out.

201

Ymryl's men had garrisoned themselves close to the centre of the town, near the large house which had once been the residence of Ilian's family, and which had, until lately, become Ymryl's palace.

Ilian regretted that Ymryl himself was not there. She looked forward to taking her vengeance on him, should her schemes be successful.

Now the hundred riders, thinly spread, had dismounted and situated themselves in a circle around the centre of the city. Some lay behind roughly thrown up barricades, others lay on roofs, while still others crouched in doorways. A hundred flame-lances were aimed into the city when Ilian rode out into the broad main avenue and cried:

'Surrender in the name of Queen Ilian!'

And her voice was high and proud.

'Surrender, Ymryl's men! We have returned to claim our city.'

The few who were on the streets turned to look in consternation, hands reaching for weapons. Men in every form of clothing, in all sorts of armour, in a score of different shapes, men with fur all over their bodies, men who were completely hairless, men with four arms or four legs, men with beastlike heads, men with tails or horns or tufted ears, men with hooves instead of feet, men with green, blue, red and black skins, men armed with bizarre weapons, the purpose of which was mysterious, men deformed, men who were dwarves and men who were giants, hermaphrodites, men with wings or with transparent skins, came pouring into the streets and saw Queen Ilian of Garathorm and laughed.

A warrior with an orange beard which came to a point at his belt called out:

'Ilian is dead. As you will be before another minute has passed.'

In reply Ilian raised her flame-lance, touched the jewelled stud, and pierced the man's forehead with a beam of red light, whereupon a dog-faced soldier threw a disc which howled and which Ilian was barely able to deflect by bringing up the small buckler she had on her right arm. She wheeled her horse around and dashed for cover. Behind her the defenders also sought cover as beams of red light darted at them from all around.

For an hour the fight raged thus, with either side using power weapons from cover, while Katinka van Bak rode from warrior to warrior, giving instructions to tighten the circle and contain the defenders in as small an area as possible. This they did, not without considerable difficulty, for though the enemy had fewer power weapons, they were more skilled in using them.

Ilian climbed a rooftop to see how the battle went. She had lost about ten of her small band, but Ymryl's men had lost more. She counted at least forty corpses. But the alien soldiers were plainly grouping for a counter-attack. Many had mounted themselves on a variety of beasts, including some captured *vayna*.

Ilian dropped back down to the ground and sought Katinka van Bak. 'They are planning to charge through, Katinka!'

'Then they must be stopped,' said the warrior woman, firmly.

Ilian got back onto her own *vayna*. The long-legged bird croaked as Ilian swung it round. It began to stride away to where Jhary-a-Conel had taken up his position in the window of a house looking towards the central square.

'Jhary! They charge!' she called.

And then a packed mass of cavalry came howling along the avenue and it seemed to Ilian for a moment that only she stood against it.

She raised her flame-lance, touched the stud. Ruby light flared, flickered from the hip, cut an erratic swathe across the bodies of the leading riders. In going down, they got in the way of those behind them and the force of the charge was weakened.

But the lance was now all but useless. The light wavered, spread, merely burned the skins of the soldiers as the sun might burn them, and they came on.

Ilian flung down the lance, drew her slender sword, took her long poignard in the hand that also held her reins, and urged the *vayna* forward. Behind her, in its saddle rest, the burning banner cracked and hissed as she gathered speed.

'For Garathorm!'

And now she knew joy. A black joy. A terrible joy.

'For Pyran and Bradne!'

And her sword sliced through the transparent flesh of a ghostly creature who grinned at her and tried to slash her with steel claws.

'For vengeance!'

And how sweet it was, that vengeance! How satisfying, that blood-letting! So close to death was she, and yet she felt more alive than she had ever felt. This was her destiny – to bear a sword into battle – to fight – to kill.

And as she fought it seemed she did not merely fight this battle but a thousand others. And in each battle she had another name, yet in each battle she felt the same grim elation.

Around her the enemy roared and rattled and it seemed that a score of swords forever sought to slay her, but she laughed at them.

And her laughter was a weapon. It chilled the blood of those she fought. It filled them with a great and unwholesome terror.

'For Fate's soldier!' she heard herself shouting. 'For the Champion Eternal. For the Struggle Without End!' And she knew not the meaning of the words, though she knew she had cried them before and would cry them again, whether she survived this encounter or not.

Now others were joining her. She saw Jhary-a-Conel's yellow horse rearing and snorting and thrashing out with its hooves, striking down warriors on all sides. The horse seemed possessed of unnatural intelligence. Its actions were no mere flailing, no panicky defence. It fought aggressively, with its master. And it grinned, displaying crooked yellow teeth, cold yellow eyes, while its rider slashed this way and that with his sword, a small smile on his lips.

And there was Katinka van Bak, tough, methodical and cool as she went about the business of slaying. She held a double-bladed battle-axe in one gloved hand, a spiked mace in the other, for she did not consider the situation suitable for the subtler sword-work. She pushed her heavy, stolid horse deep into the enemy and she chopped off limbs and crushed skulls just as surely as a housewife might prepare meat and vegetables for her husband's meal. And Katinka van Bak did not smile. She took her work seriously, doing what had to be done and feeling neither disgust nor relish.

Ilian wondered at the relish she herself felt. Her whole body tingled with pleasure. She should have been weary, but instead she felt fresher than she had ever felt before.

'For Garathorm! For Pyran! For Bradne!'

'For Bradne!' echoed a voice behind her. 'And for Ilian!'

It was Lyfeth of Ghant, wielding her sword with a mixture of delicacy and ferocity which came close to matching Ilian's own. And nearby was Yisselda of Brass, proving herself an experienced warrior, using the spike on her shield boss almost as effectively as she used her sword!

'What women we are!' cried Ilian. 'What fighters!'

She saw how disconcerted the enemy warriors were to discover the number of women who had come against them. There were few worlds, it seemed, where women fought like men. It had never been so on Garathorm, before the coming of Katinka van Bak.

Ilian saw Mysenal of Hinn grin briefly at her, his eyes shining as he rode past her towards a cluster of Ymryl's warriors whose retreat had been cut off by three or four flame-lance beams darting from the tops of nearby houses.

Two or three buildings had been ignited by the power weapons and smoke was beginning to curl through the streets. For a moment Ilian was half-blinded and found herself coughing as the acrid stuff entered her throat. Then she was through the cloud and joining Mysenal in his attack on the enemy.

Though she now bled from a dozen minor cuts and grazes, Ilian was tireless. She unhorsed one rider with a blow of her buckler and in the same movement swept her sword round to take a green-furred dwarf through the roof of his gaping mouth so that the point ran deep into his brain. As the dwarf fell, Ilian twisted the sword from his corpse in time to parry an axe which had been thrown at her by a warrior in purple armour whose pointed steel teeth clashed as he tried to draw back his arm to thrust at her with the lance he held in his other hand. Ilian leaned out in her saddle and sliced the hand from the wrist so that fist and spear dropped to the ground. The stump, spouting blood, continued the motion of casting the spear and only then did the warrior with the steel teeth realize what had happened to him and he moaned. But Ilian was riding past him, to where one of her girl warriors stood over the corpse of her dead *vayna* desperately trying to ward off the blows of three men with reptilian skins (but who were otherwise dressed dissimilarly) who were determined to slay her. Ilian clove the skull of one reptile man, smashed another unconscious so that he fell backward across his horse's rump, and pierced the heart of the last, clearing a way for the girl who darted her a quick smile of gratitude before picking up her flame-lance and running for an open doorway.

And then Ilian was in the square with a score of her warriors at her back and she called out jubilantly:

'We are through!'

Men on foot came running from every house then, those who had not taken part in the cavalry charge, and soon Ilian was surrounded again.

And soon Ilian was laughing again, as life after life was extinguished by her sparkling sword.

The sun was setting.

Ilian cried to her warriors. 'Hasten now! Let us finish this before the night falls and makes our work more difficult.'

The remnants of the enemy cavalry had been driven back into the square. The remnants of the infantry were falling back towards the great house, the house Ymryl had called his 'palace' and where Ilian had been born. It was also the house where she had shuddered, screamed and called out the hiding place of her brother.

For a moment Ilian's joy was replaced by a feeling of black despair, and she paused. The sounds of the battle seemed to fade. The whole scene became remote. And she remembered the face of Ymryl, almost boyish in seriousness, leaning forward and saying to her: 'Where is he? Where is Bradne?'

And she had told him.

Ilian shuddered. She lowered her sword, oblivious to the danger which still threatened her from all sides. Five warped creatures, their bodies and faces covered in huge warts, flung themselves upwards at her, hands clutching. She felt sharp nails dig through the links of her mail. She looked at them absently.

'Bradne . . . ' she murmured.

'Are you wounded, girl!' Katinka van Bak appeared, and an axe bit into a skull, a mace crunched into a shoulder. The warted ones squealed. 'Are you dazed?'

Ilian forced herself from the trance using her own sword to hack down a wart-covered body. 'Only for a moment,' she said.

'There's about a hundred left!' Katinka van Bak said. 'They've barricaded themselves in your father's mansion. I doubt if we'll have winkled them out before nightfall.'

'Then we must fire the building,' said Ilian coldly. 'We must burn them.'

Katinka frowned. 'I like not that. Even these should have the opportunity to surrender . . . '

'Burn them and burn the building. Burn it!' Ilian wheeled her *vayna* about to look around the square. It was piled with corpses. About fifty of her own folk still remained alive. 'It will save more fighting, will it not, Katinka van Bak?'

'It will, but . . . '

'And spare the lives of some of our folk who still survive?'

'Aye . . . ' Katinka tried to meet Ilian's eyes, but Ilian turned her face away. 'Aye. But what of the building itself? Your ancestors have dwelled in it for generations. It is the finest building in all Virinthorm. There's scarcely a finer in the whole of Garathorm. The woods of its construction are rare. Many of the varieties of tree which went to build it are now extinct . . . '

'Let it burn. I could not live there again.'

Katinka sighed. 'I will give the order, though it's not to my liking. Cannot I offer our enemies a chance to surrender to us?'

'They gave us no such chance.'

206

'But we are not them. Morally . . . '
'I'll hear nothing of morality for the moment, thank you.'
Katinka van Bak rode to do Queen Ilian's bidding.

## CHAPTER TWO

An Impossible Death

They were grim-faced, those men and women, as they stood with their hands resting on their weapons, their faces stained red by the firelight, and watched Pyran's mansion burning in the blackness of the night, smelled the smell which came from the pyre, listened to the thin, horrible sounds that still issued through the thick, black smoke from time to time.

'It is just,' said Ilian of Garathorm.

'But there are other forms of justice,' said Katinka van Bak in a quiet voice. 'You cannot burn away the guilt you feel, Ilian.'

'Can I not, madam?' Ilian laughed harshly. 'Yet how do you explain the satisfaction I feel?'

'I am not used to this,' said Katinka van Bak. She spoke for Ilian's ears alone; she spoke reluctantly. 'I've witnessed such acts of vengeance before, yet I like not the sense of unease I feel now. You have become cruel, Ilian.'

'It is ever the fate of the Champion,' said another voice. It was Jhary's. 'Ever. Do not fret, Katinka van Bak. The Champion must always seek to rid himself – or herself – of a certain ambiguous burden. And one of the means the Champion employs is deliberate cruelty – actions which go against the dictates of the Champion's conscience. Ilian thinks she bears only the guilt of her brother's betrayal. It is not so. It is a guilt which you and I, Katinka van Bak, could never experience. And we should thank all our gods for that!'

Ilian shuddered. She had barely heard Jhary's words, but she was disturbed by their import.

With a shrug, Katinka van Bak turned away. 'As you say, Jhary. You know more of such matters than do I. And there would be no Ilian at all to fight Ymryl if it were not for your knowledge.' She stalked off into the smoky shadows.

Jhary stood beside Ilian for a while. Then he, too, left her alone, staring into the blazing ruins of her old home.

The cries died and the stink of burning flesh faded until the sweet odours of the wood became predominant. Ilian felt drained of life. And as the blaze subsided, she moved closer, as if seeking warmth, for there was an awful chill in her bones now, though the night was not cold.

Still she saw Ymryl's sober features asking her that question. Still she heard her own voice replying.

When Jhary found her it was close to dawn and she was trampling through the blackened bones, the cinders and the hot ash, kicking at a charred skull here and a broken rib cage there.

'News,' said Jhary.

She looked out at him through her bleak eyes.

'News of Ymryl. He was successful in his war. He has slain Arnald and has heard what happened here last night. He's returning.'

Ilian drew deeply of the acrid air. 'Then we must prepare,' she said.

'With half our force remaining, we shall be hard-pressed to stand against Ymryl's army. He now has Arnald's strength, also – or what remains of it. At least two thousand warriors come against us! Perhaps it would be better tactics to return to the trees, harry them from time to time . . .'

'We shall continue with the plan we originally devised,' said Ilian.

Jhary-a-Conel shrugged. 'Very well.'

'Have Ymryl's flame-cannon been found?'

'They have. Hidden in cellars in a wine-press west of here. And Katinka van Bak saw that they were set up in a defensive ring during the night. Others are mounted to cover each of the main thoroughfares into the centre of the city. It is as well we acted swiftly. I for one did not expect Ymryl to return so soon.'

Ilian began to wade through the ashes. 'Katinka van Bak is an experienced general.'

'We are lucky that she is,' said Jhary.

Soon after midday the scouts came back with news that Ymryl was using similar tactics to Ilian's in approaching the city, closing in from all sides. Ilian prayed that Ymryl's scouts had not seen the hastily concealed flame-cannon. She had put about half her force to operating the power weapons. The others she had positioned in hiding elsewhere.

About an hour later, the first wave of cavalry, all shining armour and fluttering pennants, came thundering down the four broad avenues which led to the city square.

The square itself was apparently deserted, save for the corpses which had been left there.

The cavalry's tempo began to slacken as the first riders saw what lay ahead and became confused.

From somewhere high overhead there came the silvery note of a horn.

And flame-cannon roared.

And where the cavalry had been, in all four quarters was burning dust, embers drifting in the air, ash settling on the streets.

Ilian, hidden in the trees, smiled, remembering how those same flame-cannon had cut down her own folk.

The odds against her had now been improved by a matter of some several hundred, but the flame-cannon could not be used again, for they had to be filled once more with the substance which fuelled them and that substance required delicate handling and much time was involved in pouring it, drop by drop, into the chambers. Ilian saw those who had operated the cannon spring up and run back to the square, disappearing into buildings.

Silence fell again over Virinthorm.

Then, from the west, came a clattering of hooves. The leaf-filtered sunlight flashed on jeweled masks, on bright horse-armour.

From her own position in a tree some hundred yards away, Katinka van Bak called:

'It is Kalan and a Dark Empire force. They have flame weapons, too.'

Baron Kalan's snake mask glittered as he rode at headlong speed down the broad avenue. From the houses came the thin, red beams of light, issuing from Ilian's remaining flame-lances. Several of the beams seemed to pass through Kalan's body without harming him and Ilian thought that her eyes deceived her. Even the sorcerer could not be impervious to those deadly beams.

Others fell, however, before their comrades had time to return the fire, aiming their flame-lances at random in the general direction of the houses from which the attacks had come until the air was a lattice of ruby rays.

And still Kalan rode straight for the square, his horse panting as he spurred it until its blood spurted from its flanks.

Kalan was laughing. It was a laugh that was familiar to Ilian and she could not place it for a moment until she remembered that it was not unlike that laughter she had herself shouted during the previous day's battle.

Kalan rode until he came to the square and then his laughter gave way to a wail of rage as he saw the remains of the great mansion.

'My laboratories!'

He dismounted from his horse and walked into the ruins, staring about him, oblivious to any danger which might threaten him, while behind him his men fought a fierce battle with Ilian's warriors who had emerged from the houses and were engaging them hand to hand.

Ilian watched him. She was fascinated. What did he seek?

Two of Ilian's warriors detached themselves from the main party and came running at Kalan. He turned when he heard them and again he laughed, drawing his sword. The laughter echoed eerily in his snake helm.

'Leave me alone,' he called to the warriors. 'You cannot harm me.'

And now Ilian gasped. She saw one of the warriors thrust his sword into Kalan. She saw the point emerge on the other side of the sorcerer's body. She saw Kalan back away, slashing at his attacker with his own sword, cutting a deep wound in the man's shoulder. But Kalan was unwounded. The warrior groaned. Impatiently, Kalan drove his sword into the warrior's throat so that he dropped into the ashes of the mansion. The other warrior hesitated before striking at Baron Kalan, driving at the Dark Empire Lord's unarmoured fore-arm. It was a blow which should have shorn the limb from Kalan, but again Kalan was completely unhurt. At this the warrior backed off. Ignoring him, Kalan continued his frantic search amongst the charred corpses and the embers, calling back to the warrior:

'I cannot be slain. Do not waste my time and I shall not waste yours. There is something I seek here. What fool can have wrought such unnecessary destruction?' And when the warrior remained where he was, the serpent helm lifted and Kalan said, as if explaining to a stupid child: 'I cannot be slain. There is only one man who can slay me in all the infinite cosmos. And I do not see him here. Begone!'

Ilian sympathized with her warrior as she watched him stumble away.

And then Kalan chuckled. 'I have it!' He bent and picked something from the dust.

Ilian swung down from the trees and dropped into the square, confronting Kalan across a sea of corpses.

'Baron Kalan?'

He looked up. 'I have it . . . ' He made to show it to her and then he hesitated. 'What? It cannot be! Have all my powers deserted me, then?'

'You thought you had slain me?' Ilian began to advance towards him. She had seen that he was invulnerable, yet she felt she had to confront him, for she was moved by another of those strange im-pulses she could not explain. 'Ilian of Garathorm?'

'Slain? Nonsense. It was much subtler. The jewel ate your soul. It

211

was my finest creation of that sort, more sophisticated than anything else I have invented. It was meant for someone much more important than you, but the situation demanded that I use it, if I was not to die by Ymryl's hand.'

From the distance now came the sounds of battle. Ilian knew that her folk were engaging Ymryl's army. Her step did not falter as she continued to walk towards Kalan.

'I have much to avenge myself for on you, Baron Kalan,' she said.

'You cannot kill me, madam, if that's what you mean,' he told her. '*You* cannot do that.'

'But I must try.'

The Serpent Lord shrugged. 'If you must. But I would rather know how your soul escaped from my gem. I had every indication that it was trapped there for eternity. And with such a gem I could have pursued still more complicated experiments. How did it escape?'

Someone called across from the far side of the square. 'It did not, Baron Kalan. It did not escape!' It was Jhary-a-Conel's voice.

The serpent mask turned. 'What do you mean?'

'Did you not understand the nature of the soul you sought to imprison in your gem?'

'Nature? How . . . ?'

'Do you know the legend of the Champion Eternal?'

'I have read something of it, aye . . . ' The serpent mask turned from Jhary to Ilian, from Ilian to Jhary. And still Ilian continued to pace toward Baron Kalan.

'Then recall what you read.'

And Ilian stood before Baron Kalan of Vitall and with a movement of her sword she had swept the serpent helm from his shoulders to reveal his pale, middle-aged face with its wispy white beard, its thinning hair. Kalan blinked and made to cover his face, then he dropped his hands to his side, his sword hanging by its wrist-thong, one fist bunched around the thing he had sought among the ruins.

Kalan said softly: 'You still cannot slay me, Ilian of Garathorm. And even if you could, it would result in terrible consequences. Let me go. Or hold me prisoner, if you like. I have matters to consider . . . '

'Put up your sword, Baron Kalan, and defend yourself.'

'I would be reluctant to slay you,' said Kalan, his voice becoming harsher, 'for you offer an intriguing mystery to a man of science, but I *shall* kill you, Ilian, if you continue to plague me.'

'And I shall kill you, if I can.'

'I told you,' said Kalan reasonably, 'that I can only be slain by one

212

creature in the entire multiverse. And that creature is not yourself. Besides, more than you realize depends upon my remaining alive . . . '

'Defend yourself!'

Kalan shrugged and held up his sword.

Ilian thrust. Kalan parried carelessly. Her blade continued on its course, deflected only a fraction, and her point entered his flesh. Kalan's eyes widened.

'Pain!' he hissed in astonishment. 'It is pain!'

Ilian was almost as surprised as Kalan to see the blood flowing. Kalan staggered back, looking down at his wound. 'It is not possible,' he said firmly. 'It is not.'

And Ilian thrust again, this time striking directly at his heart as Kalan said: 'Only Hawkmoon can kill me. Only he. It is impossible . . . '

And he fell backwards in the ashes, causing a small cloud of black dust to spurt up around him. The look of astonishment was still printed on his dead features.

'Now we are both avenged, Baron Kalan,' said Ilian in a voice she did not recognize as her own.

She bent to see what the baron had clutched in his hand, prying it from the fingers.

It was something which gleamed like polished coal. An irregularly cut gem. She knew what it must be.

As she straightened up she noticed that the quality of the light around her had altered subtly. It was as if clouds had passed around the sun, yet the rains were not due yet for another two months.

Jhary-a-Conel came running towards her. 'So you did slay him! But I fear that action will bring more trouble to us.' He glanced at the gem she held. 'Keep that safely. If we come through this together, I will show you what you must do with it.'

Overhead, in the darkening sky, through the top-most branches of Garathorm's massive trees, there came a sound. It was like the beating of the wings of a gigantic bird. And there was a stink, too, that made the smell of the corpses seem sweet in comparison.

'What is it, Jhary?' Ilian felt fear filling her whole mind. She wanted to flee from the thing which was coming to Virinthorm.

'Kalan warned you that there would be consequences if he was slain here. You see, his experiments created the disruptions in the whole balance of the multiverse. By slaying him you have enabled the multiverse to begin healing itself, though that will bring further disruptions of what some would call a minor nature.'

'But what causes that sound, that smell?'

213

'Listen,' said Jhary-a-Conel. 'Do you hear anything else?'

Ilian listened carefully. In the distance she could hear the barking note of a war-horn. Ymryl's horn.

'He has summoned Arioch, Lord of Chaos,' said Jhary. 'And Kalan's dying has enabled Arioch to break through at last. Ymryl has a new ally, Ilian.'

## CHAPTER THREE

The Swaying of the Balance

Jhary was full of a wild, despairing mirth as he mounted his yellow horse, casting many glances at the sky. It was still dark, but the sound of that awful flapping had gone and the stink had faded.

'Only you, Jhary, know what we fight now,' said Katinka van Bak soberly. She wiped sweat from her face with her sleeve, the sword still in her hand.

Yisselda of Brass rode up. On her arm was a long, shallow cut. The blood had congealed in the wound.

'Ymryl has withdrawn his attack,' she said. 'I cannot determine what strategy he plans . . . ' Her voice tailed off as she saw Kalan's corpse still lying in the ashes. 'So,' she said, 'he is dead. Good. He had the superstition, you know, that he could only be slain by my husband, Hawkmoon.'

Katinka van Bak almost smiled. 'Aye,' she said. 'I know.'

'Have you any thought as to what Ymryl plans next?' Yisselda asked Katinka van Bak.

'He has little need of strategy now, according to what Jhary tells us,' the warrior woman replied wearily. 'He has demons aiding him now!'

'You are choosing the terminology to suit your own prejudices,' said Jhary-a-Conel. 'If I called Arioch a being of considerably advanced mental and physical powers, you would accept his existence completely.'

'I accept his existence, anyway!' snorted Katinka van Bak. 'I have heard him. I have sniffed him!'

'Well,' said Ilian in a small voice, 'we must continue our fight with Ymryl, even if it is doomed. Shall we continue our defensive strategy or alter it to one of attack?'

'It scarcely matters now,' said Jhary-a-Conel, 'but it would be nobler to die in an attack, would it not?' He smiled to himself. 'Strange how death remains unwelcome, for all I understand my fate.'

They moved through the trees, their mounts abandoned. They were stealthy and they carried the flame-lances they had taken from the

215

dead Dark Empire warriors whom Kalan had led.

Jhary led them and now he paused, raising his hand as he looked down through the leaves, wrinkling his nose.

They saw Ymryl's camp. He had made it on the very edge of the city. They saw Ymryl, his yellow horn bouncing on his naked chest. He wore only a pair of silken breeks and his feet were unshod. His arms were bound about with bracelets of leather studded with jewels and he had a broad leather belt round his waist, which carried his heavy broadsword, his broad-bladed dirk and a weapon which could shoot tiny, squat arrows across long distances. His great untidy mop of yellow hair fell across his face and his uneven teeth gleamed as he grinned somewhat nervously at his new ally.

His ally was about nine feet tall and about six feet broad with a dark, scaly skin. It was naked, hermaphrodite, and there was a pair of leathery wings folded on its back. It seemed to be in some pain as it moved about, gnawing hungrily at the remains of one of Ymryl's soldiers.

But the unnerving thing about Ymryl's ally was its face. It was a face which kept changing. At one moment it would be repulsively bestial and ugly, at another it would become the face of a beautiful youth. Only the eyes, the pain-racked eyes, did not change. Occasionally, however, they flashed with intelligence, but for the most part were cruel, fierce, primitive.

Ymryl's voice trembled, but it was triumphant. 'You will aid me now, will you not, Lord Arioch. It was the bargain we made . . . '

'Aye, the bargain,' grunted the demon. 'I have made so many. And so many have reneged of late . . . '

'I am still loyal to you, my lord.'

'I am under attack myself. Huge forces come against me on many planes, in many times. Men disrupt the multiverse. The balance has gone! The balance has gone! Chaos crumbles and Law is no more . . . '

Arioch seemed to be speaking more to himself than to Ymryl.

Ymryl said hesitantly: 'But your power? You still have your power?'

'Aye, much of it. Oh, I can aid you in your business here, Ymryl, for as long as it should last.'

'Last? What mean you, my Lord Arioch?'

But Arioch chewed the meat from the last bone and threw it down, dragging himself across the ground to peer towards the centre of the city.

Ilian shivered as she saw the face change to become fat, fleshy, jowelled, the teeth rotting. The lips moved as Arioch murmured to himself. *'It is a matter of perspective, Corum. We follow our whims . . . '* Arioch scowled. *'Ah, Elric, sweetest of my slaves . . . all turning – all turning. What means it?'* And the features changed again, to become the features of a handsome boy. *'The planes intersect, the balance tilts, the old battles become obscure, the old ways are no more. Do the gods truly die? Can the gods die?'*

And, for all she loathed the monster, Ilian felt a peculiar pang of sympathy for Arioch as she overheard his musings.

'How shall we strike, great Arioch?' Ymryl stepped up to his supernatural master. 'Will you lead us?'

'Lead you? It is not my way to lead mortals into battle. Ah!' Arioch let out a scream of agony. 'I cannot remain here!'

'You must, Arioch! Our bargain!'

'Yes, Ymryl, our bargain. I gave you the horn, that which is brother to the Horn of Fate. And there are so few still loyal to the Chaos Lords, so few worlds where we still survive . . . '

'Then you will give us power?'

Again Arioch's face changed, back to its primitive, demonic form. And Arioch growled, all the intelligence disappearing from his face. And he drew deep, snorting breaths, and his body began to change colour, to grow in size, to flare with reds and yellows as if a mighty furnace roared within him.

'He gathers his strength,' whispered Jhary-a-Conel, his lips close to Ilian's ear. 'We must strike now. Now, Ilian.'

He leapt, his flame-lance sending out its stream of ruby light. He jumped into the ranks of the great army and four warriors were cut down before any realized that an enemy had come among them. Now others of Ilian's warriors dropped from the trees, following Jhary's example. Katinka van Bak, Yisselda of Brass, Lyfeth of Ghant, Mysenal of Hinn – all jumped into the fray, jumped to certain death. And Ilian wondered why she hung back.

She saw Ymryl yell urgently at Arioch, saw Arioch reach out to touch Ymryl. Ymryl's body glowed, seeming to burn with the same fire which filled Arioch.

And Ymryl screamed, drawing his sword, and rushing upon Ilian's handful of warriors.

That was when Ilian jumped, placing herself between her folk and Ymryl.

Ymryl was possessed. His form radiated a monstrous energy as if Arioch himself possessed that mortal body. Ymryl's eyes, even, were the bestial eyes of Arioch. He snarled. He came at Ilian with his great sword hissing through the air. 'Ah, now, Ilian. This time you shall die. This time!'

And Ilian tried to block the blow, but so strong had Ymryl become that her sword was driven back against her body. She stumbled backward, again barely able to ward off Ymryl's next swipe at her. He fought with reasonless ferocity and she knew that he must kill her.

And behind Ymryl, Arioch had grown to huge proportions. His body continued to writhe, growing larger and larger, but containing less and less substance. The face altered constantly now, from second to second, and she heard a faint voice calling:

'*The balance! The balance! It sways! It bends! It melts! It is the doom of the gods! Oh, these puny creatures – these men . . .*'

And then Arioch was gone and only Ymryl was left, but an Ymryl filled with Arioch's terrible power.

Ilian continued to retreat before the rain of blows. Her arms were aching. Her legs and her back were aching. She was afraid. She did not want Ymryl to kill her.

Somewhere she heard another sound. Was it a yell of triumph? Did it mean that all her comrades were dead now, that Ymryl's soldiers had destroyed every one of them?

Was she the last of Garathorm?

She fell back as, with a terrific blow, Ymryl knocked the sword from her hand. Another blow split her buckler. Ymryl drew back his arm to deliver the death stroke.

## CHAPTER FOUR

## The Soul Gem

Ilian tried to stare Ymryl in his eyes as she died, those eyes which were no longer his own, but Arioch's.

But then the light in them began to fade and Ymryl looked about him in wonder. She heard him say:

'It is over, then? We go home?'

He seemed to be looking at scenery that was not the scenery of Garathorm. And he was smiling.

Ilian reached out and her hand grasped the hilt of her sword. With all her strength she thrust out at Ymryl and saw his blood spurt, his face become astonished, as gradually he faded into nothingness, as Arioch had faded before him.

Dazed, Ilian staggered upright, not knowing if she had killed Ymryl. Now she would never know.

Katinka van Bak lay nearby. She had a great, red wound in her body. Her face was white as if all her blood had gone. She was panting. As Ilian approached her, Katinka said:

'I heard the story of Hawkmoon's sword – the Sword of the Dawn it was called. It could summon warriors from another plane, another time. Could some other sword have summoned Ymryl . . . ?' She hardly knew what she was saying.

Jhary-a-Conel, supported by Yisselda of Brass, came limping out of the battle-dust. His leg was cut, but not deeply.

'So you saved us, after all, Ilian,' he said. 'As the Eternal Champion should!' He grinned. 'But does not, I'll admit, always do . . . '

'I saved you? No. I cannot explain this. Ymryl vanished!'

'You slew Kalan. It was Kalan who had created the circumstances which allowed Ymryl and the rest to come to Garathorm. With Kalan's death the rift in the multiverse begins to mend. In healing itself, it replaces Ymryl and all who served Ymryl back in their respective eras. I'm sure that's what happened. These are strange times, Ilian of Garathorm. Almost as strange for me as they are for you. I'm used to gods exerting their will – but Arioch – he is wretched now. Do the gods die in all planes, I wonder?'

'There have never been gods on Garathorm,' said Ilian. She bent to attend Katinka van Bak's wound, hoping that it was not as serious as it looked. But it was worse than it looked. Katinka van Bak was dying.

'They have all gone, then?' said Yisselda, hardly realizing, still, that their friend was so badly wounded.

'All – including corpses,' said Jhary. He was fumbling in the pouch at his belt. 'This will help her,' he said. 'A potion to kill pain.'

Ilian put the vial to Katinka van Bak's lips, but the warrior woman shook her head. 'No,' she said, 'it will make me sleep. I want to remain awake for what little life I have left. And I must go home.'

'Home? To Virinthorm?' said Ilian softly.

'No. To my own home. Back through the Bulgar Mountains.' Katinka sought with her eyes for Jhary-a-Conel. 'Will you take me there, Jhary?'

'We must have a litter,' he said. He called to Lyfeth, who had come up. 'Can some of your folk make a litter?'

Ilian said absently, 'You are all still alive? But how? I thought you went to your deaths . . . ?'

'The sea-folk!' said Lyfeth as she went away to help make the litter. 'Did you not see them?'

'The sea-folk? My attention was on that demon . . . '

'Just as Jhary leapt down into their camp, we saw their banners. That was why we chose to attack when we did. Look!'

Moving towards the trees to cut branches, Lyfeth pointed.

And Ilian smiled with pleasure as she saw the warriors there, each armed with a great harpoon-gun, each mounted on huge seal-like creatures. On only a few occasions had she seen the sea-folk, but she knew that they were proud and that they were strong, hunting the whales of the sea upon their amphibious beasts.

While Yisselda dressed Katinka van Bak's wounds, Ilian went to thank King Treshon, their leader.

He dismounted and bowed graciously. 'My lady,' he said. 'My queen.' Though an old man, he was still very fit and muscles rippled on his bronzed body. He wore a sleeveless mail shirt and a leather kilt, just as all his warriors did. 'Now we can make Garathorm live again.'

'Did you know of our battle?'

'No. We had spies watching Arnald of Grovent – he who finally became leader of those who took our towns. When he set off to march against Ymryl, we decided that it was the best time to strike – while they were divided and concentrating on attack from other quarters – '

'Just as we did!' Ilian said. 'It is happy for both of us that we decided upon the same strategy.'

'We were well-advised,' said King Treshon.

'Advised? By whom?'

'By yonder youth . . .' King Treshon indicated Jhary-a-Conel who was sitting next to Katinka van Bak and conversing with her in a low voice. 'He visited us a month or so since and outlined the plan we followed.'

Ilian smiled. 'He knows much, that youth.'

'Yes, my lady.'

Ilian reached into her belt purse and felt the hard edges of the black jewel. She was in a reflective mood as she trudged back to where Jhary sat, having taken her leave of King Treshon for the moment.

'You told me to keep the jewel safe,' she said. She took it from her purse, holding it up. 'Here it is.'

'I am glad it is still here,' said Jhary. 'I feared it would be whisked back to wherever Kalan's corpse now lies!'

'You planned much of what has happened here, Jhary-a-Conel, did you not?'

'Plan it? No. I serve, that is all. I do what must be done.' Jhary was pale. She noticed that he was trembling.

'What's ill? Did you sustain a worse wound that we thought?'

'No. But those forces which pulled Arioch and Ymryl from your world also demand that I leave, it seems. We must make haste to the cave.'

'The cave?'

'Where we first met.' Jhary got up and ran towards his yellow horse. 'Mount whatever there is to ride. Have two of your warriors bear Katinka's litter. Bring Yisselda of Brass with you. Quickly, to the cave!' And he was already riding.

Ilian saw that the litter was almost ready. She told Yisselda what Jhary had said and they went to find mounts.

'But why am I still in this world?' Yisselda said, frowning. 'Should not I have returned to the world where Kalan held me prisoner?'

'You feel nothing – nothing pulling you from here?' Ilian said.

'Nothing.'

Impulsively Ilian reached forward and kissed Yisselda lightly on the cheek. 'Farewell,' she said.

Yisselda was surprised. 'You do not come with us to the cave?'

'I come with you. But I wished to say goodbye. I cannot explain why.'

Ilian felt a mood of peace begin to descend on her. Again she touched the black jewel in her pouch. She smiled.

Jhary was standing in the cave-mouth when they arrived. He looked even weaker than before. He held his black and white cat tightly to his chest.

'Ah,' he said. 'I thought I would not be here. Good.'

Lyfeth of Ghant and Mysenal of Hinn had insisted on carrying Katinka van Bak's litter themselves. They made to carry it into the cave, but Jhary stopped them. 'I am sorry,' he said. 'You must wait here. If Ilian does not return, you must elect a new ruler in her place.'

'A new ruler? What do you intend to do with her?' Mysenal leapt forward, hand on his sword. 'What harm can befall her in that cave?'

'No harm. But Kalan's jewel still contains her soul . . . ' Jhary was sweating. He gasped and shook his head. 'I cannot explain now. Be assured I will protect your queen . . . '

And he followed Yisselda and Ilian, who were now carrying Katinka van Bak's litter, into the cave.

Ilian was astonished at how deep the cave was. It seemed to go on and on into the mountainside. And it became colder as they went deeper. Yet she said nothing, trusting Jhary.

She turned only once, when she heard Mysenal's excited voice in the distance, shouting: 'We blame you for nothing, now, Ilian! You are absolved . . . '

And she wondered at Mysenal's tone and why he should feel such urgency in expressing that sentiment. Not that it meant a great deal to her. She knew her guilt, whatever others said.

And then Katinka van Bak said weakly from her litter, 'Is this not the spot, Jhary-a-Conel?'

Jhary nodded. Since the light had faded, he had carried an odd globe in his hand – a globe which gleamed with light. He set this down upon the floor of the cavern and then Ilian gasped at what she saw. It was the corpse of a tall and handsome man, dressed all in furs. There was no wound on his body, nothing to indicate how he died. And his face reminded her of someone's. She closed her eyes. 'Hawkmoon . . . ' she murmured. 'My name . . . '

Yisselda was sobbing as she knelt down beside the corpse.

'Dorian! My love! My love!' She turned to look up at Jhary-a-Conel. 'Why did you not warn me of this?'

Jhary ignored her and turned instead to Ilian who was leaning dazedly against the wall of the cave. 'Give me the jewel,' he said. 'The

222

black jewel, Ilian. Give it to me.'

And when Ilian felt for the gem in her purse she found something that was warm, that vibrated.

'It is alive!' she said. 'Alive!'

'Aye.' He spoke urgently in a low, thin voice. 'Hurry. Kneel beside him . . .'

'The corpse?' Ilian drew back distastefully.

'Do as I say!' Jhary weakly dragged Yisselda back from Hawkmoon's body and made Ilian kneel. She did so reluctantly. 'Now, place the jewel upon his forehead – place it where you see the scar.'

Trembling, she did as he ordered.

'Place your own forehead against the gem.'

She bent and her forehead touched the pulsing jewel and suddenly she was falling *into* the jewel and *through* the jewel, and as she fell, someone else fell towards her – as if she fell towards a mirror image of herself. She cried out . . .

She heard Jhary's weak, 'Farewell!' and she tried to answer, but she could not. On and on she fell, through corridors of sensations, of memories, of guilt and of redemption . . .

And she was Asquiol and she was Arflane and she was Alaric. She was John Daker, Erekosë and Urlik. She was Corum and Elric and she was Hawkmoon . . .

'Hawkmoon!' she cried the name with her own lips and it was a battle-cry. She fought Baron Meliadus and Asrovaak Mikosevaar at the battle of the Kamarg. She fought Meliadus again at Londra and Yisselda was beside her. And she and Yisselda looked upon the battle-field when it was all over and they saw that of their comrades only they survived . . .

'Yisselda!'

'I am here, Dorian. I am here!'

He opened his eyes and he said: 'So Katinka van Bak did not betray me! But what a devious ruse to bring me to you. Why should she concoct so complicated a scheme?'

Katinka whispered from her litter. 'Perhaps you will find out one day, but not from me, for I save my breath. I need you two to take me out of these mountains, to Ukrainia where I wish to die.'

Hawkmoon got up. He was horribly stiff, as if he had lain in the same spot for months. He saw the blood on the bandages. 'You are wounded! I did not strike out. At least, I cannot recall . . .' He put his hand to his forehead. There was something warm there, like blood, but when he drew his fingers away there was only a faint, dark

223

radiance which flickered for a moment before it vanished. 'Then how – Jherek? Surely not . . . '

Katinka van Bak smiled. 'No. Yisselda will tell you how I got this.'

Another woman said in a soft and vibrant voice from behind Hawkmoon, 'She sustained her wound helping to save a country that was not her own.'

'Not for the first time has she been wounded thus,' said Hawkmoon turning. He stared at a face of extraordinary beauty and yet it was a face that had a sadness in it. A sadness that he felt he might define if he thought for a moment. 'We have met before?'

'You have met before,' said Katinka, 'but now you must part swiftly, for there will be other disruptions if you occupy the same plane for much longer. Believe my warning, Ilian of Garathorm. Go back now. Go back to Mysenal and Lyfeth. They will help you restore your country.'

'But . . . ' Ilian hesitated 'I would speak longer with Yisselda and this Hawkmoon.'

'You have not the right. You are two aspects of the same thing. Only on certain occasions can you meet. Jhary told me that. Go back. Hurry!'

Reluctantly the beautiful girl turned, her golden hair swinging, her chain-mail clinking. She began to walk into the darkness and soon she had vanished from sight.

'Where does the tunnel lead, Katinka van Bak,' Hawkmoon asked, 'to Ukrainia?'

'Not to Ukrainia. And soon it will lead to nowhere at all. I hope she fares well, that maid. She has much to do. And I have a feeling that she will meet Ymryl again.'

'Ymryl?'

Katinka van Bak sighed. 'I told you I would not waste my breath. I need it to keep me alive until we reach Ukrainia. Let us hope the sleigh still waits for us below.'

And Hawkmoon shrugged. He turned to look tenderly upon Yisselda. 'I knew you lived,' he said. 'They called me mad. But I knew you lived.'

They embraced. 'Oh, Dorian, such adventures I have had,' said Yisselda.

'Tell him about them later,' said the dying Katinka van Bak pettishly from her litter. 'Now pick up this stretcher and get me to that sleigh!'

As she stopped to take one end of the litter, Yisselda said: 'And how do the children fare, Dorian?'

And she wondered why Hawkmoon continued the rest of the journey through the tunnel in silence.

*This ends the Second of the Chronicles of Castle Brass*

# THE QUEST FOR TANELORN

To all those nomads who have
decided to settle in a nice spot . . .

# BOOK ONE

# THE WORLD INSANE: CHAMPION OF DREAMS

## CHAPTER ONE

## An Old Friend at Castle Brass

'Lost?'

'Aye.'

'But only dreams, Hawkmoon. Lost dreams?' The tone was nearly pathetic.

'I think not.'

Count Brass moved his great body away from the window so that light fell suddenly on Hawkmoon's gaunt face. 'Would that I had two grandchildren. Would that I had. Perhaps one day . . . '

It was a conversation which had been repeated so many times that it had become almost a ritual. Count Brass did not like mysteries; he did not respect them.

'There was a boy and a girl.' Hawkmoon was still tired, but there was no longer any madness in him. 'Manfred and Yarmila. The boy much resembled you.'

'We have told you this, father.' Yisselda, hands folded under her breasts, moved from the shade near the fireplace. She wore a green gown, cuffs and collar ermine-trimmed. Her hair was drawn back from her face. She was pale. She had been pale since her return, with Hawkmoon, to Castle Brass, more than a month ago. 'We told you – and we must find them.'

Count Brass ran heavy fingers through his greying red hair, his red brows furrowed. 'I did not believe Hawkmoon – but I believe you both now, though I do not wish to.'

'It is why you argue so, father.' Yisselda placed a hand upon his brocaded arm.

'Bowgentle could explain these paradoxes, possibly,' Count Brass continued, 'but there is no other who could find the kind of words which a plain-thinking soldier like myself could easily understand. You are of the belief that I have been brought back from the dead, yet I've no memory of dying. And Yisselda has been rescued from Limbo, when I, myself, thought her slain at the Battle of Londra. Now you speak of children, also somewhere in Limbo. A horrifying thought. Children experiencing such terrors! Ah! No! I will not consider it.'

'We have had to, Count Brass.' Hawkmoon spoke with the authority of a man who had faced many hours alone with his darkest thoughts. 'It is why we are determined to do everything we can to find them. It is why, today, we leave for Londra where we hope Queen Flana and her scientists can help us.'

Count Brass fingered his thick red moustaches. The mention of Londra had aroused other thoughts in his mind. There was a slight expression of embarrassment on his face. He cleared his throat.

There was kindly humour in Yisselda's eyes as she said, 'Is there a message we can give Queen Flana?'

Her father shrugged. 'The usual courtesies, of course. I intend to write. Perhaps I will have time to give you a letter before you leave.'

'She would be glad to see you in person again.' Yisselda glanced meaningly at Hawkmoon, who rubbed at the back of his neck. 'In her last letter she told me how much she had enjoyed your visit, father. She remarked on the wisdom of your counsel, the practical common sense of your advice in matters of State. There was a hint that she could offer you an official position at the Court of Londra.'

Count Brass's ruddy features seemed to take on a deeper shade of colour, a blush. 'She mentioned something of that. But she does not need me in Londra.'

'Not for your advice, certainly,' said Yisselda. 'Your support . . . ? She was fond of men, once. But with D'Averc's terrible death – I have heard that she has had no thoughts of marrying. I have heard that she has considered the question of an heir, but that there is only one man who could, in her opinion, compare with Huillam D'Averc. I speak clumsily . . . '

'Indeed you do, daughter. It is understandable, for your mind is full of other thoughts. I am touched, however, by your willingness to concern yourself with my very minor affairs.' Count Brass smiled and put his arm out to Yisselda. The brocade sleeve fell away to reveal his bronzed, heavily muscled forearm. 'But I am too old to marry. If I planned marriage, certainly I could think of no better wife than Flana. But the decision I made many years ago to live in virtual retirement in the Kamarg remains. Besides, I have my duty to the folk of the Kamarg. Would I abandon that?'

'We could take up that duty, as we did once when you were . . . ' She paused.

'Dead?' Count Brass frowned. 'I am grateful that I do not have such memories of you, Yisselda. When I returned from Londra and found you here I was full of joy. I asked for no explanation. It was enough that you lived. But then, I had seen you die at Londra some years before. It was a memory I was happy to doubt. A memory of children, though – to be haunted by such ghosts, by the knowledge that they are alive somewhere and afraid – Oh, that is terrifying!'

'It is a familiar terror,' said Hawkmoon. 'Hopefully we shall find them. Hopefully they know nothing of all this. Hopefully, in whatever other plane they now inhabit, they are happy.'

There came a knock on the door of Count Brass's study. He answered it in his gruff voice: 'Enter.'

Captain Josef Vedla opened the door, closed it behind him and stood in silence for a moment. The old soldier was clad in what he chose to call his civilian clothing – doeskin shirt, buckskin jerkin and breeks, boots of old, black leather. At his belt was a long dirk, apparently there not for any particular usefulness save to act as a familiar rest for his left hand. 'The ornithopter is almost ready,' he said. 'It will take you to Karlye. The Silver Bridge is completed, rebuilt in all its old beauty, and by means of it you may cross, Duke Dorian, as you wished, to Deau-Vere.'

'Thank you, Captain Vedla. It will please me to make this journey from the Kamarg by the route I used when I first came to Castle Brass.'

Her hand still in that of her father, Yisselda stretched her other hand out and took Hawkmoon's. Her steady eyes regarded his face and her grip tightened for a second on his fingers. He drew a deep breath. 'Then we must go,' he said.

'There was other news . . . ' Josef Vedla hesitated.

'Other news?'

'Of a rider, sir. He has been seen by our guardians. We received a heliograph message a few minutes ago. He comes towards the town . . . '

'Has he annouced himself at our borders?' Count Brass asked.

'That is what is strange, Count Brass. He was not seen at the borders. He was halfway into the Kamarg before he was sighted.'

'That is unusual. Our guardians are normally vigilant . . . '

'They are quite as vigilant today. He did not enter by any of the known roads.'

'Well, doubtless we'll have the opportunity of asking him how he avoided being seen,' said Yisselda calmly. 'After all, it is one rider, not an army.'

Hawkmoon laughed. For a moment they had all been overworried. 'Have him met, Captain Vedla. Invite him to the castle.'

Vedla saluted and left.

Hawkmoon went to the window and looked over the roofs of Aigues-Mortes to the fields and lagoons beyond the old town. The sky was a clear, pale blue and the distant water reflected it. A light, winter wind was blowing at the reed beds. He saw a movement on the wide, white road that came through the marshes to the town. He saw the rider. He was coming swiftly, at a steady canter, sitting upright in his saddle, sitting proudly, it seemed to Hawkmoon. And the rider's outline was familiar. Rather than peer at the distant figure, Hawkmoon turned away from the window, prepared to wait until it was close and could be identified easily.

'An old friend – or an old enemy,' he said. 'I recognize something about his stance.'

'We have had no announcement,' said Count Brass. He shrugged. 'But these are not the old days. These are calmer times.'

'For some,' said Hawkmoon, then he regretted the self-pity of his tone. He had had too much of such emotions. Now that he was rid of them he was, perhaps, overly sensitive to any traces of their return he detected in himself. From an over-indulgence in such feelings, he had now gone to a mood of intense stoicism which was a relief to all save those who knew him best and had the greatest affection for him. Sensitive to his thoughts, Yisselda reached to place delicate fingers upon his lips and then his cheek. Gratefully, he smiled at her, drawing her to him and kissing her lightly upon the forehead.

'Now I must prepare for our journey,' she said.

Hawkmoon was already dressed in the clothes in which he intended to travel.

'Will you and father wait here to receive our visitor?' she asked Hawkmoon.

He nodded. 'I think so. There is always hope that . . . '

'Do not expect it, my dear. There is little chance that he will bring news of Manfred and Yarmila.'

'True.'

With another smile at her father, Yisselda left the room.

Count Brass strode to a table of polished oak on which a tray had been set. He lifted a pewter mug. 'Would you share a glass of wine with me, Hawkmoon, before you go?'

'Thank you.'

Hawkmoon joined Count Brass at the table, accepting the carved wooden goblet the old warrior handed him. He sipped the wine and resisted the temptation to return to the window to see if he recognized the traveller.

'More than ever, I regret that Bowgentle is not here to advise us,' said Count Brass. 'All this talk of other planes of existence, of other possibilities, of dead friends still alive – it smacks of the occult. All my life I have looked with a cold eye upon superstitions; I have scoffed at pseudo-philosophical speculation. But I have not the kind of mind which can easily distinguish between mumbo-jumbo and that which falls into the province of the genuinely metaphysical.'

'Do not misinterpret what I say as morbid brooding,' Hawkmoon replied, 'but I have reason to hope that Bowgentle may, one day, be restored to us.'

'The difference between us, I suppose,' said Count Brass, 'is that you, for all your rediscovered toughness of mind, continue to allow yourself to entertain many forms of hope. Long ago, I dismissed Faith altogether – at least from my conscious thoughts. Yet you, Hawkmoon, discover it over and over again.'

'Aye – through many lives.'

'What?'

'I refer to my dreams. To those strange dreams of myself in so many different incarnations. I had identified those dreams with my madness, but now I am not so sure. They still come to me, you know.'

'You have not mentioned them since you returned here with Yisselda.'

'They have not tormented me as they once did. But they are familiar, still.'

'Every night?'

'Aye. Every night. The names – Elric, Erekosë, Corum – those are the chief ones. And there are others. And sometimes I see the Rune-staff, and sometimes a black sword. All seem significant. And sometimes, when I am alone, particularly when I ride the marshlands, they come to me in my waking hours. Faces, familiar and unfamiliar, float before me. Snatches of words are heard. And most common is that frightening phrase "Champion Eternal!" . . . Formerly I would have thought that only a madman could think of himself as a demigod . . . '

'I, too,' said Count Brass, pouring more wine for Hawkmoon. 'But it is others who make their heroes into demigods. Would that the world had no need for heroes.'

'A sane world will not need them.'

'But perhaps a sane world is a world without humankind.' Count Brass's smile was bleak. 'Perhaps it is we who make it what it is?'

'If an individual can make himself whole, so can our race,' said Hawkmoon. 'If I have Faith, Count Brass, that is why I retain it.'

'I wish that I shared such Faith. I see Man as destined, ultimately, to self-destruction. All that I hope for is that that destiny can be averted for as long as possible, that Man's most foolish actions can be restrained, that a little equilibrium can be maintained.'

'Equilibrium. The idea symbolized by the Cosmic Balance, by the Runestaff. Have I told you that I have come to doubt that philosophy? Have I told you that I have come to the conclusion that equilibrium is not enough – not in the sense you mean? Equilibrium in an individual is a fine thing – a balance between the needs of the mind and the needs of the body – maintained without self-consciousness. Certainly, let us aim for that. But what of the world? Would we tame it too much?'

'You have lost me, my friend.' Count Brass laughed 'I was never a cautious man, in the ordinary sense of the word, but I became a weary one. Perhaps it is weariness which now informs your thoughts?'

'It is anger,' said Hawkmoon 'We served the Runestaff. It costs us dear to serve it. Many died. Many were tormented. We still know a terrible despair. And we were told that we could call on its help when we needed it. Do we not need it now?'

'Perhaps we do not need it enough.'

Hawkmoon's laugh was grim. 'If you are right, I do not look forward much to a future when we *shall* need it enough!'

And then his head was filled by a revelation and he rushed to the window. But by now the figure had left the road and entered the town and could not be seen. 'I know that rider!'

There came a knock at the door. Hawkmoon went to it and flung it open.

And there he stood, tall and cocky and proud, with his hand on his hip and the heel of his other hand resting on the pommel of his plain sword, a folded cloak over his right shoulder, his bonnet at a tilt and a crooked grin on his red, raw face. It was the Orkneyman, the brother of the Warrior in Jet and Gold. It was Orland Fank, Servant of the Runestaff.

'Good day to ye, Duke of Köln,' he said.

Hawkmoon's brow was furrowed and his smile was bleak. 'Good day to you, Master Fank. Do you come asking favours?'

'The folk of Orkney ask nothing for nothing, Duke Dorian.'

'And the Runestaff – what does that ask?'

Orland Fank took a few paces into the room, Captain Vedla at his heels. He stood beside the fire and warmed his hands at it, glancing about him. There was sardonic amusement in his eyes, as if he relished their puzzlement.

'I thank ye for sending your emissary here with your invitation to guest at Castle Brass,' said Fank, winking up at Vedla, who was disconcerted still. 'I was not sure how ye'd receive me.'

'You were right to wonder, Master Fank.' Hawkmoon's own expression matched Fank's. 'I seem to remember something of an oath you swore, when we parted. Since then we have battled dangers quite as momentous as those we fought in the service of the Runestaff – and the Runestaff has been not one wit in evidence.'

Fank frowned. 'Aye, that's true. But blame neither myself nor the staff for that. Those forces affecting you and yours also affected the Runestaff. It is gone from this world, Hawkmoon of Köln. I have sought it in Amarehk, in Asiacommunista, in all the lands of this Earth. Then I heard rumours of your madness – of peculiar happenings here in the Kamarg – and I came, barely stopping, all the way from the Courts of Muskovia to visit you and ask you if you have an explanation for the events of the past year or so.'

'You – the Runestaff's oracle – come to ask us for information?' Count Brass let forth a bellow of laughter and slapped at his thigh. 'Oh, this is indeed a turning world!'

'I have information to exchange!' Fank drew himself up to face Count Brass, his back to the fire, his hand on his sword's hilt. All his amusement was suddenly gone from him and Hawkmoon noticed how drawn his face seemed, how tired his eyes were.

Hawkmoon poured out a cup of wine and handed it swiftly to Fank who accepted it, flashing Hawkmoon a quick glance of gratitude.

Count Brass regretted his outburst and his expression became sober. 'I am sorry, Master Fank. I am a poor host.'

'And I a poor guest, Count. I see from the activity in your courtyard that someone leaves Castle Brass today.'

'Yisselda and I go to Londra,' said Hawkmoon.

'Yisselda? So it is true. I heard different tales – that Yisselda was dead, that Count Brass was dead – and I could not deny or confirm them, for I found my memory playing peculiar tricks. I lost confidence in my own recollection of events . . . '

'We have all had that experience,' said Hawkmoon. And he told Fank of everything he could remember (it was garbled, there were some things he could only half remember, some things he could only guess at) concerning his recent adventures, which seemed to him unreal, and his recent dreams which seemed much more tangible. Fank continued to stand before the fire, his hands folded on his back, his head upon his chest, listening with absolute concentration to every word. Occasionally he would nod, sometimes he would grunt, and

237

very rarely he would ask for clarification of some phrase. While he listened, Yisselda, dressed in heavy jerkin and breeks for her journey, entered, and seated herself silently by the window, only speaking when, towards the end of Hawkmoon's account, she could add information of her own.

'It is true,' she said, when Hawkmoon had finished. 'The dreams seem the reality, and the reality seems the dream. Can you explain that, Master Fank?'

Fank sniffed, rubbing at his nose. 'There are many versions of reality, my lady. Some would say that our dreams reflect events in other planes. There is a great disruption taking place, but I do not think it was caused by the experiments of Kalan and Taragorm. As far as their work goes, I think the damage has been largely repaired. I think they were able to exploit this larger disruption for a while. Possibly they exacerbated the condition, but that is all. Their efforts were puny. They could not have caused all this. I suspect a vaster conflict. I suspect that there are forces at work so huge and terrifying that the Runestaff has been called from this individual plane to serve in a war of which we have received only a hint. A great war in which the destiny of the planes will be fixed for a period of time most would consider Eternity. I speak of something I know little about, my friends. I have only heard the phrase 'The Conjunction of the Million Spheres', spoken by a dying philosopher in the mountains of Asiacommunista. Means the phrase anything to you?'

The phrase was familiar to Hawkmoon, yet he was sure he had not heard it before, even in his strange dreams. He told Fank that.

'I had hoped ye'd know more, Duke Dorian. But I believe that phrase to have considerable significance to us all. Now I learn that ye seek lost children, while I seek the Runestaff. What of the world "Tanelorn"? Means that anything?'

'A city,' said Hawkmoon. 'The name of a city.'

'Aye. That is what I heard. Yet I have found no city of that name anywhere in this world. It must lie in some other. Would we find the Runestaff there? Would we find your children there?'

'In Tanelorn?'

'In Tanelorn.'

## CHAPTER TWO

## On the Silver Bridge

Fank had elected to remain at Castle Brass and so Hawkmoon and Yisselda climbed into the cushioned cabin of the great ornithopter. Ahead, in his small, open cockpit, the pilot began to manipulate the controls.

Count Brass and Fank stood outside the door of the castle watching as the heavy metallic wings began to beat and the strange motors of the ancient craft murmured, whispered and crooned. There came a fluttering of enamelled silver feathers, a lurch, a wind which set Count Brass's red hair pouring back from his head and caused Orland Fank to hang on to his bonnet; then the ornithopter began to rise.

Count Brass raised a hand in farewell. The machine banked a little as it rose over the red and yellow roofs of the town, then it wheeled once, turned to avoid a cloud of wild, giant flamingos which blossomed suddenly from one of the lagoons to the west, gained height and speed with each beat of its clashing wings, and soon it seemed to Hawkmoon and Yisselda that they were entirely surrounded by the cold, lovely blue of the winter sky.

Since their conversation with Orland Fank, Hawkmoon had been in a thoughtful mood and Yisselda, respecting this mood, had made no attempt to talk to him. Now he turned to her, smiling gently.

'There are still wise men in Londra,' he said. 'Queen Flana's court has attracted many scholars, many philosophers. Perhaps some will be able to help us.'

'You know of Tanelorn?' she said. 'The city Fank mentioned.'

'Only the name. I feel I *should* know much. I feel that I have been there, at least once, possibly many times, yet you and I both know that I have not.'

'In your dreams? Have you been there in your dreams, Dorian?'

He shrugged. 'Sometimes it seems to me that I have been everywhere in my dreams – in every age of the Earth – even beyond the Earth and to other worlds. I am convinced of one thing; that there are a thousand other Earths, even a thousand other galaxies – and that events in our world are mirrored in all the rest; that the same destinies are played out in subtly different ways. But whether those destinies are controlled by ourselves or by other, superhuman, forces, I do not know. Are there such things as Gods, Yisselda?'

'Men make Gods. Bowgentle once offered the opinion that the mind of Man is so powerful that it can make "real" anything it desperately needs to be real.'

'And perhaps those other worlds are real because, at some time in our history, enough people needed them. Could that be how alternative worlds are created?'

She shrugged. 'It is not something you and I are likely to prove, no matter how much information we are given.'

Tacitly, they both dropped this line of thought, contenting themselves with the magnificence of the views which passed below them as they peered through the portholes of the cabin. Steadily the ornithopter headed northward to the coasts, at length passing over the tinkling towers of Parye, the Crystal City, now restored in all its finery. The sunlight was reflected and transformed into rainbow colours by the scores of prisms, the spires of Parye, created by means of that city's timeless and cryptic technologies. They observed whole buildings, gilded and ancient, wholly enclosed in vast, apparently solid eight-, ten-, and twelve-sided crystal structures.

Half blinded, they fell back from the portholes, still able to see the sky all around them filled with soft, pulsating colours, still able to hear the gentle, musical ringing of the glass ornaments which the citizens of Parye used to decorate their quartz-paved streets. Even the warlords of the Dark Empire had let Parye stand; even those insane and bloody-handed destroyers had held the Crystal City in awe – and now she was fully restored to all her great beauty and it was said that the children of Parye were born blind, that it was often three years before their eyes were capable of accepting the everyday visions granted to those who habitually dwelled therein.

Parye behind them, they now entered grey cloud and the pilot, kept warm by the heater in his cockpit and the thick flying garments he wore, sought clearer sky above the cloud, found none, and dropped lower until they were barely two hundred feet from the flat, dull winter fields of the country lying inland from Karlye. A light drizzle was falling and, as the drizzle turned to driving rain, the sun began to set, so that they came to Karlye at dusk, seeing the warm lights welcoming them from the windows of the city's cobble-stone buildings. They circled over Karlye's quaintly designed roof tops of dark red and light grey slates, dropping, at length, into the bowl of the circular, grass-sown, landing field around which the city was built. For an ornithopter (never the most comfortable of flying machines) the vessel landed smoothly, with Hawkmoon and Yisselda clinging firmly to the straps provided until the bumping had stopped and the pilot, his transparent visor streaming with moisture, turned to indicate to them that they might leave. The rain beat heavily now upon the cabin's canopy and Hawkmoon and Yisselda dressed themselves in thick capes which covered them to their feet. Across the landing field men came running, bodies bent into the wind, and behind them was a hand-drawn carriage. Hawkmoon waited until the carriage had been positioned as close as possible to the ornithopter, then he drew open the oddly shaped door and helped Yisselda to cross the sodden ground to the vehicle. They climbed in, and with a rather exaggerated lurch, the carriage moved towards the buildings on the far side of the field.

'We'll lodge in Karlye tonight,' said Hawkmoon, 'and leave early in the morning for the Silver Bridge.'

Count Brass's agents in Karlye had already secured rooms for the Duke of Köln and Yisselda of Brass; these were situated not far from the landing field, in a small but extremely comfortable inn which was one of the few buildings to have survived the conquerings of the Dark Empire. Yisselda remembered that she had stayed here with her father when she was a child and at first she felt a simple delight until her own childhood reminded her of her lost Yarmila, and then her brow became clouded. Hawkmoon, realizing what had happened, put his arm around her shoulders to comfort her when, after eating a good supper, they went upstairs to bed.

The day had tired them and neither was of a disposition to stay awake talking, for there was little left to talk about, so they slept.

But Hawkmoon's sleep was almost immediately populated by his all too familiar dreams – faces and images jostling for his attention – eyes imploring him, hands beseeching him, as if a whole world, perhaps a whole universe, cried out for his attention and his aid.

*And he was Corum – alien Corum of the Vadhagh – riding against the foul Fhoi Myore, the Cold Folk from Limbo ...*

*And he was Elric – Last Prince of Melniboné – a shouting battle-blade in his right hand, his left upon the pommel of an oddly wrought saddle, the saddle on the back of a huge reptilian monster whose saliva turned to fire wherever it dripped ...*

*And he was Erekosë – poor Erekosë – leading the Eldren to victory over his own human people – And he was Urlik Skarsol, Prince of the Southern Ice, crying out in despair at his fate, which was to bear the Black Sword ...*

241

TANELORN . . .

*Oh, where was Tanelorn . . . ?*

*Had he not been there, at least once? Did he not recall a sense of absolute peace of mind, of wholeness of spirit, of the happiness which only those who have suffered profoundly may feel*

TANELORN . . .

*'Too long have I borne my burden – too long have I paid the price of Erekosë's great crime . . . ' It was his voice which spoke, but it was not his lips which formed the words – they were other lips, unhuman lips . . . 'I must have rest – I must have rest . . . '*

*And now there came a face – a face of ineffable evil, but it was not a confident face – a dark face – was it desperate? Was it his face? Was this his face, too?*

*AH, I SUFFER!*

*This way and that, the familiar armies marched. Familiar swords rose and fell. Familiar faces screamed and perished, and blood flowed from body after body – a familiar flowing . . .*

*TANELORN – have I not earned the peace of Tanelorn?*

*Not yet, Champion. Not yet . . .*

*It is unjust that I, alone, should suffer so!*

*You do not suffer alone. Mankind suffers with you.*

*It is unjust!*

*Then make justice!*

*I cannot. I am only a man.*

*You are the Champion. You are the Eternal Champion.*

*I am a man!*

*You are a man. You are the Champion Eternal.*

*I am only a man!*

*You are only the Champion.*

*I am Elric! I am Urlik! I am Erekosë! I am Corum! I am too many. I am too many!*

*You are one.*

And now, in his dreams (if dreams they were), Hawkmoon felt, for a brief instant, a sense of peace, an understanding too profound for words. He was one. He was one . . .

But then it was gone and he was many again. And he yelled in his bed and he begged for peace.

And Yisselda was clinging to his threshing body. And Yisselda was weeping. And light fell on his face from the window. It was dawn.

'Dorian. Dorian. Dorian.'

'Yisselda.'

He drew a deep breath. 'Oh, Yisselda.' And he was grateful that at least she had not been taken from him, for he had no other consolation but her in all the world, in all the many worlds he experienced while he slept; so he held her close to him in his strong warrior's arms, and he wept for a little while, and she wept with him. Then they rose from the bed and dressed themselves and in silence they left the inn without breakfasting, mounting the good horses which waited for them. They rode away from Karlye, along the coast road, through the rain which swept from the grey, turbulent sea, until they came to the Silver Bridge which spanned thirty miles of water between the mainland and the isle of Granbretan.

The Silver Bridge was not as Hawkmoon had seen it, all those many years before. Its tall pylons, obscured now by mist, by rain, and, at their tops, by cloud, no longer bore motifs of warfare and Dark Empire glories; instead they were decorated with designs supplied by all the cities of the continent which the Dark Empire warlords had once pillaged – a great variety of designs, celebrating the harmony of Nature. The vast causeway still measured a quarter of a mile wide, but previously, when Hawkmoon had crossed it, it had carried war-machines, the loot of a hundred great campaigns, the beast-warriors of the Dark Empire. Now trading caravans came and went along its two main roads; travellers from Normandia, from Italia, Slavia, Rolance, Scandia, from the Bulgar Mountains, from the great German city-states, from Pesht and from Ulm, from Wien, from Krahkov and even from distant, mysterious Muskovia. There were waggons drawn by horses, by oxen, by elephants, even. There were trains of camels, mules and donkeys. There were carts propelled by mechanical devices, often faulty, often faltering, whose principles were understood by only a handful of clever men and women (and most of them could understand only in the abstract) but which had worked for a thousand years or more; there were men on horseback and there were men who had walked hundreds of miles to cross the wonder that was the Silver Bridge. Clothing was often outlandish, some of it dull, patched, dusty, some of it vulgar in its magnificence. Furs, leather, silks, plaids, the skins of strange beasts, the feathers of rare birds, decorated the heads and backs of the travellers, and some who were clad in the greatest finery suffered the most in the chill rain which soaked through the subtly dyed fabrics and quickly found the unadorned flesh beneath. Hawkmoon and Yisselda travelled in heavy, warm gear that was plain, bereft of any decoration, but their steeds were sturdy and carried them without tiring, and soon they had joined the throng heading westward towards a land once feared by all but now transformed, under Queen Flana, into a centre of art and

243

trade and learning and just government. There would have been several quicker ways of reaching Londra, but Hawkmoon's desire was strong to reach the city by the same means he had first left it.

His spirits improved as he looked at the quivering hawsers supporting the main causeway, at the intricate workmanship of the silversmiths who had fashioned decorations many inches thick to cover the strong steel of the pylons which had been built not only to bear millions of tons in weight but also to withstand the perpetual pounding of the waves, the pressure of the deepest currents so far beneath the surface. Here was a monument to what man could achieve, both useful and beautiful, without need of supernatural agencies of any sort. All his life he had despised that sad and insecure philosophy which argued that man, alone, was not great enough to achieve marvels, that he must be controlled by some superhuman force (gods, more sophisticated intelligences from somewhere beyond the Solar System) to have achieved what he had achieved. Only those frightened of the power within their own minds could have need of such views, thought Hawkmoon, noticing that the sky was clearing and a little sunlight was beginning to touch the silver hawsers and make them glint more brightly than before. He drew in a deep breath of the ozone-laden air, smiling as gulls wheeled about the upper levels of the pylons, pointing out the sails of a ship just before it passed under the bridge and beyond their view, commenting on the beauty of a particular bas-relief, the originality of a particular piece of silverwork. Both he and Yisselda became calmer as they took an interest in all the sights and they spoke of the pleasure they would experience if Londra were half as beautiful as this reborn bridge.

And then it seemed to Hawkmoon that a silence fell upon the Silver Bridge, that the clatter of the waggons and the hooves of the beasts disappeared, that the crying of the gulls ceased, that the sound of the waves went away, and he turned to mention this to Yisselda and she had gone. And he looked about him and he realized, in dawning terror, that he was quite alone on the ridge.

There was a thin cry from very far away – a cry which might have been Yisselda calling to him – then that, too, was gone.

And Hawkmoon made to wheel his horse about, to ride back the way he had come in the hope that, if he moved swiftly, he could rejoin Yisselda.

But Hawkmoon's horse refused to be handled. It was snorting. It stamped at the metal of the bridge. It whinnied.

And Hawkmoon, betrayed, screamed a single, agonized word.
'NO!'

## CHAPTER THREE

## In the Mist

'No!'

It was another voice – a booming, pain-racked voice, far louder than Hawkmoon's, louder than thunder.

And the bridge swayed and the horse reared and Hawkmoon was thrown heavily to the metal causeway. He tried to rise; he tried to crawl back to where he was sure he would find Yisselda.

'Yisselda!' he cried.

'Yisselda!'

And wicked laughter sounded behind him.

He turned his head, lying spreadeagled on the swaying bridge. He saw his horse, its eyes rolling, tumble over, slide to the edge, to be pinned against a rail, its legs kicking at the air.

Now Hawkmoon tried to reach for the sword beneath his cloak, but he could not free it. It was pinned beneath him.

The laughter came again, but its pitch and its tone changed; it was less confident. Then the voice gave out its bellowing echo:

'No!'

Hawkmoon knew a terrible fear, a fear greater than anything he had previously confronted. His impulse was to crawl away from the source of that fear, but he forced himself to turn his head again and look at the face.

The face filled his whole horizon, glaring out of the mist which swirled around the swaying bridge. The dark face of his dreams, its eyes were filled with glaring menace, with a complicated terror of its own, and the huge lips formed the word which was a challenge, a command, a plea:

'No!'

Then Hawkmoon climbed to his feet and stood with his legs apart, balancing himself, staring back at the face, staring by virtue of an effort of will which astonished him.

'Who are you?' said Hawkmoon. His voice was thin, the mist seemed to absorb the words. 'Who are you? Who are you?'

'No!'

The face was apparently without a body. It was beautiful and sinister and of a dark, indeterminate colour. The lips were a glowing unhealthy red; the eyes were perhaps black, perhaps blue, perhaps brown, and there was a kind of gold in the pupils.

Hawkmoon knew that the creature was in torment, but he knew, too, that it menaced him, that it would destroy him if it could. Again his hand went to his sword, but fell away as he realized how useless the blade would be, what an empty gesture it would be if he drew it.

'SWORD . . . ' said the being. 'SWORD . . . ' The word had considerable meaning. 'SWORD . . . ' Once again its tone changed, to that of an unrequited lover, pleading for the return of the object of its love and hating itself for its wretchedness, hating, too, that which it loved. There was a threat in its voice; there was death there.

'ELRIC? URLIK? ME . . . I WAS A THOUSAND . . . ELRIC? ME . . . ?'

Was this some fearful manifestation of the Champion Eternal – of Hawkmoon himself? Did he look upon his own soul?

'ME . . . THE TIME . . . THE CONJUNCTION . . . I CAN HELP . . . '

Hawkmoon dismissed the thought. It was possible that the being represented something within himself, but it was not the whole of him. He knew that it had a separate identity and he knew, also, that it needed flesh, it needed form, and that was what he could give it. Not his own flesh, but something which was his.

'Who are you?' Hawkmoon felt strength enter his voice as he forced himself to look upon the dark, glaring face.

'ME . . . '

The eyes focused on Hawkmoon and they glowed with hatred. Hawkmoon's instinct was to step backward, but he held his ground and returned the glare of those evil, gigantic eyes. The lips snarled and revealed jagged, flaming teeth. Hawkmoon trembled.

Words came to Hawkmoon and he spoke them firmly, though he did not know their origin, or their import, only that they were the right words.

'You must go,' he said. 'You have no place here.'

'I MUST SURVIVE – THE CONJUNCTION – YOU WILL SURVIVE WITH ME, ELRIC . . . '

'I am not Elric'

'YOU ARE ELRIC!'

'I am Hawkmoon.'

'WHAT OF IT? A MERE NAME. IT IS AS ELRIC THAT I LOVE YOU MOST. I HAVE HELPED YOU SO WELL . . . '

'You mean to destroy me,' said Hawkmoon, 'that I do know, I'll accept no help from you. It is your help which has chained me through millennia. It will be the last action of the Champion Eternal to take part in your destruction!'

'YOU KNOW ME?'

'Not yet. Fear the time when I *shall* know you!'

'ME ...'

'You must go. I begin to recognize you.'

'NO!'

'You must go.' Hawkmoon felt his voice begin to quaver and he doubted if he could look upon that terrible face for another moment.

'Me ...' The voice was fainter, it threatened less, it pleaded more.

'You must go.'

'*Me* ...'

Then Hawkmoon summoned all that remained of his will and he laughed at it.

'Go!'

Hawkmoon spread his arms wide as he began to fall, for face and bridge had vanished at the same moment.

He fell through chilling mist, head over heels, his cloak flapping about him and tangling itself in his legs – through chilling mist and into cold water. He gasped. His mouth filled with the salt of the sea. He coughed and his lungs were full of shards of ice. He forced the water out, striking upwards, trying to reach the surface. He began to drown.

His body heaved as it tried to draw in air and force out water, but there was only water for it to breathe. Once he opened his eyes and saw his hands, and his hands were the bone-white hands of a corpse; white hair drifted about his face. He knew his name was no longer Hawkmoon, so he closed his eyes tight shut again and repeated his old battle cry, the battle cry of his ancestors which he had voiced a hundred times in his wars against the Dark Empire.

*Hawkmoon ... Hawkmoon ... Hawkmoon ...*

'Hawkmoon!'

This was not his own shout. It came from above him, from out of the mist. He forced his body to the surface. He blew the water from his lungs. He gasped at the freezing air.

'Hawkmoon!'

There was a dark outline on the surface of the ocean. There was a regular splashing sound.

'Here!' cried Hawkmoon.

The small rowing boat came slowly towards him, its oars rising and falling. A small figure sat in it. He was swathed in a heavy sea-cloak, there was a wide-brimmed, dripping hat obscuring the greater part of his features, but the grin on his lips was unmistakable, and unmistakable, too, was his companion who sat in the prow of the boat looking with apparent concern in its yellow eyes at Hawkmoon. It was a very wet little creature, that black and white cat. It spread its wings once, to shake moisture from them. It mewed.

Hawkmoon clutched the wooden side of the boat and Jhary-a-Conel methodically shipped his oars before reaching carefully down to help the Duke of Köln aboard.

'It is wise for such as me to trust to his instincts,' said Jhary-a-Conel, handing Hawkmoon a flask of some strong spirit. 'Do you know where we are, Dorian Hawkmoon?'

Unable to speak for the water still in his lungs and stomach, Hawkmoon lay back in the boat and shivered and vomited until Jhary-a-Conel, self-styled Companion to Heroes, began once more to row.

'I thought it first a river, then a lake,' said Jhary conversationally, 'then I decided it must be a sea. You have swallowed a great deal of it. What do you say?'

Hawkmoon spat the last of the water over the side. He wondered at his impulse to laugh. 'A sea,' he said. 'How came you to be boating on it?'

'An impulse.' Jhary seemed to notice the small black and white cat for the first time and showed surprise. 'Aha! So I am Jhary-a-Conel, am I?'

'You were uncertain?'

'I think I had another name when I began to row. Then the mist came.' Jhary shrugged. 'No matter. For me, it's a familiar enough event. Well, well, Hawkmoon, how came you to be *swimming* in this sea?'

'I fell from a bridge,' said Hawkmoon simply, not wishing, for the moment, to discuss the experience. He did not bother to ask Jhary-a-Conel whether they were nearer to France or to Granbretan, particularly since it was just beginning to dawn on him that he had no business remembering Jhary's name or feeling such a close familiarity with him. 'I met you in the Bulgar Mountains, did I not? With Katinka van Bak?'

'I seem to recall something of that. You were Ilian of Garathorm for a while, then Hawkmoon again. How swiftly your names change, these days! You threaten to confuse me, Duke Dorian!'

'You say my names change. You have known me in different guises?'

'Certainly. Enough for this particular conversation to have a boring familiarity.' Jhary-a-Conel grinned.

'Tell me some of those names.'

Jhary frowned. 'My memory is poor on such matters. Sometimes it seems to me I can recall a great deal of past (and future) incarnations. At other times, like this one, my mind refuses to consider anything but immediate problems.'

'I find that inconvenient,' said Hawkmoon. He looked up, as if he might see the bridge, but there was only mist. He prayed that Yisselda was safe, that she was still on her way to Londra.

'Oh, so do I, Duke Dorian. I wonder if I have any business here at all, you know.' Jhary-a-Conel pulled strongly at his oars.

'What of the "Conjunction of the Million Spheres"? Does your faulty memory serve you with any information concerning that phrase?'

Jhary-a-Conel frowned. 'It rings a distant bell. An event of some importance, I should have thought. Tell me more.'

'There is no more I can tell you. I had hoped . . . '

'If I should remember anything, I will tell you.'

The cat mewled again and Jhary craned his head around. 'Aha! Land of some sort. Let us hope it is friendly.'

'You have no idea where we are, then?'

'None at all, Duke Dorian.' The bottom of the boat scraped against shingle. 'Somewhere in one of the Fifteen Planes, it's to be hoped.'

## CHAPTER FOUR

The Gathering of the Wise

They had walked for five miles over chalky hills and seen no sign that this land was inhabited. Hawkmoon had told Jhary-a-Conel of everything that had befallen him, of everything which puzzled him. He remembered little of the adventure of Garathorm and Jhary remembered more, speaking of the Lords of Chaos, of Limbo and the perpetual struggle between the Gods, but all their conversation, as conversation often will, caused further confusion and at length they agreed to put an end to their various speculations.

'Only one think I know, and I know that in my bones,' said Jhary-a-Conel, 'and that is that you need not fear for your Yisselda. I must admit that I am, by nature, optimistic – against considerable evidence on occasion – and I know that in this venture we stand to win much or lose all. That creature you encountered on the bridge must have considerable power if he could wrench you from your own world, and there is no question, of course, that he means you ill, but I have no inkling of his identity or when he will find us again. It seems to me that your ambition to find Tanelorn is pertinent.'

'Aye,' Hawkmoon looked around him. They stood on the crown of one of many low hills. The sky was clearing and the mist had vanished altogether and there was an eerie silence and the landscape was remarkable in that all that seemed to live was the grass itself; there were no birds, no signs of the kind of wildlife which might be expected to flourish here in the absence of man. 'Yet our chances of finding Tanelorn seem singularly poor at this particular moment, Jhary-a-Conel.'

Jhary reached up to his shoulder to stroke the black and white cat which had sat there patiently since they had begun their march inland. 'I am bound to agree,' he said. 'Nonetheless it seems to me that our coming to this silent land was not merely fortuitous. We are bound to have friends, you know, as well as enemies.'

'Sometimes I doubt the worth of the kind of friends you mean,' Hawkmoon said bitterly, remembering Orland Fank and the Runestaff. 'Friends or enemies – we are still their pawns.'

'Well,' said Jhary-a-Conel with a grin, 'not pawns, perhaps – you must judge your worth better than that – why, I myself am at least a knight!'

'My objection,' said Hawkmoon firmly, 'is to being placed on the board at all.'

'Then it is for you to remove yourself from it,' Jhary said mysteriously, adding: 'even if it should mean the destruction of the board itself.' He refused to amplify this remark, saying that it was intuition, not logic, which had led him to make it. But the remark had considerable resonance in Hawkmoon's mind and, oddly, it improved his spirits considerably. With increased energy, he set off again, taking such great strides that Jhary was hard put to keep up with him and soon began to complain, begging Hawkmoon to slow a little.

'We are not exactly certain where we are going, after all,' said Jhary.

Hawkmoon laughed. 'Indeed! But at this moment, Jhary-a-Conel, I care not if we head for Hell!'

The low hills rolled on in all directions and by nightfall their legs were aching greatly and their stomachs felt exceptionally empty and still there was no sign that this world was populated by any living thing but themselves.

'We should be grateful, I suppose,' said Hawkmoon, 'that the weather is reasonably clement.'

'Though dull,' added Jhary. 'Neither hot nor cold. Could this be some pleasanter corner of Limbo, I wonder.'

Hawkmoon's attention was no longer with his friend. He was peering through the dusk. 'Look, Jhary. Yonder. Do you see something?'

Jhary followed Hawkmoon's pointing hand. He screwed up his eyes. 'On the brow of the hill?'

'Aye. Is it a man?'

'I think it is.' Impulsively, Jhary cupped his hands around his mouth, shouting: 'Hey! Can you see us? Are you a native of these parts, sir?'

Suddenly the figure was very much closer. It had an aura of black fire flickering around its whole body. It was clad in black, shining stuff that was not metal. Its dark face was hidden by a high collar, but enough was visible for Hawkmoon to recognize it.

'Sword . . . ' said the figure. 'Me,' it said. 'Elric.'

'Who are you?' This was Jhary speaking. Hawkmoon could not speak – his throat was cramped, his lips dry. 'Is this your world?'

Fierce agony burned in the eyes; fierce hatred burned there. The figure made a motion towards Jhary – a belligerent motion as if he would tear the little man apart – but then something stopped him. He drew back. He looked at Hawkmoon again. He was snarling. 'Love,' he said. 'Love.' He spoke the word as if it was new to him, as if he were trying to learn it. The black flame around his body flared, flickered and dimmed, like a breeze-blown candle. He gasped. He pointed at Hawkmoon. He raised his other hand, as if to bar Hawkmoon's path. 'Do not go. We have been too long together. We cannot part. Once I commanded. Now I plead with you. What have I done for you but help you in all your many manifestations? Now they have taken my form away. You must find it, Elric. That is why you live again.'

'I am not Elric. I am Hawkmoon.'

'Ah, yes. I remember now. The jewel. The jewel will do. But the sword is better.' The beautiful features writhed in pain. The horrid eyes glared, so filled with anguish at that moment. The fingers curled like hawk's claws. The body shuddered. The flame waned.

'Who are you?' said Hawkmoon this time.

'I have no name, unless you give me one. I have no form, unless you find it for me. I have only power. Ah! And pain!' The figure's features writhed again. 'I need . . . I need . . . '

Jhary made an impatient movement towards his hip, but Hawkmoon's hand stayed him. 'No. Do not draw it.'

'The sword,' said the creature eagerly.

'No,' said Hawkmoon quietly. And he did not know what he refused the creature. It was dark now, but the figure's darker aura pierced the ordinary blackness of the night.

'A sword!' It was a demand. A scream. 'A sword!'

For the first time, Hawkmoon realized that the creature had no weapons of its own. 'Find arms, if you wish them,' he said. 'You shall not have ours.'

Lightning leaped suddenly from the ground around the creature's feet. It gasped. It hissed. It shrieked. 'You will come to me! You will need me! Foolish Elric! Silly Hawkmoon! Stupid Erekosë! Pathetic Corum! You will need me!'

The scream seemed to last for several moments, even after the figure had vanished.

'It knows all your names,' said Jhary-a-Conel. 'Do you know what it is called?'

Hawkmoon shook his head. 'Not even in my dreams.'

'It is new to me,' Jhary told him. 'In all my many lives I do not think I have encountered it before. My memory is never good, at the best of times, but I would know if I had seen that being before. This is a strange adventure, an adventure of unusual significance.'

Hawkmoon interrupted his friend's musings. He pointed down into the valley. 'Would you say that was a fire, Jhary? A camp fire. Perhaps we are to meet the denizens of this world at long last.'

Without debating the wisdom of approaching the fire directly, they began to plod down the hill, coming at last to the floor of the valley. The fire was only a short distance from them now.

As they approached Hawkmoon saw that the fire was surrounded by a group of men, but what was peculiar about the scene was that each of the men was mounted on a horse and each horse faced inward so that the group made a perfect, silent circle. So still were the horses, so stolidly did the riders sit in their saddles, that if it had not been for the sight of their breath steaming from their lips, Hawkmoon would have guessed them to be statues.

'Good evening,' he said boldly, but he received no reply from any of them. 'We are travellers who have lost our way and would appreciate your help in finding it again.'

The rider nearest to Hawkmoon turned his long head. 'It is why we are here, Sir Champion. It is why we have gathered. Welcome. We have been waiting for you.'

Now that Hawkmoon saw it closer to, he realized that the fire was no ordinary fire. Rather it was a radiance, emanating from a sphere about the size of his fist. The sphere hovered a foot above the ground. Within it Hawkmoon thought he could see other spheres circulating. He returned his attention to the mounted men. He did not recognize the one who had spoken: a tall, black man, his body half naked, his shoulders swathed in a cloak of white fox fur. He made a short, polite bow. 'You have the advantage of me,' he said.

'You know me,' the black man told him, 'in at least one of your parallel existences. I'm named Sepiriz, the Last of the Ten.'

'And is this your world?'

Sepiriz shook his head. 'This is no one's world. This world still waits to be populated.' He looked beyond Hawkmoon at Jhary-a-Conel. 'Greetings, Master Moonglum of Elwher.'

'I am called Jhary-a-Conel at present,' Jhary told him.

'Yes,' said Sepiriz. 'Your face is different. And your body, now I look closely. Still, you did well in bringing the Champion to us.'

Hawkmoon glanced at Jhary. 'You knew where we were going?'

Jhary spread his hands. 'Only in the back of my mind. I could not have told you, if you had asked.' He stared frankly at the circle of horsemen. 'So you are all here.'

'You know them all?' asked Hawkmoon.

'I think so. My Lord Sepiriz – from the Chasm of Nihrain are you not? And Abaris, the Magi.' This an old man clad in a rich gown embroidered with curious symbols. He smiled a quiet smile, acknowledging his name 'And you are Lamsar the Hermit,' said Jhary-a-Conel to the next horseman, who was even older than Abaris, and dressed in oiled leather to which patches of sand clung. His beard too, had sand in it. 'I greet you,' he murmured.

In astonishment, Hawkmoon recognized another of the riders. 'You are dead,' he said. 'You died in defense of the Runestaff at Dnark.'

There came laughter from within the mysterious helm as the Warrior in Jet and Gold, Orland Fank's brother, flung back his armoured head. 'Some deaths are more permanent than others, Duke of Köln.'

'And you are Aleryon of the Temple of Law,' said Jhary to another old man, a pale, beardless man. 'Lord Arkyn's servant. And you are Amergin the Archdruid. I know you, too.'

Amergin, handsome, his hair bound with gold, his white garments loose on his lean body, inclined a grave head.

The last rider was a woman, her face completely covered by a golden veil, her filmy robes all of a kind of silver colour. 'Your name, lady, escapes me,' said Jhary, 'though I think I recognize you from some other world.'

And Hawkmoon found himself saying, 'You were slain on the South Ice. The Lady of the Chalice. The Silver Queen. Slain by . . . '

'By the Black Sword? Count Urlik, I would not have known you.' Her voice was sad and it was sweet and suddenly Hawkmoon saw himself, clad all in furs and armour, standing on a plain of glinting ice, a huge and horrible sword in his hand, and he shut his eyes tight and groaned. 'No . . . '

'It is over,' she said. 'It is over. I did you a great disservice, Sir Champion. Now I would help you further.'

The seven riders dismounted as one and moved closer to the small sphere.

'What is that globe?' asked Jhary-a-Conel nervously. 'It is magical, is it not?'

'It is what allows all seven of us to remain upon this plane,' said Sepiriz. 'We are, as you know, considered wise in our own worlds. This gathering was called so that we could debate events, for all of us have had the same experience. Our wisdom came from beings greater than ourselves. They gave us their knowledge when we called upon them for it. But, of late, it has been impossible to seek that knowledge. They are all engaged in matters of such moment that they have no time for us. To some of us these beings are known as the Lords of

Law and we serve them as their messengers – in return they illuminate our minds. But we have had no word from those great Lords and
we fear that they are under attack from a force greater than any they
have previosly encountered.'

'From Chaos?' Jhary asked.

'Possibly. But we have learned, too, that Chaos is under attack
also, and not from Law. The Cosmic Balance itself, it seems, is
threatened.'

'And that is why the Runestaff has been called from my world,'
said Hawkmoon.

'That is why,' agreed the Warrior in Jet and Gold.

'And do you have any inkling of the nature of this threat?' Jhary
asked.

'None, save that it seems to have something to do with the Conjunction of the Million Spheres. But you know of that, Sir
Champion.' Sepiriz was about to continue when Jhary raised a hand
to stop him.

'I know the phrase, but no more. My bad memory – which saves
me from so much grief – tricks me again . . . '

'Ah,' said Sepiriz, frowning. 'Then perhaps we should not speak of
it . . . '

'Speak of it, I beg you,' said Hawkmoon, 'for the phrase means
much to me.'

'Law and Chaos are engaged in a great war – a war fought on all
the planes of the Earth – a war in which humanity is completely,
unwittingly, involved. You, as humanity's Champion, fight in each of
your manifestations – ostensibly on the side of Law (though even that
is disputed).' Sepiriz sighed. 'But Law and Chaos exhaust themselves.
Some think they lose the power to maintain the Cosmic Balance and
that when the Balance fades, then all existence ends. Others believe
the Balance and the Gods all doomed, that the time of the Conjunction of the Million Spheres has come to us. I have said nothing of this
to Elric, in my native world, for he is already greatly confused. I do
not know how much to tell you, Hawkmoon. The morality of guessing at such monumental problems disturbs me. Yet if Elric is to blow
the Horn of Fate – '

'And Corum is to release Kwll,' added Aleryon.

'And Erekosë to come to Tanelorn,' said the Lady of the Chalice.

' – then it can only result in a cosmic disruption of unimaginable
magnitude. Our wisdom fails us. We are almost afraid to act; there is
nothing to advise us. No one to tell us what the best course may
be . . . '

'No one, save the Captain,' said Abaris of the Magi.

'And how do we know that he does not work for his own ends? How do we know if he is as altruistic as he makes out?' Lamsar the Hermit spoke in a tone of worried bewilderment. 'We know nothing of him. He has only recently appeared in the Fifteen Planes.'

'The Captain?' Hawkmoon said eagerly. 'Is he a being who radiates darkness?' He described the creature he had seen on the bridge and, earlier, in this world.

Sepiriz shook his head. 'That being some of us have seen briefly – but he, too, is mysterious. That is why we are so uncertain – these different creatures come to the multiverse and we know nothing of them. Our wisdom fails us . . . '

'Only the Captain has confidence,' said Amergin. 'He must go to him. We cannot help.' He looked intently at the shining globe in their midst. 'The little sphere – is the light fading?'

Hawkmoon looked at the sphere and saw that Amergin was right. 'Is that significant?' he asked.

'It means that we have little time left here,' said Sepiriz. 'We are to be recalled to our own worlds, our own times. We shall never be able to meet again in this way.'

'Tell me more of the Conjunction of the Million Spheres,' said Hawkmoon.

'Seek Tanelorn,' said the Lady of the Chalice.

'Avoid the Black Sword,' said Lamsar the Hermit.

'Go back to the ocean,' said the Warrior in Jet and Gold. 'Take passage on the Dark Ship.'

'And what of the Runestaff?' Hawkmoon said. 'Must I continue to serve that?'

'Only if it will serve you,' said the Warrior in Jet and Gold.

Now the light from the sphere was very dim and the seven were mounting their horses; they had become shadows.

'And my children,' Hawkmoon called. 'Where are they?'

'In Tanelorn,' said the Lady of the Chalice. 'They wait to be reborn.'

'Explain!' Hawkmoon pleaded. 'Lady – explain!'

But her shadow was the first to fade with the last of the light from the sphere. Soon only the black giant Sepiriz remained and his voice was very faint.

'I envy you your greatness, Champion Eternal, but I do not envy you your struggle.'

And into the blackness Hawkmoon shouted:

'It is not enough! It is not enough! I must know more!'

Jhary placed a sympathetic hand upon his arm. 'Come, Duke Dorian, we shall only learn more by doing as they instructed. Come, let us go back to the ocean.'

But then Jhary was gone and Hawkmoon was alone.

'Jhary-a-Conel? Jhary?'

Hawkmoon began to run through the night, to run through the silence, his mouth gaping to emit a scream which would not come, his eyes stinging with tears which would not flow, and in his ears he could hear nothing but his own heart beating like a funeral drum.

## CHAPTER FIVE

On the Shore

And now it was dawn and the mist was on the sea, spilling aboard the stony land; and there were lights, silver-grey, drifting in the mist, and the cliffs behind Hawkmoon were ghastly. He had not slept. He felt a ghost in a ghost's world. He was abandoned, and still he had not wept. His eyes stared into the mist, his cold hand gripped the cold pommel of his sword, his white breath streamed from lips and nostrils, and he waited as a morning hunter awaits his prey, making no sound himself lest he fail to hear that betraying small noise which will reveal the object of his watch. Having no other possible action but to obey the advice of the seven wise ones who had spoken to him in the previous night, he waited for the ship which they had told him would come. He waited, uncaring if it came or not, but he knew that it would come.

Now a spot of red gleamed above his head and he thought at first it was the sun, but the tint was too deep, it was ruby coloured. Some star gleaming from an alien firmament, he thought. The red light tinged the mist, turning it pink. At the same time he heard a rhythmical creaking from the water and he knew that a ship was heaving-to. He heard an anchor fall, heard the murmur of voices, heard the rattle of a pulley and a bumping as of a small boat being lowered. He returned his attention to the red star, but it was gone, only its light was left. The mist parted. He saw a high ship in outline, its fore and aft decks considerably taller than the main deck; a lantern shone at prow and stern, rising and falling with the waves. The sails were furled, mast and rails were carved intricately, the style of the workmanship wholly unfamiliar.

'Please . . . '

Hawkmoon looked to his left and there stood the creature, its black aura dancing about it, its burning eyes entreating him.

'You irritate me, sir,' said Hawkmoon. 'I have no time for you.'

'Sword . . . '

'Find yourself a sword – then I'll be happy to fight you, if that is what you desire.' He spoke with a confidence of tone not matched by the fear which steadily grew in him. He refused to look at the figure.

258

'The ship . . . ' said the creature. 'Me . . . '

'What?' Hawkmoon turned and saw that the eyes were leering at him now with full awareness of his state of mind.

'Let me come with you,' said the creature. 'I can help you there. You will need help.'

'Not yours,' said Hawkmoon, glancing at the water and seeing the boat which had been sent for him.

An armoured man stood upright in the boat. His armour had been fashioned to follow certain rules of geometry, rather than to serve in the practical business of protection against an enemy's weapons. His great, beaked helmet hid much of his face, but bright, blue eyes were evident, and a curling, golden beard.

'Sir Hawkmoon?' The armoured man's voice was light, friendly. 'I am Brut, a knight of Lashmar. I believe we are engaged upon a common quest.'

'A quest?' Hawkmoon noticed that the dark figure had disappeared.

'For Tanelorn?'

'Aye. I seek Tanelorn.'

'Then you will find allies aboard the ship.'

'What is the ship? Where is it bound?'

'Only those who sail with her know that.'

'Is there one called "Captain" aboard?'

'Aye, our Captain. He is aboard.' Brut climbed from the boat and held it against the movement of the waves. Those who rowed turned their heads to look at Hawkmoon. They were all experienced faces, the faces of men who had fought in more than a single battle. Warrior Hawkmoon knew other warriors when he saw them.

'And who are these?'

'Comrades of ours.'

'What makes us comrades?'

'Why,' Brut smiled with good humour belying the import of his words, 'we are all damned, sir.'

For some reason this statement relieved rather than disturbed Hawkmoon. He laughed, striding forward, letting Brut help him into the boat. 'Do any but the damned seek for Tanelorn?'

'I have never heard of any others.' Brut clapped a hand on Hawkmoon's shoulder as he joined him. The boat was seized by the waves and the warriors bent their backs again, turning round and rowing for where the ship awaited them, its dark, polished timbers still catching a little of the ruby coloured light from above. Hawkmoon admired its lines, admired its high, curved prow.

'It is a ship belonging to no fleet I've ever seen,' he said.

'It belongs to no fleet at all, Sir Hawkmoon.'

Hawkmoon looked back, but the land had vanished. Only familiar mist was there.

'How came you to that shore?' Brut asked him.

'You know not? I thought you would. I had hoped for answers to my questions. I was told to wait for the ship there. I became lost — thrown from my own world and the ones I love by a creature which hates me and professes to love me.'

'A god?'

'A god without the usual qualities, if he be a god,' Hawkmoon said dryly.

'I have heard that the gods are losing their most impressive qualities,' said Brut of Lashmar. 'Their powers are stretched so thin.'

'In this world?'

'This is no "world,"' said Brut, almost in surprise.

The boat reached the ship and Hawkmoon saw that a stout ladder had been uncurled in readiness for them. Brut held the bottom for him, signing for him to climb. Quelling his caution, which desired him to consider his actions before going aboard the ship, Hawkmoon began to ascend.

There came a cry from above. Davits were swung out to take the boat up. A wave caught the ship and it swayed, moaning. Hawkmoon climbed slowly. He heard the crack of an unfurling sail; he heard a creak as a capstan turned. He raised his eyes, but they were blinded by a sudden beam from the red star overhead, which was again revealed by a rent in the clouds.

'That star,' he called. 'What is it, Brut of Lashmar? Do you follow it?'

'No,' said the blond soldier. His voice was suddenly bleak. 'It follows us.'

# BOOK TWO

# SAILING BETWEEN THE WORLDS: SAILING FOR TANELORN . . .

## CHAPTER ONE

The Waiting Warriors

Hawkmoon looked about him while Brut of Lashmar joined him on deck. Already a wind had sprung up and was filling the great, black sail. It was a familiar wind. Hawkmoon had experienced it at least once before, when he and Count Brass had fought Kalan, Taragorm and their minions in the caverns below Londra, when the very essence of Time and Space had been disrupted thanks to the efforts of the Dark Empire's two greatest sorcerer scientists. But, for all that it was a familiar wind, Hawkmoon did not care to feel its breath upon his flesh and he was grateful when Brut escorted him along the deck and flung open the door of the stern cabin. Heat poured out, welcoming him. A big lantern swayed here, hanging from four silver chains, its light spreading through the relatively large space, diffused by red-grey glass. In the centre of the cabin stood a heavy sea-table, its legs firmly clamped to the boards. A number of big, carved chairs were fixed around this table and some of the chairs were occupied, while elsewhere men stood up. All looked curiously at Hawkmoon as he entered.

'This is Dorian Hawkmoon, Duke of Köln,' said Brut. 'I'll rejoin my fellows in my own cabin. I'll call for you again soon, Sir Hawkmoon, for we'll need to pay our respects to the Captain.'

'Does he know who I am? Does he know I'm aboard?'

'Of course. He selects a crew carefully, does the Captain.' Brut laughed and his laughter was echoed by the grim, hard men in the cabin.

Hawkmoon's attention was drawn to one of the standing men – a warrior with unusual features, wearing armour of such delicate workmanship that it had an almost ethereal quality to it. Over his right eye was a brocaded patch and on his left hand a glove of what Hawkmoon guessed to be silvered steel (except he knew in his heart that it was not). The warrior's pointed face and slanting, slender brows, his eye which was purple, with a pupil of soft yellow and his filmy, pale hair, all spoke of his membership of a race only slightly related to Hawkmoon's. Yet Hawkmoon felt a kinship with him that was strong, that was magnetic (and that was frightening, too).

'I am Prince Corum of the Scarlet Robe,' said the warrior, striding forward. 'You are Hawkmoon, are you not, of the Runestaff?'

'You know of me?'

'I have seen you, often. In visions, sir – in dreams. Do you not know me?'

'No . . . ' But Hawkmoon did know Prince Corum. He had seen him, too, in visions. 'I admit that – yes, I do know you . . . '

Prince Corum smiled a sad, grim smile.

'How long have you been aboard this ship?' Hawkmoon asked him, sitting down in one of the chairs and accepting a goblet of wine offered him by one of the other warriors.

'Who knows?' said Corum. 'A day or a century. It is a dream ship. I boarded it thinking I would reach the past. The last I remember of any event before boarding was being slain – betrayed by one I thought I loved. Then I was on a misty shore, convinced that my soul had gone to Limbo, and this ship hailed me. Having nought else to do, I joined it. Since then others have filled the berths here. There is one left, I am told, then we have a full complement. I gather we sail now to pick up this last passenger.'

'And our destination?'

Corum took a draught from his own wine cup. 'I have heard the name Tanelorn spoken, but the Captain told me nothing of that. Perhaps the name is spoken in hope. I have received no evidence of any specific destination.'

'Then Brut of Lashmar was deceiving me.'

'Deceiving himself, more like,' said Corum. 'But perhaps Tanelorn is where we are bound. I have been there once, I seem to remember.'

'And did you find peace there?'

'Briefly, sir, I think.'

'Your memory, then, is poor?'

'It is no worse than the memories of most of us who sail on the Dark Ship,' said Corum.

'Have you heard of the Conjunction of the Million Spheres?'

'Yes, it strikes a chord. A time of great changes, is it not, on all the planes? When the planes intersect at specific points in their histories. When our normal perception of Time and of Space becomes meaningless and when it is possible for radical alterations to be made in the nature of reality itself. When old gods die . . . '

'And new ones are born?'

'Perhaps. If they are needed.'

'You can amplify, sir?'

'If my memory were jogged, Dorian Hawkmoon, I am sure that I could. There is much in my head which will not, as it were, come forward. Knowledge is there, but also pain – and perhaps the pain and the knowledge are too closely linked, so that one is buried with the other. I believe I have been mad.'

'I, too,' said Hawkmoon. 'But I have been sane, also. Now I'm neither. It is an odd feeling.'

'I know it well, sir.' Corum turned, indicating the other occupants of the cabin with his cup. 'You must meet your comrades. This is Emshon of Ariso...' A fierce-faced little man with heavy moustaches and a glowering manner looked up from the table, grunting at Hawkmoon. He had a thin tube in his hand which he lifted frequently to his lips. Within the tube were herbs of some kind, smouldering, and it was their smoke which the dwarfish warrior inhaled. 'Greetings, Hawkmoon,' he said. 'I hope you're a better sailor than myself, for this damned ship's inclined to pitch like an unwilling virgin at times.'

'Emshon has a gloomy disposition,' said Corum, smiling, 'and something of a coarse manner of speech, but he's agreeable enough company most of the time. And this is Keeth Woecarrier, who is convinced he brings doom to all he rides with...'

Keeth looked shyly away, uttering something which none could hear. From beneath his bearskin cloak he raised a huge hand in greeting, and all that Hawkmoon heard of his words was: 'It's true. It's true.' He was a big, lumbering soldier, dressed in patched leather and wool, with a skin cap upon his head.

'John ap-Rhyss.' This was a tall, thin man with hair falling well below his shoulders and a drooping moustache adding to his melancholy look, clad all in faded black, save for a bright insignia stitched to his shirt above his heart. He wore a dark wide-brimmed hat and his grin of greeting was sardonic. 'Hail to you, Duke Dorian. We have heard of your exploits in the land of Yel. You fight the Dark Empire, do you not?'

'I did,' said Hawkmoon. 'But that fight is now won.'

'Have I been away so long?' John ap-Rhyss frowned.

'It is useless to measure Time in the ordinary way,' Corum said warningly. 'Accept that in Hawkmoon's immediate past the Dark Empire is defeated – in yours, it is still strong.'

'I am called Turning Nikhe,' said the one closest to John ap-Rhyss. He was bearded, red-haired, with a quiet, wry manner. In contrast to ap-Rhyss, he was covered all over in jingling talismans, in beads, decorated leather, embroidery, charms of gold, silver and brass. His sword-belt was embedded with semi-precious jewels, with

265

little falcons of bronze, with stars and arrows. 'I have my name because I once changed sides during a battle, and am considered a traitor in certain parts of my own world (though I had my reasons for doing what I did). Be warned of that, however. I am not a land soldier, as most of you, but a sailor. My own ship was rammed by ships of King Fesfaton's navy. I was drowning when rescued by this vessel. I had thought I'd be needed for crew, but find myself a passenger.'

'Who crews the ship, then?' Hawkmoon asked for he had seen none but these warriors.

Turning Nikhe laughed in his red beard. 'Forgive me,' he said. 'But there are no sailors aboard, save you count the Captain.'

'The ships sails herself,' said Corum quietly. 'And we have speculated on whether she is commanded by the Captain or whether she commands him.'

'It is a sorcerous ship and I wish I had no part of her,' said one who had not yet spoken. He was fat, sporting a steel breastplate engraved with naked women in all manner of poses. Beneath this he wore a red silk shirt and there was a black neckerchief at his throat. He had golden rings in the lobes of his large ears and his black hair fell in ringlets to his shoulders. His black beard was trimmed and tapered and his moustache curled over his swarthy cheeks, almost to his hard, brown eyes. 'I am Baron Gotterin of Nimplaset-in-Khorg and I know where this ship is bound.'

'Where, sir?'

'For Hell, sir. I am dead, as we all are – though some are too cowardly to admit it. On Earth I sinned with zest and with imagination and am in no doubt of my fate.'

'Your imagination fails you now, Baron Gotterin,' said Corum dryly. 'You take a view which is exceptionally conventional.'

Baron Gotterin shrugged his big shoulders and took a deep interest in the contents of his wine cup.

An old man stepped out of the shadows. He was thin, but strong, and he wore garments of stained, yellow leather which accentuated his pallor. On his head was a dented battle cap, of wood and iron, the wood studded with brass nails. His eyes were bloodshot, moody and his mouth had a morose set to it. He scratched the back of his neck, saying: 'I'd rather be in Hell than imprisoned here,' he said. 'I'm a soldier, as we all are, and keen to be at my trade. I am most dreadfully bored.' He nodded to Hawkmoon. 'I'm called Chaz of Elaquol and I have the distinction of never having served in a victorious army. I was fleeing, defeated as usual, when I was driven by my pursuers into the sea. My luck is useless in battle, but I have never been captured. This, however, was the strangest rescue of them all!'

'Thereod of the Caves,' said one even paler than Chaz, presenting himself. 'I greet you, Hawkmoon. This is my first voyage, so I find all its aspects interesting.' He was the youngest of the company, with an awkward manner of moving. He wore the faintly scintillating skins of some reptile and there was a cap on his head of the same stuff, and he had a sword so long that it jutted a foot above his back (on which it was slung) and almost touched the floor.

The last to be introduced had to be shaken awake by Corum. He sat at the far end of the table, an empty goblet still in his gloved hand, his face hidden by the fair hair hanging over it. He belched, grinned apologetically, looked at Hawkmoon with friendly, foolish eyes, poured himself more wine, drank off the whole goblet, made to speak, failed, and closed his eyes again. He began to snore.

'That's Reingir,' said Corum, 'nicknamed "The Rock," though how he came by the name he has never been sober enough to tell us! He was drunk when he came aboard and has kept himself in that state ever since, though he's amiable enough and sometimes sings for us.'

'And you know not why we have all been gathered?' Hawkmoon asked, 'We are all soldiers, but appear to have little else in common.'

'We have been picked to fight some enemy of the Captain's,' said Emshon. 'All I know is that it's not *my* fight and I would have preferred to have been consulted before being selected. I had a plan to storm the Captain's cabin and take over the ship, sailing for pleasanter climes than these (have you noticed it is always misty?) but these "heroes" would have none of it. You've precious little in the way of guts. The Captain would only have to fart and you'd scatter!'

The others took this with amusement. Evidently, they were used to Emshon's *braggadocio*.

'Do you know why we're here, Prince Corum?' Hawkmoon asked. 'Have you spoken with the Captain?'

'Aye – spoken at some length. But I'll say nothing until you've seen him.'

'And when will that be?'

'Quite soon, I'd think. Each of us has been summoned shortly after coming aboard.'

'And told next to nothing!' complained Chaz of Elaquol. 'All I want to know is when the fight begins. And I pray that it's won. I'd like to be on a winning side before I die!'

John ap-Rhyss smiled, showing his teeth. 'You do not instil us with confidence, Sir Chaz, with your many tales of defeat.'

Chaz said seriously, 'I care not if I survive the coming battle or not, but I have a feeling in my bones that it will be successful for some of us.'

'Only some?' Emshon of Ariso snorted and made a bad-tempered gesture. 'Successful for the Captain, maybe.'

'I am inclined to think that we are privileged,' said Turning Nikhe quietly. 'There is not one of us here who was not close to death before the Dark Ship found us. If we are to die, then it will probably be in some great cause.'

'You are a romantic, sir,' said Baron Gotterin. 'I am a realist. I believe nothing of what the Captain has told us. I know for certain that we go to our punishments.'

'Everything you say, sir, proves only one thing – that you possess a dull and primitive conscience!' Emshon was plainly pleased with his own remark. He smirked.

Baron Gotterin turned away and found himself staring into the melancholy eye of Keeth Woecarrier who made an embarrassed noise and looked at the floor.

'This bickering frets me,' said Thereod of the Caves. 'Will anyone join me in a game of chess?' He indicated a large board fastened by leather straps to a bulwark.

'I'll play,' said Emshon, 'though I tire of beating you.'

'The game is new to me,' said Thereod mildly. 'But I learn, Emshon, that you'll admit.'

Emshon rose from the table and helped Thereod unstrap the board. Together they carried it to the table and clipped it into place. From a chest Thereod took out a box of pieces and began to arrange them. Some of the others gathered to watch the game.

Hawkmoon addressed Corum. 'Are all of these counterparts of ourselves?'

'Counterparts or other incarnations, do you mean?'

'Other manifestations of the so-called Champion Eternal,' said Hawkmoon. 'Do you know the theory? It explains why we recognize each other, why we have seen each other in visions.'

'I know the theory well,' said Corum. 'But I do not believe most of these warriors are our counterparts, as you call them. Some, like

John ap-Rhyss, are from the same worlds. No, in this company, I think only you and I share – what? – a soul?'

Hawkmoon looked hard at Corum. And then he shivered.

## CHAPTER TWO

# The Blind Captain

Hawkmoon had no idea how much time had passed before Brut came back to the cabin, but Emshon and Thereod had played two games of chess and were half-way through another.

'The Captain is ready to receive you, Hawkmoon.' Brut looked tired; mist streamed in through the open door before he could slam it shut.

Hawkmoon got up from his chair. His sword caught under the table and he freed it so that it swung to its usual position on his thigh. He drew his cloak about him, fastening the clasp.

'Don't spring so readily to his bidding,' Emshon said grumpily, raising his eyes from the board. 'He needs us, does the Captain, for whatever his venture is.'

Hawkmoon smiled. 'I must satisfy my curiosity, Emshon of Ariso.'

He followed Brut from the cabin and along the chilly deck. He thought that he had noticed a large wheel forward, when he boarded, and now he saw one at the stern. He commented on this to Brut.

Brut nodded. 'There are two. But only one steersman. Apart from the Captain, he seems to have been the only other being on board.' Brut pointed through the thick, white mist, and there was the outline of a man, his two hands upon the wheel. He stood extraordinarily still, dressed in thick, quilted jerkin and leggings. He seemed fixed to the wheel, fixed to the deck, and Hawkmoon could have found himself doubting if the man lived at all . . . He could tell from the motion of the ship that she sailed with more than natural speed and, looking up at the sail, he saw that it was full, but no wind blew now, not even that unearthly wind with which he had become familiar. They passed a cabin identical to that which they had left and then reached the high forward deck. Under this was a door whose substance was not the same as the dark wood of the rest of the ship. It was of metal, but a metal which had a vibrant, organic quality to it, a russet cast which reminded Hawkmoon of the pelt of a fox.

'This is the Captain's cabin,' said Brut. 'I'll leave you here, Hawkmoon. I hope you receive answers to at least some of your questions.'

Brut walked back to his own cabin, leaving Hawkmoon contemplating the strange door. He stretched out a hand to touch the metal. It was warm. It sent a shock through him.

'Enter, Hawkmoon,' said a voice from within. It was a richly timbred voice, but it sounded remote.

Hawkmoon looked for a handle, but found none. He began to press on the door, but already it was opening. Bright, ruby light struck eyes grown used to the dimness of the stern cabin. Hawkmoon blinked, but moved towards the light, while the door closed behind him. The air was warm and sweetly scented; brass and gold and silver fixtures glinted; glass shone. Hawkmoon saw rich hangings, a deep, many-hued carpet, red lamps fixed to bulkheads, subtle carvings; there were purples, dark reds, dark greens and yellows; there was a polished desk, its rails of gleaming, twisted gold, and on the desk were instruments, charts, a book. There were chests, a curtained bunk. Beside the desk stood a tall man who might, in face and figure, have been a relative of Corum's. He had the same tapering head, the fine red-gold hair, the almond, slanting eyes. His loose garments were all of the same shade of buff and the sandals on his feet were of silver, while silver laces were wound about his calves. On his head was a circlet of blue jade. But it was the eyes which drew Hawkmoon's attention. They were a milky white, flecked with blue, and they were blind. The Captain smiled.

'Greetings, Hawkmoon. Have you been given our wine, yet?'

'I had some wine, aye.' Hawkmoon watched as the man moved deftly towards a chest on which were set out a silver jug and silver cups.

'You will have some more?'

'I thank you, sir.'

The Captain poured the wine and Hawkmoon picked up his cup. He sipped and the wine filled him with a sense of well-being. 'I have not had this vintage,' he said.

'It will restore you,' said the Captain, taking a cup for himself. 'And will have no ill-effects, I assure you.'

'There is a rumour on board, sir, that your ship is bound for Tanelorn.'

'There are many who sail with us who yearn for Tanelorn,' said the Captain, turning his blind head to face Hawkmoon. For a moment Hawkmoon thought that the Captain looked not at his face but directly into his soul. He crossed the cabin to one of the portholes and looked out at the white, swirling mist. The steady rising and falling forward motion of the ship seemed to become more pronounced.

'You answer cryptically,' said Hawkmoon. 'I had hoped that you would be more direct with me.'

'I am as direct as I can be, Duke Dorian, be assured of that.'

'Assurances . . .' began Hawkmoon, then held back the rest of the sentence.

'I know,' said the Captain. 'They are of little use to a mind in the torment which you must feel. But I believe that my ship takes you closer to Tanelorn and to your children.'

'You know that I seek my children?'

'Yes. I know that you are a victim of the disruptions which have come about as a result of the Conjunction of the Million Spheres.'

'Can you tell me more of that, sir?'

'You know already that there are many worlds which exist in relation to your own, but separated by barriers which cut them off from your perception? You know that their histories are often similar, that the beings sometimes called the Lords of Law and the Lords of Chaos war permanently for domination of those worlds and that certain men and women have a destiny which involves them in those wars?'

'You speak of the Eternal Champion?'

'Of him and of those who share his fate.'

'Jhary-a-Conel?'

'That is one of his names. And Yisselda is another name. She has many counterparts, too.'

'And what of the Cosmic Balance?'

'Of the Cosmic Balance and the Runestaff little is known.'

'You do not serve either?'

'I do not believe so.'

'That, at least, is a relief to my ears,' said Hawkmoon, replacing his finished cup upon the chest. 'I have become tired of talk of great destinies.'

'I will speak of nothing but the practical business of survival,' the Captain told him. 'My ship has always sailed *between* the worlds – guarding, perhaps, the many borders where they are weakest. We have known no other life, I think, my steersman and I. I envy you that, Sir Champion – I envy you the variety of your experience.'

'I have a mind to exchange destinies, if you would like to, Captain.'

The blind man laughed quietly. 'I do not think that that is possible.'

'So my being aboard your ship has something to do with the Conjunction of the Million Spheres?'

'Everything. As you are aware, the event itself is rare enough. And this time the Lords of Law and Chaos and their many minions battle with particular ferocity to see which of them shall control the worlds when the Conjunction is passed. They involve yourself in all your guises, for you are important to them, make no mistake of that. As Corum, you have created a special problem for them.'

'Corum and I are the same, then?'

'Different manifestations of the same Hero, drawn from different worlds at different times. A dangerous business – normally two aspects of the Champion co-existing in the same world at the same time would be an alarming prospect – and we have four such aspects to consider. You have not yet met Erekosë?'

'No.'

'He inhabits the forward cabin. Eight other warriors are there, too. They await only Elric. We sail now to find him. He must be drawn from what would be your past, just as Corum has been drawn from what would be your future if you shared the same world. Such are the forces at work which make us risk monumental stakes! I pray that it will prove worthwhile.'

'And what are the forces at work?'

'I tell you what I have told the other two and what I will tell Elric. I can tell you no more, so ask no further questions when I have finished. Do you agree to that?'

'I must,' said Hawkmoon simply.

'When the time comes,' said the Captain, 'I will tell you all that there is left.'

'Continue, sir,' said Hawkmoon politely.

'Our destination is an island – a rare thing, for it is an island indigenous to these waters – inhabiting what you would call Limbo and, at the same time, inhabiting all the worlds on which mankind struggles. That island – or rather the city which stands upon the island – has been attacked many times and both Law and Chaos would control it, yet none has ever succeeded. Once it had the blessing of a people known as the Grey Lords, but they have since disappeared – none knows where. In their place have come enemies of immense power – beings who would destroy all the worlds forever. It is the Conjunction which has allowed them to enter this "multiverse" of ours. And having entered, having gained this foothold on our borders, they will not leave until they have effectively killed everything living.'

'They must be powerful indeed. And this ship has been called to gather a band of warriors to join forces with those who fight that enemy?'

'The ship goes to fight the enemy, yes.'

'But we must perish, surely?'

'No. Individually you in any one of your aspects would not have the power to destroy this enemy. That is why the others have been called. Later, I will tell you more.' The Captain paused, as if listening to something in the waters surrounding the ship. 'There! I think we are ready to find our last passenger. Go now, Hawkmoon. Forgive my manner, but you must leave me.'

'When will I learn more, sir?'

'Soon.' The Captain gestured at the door, which had opened. 'Soon.'

His head full of the information the Captain had given him, Hawkmoon stumbled back into the mist.

Far away, he could just hear the booming of surf, and he knew that the ship neared land. For a moment he though he would remain on deck and view that land if he could, but then something made him change his mind and he hurried towards the stern cabin, casting a last look back at the rigid, mysterious figure of the steersman who was still at the forward wheel.

CHAPTER THREE

The Island of Shadows

'And did the Captain illuminate you, Sir Hawkmoon?' Emshon fingered his chess queen as Hawkmoon entered the cabin.

'A little,' said Hawkmoon, 'though he mystified me more. Why do our numbers seem significant? Ten men to a cabin?'

'Is it not the maximum the cabins can hold comfortably?' asked Thereod, who seemed to be winning the game.

'There must be a considerable amount of space below,' Corum said. 'That cannot be the reason.'

'And what of sleeping qurters?' said Hawkmooon. 'You have been aboard longer than I. Where do you sleep?'

'We do not sleep,' said Baron Gotterin. The fat soldier jerked a thumb at the snoring Reingir. 'Save for that one. And he sleeps all the time.' He fingered his oiled beard. 'Who sleeps in Hell?'

'You have sung the same toneless song since you came aboard,' John ap-Rhyss said. 'A more polite man would be silent or find some new song to sing.'

Gotterin sneered and turned his back on his critic.

The tall, long-haired man from Yel sighed and resumed his drinking.

'The last of us is due to board soon, I gather,' said Hawkmoon. He looked at Corum. 'One named Elric. Is the name familiar?'

'It is. Is it not familiar to you?'

'Elric, Erekosë and myself fought together once, at a time of great crisis. The Runestaff saved us, then, at the fight at the Tower of Voilodion Ghagnasdiak.'

'What do you know of the Runestaff? Has it aught to do with the Cosmic Balance of which I have heard so much of late?'

'Possibly,' said Corum, 'but do not look to me for understanding of such mysteries, friend Hawkmoon. I am as bewildered as yourself.'

'Both seem to stand for Equilibrium.'

'True.'

'And yet I learn that the equilibrium is one maintaining the power of the gods. Why do we fight to maintain their power?'

Corum smiled reminiscently. 'Do we?' he said.

'Do we not?'

'Usually, I suppose,' said Corum.

'You become as irritating as the Captain,' said Hawkmoon with a laugh. 'What do you mean?'

Corum shook his head. 'I am not sure.'

Hawkmoon realized that he felt better than he had done for some while. He commented on this.

'You have drunk the Captain's wine,' said Corum. 'It is what sustains us, I think. There is more here. I offered you only the ordinary stuff, but if you desire . . .'

'Not now. But it sharpens the brain – it sharpens the brain.'

'Does it?' said Keeth Woecarrier from the shadows. 'I fear it dulls mine. I am confused.'

'We are all confused,' said Chaz of Elaquol dismissively. 'Who would not be?' He half drew his sword and then plunged it back into the scabbard. 'I am only clear-headed when I fight.'

'I gather that we shall be fighting soon,' Hawkmoon told him.

This drew the interest of them all and Hawkmoon repeated the little the Captain had said. The warriors fell, again, to speculating, and even Baron Gotterin brightened, speaking no more of Hell and punishment.

Hawkmoon had an inclination to avoid Prince Corum's company, not because he disliked the man (he found him most likeable) but because he was disturbed by the idea that he shared the cabin with one who was another incarnation of himself. Corum seemed to have a common feeling.

And so the time passed.

Later, the door of the cabin opened and two tall men stood there. One was of a darkish countenance, heavy and broad-shouldered, with many scars upon his face which was, though careworn, strikingly handsome. It was hard to tell his age, though he was probably close to forty, and his dark hair had a little silver in it. His deep-set eyes were intelligent, revealing something of a private grief. He was dressed in thick leather strengthened at the shoulders, elbows and wrists with steel plates which were much dented and scraped. He recognized Hawkmoon and nodded to Corum as if they had already met. His companion was slim and physically had much in common with Corum and the Captain. His eyes were crimson, smouldering like the coals of some supernatural fire, and they stared from a face which was bone-white, bloodless – the face of a corpse. His long hair, too, was white. His body was swathed in a heavy leather cloak, the

276

hood thrown back. From under the cloak jutted the outlines of a great broadsword and Hawkmoon wondered why he should feel a frisson of fear when he observed that outline.

Corum recognized the albino. 'Elric of Melniboné! My theories become more meaningful!' He glanced eagerly at Hawkmoon, but Hawkmoon hung back, not sure that he welcomed the white swordsman. 'See, Hawkmoon, this is the one of whom I spoke.'

The albino was surprised, baffled. 'You know me, sir?'

Corum was smiling. 'You recognize me, Elric. You must! At the Tower of Voilodion Ghagnasdiak? With Erekosë – though a different Erekosë.'

'I know of no such tower, no name which resembles that, and this is the first I have seen of Erekosë.' Elric looked to his companion, Erekosë, as if seeking help. 'You know me and you know my name, but I do not know you. I find this disconcerting, sir.'

The other spoke for the first time, his voice deep and vibrant and melancholy. 'I, too, had never met Prince Corum before he came aboard,' said Erekosë, 'yet he insists we fought together once. I am inclined to believe him. Time on the different planes does not always run concurrently. Prince Corum might well exist in what we would term the future.'

Hawkmoon found that his brain was refusing to hear any more. He longed for the relative simplicity of his own world. 'I had thought to find some relief from such paradoxes here,' he said. He rubbed at his eyes and his forehead, fingering, for an instant, the scar where the Black Jewel had once been imbedded. 'But it seems there is none at this present moment in the history of the planes. Everything is in flux and even our identities, it seems, are prone to alter at any moment.'

Corum was insistent, still addressing Elric. 'We were Three! Do you not recall it, Elric? The Three Who Are One?'

Evidently Elric knew nothing of which Corum spoke.

'Well,' said Corum with a shrug, 'now we are Four. Did the Captain say anything of an island we are supposed to invade?'

'He did.' The newcomer looked from face to face. 'Do you know who these enemies might be?'

Hawkmoon had a fellow feeling for the albino, then. 'We know no more or less than do you, Elric. I seek a place called Tanelorn and two children. Perhaps I seek the Runestaff, too. Of that I am not entirely sure.'

Corum, still eager to jog Elric's memory, said: 'We found it once. We three. In the Tower of Voilodion Ghagnasdiak. It was of considerable help to us.'

Hawkmoon wondered if Corum were mad. 'As it might be to me,' he said. 'I served it once. I gave it a great deal.' He stared hard at Elric, for the white face was becoming more familiar with every passing moment. He realized that he did not fear Elric. It was the sword which the albino bore – there was what Hawkmoon feared.

'We have much in common, as I told you, Elric.' Erekosë was plainly trying to remove the tensions from the atmosphere. 'Perhaps we share masters in common, too?'

Elric made something of an arrogant shrug. 'I serve no master but myself!'

Hawkmoon found himself smiling at this. The other two also smiled.

And when Erekosë murmured: 'On such ventures as these one is inclined to forget much, as one forgets a dream,' Hawkmoon found himself saying, with considerable conviction: 'This *is* a dream. Of late I've dreamt many such.'

And Corum, now acting as mediator himself, said: 'It is all dreaming, if you like. All existence.'

Elric made a dismissive gesture which Hawkmoon found a trifle irritating. 'Dream or reality, the experience amounts to the same, does it not?'

Erekosë's smile was soulful. 'Quite right.'

'In my own world,' said Hawkmoon sharply, 'we had a clear idea of the difference between dream and reality. Does not such vagueness produce a peculiar form of mental lethargy in us?'

'Can we afford to think?' Erekosë asked, almost savagely. 'Can we afford to analyse too closely? Can you, Sir Hawkmoon?'

And Hawkmoon knew, suddenly, what Erekosë's doom was. He knew that it was his doom, too. And he fell silent, shamed.

'I remember,' said Erekosë, more softly now. 'I was, am, or will be Dorian Hawkmoon. I remember.'

'And that is your grotesque and terrifying fate,' said Corum. 'We all share the same identity – but only you, Erekosë, remember them all.'

'I wish my memory were not so sharp,' said the heavy man. 'For so long have I sought Tanelorn and my Ermizhad. And now comes the Conjunction of the Million Spheres, when all the worlds intersect and there are pathways between them. If I can find the right path, then I shall see Ermizhad again. I shall see all that I hold dearest. And the Eternal Champion will rest. We shall all rest, for our fates are so closely linked together. The time has come again for me. This, I now know, is the second Conjunction I shall witness. The first wrenched me from a world and set me to warring. If I fail to take advantage of the second, I shall never know peace. This is my only opportunity. I pray that we do sail for Tanelorn.'

'I pray with you,' said Hawkmoon.

'So you should,' said Erekosë. 'So you should, sir.'

When the other two had gone, Hawkmoon agreed to join Corum in a game of chess (though he was still reluctant to spend much time in the other's company), but the game became strange – each able to anticipate exactly what his opponent would do. Corum took the experience with apparent lightness. Laughing he sat back in his chair. 'There is little point to continuing, eh?'

Hawkmoon agreed with relief and, with relief, saw the door open and Brut of Lashmar entered, a jug of hot wine in one gloved hand.

'I bring the compliments of the Captain,' he said, placing the jug in an indentation at the centre of the table. 'Did you sleep well?'

'Sleep?' Hawkmoon was surprised. 'Have you slept? Where do you sleep?'

Brut frowned. 'You were not informed, then, of the bunks below. How have you remained awake so long?'

Corum said hastily: 'Let us not pursue the question.'

'Drink the wine,' said Brut quietly. 'It will revive you.'

'Revive us?' Hawkmoon felt a wildness, a bitterness, rise in him. 'Or make us share the same dream?'

Corum poured wine for both of them and almost forced the cup into Hawkmoon's hand. He looked alarmed.

Hawkmoon made to dash the wine away, but Corum put his silver hand on Hawkmoon's arm. 'No, Hawkmoon. Drink. If the wine makes the dream coherent to all of us, then it is better.'

Hawkmoon hesitated, thought for an instant, disliked the drift of his thoughts, and he drank. The wine was good. It had the same influence as that which he had drunk in the Captain's company. His spirits improved. 'You are right,' he said to Corum.

'The Captain would have the Four join him now,' said Brut soberly.

'Has he more information for us?' Hawkmoon asked, aware that the other warriors in the cabin listened eagerly. One by one they came up to the wine jug and helped themselves from it. They drank as he had drunk, quickly.

Hawkmoon and Corum rose and followed Brut from the cabin. Walking along the deck, through the mist, Hawkmoon tried to see beyond the rail, but saw only mist. Then he noticed a man standing at the rail, his attitude introspective. He recognized Elric and called out in a friendlier tone than he had used before:

'The Captain has requested that we Four visit him in his cabin.'

Hawkmoon saw Erekosë leave his cabin, nodding to them. Elric left the rail and led the way up the deck to the forward deck and the red-brown door. He knocked; they entered the warmth and luxury of the cabin.

And the Captain's blind face greeted them, and he made a sign towards the chest, where the silver jug and the silver wine cups were, and he said:

'Please help yourselves, my friends.'

Hawkmoon found now that he was eager to drink, as were his companions.

'We are nearing our destination,' said the Captain. 'It will not be long before we disembark. I do not believe our enemies expect us, yet it will be a hard fight against those two.'

Hawkmoon had received the impression that they fought many. 'Two? Only two?'

'Only two.'

Hawkmoon glanced at the others, but they did not meet his gaze. They were looking at the Captain.

'A brother and a sister,' said the blind man. 'Sorcerers from quite another universe than ours. Due to recent disruptions in the fabric of our worlds – of which you know something, Hawkmoon, and you, too, Corum – certain beings have been released who would not otherwise have the power they now possess. And possessing great power, they crave for more – for all the power that there is in our universe. These beings are amoral in a way in which the Lords of Law and Chaos are not. They do not fight for influence upon the Earth, as those gods do. Their only wish is to convert the essential energy of our universe to their own uses. I believe they foster some ambition in their particular universe which would be furthered if they could achieve their wish. At present, in spite of conditions highly favourable to them, they have not attained their full strength, but the time is not far off before they do attain it. Agak and Gagak is how they are called in human tongue and they are outside the power of any of our gods, so a more powerful group has been summoned – yourselves.'

Hawkmoon made to ask how they could be more powerful than gods, but he controlled the impulse.

'The Champion Eternal,' the Captain continued, 'in four of his incarnations (and four is the maximum number we can risk without precipitating further unwelcome disruptions amongst the planes of

Earth) – Erekosë, Elric, Corum and Hawkmoon. Each of you will command four others, whose fates are linked with your own and who are great fighters in their own right, though they do not share your destinies in every sense. You may each pick the four with whom you wish to fight. I think you will find it easy enough to decide. We make landfall quite shortly now.'

Hawkmoon wondered if he disliked the Captain. He felt that he challenged him when he said: 'You will lead us?'

The Captain seemed genuinely regretful. 'I cannot. I can only take you to the island and wait for those who survive – if any survive.'

Elric frowned, voicing Hawkmoon's own reservations. 'This fight is not mine, I think.'

But the Captain's answer was given with conviction, with authority. 'It is yours – and it is mine. I would land with you if that were permitted me, but it is not.'

'Why so?' This was Corum speaking.

'You will learn that one day.' A cloud seemed to pass over the Captain's blind features. 'I have not the courage to tell you. I bear you nothing but good will, however. Be assured of that.'

Hawkmoon found himself thinking cynically, once again, about the value of assurances.

'Well,' said Erekosë, 'since it is my destiny to fight, and since I, like Hawkmoon, continue to seek Tanelorn, and since I gather there is some chance of my fulfilling my ambition if I am successful, I for one agree to go against these two, Agak and Gagak.'

Hawkmoon shrugged and nodded. 'I go with Erekosë – for similar reasons.'

Corum sighed. 'And I.'

Elric looked about him at the other three. 'Not long since, I counted myself without comrades. Now I have many. For that reason alone I will fight with them.'

Erekosë was pleased by this. 'It is perhaps the best of reasons.'

The Captain spoke again, his blind eyes seeming to stare beyond them. 'There is no reward for this work, save my assurance that your success will save the world much misery. And for you, Elric, there is less reward than the rest may hope for.'

Elric seemed to disagree, but Hawkmoon could not read the albino's face when he said, 'Perhaps not.'

'As you say.' The Captain's tone had changed. He was more relaxed. 'More wine, my friends?'

They drank the wine he offered them and waited while he continued. His face was raised now. He addressed the sky, his voice distant.

'Upon this island is a ruin – perhaps it was once a city called Tanelorn – and at the centre of the ruin stands one whole building. It is this building which Agak and his sister use. It is that which you must attack. You will recognize it, I hope, at once.'

'And we must slay this pair?' Erekosë spoke as if the work were nothing.

'If you can. They have servants who help them. These must be slain, also. Then the building must be fired. This is important.' The Captain paused. 'Fired. It must be destroyed in no other way.'

Hawkmoon noticed that Elric was smiling. 'There are few other ways of destroying buildings, Sir Captain.'

It seemed a pointless observation to Hawkmoon and he thought that the Captain responded with great politeness, bowing slightly and saying, 'Aye, it's so. Nonetheless, it is worth remembering what I have said.'

'Do you know what these two look like, these Agak and Gagak?' said Corum.

The Captain shook his head. 'No. It is possible that they resemble creatures of our own worlds. It is possible that they do not. Few have seen them. It is only recently that they have been able to materialize at all.'

'And how may they best be overwhelmed?' Hawkmoon spoke almost banteringly.

'By courage and ingenuity,' the Captain said.

'You are not very explicit, sir,' said Elric in a tone which echoed Hawkmoon's.

'I am as explicit as I can be. Now, my friend, I suggest you rest and prepare your arms.'

They issued into the writhing mist. It clung to the ship like a desperate beast. It stirred. It threatened them.

Erekosë's mood had changed. 'We have little free will,' he said morosely, 'for all we deceive ourselves otherwise. If we perish or live through this venture, it will not count for much in the overall scheme of things.'

'I think you are of a gloomy turn of mind, friend,' Hawkmoon told him sardonically. He would have continued, but Corum interrupted.

'A realistic turn of mind.'

They reached the cabin shared by Erekosë and Elric. Corum and Hawkmoon left them there and tramped up the deck, through the white, clinging stuff, to their own cabin, there to pick the four who would follow them.

'We are the Four Who Are One,' said Corum. 'We have great

power. I know that we have great power.'

But Hawkmoon was wearying of talk he found altogether too mystical for his own, normally practical, turn of mind.

He hefted the sword he was honing. 'This is the most trustworthy power,' he said. 'Sharp steel.'

Many of the other warriors murmured their agreement.

'We shall see,' said Corum.

But as he polished the blade, Hawkmoon could not help but be reminded of the outline of that other sword he had observed beneath Elric's cloak. He knew that he would recognize it when he saw it. He did not know, however, why he feared it so much, and this lack of knowledge also disturbed him. He found himself thinking of Yisselda, of Yarmila and Manfred, of Count Brass and the Heroes of the Kamarg. This adventure had begun partly because he had hoped to find all his old comrades and loved ones again. Now he was threatened with never seeing any of them again. And yet it was worth fighting in the Captain's cause if Tanelorn, and consequently his children, could be found. And where was Yisselda? Would he find her, too, in Tanelorn?

Soon they were ready. Hawkmoon had with him John ap-Rhyss, Enshon of Ariso, Keeth Woecarrier and Turning Nikhe, while Baron Gotterin, Theorod of the Caves, Chaz of Elaquol and Reingir the Rock, awakened at last from his drunken snoozings and stumbling blearily in the wake of the rest, made up Corum's party. Privately, Hawkmoon felt he had the pick of the men.

Into the mist they marched, and to the side of the ship. The anchor was already rattling, the ship already settling. They could see rocky land – an isle which looked distinctly inhospitable. Could it possibly shelter Tanelorn, the fabulous city of peace?

John ap-Rhyss sniffed suspiciously, wiping the mist from his moustache, his other hand playing with the hilt of his sword. 'I have seen no place less welcoming,' he said.

The Captain had left his cabin. His steersman stood next to him. Both held armfuls of brands.

With a shock, Hawkmoon saw that the steersman's face was the twin of the Captain's – but the eyes were not blind. They were sharp, they were full of knowledge. Hawkmoon could hardly bear to look at the face as he accepted his brand and tucked it into his belt.

'Only fire will destroy this enemy forever.' The Captain now handed Hawkmoon a tinder box with which to light the brand when the time came. 'I wish you success, warriors.'

Now each man had a brand and a tinder box. Erekosë was first over the side, swinging down the rope ladder, unclipping his sword so that it would not touch the water, and plunging into the milky sea up to his waist. The others followed him, wading through the shallows until they stood upon the shore, looking back at the ship.

Hawkmoon noticed that the mist did not extend as far as the land, which had now taken on some colour. Normally, he would have thought how dull the surroundings were, but in contrast to the ship they were bright – red rocks festooned with lichen of several shades of yellow. And above his head was a great disc, bloody and still, which was the sun. It cast a great many shadows, thought Hawkmoon.

It was only slowly that he began to notice just how many shadows were cast – shadows which could not possibly belong to the rocks alone – shadows of all sizes, of all shapes.

Some, he saw, were the shadows of men.

## CHAPTER FOUR

A City Haunted By Itself

The sky was like a wound gone bad, full of dreadful, unhealthy blues, browns, dark reds and yellows, and there were shadows in it which, unlike those on the land, sometimes moved.

One called Hown Serpent-Tamer, a member of Elric's party, whose armour was sea-green and scintillating, said: 'I have rarely been ashore, it's true, but I think the quality of this land is stranger than any other I've known. It shimmers. It distorts.'

'Aye,' said Hawkmoon. He had noticed the same sweep of flickering light which passed from time to time over the island and distorted the outlines of the surrounding ground.

A barbaric warrior, with braids and glaring eyes, called Ashnar the Lynx, was plainly much discomforted by all of this. 'And from whence come all these shadows?' he growled. 'Why cannot we see that which casts them?'

They continued to march inland, though all were reluctant to leave the shore and the ship behind. Corum seemed the least disturbed. He spoke in a tone of philosophical curiosity.

'It could be that these are shadows cast by objects existing in other dimensions of the Earth,' said the Prince in the Scarlet Robe. 'If all dimensions meet here, as has been suggested, that could be a likely explanation. This is not the strangest example I have witnessed of such a conjunction.'

A black man, whose face bore a peculiar V-shaped scar, and who was called Otto Blendker, fingered the sword belt which crossed his chest and grunted. 'Likely? Pray let none give me an *unlikely* explanation, if you please!'

Thereod of the Caves said: 'I have witnessed a similar peculiarity in the deepest caves of my own land, but nothing so vast. There, I was told, dimensions met. So Corum is doubtless right.' He shifted the long, slender sword on his back. He spoke no more to the party in general, but fell to conversing with the dwarfish Emshon of Ariso who was, as usual, grumbling about something.

Hawkmoon was still considering if they had been duped by the Captain. They still had no proof that the blind man truly meant them well. For all Hawkmoon knew the Captain himself had designs upon the worlds and was using them against their fellows. But he voiced nothing of this to the others, all of whom seemed prepared to do the Captain's bidding without question.

Once more Hawkmoon found himself eyeing the shape of the sword beneath Elric's cloak and wondering why it perturbed him so much. He became lost in his own thoughts, looking as little as possible at the disturbing landscape around him, reviewing the events which had led to his finding himself in this company. He was aroused from his reverie by Corum's voice saying:

'Perhaps this is Tanelorn – or, rather, all the versions of Tanelorn there have ever been. For Tanelorn exists in many forms, each form depending upon the wishes of those who most desire to find her.'

Hawkmoon looked and he saw the city. It was a crazy assortment of ruins, displaying every possible idiosyncratic style of architecture, as if some god had collected examples of buildings from every world of the multiverse and placed them here, willy-nilly. All were in ruins. They stretched away to the horizon – tottering towers, shattered minarets, crumbling castles – and all cast shadows. Moreover, in this city, too, there were many shadows which had no apparent origin. Shadows of buildings not visible to their eyes.

Hawkmoon was shocked. 'This is not the Tanelorn I expected to find,' he said.

'Nor I.' Erekosë spoke in a tone which echoed Hawkmoon's.

'Perhaps it is not Tanelorn.' Elric stopped short, his crimson eyes scanning the ruins. 'Perhaps it is not.'

'Or perhaps this is a graveyard.' Corum frowned. 'A graveyard containing all the forgotten versions of that strange city?'

Hawkmoon refused to pause. He kept walking until he had reached the ruins, and the others began to follow him, until they were all clambering through the broken stones, inspecting here a piece of engraving, there a fallen statue. Behind him, Hawkmoon heard Erekosë speaking in a low voice to Elric.

'Have you noticed,' said Erekosë, 'that the shadows now represent something?'

Hawkmoon heard Elric reply. 'You can tell from the ruins what some of the buildings looked like when they were whole. The shadows are the shadows of those buildings – the original buildings before they became ruined.'

Hawkmoon looked for himself and saw that Elric was right. It was a city haunted by itself.

'Just so,' said Erekosë.

Hawkmoon turned. 'We were promised Tanelorn. We were promised a corpse!'

'Possibly,' said Corum, thoughtfully. 'But do not come to too hasty a conclusion, Hawkmoon.'

'I would judge the centre to be over there, ahead of us,' said John ap-Rhyss. 'Would that be the best place to look for those we fight?'

The others agreed and they altered the direction of their march a little, making for a cleared space amongst the ruins where a building could be seen, its outline sharp and clean where the outlines of the others were indistinct. Its colours, too, were brighter, with planes of curved metal going at all angles, connected by tubes which might have been of crystal and which glowed and throbbed.

'It resembles a machine more than a building.' Hawkmoon found his curiosity aroused.

'And a musical instrument more than a machine.' Corum's single eye viewed the building with a certain awe.

The four heroes stopped and their men stopped with them.

'This must be the dwelling of the sorcerers,' said Emshon of Ariso. 'They do themselves well, eh? And look – it is really two identical buildings, connected by those tubes.'

'A home for the brother and a home for the sister,' said Reingir the Rock. He belched and looked apologetic.

'Two buildings,' Erekosë remarked. 'We were not prepared for this. Shall we split up and attack both?'

Elric shook his head. 'I think we should go together into one, else our strength will be weakened.'

'I agree,' said Hawkmoon, wishing he knew why he was so reluctant, nonetheless, to follow Elric into the building.

'Well, let us set to it,' Baron Gotterin said. 'Let us enter Hell, if this is not Hell already.'

Corum gave the Baron an amused glance. 'You are certainly determined to prove your theory!'

Again Hawkmoon took the initiative, heading over the level ground towards what he guessed to be the doorway of the nearest building – a dark, asymmetrical gash. As the twenty warriors approached, experienced eyes wary for attack by any possible defenders, the building seemed to take on a brighter glow, seemed to pulse with a steady beat, seemed to emit peculiar, almost inaudible, whispering noises. Used to the sorcerous technology of the Dark Empire, Hawkmoon still found himself fearing the place, and suddenly he was holding back, letting Elric lead the way in, his four chosen comrades with him. Hawkmoon and his men went next through the black portal and they were in a passage which curved sharply almost as soon as they had entered; a humid passage which brought sweat to their faces. Again they paused, glancing at one another. Then they began to move again, ready to meet whatever defenders there were.

They had gone some distance along the passage before its walls and floor began to shake so heavily that Hown Serpent-tamer was flung downwards, to lie sprawled and swearing while the others barely managed to keep their balance, and at the same time there came a booming, faraway voice from ahead – a voice full of querulous outrage.

'Who? Who? Who?'

Hawkmoon, gripped by inapposite humour, thought it the voice of a mad and gigantic owl.

'Who? Who? Who invades me?'

With the help of the others, Hown had regained his footing. They pushed on as the passage's motion became somewhat less violent, while the voice continued to mutter, distracted, as if to itself.

'What attacks? What?'

None had any explanation for the voice. All were bewildered by it. They said nothing, letting Elric lead them into a fairly large hall.

Within the hall the air was even warmer and hard to breathe. Viscous fluid dripped from the ceiling and oozed down the walls. Hawkmoon found himself disgusted and quelled a strong desire to turn back. Then Ashnar the Lynx yelped and pointed at the beasts which squeezed themselves through the walls and came slithering at them, mouths gaping. They were snake-like things and the sight of them brought bile to Hawkmoon's throat.

'Attack!' The voice cried again. 'Destroy this! Destroy it!' There was a terrible, mindless quality to the command.

Instinctively the warriors formed themselves into four groups, standing back to back to meet the attack.

Instead of real teeth, the beasts had sharp bone ridges in their mouths, like twin knives, making a horrid clashing sound as they drew their shapeless, disgusting bodies through the slime of the floor.

Elric was the first to draw his sword and Hawkmoon was distracted for a second as he saw the huge black blade rise over the albino's head. He could have sworn that he heard the blade moan, that it glowed with a life which was its own. But then he was cutting at the beasts which slithered all around him, striking into flesh which parted with nauseating ease and which gave off a stink threatening to overwhelm them all. The air grew thicker and the fluid on the floor was deeper and Elric was shouting to them. 'Move on through them!'

he cried. 'Hacking a path through as you go. Head for yonder opening.'

Hawkmoon saw the doorway and he knew that Elric's plan was the best they could hope for. He began to press forward, his men moving with him, destroying a multitude of the horrid beasts as they went. As a result the stench increased and Hawkmoon was gagging now.

'The creatures are not hard to fight!' Hown Serpent-tamer was panting. 'But each one we kill robs us a little of our own chances of life.'

'Cunningly planned by our enemies, no doubt,' answered Elric.

Elric was the first to reach the passage, waving them to join him.

Thrusting, swinging, slicing, they gained the door and the beasts were reluctant to follow. Here the air was a little more breathable. Hawkmoon leaned against the wall of the passage, listening to the others debate, but unable to join the conversation.

'*Attack! Attack!*' ordered the faraway voice. But no further attack came.

'I like not this castle at all.' Brut of Lashmar fingered a tear in his cloak. 'High sorcery commands it.'

'It is only what we knew,' said Ashnar the Lynx, his barbarian's eyes darting this way and that.

Otto Blendker, another of Elric's men, wiped sweat from his black brow. 'They are cowards, these sorcerers. They do not show themselves.' He was almost shouting. 'Is their aspect so loathsome that they are afraid lest we look upon them?' Hawkmoon realized that Blendker was speaking for the benefit of the two sorcerers, Agak and Gagak, hoping to shame them into appearing. But there was no response. Soon they were pushing on through the fleshy passages, which changed dimensions frequently and were sometimes all but impassable. The light, too, was inconstant, and often they moved in complete darkness, linking hands so as not to become separated.

'The floor rises all the time,' murmured Hawkmoon to John ap-Rhyss, who was nearest to him. 'We must be fairly close to the top of the building.'

ap-Rhyss made no reply. His teeth were clenched as if he tried not to betray his fear.

'The Captain said that the sorcerers could probably change shape,' Emshon of Ariso said. 'They must change frequently, for these passages are not designed for creatures of any one particular size.'

Elric, at the head of the twenty, said: 'I become impatient to confront these shape changers.'

Ashnar the Lynx, next to him, growled: 'They said there'd be treasure here. I thought to stake my life against a fair reward, but there's nought here of value.' He touched the wall. 'Not even stone or brick. What are these walls made of, Elric?'

Hawkmoon had wondered the same thing and he hoped that the albino would offer an explanation, but Elric was shaking his head. 'That had puzzled me, also, Ashnar.'

Hawkmoon heard Elric draw in his breath, saw him raise his strange, heavy sword – and there were new attackers coming at them. These were beasts with red, snarling mouths and their bristling fur was orange. Yellow fangs dripped saliva. Elric was the first to be threatened, driving his sword deep into the first beast's belly even as its claws fell on him. It was like a huge baboon and the thrust had not killed it.

Then Hawkmoon was engaged with another of the apes, slashing at it while it feinted, side-stepping his blows, and Hawkmoon was aware that he had little chance, individually, against it. He saw Keeth Woecarrier, careless of his safety, come blundering to his aid, big sword swinging, a look of resignation upon his melancholy face. The ape turned its attention to the Woecarrier, throwing the whole weight of its body at him. Keeth's blade ran it through the chest, but its fangs were on the large man's throat and blood was bursting from the jugular almost in an instant.

Hawkmoon thrust under the ape's ribs, knowing that it was too late to save Keeth Woecarrier whose body was already sinking to the damp floor. Corum appeared, stabbing the creature from the other side. It snarled, turning on them, claws reaching for them. Its eyes glazed. It stumbled. It fell backwards on to the Woecarrier's corpse.

Hawkmoon did not wait to be attacked, but sprang over the corpses to where Baron Gotterin was locked in the grip of another orange ape. Teeth snapped, tearing the fat face free of the skull. Gotterin yelled once, almost in triumph, almost as if he felt his theory vindicated. Then he died. Ashnar the Lynx used his sword like an axe, lopping off the head of Gotterin's assassin. He stood upon the body of another slain ape. Miraculously, he had taken two of the beasts single-handed. He was roaring out some toneless battle song. He was full of joy now.

Hawkmoon grinned at the barbarian and rushed to Corum's assistance, making a deep cut through the neck and back of the baboon. Blood shot into his eyes and blinded him for a moment so that he thought he was doomed. But the beast was finished. It twitched for only a few seconds longer. Corum pushed it from him with the pommel of his sword.

Hawkmoon saw that Chaz of Elaquol was also dead, but that Turning Nikhe still lived, nursing a deep gash in his face, grinning the while. Reingir the Rock lay upon his back, his throat torn out, while John ap-Rhyss, Emshon of Ariso and Thereod of the Caves had managed to survive the fight with only minor wounds. Erekosë's men had fared less well. One had his arm hanging by strips of flesh alone, another had lost an eye and another had had his hand bitten clean off. The others were tending them as best they could. Brut of Lashmar, Hown Serpent-tamer, Ashnar the Lynx and Otto Blendker were also reasonably unhurt.

Ashnar looked triumphantly upon the bodies of the two apes. 'I begin to suspect this venture of being uneconomical,' he said. He was panting as a hound might pant after a successful kill. 'The less time we take over it, the better. What think you, Elric?'

'I would agree.' Elric shook blood from his fearsome sword. 'Come.'

Without waiting for the others, he began to lead the way towards a chamber ahead. The chamber glowed with a peculiar pink light. Hawkmoon and the others followed him into it.

Now Elric was looking down in horror. He bent and grasped something. And Hawkmoon felt his own legs seized. They were snakes, covering the floor of the chamber – long, thin reptiles, flesh-coloured and eyeless – tightening their coils about his ankles. Wildly, Hawkmoon hacked downwards, severing two or three of the heads, but the coils did not relax. Around him, his surviving comrades were shouting with fear, trying to free themselves.

And then the one called Hown Serpent-tamer, the warrior in the sea-green armour, began to sing.

He sang in a voice which was like the sound of a waterfall in a mountain stream. He sang casually, for all the urgency in the set of his face, and slowly the snakes began to release their hold upon the men, slowly they fell back to the floor, appearing to sleep.

'Now I understand how you came by your surname,' said Elric in relief.

'I was not sure the song would work on these,' said the Serpent-tamer, 'for they are unlike any serpents I have ever seen in the seas of my own world.'

They left the snakes behind, climbing higher, finding it difficult to keep a purchase on the yielding, slimy floor. The heat was increasing all the time and Hawkmoon felt that he might soon faint if he did not soon breathe fresher air. He became reconciled to going down on his stomach in order to squeeze through tiny, rubbery gaps in the passage; to spreading his arms at times in order to maintain his balance as tall caverns shook and rained sticky liquid on his head; to slapping at small creatures, rather like insects, which from time to time attacked; to hearing the sourceless voice crying:

'Where? Where? Oh, the pain!'

The little beasts flew around them in clouds, nipping at their faces and hands, hardly visible yet always present.

'Where?'

Virtually blinded, Hawkmoon forced his body on, restraining the urge to vomit, desperate for sweet air, seeing warriors fall and being hardly able to help them up again. Upward, higher and higher, rose the passage, twisting in every direction, and Hown Serpent-tamer continued to sing, for there were still many snakes on the floor.

Ashnar the Lynx had lost his short-lived ebullience. 'We can survive this only a little longer. We shall be in no condition to meet the sorcerer if we ever find him or his sister.'

'My thoughts, too,' said Elric. 'Yet what else may we do, Ashnar?'

'Nothing,' Hawkmoon heard Ashnar murmur. 'Nothing.'

And the same word was repeated, sometimes louder, sometimes softer:

'Where?' it said.

'Where?' it demanded.

'Where? Where? Where?'

And soon the voice had grown to a shout. It rang in Hawkmoon's ears. It grated on his nerves.

'Here,' he muttered. 'Here we are, sorcerer.'

Then they had come to the end of the passage at last and saw an archway of regular proportions, and beyond the archway a well-lit chamber.

'Agak's room, without doubt,' said Ashnar the Lynx.

They stepped into an octagonal chamber.

## CHAPTER FIVE

## Agak and Gagak

There were eight milky colours to each of the eight inwardly sloping sides of the chamber; each colour changing in unison with the others. From time to time a side would become almost transparent and it was possible to see through it to the ruins of the city below, the other building, still connected by a network of tubes and threads.

There were noises within the chamber – a sighing, a whispering, a bubbling. They came from a great pool set into the centre of the floor.

Reluctantly, they filed into the chamber. Reluctantly they looked into the pool and saw that the substance there might be the stuff of life itself, for it moved constantly, it formed shapes – faces, bodies, limbs of all manner of men and beasts; structures which rivalled those of the city outside for architectural variety; whole landscapes in miniature; unfamiliar firmaments, suns and planets; creatures of unlikely beauty and of convincing ugliness; scenes of battles, of families at peace in their households, of harvests, ceremonies, pomp; ships both outlandish and familiar, some of which flew through the skies, or through the darks of space, or below the waves, in nameless materials, unusual timbers, peculiar metals.

In fascination, Hawkmoon stared and stared, until a voice roared from the pool, revealing its source at last.

'WHAT? WHAT? WHO INVADES?'

Hawkmoon saw Elric's face in the pool. He saw Corum's face there and he saw Erekosë's. When he recognized his own, he turned away.

'WHO INVADES? AH! I AM TOO WEAK!'

Elric was the first to reply:

'We are of those you would destroy. We are those on whom you would feed.'

'AH! AGAK! I AM SICK! WHERE ARE YOU?'

Hawkmoon exchanged puzzled glances with Corum and with Erekosë. None could explain the sorcerer's response.

Shapes rose from the liquid and fell apart, fell back into the pool.

Hawkmoon saw Yisselda there, and other women who reminded him of Yisselda, though they did not resemble her. He cried out, starting forward. Erekosë restrained him. The figures of the women disintegrated and were replaced by the twisting towers of an alien city.

'I WEAKEN . . . MY ENERGY NEEDS TO BE REPLENISHED . . . WE MUST BEGIN NOW, AGAK . . . IT TOOK US SO LONG TO REACH THIS PLACE, I THOUGHT I COULD REST. BUT THERE IS DISEASE HERE. IT FILLS MY BODY. AGAK. AWAKEN AGAK. AWAKEN!'

Hawkmoon controlled the shudders which began to rack his body.

Elric was staring intently into the pool, an expression of dawning realization on his pale face.

'Some servant of Agak's, charged with the defense of the chamber?' This was Hown Serpent-tamer's suggestion.

'Will Agak awake?' Brut glanced around the eight-sided chamber. 'Will he come?'

'Agak!' Ashnar the Lynx raised his braided head in a challenge. 'Coward!'

'Agak!' cried John ap-Rhyss, drawing his sword.

'Agak!' shouted Emshon of Ariso.

The others all took up the shout; all save the four heroes.

Hawkmoon was beginning to guess what the words had meant. And something was growing inside his mind – another understanding, an understanding of how the sorcerers must be slain. His lips formed the word 'No,' but could not voice it. He looked again into the faces of the three other aspects of the Champion Eternal. He saw that the others were also afraid.

'We are the Four Who Are One.' Erekosë's voice was shaking.

'No . . .' Elric spoke now. He was making some sort of attempt to sheath his black sword, but the sword seemed to be refusing to enter the scabbard. There was panic and horror in the albino's crimson eyes.

Hawkmoon took a small step backward, hating the images which now filled his head, hating the impulse which had seized his will.

'AGAK! QUICKLY!'

The pool boiled.

Hawkmoon heard Erekosë saying:

'If we do not do this thing, they will eat all our worlds. Nothing will remain.'

Hawkmoon did not care.

Elric, closest to the pool, was clutching his bone-white head and swaying, threatening to fall. Hawkmoon made a movement towards him, hearing the albino groan, hearing Corum's urgent, echoing voice behind him, feeling desperate, wholehearted comradeship with his three counterparts.

'We must do it, then,' said Corum.

Eric was panting. 'I will not,' he said. 'I am myself.'

'And I!' Hawkmoon stretched out a hand, but Elric did not see it.

'It is the only way for us,' said Corum, 'for the single thing that we are. Do you not see that? We are the only creatures of our worlds who possess the means of slaying the sorcerers – in the only manner in which they can be slain!'

Hawkmoon's eyes met Elric's; they met those of Corum; they met Erekosë's. And Hawkmoon knew and the individual that was Hawkmoon recoiled from the knowledge.

'We are the Four Who Are One.' Erekosë's tones were firm. 'Our united strength is greater than the sum. We must come together, brothers. We must conquer here before we can hope to conquer Agak.'

'No . . .' said Elric, voicing Hawkmoon's emotion.

But something greater than Hawkmoon was at work within him. He moved to one corner of the pool and stood there, seeing that the others had taken up positions at each of the other corners.

'AGAK!' said the voice. 'AGAK!' And the pool's activity became more violent.

Hawkmoon could not speak. He saw that the faces of his three counterparts were as frozen as his own. He was only dimly aware of the warriors who had followed them here. They were moving away from the pool, guarding the entrance, looking about them for signs of attack, protecting the Four, but their eyes held terror.

Hawkmoon saw the great black sword move upwards, but he could feel no more fear of it as his own sword rose to meet it. Then all four swords were touching, their tips meeting over the exact centre of the pool.

At the moment when the tips met, Hawkmoon gasped, feeling a power fill his soul. He heard Elric shout and knew that the albino was experiencing the same sensation. Hawkmoon hated the power. It enslaved him. He wished to escape from it, even now.

'*I understand.*' It was Corum's voice, but the lips were Hawkmoon's. '*It is the only way.*'

'*Oh, no, no!*' And Hawkmoon's voice sprang from Elric's throat.

Hawkmoon felt his name go away.

'AGAK! AGAK!' The substance of the pool writhed, boiled and leaped. 'QUICKLY! WAKE!'

Hawkmoon knew that his identity was fading. He was Elric. He was Erekosë. He was Corum. And he was Hawkmoon, too. A little of him was still Hawkmoon. And he was a thousand others – Urlik,

Jherek, Asquiol . . . He was a part of a gigantic, a noble beast . . .

His body had changed. He hovered over the pool. The vestige of Hawkmoon could see it for a second before that vestige joined the central being.

On each side of its head was a face and each face belonged to one of the companions. Serene and terrible, the eyes did not blink. It had eight arms and the arms were still; it squatted over the pool on eight legs, and its armour and accoutrements were of all colours blending and at the same time separate.

The being clutched a single great sword in all eight hands and both he and the sword glowed with a ghastly golden light.

'Ah,' he thought, '*now I am whole.*'

The Four Who Were One reversed its monstrous sword so that the point was directed downward at the frenetically boiling stuff in the pool below. The stuff feared the sword. It mewled.

'*Agak, Agak . . .*'

The being of whom Hawkmoon was a part gathered its great strength and began to plunge the sword down.

Shapeless waves appeared on the surface of the pool. Its whole colour changed from sickly yellow to an unhealthy green. '*Agak, I die . . .*'

Inexorably the sword moved down. It touched the surface.

The pool swept back and forth; it tried to ooze over the sides and on to the floor. The sword bit deeper and the Four Who Were One felt new strength flow up the blade. There came a moan; slowly the pool quietened. It became silent. It became still. It became grey.

Then the Four Who Were One descended into the pool to be absorbed.

*Hawkmoon rode for Londra and with him were Huillam D'Averc, Yisselda of Brass, Oladahn of the Bulgar Mountains, Bowgentle the philosopher, and Count Brass. Each of these wore a mirror helm which reflected the rays of the sun.*

*Hawkmoon held the Horn of Fate in his hands. He put it to his lips. He blew the blast to herald in the night of the new earth. The night that would precede the new dawn. And though the horn's note was triumphant, Hawkmoon was not. He stood full of infinite loneliness and infinite sorrow, his head tilted back as the sound rang on.*

*Hawkmoon relived the torment he had suffered in the forest, when Glandyth had struck off his hand. He screamed as the pain came to his wrist once more and then there was fire in his face and he knew that Kwll had plucked his brother's jeweled eye from his skull, now*

296

that his powers were restored. Red darkness swam in his brain. Red fire drained his energy. Red pain consumed his flesh.

And Hawkmoon spoke in tones of the most terrible torment. 'Which of the names will I have next time you call?'

'Now Earth is peaceful. The silent air carries only the sounds of quiet laughter, the murmur of conversation, the small noises of small animals. We and Earth are at peace.'

'But how long can it last?'

'Oh, how long can it last?'

The beast that was the Champion Eternal could see clearly now.

It tested its body. It controlled every limb, every function. It had triumphed; it had revitalized the pool.

Through its single octagonal eye it looked in all directions at the same time over the wide ruins of the city; then it focused all its attention upon its twin.

Agak had awakened too late, but he was awakening at last, roused by the dying cries of his sister Gagak whose body the mortals had first invaded and whose intelligence they had overwhelmed, whose eye they now used and whose powers they would soon attempt to utilize.

Agak did not need to turn his head to look upon the being he still saw as his sister. Like hers, his intelligence was contained within the huge octagonal eye.

'Did you call me, sister?'

'I spoke your name, that is all, brother.' There were enough vestiges of Gagak's lifeforce in the Four Who Were One for it to imitate her manner of speaking.

'You cried out?'

'A dream.' The Four paused and then it spoke again: 'A disease. I dreamed that there was something upon this island which made me unwell.'

'Is that possible? We do not know sufficient about these dimensions or the creatures inhabiting them. Yet none is as powerful as Agak and Gagak. Fear not, sister. We must begin our work soon.'

'It is nothing. Now I am awake.'

Agak was puzzled. 'You speak oddly.'

'The dream . . .' answered the creature which had entered Gagak's body and destroyed her.

'We must begin,' said Agak. 'The dimensions turn and the time has come. Ah, I feel it. It waits for us to take it. So much rich energy. How we shall conquer when we go home!'

'I feel it,' replied the Four, and it did.

It felt its whole universe, dimension upon dimension, swirling all about it. Stars and planets and moons through plane upon plane, all full of the energy upon which Agak and Gagak had desired to feed. And there was enough of Gagak still within the Four to make the Four experience a deep, anticipatory hunger which, now that the dimensions attained the right conjunction, would soon be satisfied.

The Four was tempted to join with Agak and feast, though it knew if it did so it would rob its own universe of every shred of energy. Stars would fade, worlds would die. Even the Lords of Law and Chaos would perish, for they were part of the same universe. Yet to possess such power it might be worth committing such a tremendous crime . . .

It controlled this desire and gathered itself for its attack before Agak became too wary.

'Shall we feast, sister?'

The Four realized that the ship had brought it to the island at exactly the proper moment. Indeed, they had almost come too late.

'Sister?' Agak was again puzzled. 'What . . . ?'

The Four knew it must disconnect from Agak. The tubes and wires fell away from his body and were withdrawn into Gagak's.

'What's this?' Agak's strange body trembled for a moment. 'Sister?'

The Four prepared itself. For all that it had absorbed Gagak's memories and instincts, it was still not confident that it would be able to attack Agak in her chosen form. And since the sorceress had possessed the power to change her form, the Four began to change, groaning greatly, experiencing dreadful pain, drawing all the materials of its stolen being together so that what had happened to be a building now became pulpy, unformed flesh. And Agak, stunned, looked on.

'Sister? Your Sanity . . .'

The building, the creature that was Gagak, threshed, melted and erupted.

It screamed in agony.

It attained its form.

It laughed.

CHAPTER SIX

## The Battle for Everything

Four faces laughed upon a gigantic head. Eight arms waved in
triumph, eight legs began to move. And over that head it waved a
single, massive sword.

And it was running.

It ran upon Agak while the alien sorcerer was still in his static
form. Its sword was whirling and shards of ghastly golden light fell
away from it as it moved, lashing the shadowed landscape. The Four
was as large as Agak. And at this moment it was as strong.

But Agak, realizing his danger, began to suck. No longer would
this be a pleasurable ritual shared with his sister. He must suck at the
energy of this universe if he was to find the strength to defend himself, to gain what he needed to destroy his attacker, the slayer of his
sister.

Worlds died as Agak sucked.

But not enough.

Agak tried cunning:

'This is the centre of your universe. All its dimensions intersect
here. Come, you can share the power. My sister is dead. I accept her
death. You shall be my partner now. With this power we shall conquer a universe far richer than this!'

'No!' said the Four, still advancing.

'Very well, but be assured of your defeat.'

The Four swung its sword. The sword fell upon the faceted eye
within which Agak's intelligence pool bubbled, just as his sister's had
once bubbled. But Agak was stronger already and healed himself at
once.

Agak's tendrils emerged and lashed at the Four and the Four cut at
the tendrils as they sought its body. And Agak sucked more energy to
himself. His body, which the mortals had mistaken for a building,
began to glow burning scarlet and to radiate an impossible heat.

The sword roared and flared so that black light mingled with the
gold and flowed against the scarlet.

And all the while the Four could sense its own universe shrinking
and dying.

'Give back, Agak, what you have stolen!' said the Four.

Planes and angles and curves, wires and tubes, flickered with deep red heat and Agak sighed. The universe whimpered.

*'I am stronger than you,'* said Agak. *'Now!'*

And Agak sucked again.

The Four knew that Agak's attention was diverted for just that short while as he fed. And the Four knew that it, too, must draw energy from its own universe if Agak were to be defeated. So the sword was raised.

The sword was flung back, its blade slicing through tens of thousands of dimensions and drawing their power to it. Then it began to swing back.

It swung and black light bellowed from its blade.

It swung and Agak became aware of it. His body began to alter.

Down towards the sorcerer's great eye, down towards Agak's intelligence pool swept the black blade.

Agak's many tendrils rose to defend the sorcerer against the sword, but the sword cut through them as if they were not there and it struck the eight-sided chamber which was Agak's eye and it plunged on down into Agak's intelligence pool, deep into the stuff of the sorcerer's sensibility, drawing up Agak's energy into itself and thence into its master, the Four Who Were One.

And something screamed through the universe.

And something sent a tremor through the universe.

And the universe was dead, even as Agak began to die.

The Four did not dare wait to see if Agak were completely vanquished.

It swept the sword out, back through the dimensions, and everywhere the blade touched the energy was restored.

The sword rang round and round.

Round and round. Dispensing the energy.

And the sword sang its triumph and its glee.

And little shreds of black and golden light whispered away and were re-absorbed.

*Hawkmoon knew the nature of the Champion. He knew the nature of the Black Sword. He knew the nature of Tanelorn. For at this moment that part of him which was Hawkmoon had experience of the whole multiverse. It inhabited him. He contained it. There were no mysteries at that moment.*

*And he recalled that one of his aspects had read something in the Chronicle of the Black Sword, that record of the Champion's exploits:* 'For the Mind of Man alone is free to explore the lofty vastness of the cosmic infinite, to transcend ordinary consciousness, or roam the subterranean corridors of the human brain with its boundless dimensions. And universe and individual are linked, the one mirrored in the other, and each contains the other . . .'

*'Ha!' cried that individual which was Hawkmoon. And he triumphed; he celebrated. This was the end of the Champion's doom!*

For a moment the universe had been dead. Now it lived and Agak's energy had been added to it.

Agak lived, too, but he was frozen. He had attempted to change his shape. Now he still half resembled the building Hawkmoon had seen when he first came to the island, but part of him resembled the Four Who Were One. Here was part of Corum's face, here a leg, there a fragment of sword blade – as if Agak had believed, at the end, that the Four could only be defeated if its own form were assumed, just as the Four had assumed Gagak's form.

'We had waited so long . . .' Agak sighed and then he was dead.

And the Four sheathed its sword.

*Hawkmoon thought . . .*

Then came a howling through the ruins of the many cities and a strong wind blustered against the body of the Four so that it was forced to kneel on its eight legs and bow its four-faced head before the gale.

*Hawkmoon felt . . .*

Then, gradually, it assumed again the shape of Gagak, the sorceress, and then it lay within Gagak's stagnating intelligence pool . . .

*Hawkmoon knew . . .*

. . . and then it rose over it, hovered for a moment, withdrew its sword from the pool.

*Hawkmoon was Hawkmoon. Hawkmoon was the Champion Eternal on his last great quest . . .*

Then four beings fled apart and Elric and Hawkmoon and Erekosë and Corum stood with sword blades touching over the centre of the dead brain.

Hawkmoon sighed. He was full of wonderment. He was full of fear. Then the terror began to fade, to be replaced by an exhaustion which had something of contentment in it.

'Now I have flesh again. Now I have flesh,' said a pathetic voice.

And it was the barbarian Ashnar, his face all ruined, his eyes all crazy. He had dropped his sword and had not noticed. He kept touching himself, digging at his face with his nails. And he giggled.

301

John ap-Rhyss raised his head from the floor. He looked at Hawkmoon in hatred, then he looked away again. Emshon of Ariso, his sword, too, forgotten, crawled forward to help John ap-Rhyss rise to his feet. There was a cold silence in the manner of both men.

Others were mad or dead. Elric was helping Brut of Lashmar up.

'What did you see?' asked the albino.

'More than I deserved, for all my sins. We were trapped – trapped in that skull . . .' The Knight of Lashmar broke down, his sobbing that of a little child. Elric held Brut, stroking his blond hair, unable to say anything which might ease the burden of his experience.

Erekosë murmured, almost to himself. 'We must go.' As he walked towards the door, his feet threatened to slide from under him.

'It was not fair,' said Hawkmoon to John ap-Rhyss and Emshon of Ariso, 'that you should suffer with us. It was not fair.'

John ap-Rhyss spat at the floor.

## CHAPTER SEVEN

## The Heroes Part

Outside, standing amongst the shadows of buildings that were not there, or only partly standing; standing beneath a bloody sun which had not moved a fraction in the sky since they had landed on the island; Hawkmoon watched the bodies of the sorcerers burn.

The fire took eagerly, shrieking and howling as it consumed Agak and Gagak, and its smoke was whiter than Elric's face, redder than the sun. The smoke filled the sky.

Hawkmoon could remember little of what had befallen him inside Gagak's skull, but he was full of bitterness at that moment.

'I wonder if the Captain knew why he sent us here?' said Corum.

'Or if he suspected what would happen?' Hawkmoon wiped at his mouth.

'Only we – only that being – could battle Agak, and Gagak in anything resembling their own terms.' Erekosë's eyes were full of a private knowledge. 'Other means would not have been successful. No other creature could have the particular qualities, the enormous power needed to slay such strange sorcerers.'

'So it seems,' said Elric. The albino had become taciturn, introspective.

Corum said encouragingly, 'Hopefully you will forget this experience as you forgot – or will forget – the other.'

Elric was not to be consoled. 'Hopefully, brother.'

Now Erekosë made an effort to break their mood. He chuckled. 'Who could recall that?'

Hawkmoon was bound to agree with him. Already the sensations were fading; already the experience had the feeling of an unusually powerful dream. He looked round at the soldiers who had fought with him; still none would meet his eye. Plainly they blamed him and his other manifestations for a horror they should not have had to confront. Ashnar the Lynx, tough-minded barbarian, was witness to the dreadful emotions they had had to suppress, to control, and now Ashnar gave out a chilling shriek and began to run towards the blaze. He ran until he had almost reached it and Hawkmoon thought he would throw himself upon the pyre, but he changed his direction at the last moment and ran instead into the ruins, swallowed by shadows.

'Why follow him?' said Elric. 'What can we do for him?' There was pain in his crimson eyes as he regarded the body of Hown Serpent-tamer, who had saved all their lives. Elric shrugged, but it was not a careless shrug. He shrugged as a man might who sought to adjust a particularly heavy load upon his shoulders.

John ap-Rhyss and Emshon of Ariso helped the dazed Brut of Lashmar to walk as they moved back from the fire, back towards the shore.

Hawkmoon said to Elric, as they walked, 'That sword of yours. It has a familiar look. It is no ordinary blade, eh?'

'No,' agreed the albino. 'It is not an ordinary blade, Duke Dorian. It is ancient, timeless, some say. Others think it was forged for my ancestors in a battle against gods. It has a twin, but that is lost.'

'I fear it,' said Hawkmoon. 'I know not why.'

'You are wise to fear it,' Elric told him. 'It is more than a sword.'

'A demon, too?'

'If you like.' Elric would say no more.

'It is the doom of the Champion to bear that blade at the Earth's most crucial crises,' Erekosë said. 'I have borne it and would not bear it again, if I had the choice.'

'The choice is rarely the Champion's,' Corum added with a sigh.

Now they had come to the beach again and hovered there, contemplating the white mist surging on the water. The dark silhouette of the ship was plainly visible.

Corum, Elric and some of the others began to go forward into the mist, but Hawkmoon, Erekosë and Brut of Lashmar all hesitated at the same time. Hawkmoon had come to a decision.

'I will not rejoin the ship,' he said. 'I feel I've served my passage now. If I can find Tanelorn, this, I suspect, is where I must look.'

'My own feelings.' Erekosë moved his body so that he was looking again at the ruins.

Elric's glance at Corum was questioning and Corum smiled in answer.

'I have already found Tanelorn. I go back to the ship in hope that soon it will deposit me upon a more familiar shore.'

'That is my hope.' Elric offered Brut, whom he supported, the same questioning stare.

Brut was whispering. Hawkmoon caught some of the words. 'What was it? What happened to us?'

'Nothing.' Elric gripped Brut's shoulder and then released it.

Brut broke free. 'I will stay. I am sorry.'

'Brut?' Elric frowned.

'I am sorry. I fear you. I fear that ship.' Brut stumbled backwards, stumbled inland.

'Brut?' Elric reached out a hand.

'Comrade,' said Corum, laying his silver hand upon Elric's own shoulder, 'let us be gone from this place. It is what is back there that I fear more than the ship.'

With one last moody look at the ruins, Elric said: 'With that I agree.'

'If that is Tanelorn, it is not, after all, the place I sought,' muttered Otto Blendker.

Hawkmoon expected John ap-Rhyss and Emshon of Ariso to go with Blendker, but they remained stolidly where they were.

'Will you stay with me?' said Hawkmoon in surprise.

The tall, long-haired man of Yel and the short, belligerent warrior of Ariso nodded together.

'We stay,' said John ap-Rhyss.

'You have no love for me, I thought.'

'You said that we suffered an injustice,' John ap-Rhyss told him. 'Well, that is true. It is not you we hate, Hawkmoon. It is those forces which control us all. I am glad that I am not Hawkmoon, yet I envy you in a way.'

'Envy?'

'I agree,' said Emshon soberly. 'To play such a role, one would give much.'

'One's soul?' said Erekosë.

'What is that?' asked John ap-Rhyss, refusing to meet the eye of the heavy-bodied man. 'A cargo we abandon too soon in our voyage, perhaps. Then we spend the rest of our lives trying to discover where we lost it.'

'Is that what you seek?' Emshon asked him.

John ap-Rhyss grinned a wolf's grin at him. 'Say so, if you wish.'

'Farewell to you, then,' said Corum, saluting them. 'We continue with the ship.'

'And I.' Elric drew his cloak about his face. 'I wish you success in your quest, brothers.'

'And you in yours,' said Erekosë. 'The Horn must be blown.'

'I do not understand you.' Elric's tone was cold. He turned and began to wade into the water, not waiting for an explanation.

Corum smiled. 'Removed from our times, plagued by paradoxes, manipulated by beings who refuse to enlighten us – it is tiresome, is it

305

not?'

'Tiresome,' said Erekosë laconically. 'Aye.'

'My struggle has ended, I think,' said Corum. 'I believe that soon I will be allowed to die. I have served my turn as Champion Eternal. I join my Rhalina, my mortal bride.'

'I must still seek for my immortal Ermizhad,' said Erekosë.

'My Yisselda lives, I'm told,' Hawkmoon added. 'But I seek my children.'

'All the parts of the thing that is the Eternal Champion come together,' said Corum. 'This could be the last quest for all of us.'

'And shall we know peace, then?' Erekosë asked.

'Peace comes to a man only after he has struggled with himself,' said Corum. 'Is that not your experience?'

'It is the struggling which is so hard,' Hawkmoon told him.

Corum said no more. He followed Elric and Otto Blendker into the sea. Soon they had disappeared into the mist. Soon they heard faint shouts. Soon they heard the anchor raised. The ship was gone.

Hawkmoon was relieved, for all he did not relish the idea of what lay ahead of him. He turned.

The black figure was back. It was grinning at him. It was an evil, intimate grin.

'Sword,' it said. And it pointed after the ship. 'Sword. You will need me, Champion. Soon.'

Erekosë showed terror for the first time. Like Hawkmoon, his first instinct was to draw his blade, but something stopped him. John ap-Rhyss and Emshon of Ariso shouted in astonishment and Hawkmoon stayed their hands. 'Do not draw,' he said.

Brut of Lashmar merely stared at the apparition with his glazed, tired eyes.

'Sword,' said the creature. His black aura made it seem that he danced a peculiar, jerky jig, but his body was quite still. 'Elric? Corum? Hawkmoon? Erekosë? Urlik . . . ?'

'Ah!' cried Erekosë. 'Now I know you. Go! Go!'

The black figure laughed. 'I can never go. Not while the Champion needs me.'

'The Champion needs you no longer,' said Hawkmoon, without knowing what he meant.

'He does! He does!'

'Go!'

The wicked face continued to grin.

'There are two of us now,' said Erekosë. 'Two are stronger.'

'But it is not allowed,' said the figure. 'It has never been allowed.'

'This is a different time, the Time of the Conjunction.'

'No!' cried the apparition.

Erekosë's laugh was contemptuous.

The black figure darted forward, became huge; darted back, became tiny; resumed its normal size, fled across the ruins, its own shadow capering behind it, not always in unison. The great, heavy shadows of that collection of cities seemed about to fall on the figure, for he recoiled from many of them.

'No!' they heard him cry. 'No!'

John a-Rhyss said: 'Was that what was left of the sorcerer?'

'It was not,' said Erekosë. 'It is what is left of our nemesis.'

'You know it, then?' said Hawkmoon.

'I think so.'

'Tell me. It has haunted me since my adventure began. I think it was responsible for parting me from Yisselda, from my own world.'

'It has not the power for that, I'm sure,' said Erekosë. 'Doubtless, however, it was pleased to take advantage. I have only seen it once before, very briefly, in this manifestation.'

'What is it called?'

'Many names,' said Erekosë thoughtfully.

They began to move back into the ruins. The apparition had vanished again. Ahead they saw two new shadows; two huge shadows. They were the shadows of Agak and Gagak as they had looked when the heroes had first arrived here. The bodies had by this time burned to nothing. But the shadows remained.

'Tell me one?' Hawkmoon asked.

Erekosë pursed his lips before replying, then he darted a look directly into Hawkmoon's eyes. 'I think I understand why the Captain was reluctant to speculate, to divulge any information he could not be completely sure of. It is dangerous, in these circumstances, to jump to conclusions. Perhaps I am wrong, after all.'

'Oh!' cried Hawkmoon. 'Tell me what you suspect, then, Erekosë, if it is merely suspicion.'

'I think one of the names is Stormbringer,' the scarred man told him.

'And now I know why I feared Elric's sword,' Hawkmoon said.

They spoke no more of this.

BOOK THREE

# IN WHICH MANY THINGS ARE FOUND TO BE ONE THING

CHAPTER ONE

Prisoners in Shadows

'We are like ghosts, are we not?'

Erekosë lay upon a pile of broken stone and stared up at the red, motionless sun. 'A converse of ghosts . . .' He smiled to show that he spoke idly, merely to pass time.

'I am hungry,' said Hawkmoon. 'That proves two things to me – that I'm made of ordinary flesh and that it has been a long while since our comrades returned to the ship.'

Erekosë sniffed at the cool air. 'Aye. I wonder, now, why I remained. Perhaps it is our fate to be marooned here – an irony, eh? Seeking Tanelorn we are allowed to exist in *all* the Tanelorns. Could this be all that remains?'

'I suspect not,' said Hawkmoon. 'Somewhere we'll find a gateway to the worlds we want.'

Hawkmoon sat on the shoulder of a fallen statue, trying to distinguish from the many shadows some shadow he might recognize.

Some yards away John ap-Rhyss and Emshon of Ariso were searching in the rubble for a box Emshon was sure he had seen on their way to do battle with Agak and Gagak and which, he had told John ap-Rhyss, was bound to contain something of value. Brut of Lashmar, a little better recovered, stood near them, not joining in the search.

Yet it was Brut who noticed later that a number of shadows which had previously been static were now in motion. 'Look, Hawkmoon,' he said. 'Is the city coming alive?'

The rest of the city remained as it had always been, but in one small corner of it, where the silhouette of a particularly ornate and delicate house was cast against the stained, white wall of a ruined temple, three or four of the human shadows were moving. And still they were only shadows – the men who cast them were not visible. It was like a play Hawkmoon had once witnessed, with puppets manipulated behind a screen.

Erekosë was on his feet, clambering towards the scene, Hawkmoon close at his heels and the others following a little less speedily.

And very faintly they could hear sounds – the clatter of weapons, shouts, the shuffle of booted feet on stone.

311

Erekosë stopped when his own height was almost equalled by the height of the shadows. Cautiously he reached out to touch one, stepping forward.

And Erekosë had vanished!

All that remained of him was his shadow. It had joined the others. Hawkmoon saw the shadow draw its sword and range itself beside another shadow, which seemed to him familiar. It was the shadow of a man no larger than Emshon of Ariso who watched the shadow-play with his mouth open, his eyes glazed.

Then the motion of the fighting men began to slow again. Hawkmoon was wondering how he might rescue Erekosë when the tall hero had reappeared, dragging another with him. The other shadows had frozen once more.

Erekosë was panting. The man with him was lacerated with a score of small wounds, but did not seem badly hurt. He was grinning in relief, wiping a whitish dust from the orange fur which covered his body, sheathing his sword, wiping his whiskers with the back of his paw-like hand. It was Oladahn. Oladahn of the Bulgar Mountains, kin to the Mountain Giants, Hawkmoon's closest friend and companion through most of his greatest adventures. Oladahn, who had died at Londra, who Hawkmoon had seen next as a glassy-eyed ghost in the swamps of the Kamarg and lastly upon the decks of *The Romanian Queen*, where, bravely, he had attacked Baron Kalan's crystal pyramid and, as a consequence, vanished.

'Hawkmoon!' Oladahn's joy at seeing his old comrade made him forget all else. He ran forward and embraced the Duke of Köln.

Hawkmoon found himself laughing with pleasure. He looked up at Erekosë. 'How you saved him I know not. But I am grateful to you.'

Erekosë, infected by their joy, laughed, too. 'How I saved him, I know not!' He glanced back at the static shadows. 'I found myself in a world scarcely more substantial than this one. I helped fight off those who attacked your friend – in desperation, as our movements became sluggish, I fell back – and here we are again!'

'How came you to that place, Oladahn?' Hawkmoon asked.

'My life has been confusing and my adventures peculiar since I last saw you aboard that ship,' Oladahn said. 'For a while I was the prisoner of Baron Kalan, unable to move my limbs, yet with my mind functioning normally. That was not pleasant. Then, suddenly, I was freed. I found myself upon a world involved in a battle between four or five different factions and served with one army and another, never quite understanding the issues involved. Then I was back in the Bulgar Mountains, wrestling a bear and getting the worst of the encounter. Then I came to a metal world, where I was the only creature of flesh amongst a motley variety of machines. About to be mangled by one of the machines (which was not without a certain philosophical intelligence) I was saved by Orland Fank – you remember him? – and taken to the world I have just escaped from. Fank and I sought the Runestaff there, a world of cities and of conflict. On an errand for Fank in a particularly violent quarter of one of the cities, I was set upon by more men than I could deal with. About to be slain, I found myself again frozen. This condition lasted for hours or for years (that I shall never know) until just before I was rescued by your comrade here. Tell me, Hawkmoon, what became of our other friends?'

'It's a long tale and it has little point, since I can explain few of the events in it,' Hawkmoon told him. He recounted something of his adventures, of Count Brass, Yisselda and his missing children, of the defeat of both Taragorm and Baron Kalan, of the disruption their insane vengeance and scheming had brought to the multiverse, ending: 'But of D'Averc and Bowgentle I can tell you nothing. They vanished much as you vanished. I would guess that their adventures are a match for yours. It is significant, is it not, that you have been snatched from inevitable death so many times?'

'Aye,' said Oladahn. 'I thought I had a supernatural protector – though I became tired of leaping, as it were, from the cooking pot into the stove! What have we here?' Stroking his whiskers, he looked about him, nodding politely to Brut, John and Emshon who were all staring at him in restrained amazement. 'It would seem significant that I have been allowed to join you again. But where is Fank?'

'I left him at Castle Brass, though he said nothing of meeting you. Doubtless he resumed his quest for the Runestaff and found you during that adventure.' Hawkmoon described everything he could of the nature of the island on which they now stood.

This description left Oladahn scratching at the red fur of his head and shrugging his shoulders. Almost before Hawkmoon had finished, he was looking at the various rents in his jerkin and divided kilt, picking at the drying blood on his various wounds.

'Well, friend Hawkmoon,' he said, distracted, 'I'm content enough to be at your side again. Is there anything to eat?'

'Nothing,' John ap-Rhyss said feelingly. 'We'll starve to death if we can find no game on this island. And nothing appears to live here, save ourselves.'

As if in answer to this declaration, there came a howling from the other side of the city. They looked towards the source of the sound.

313

'A wolf?' Oladahn asked.

'A man, I think,' said Erekosë. He had not sheathed his sword and he used it to point.

Ashnar the Lynx came running towards them, leaping over stones, darting around tottering towers, his own sword raised above his head, his mad eyes glaring, the little bones in his braids dancing about his savage skull. Hawkmoon thought he attacked, but then he saw that Ashnar was pursued by a tall, lean, red-faced man in a bonnet and kilt, a plaid flying from his shoulders, his sword bouncing in the scabbard at his side.

'Orland Fank!' cried Oladahn. 'Why does he chase that man?'

Hawkmoon could hear Fank's shouts now. 'Come here, will ye? Come here man! I mean ye no harm!'

Then Ashnar had tripped and fallen, whimpering and scrabbling amongst dusty stones. Fank reached him, knocked the sword from his hand, gathered a fistful of braids and raised the barbarian's head.

Hawkmoon called: 'He is mad, Fank. Be gentle with him.'

Fank looked up. 'So it's Sir Hawkmoon, is it? And Oladahn? I wondered what had become of ye – deserted me, did you?'

'Almost,' answered the kin of the Mountain Giants feelingly, 'to Brother Death into whose arms you sent me, Master Fank.'

Fank grinned, letting go of Ashnar's hair.

The barbarian made no effort to rise, merely lay in the dust and moaned.

'What harm has that man offered you?' Erekosë asked Fank sternly.

'None. I could find no other human being in this gloomy conglomeration. I wanted to question him. When I approached him he let forth his heathen howling and tried to escape.'

'How found you this place?' Erekosë asked.

'By an accident. My quest for a certain artifact has led me through several of the Earth's many planes. I heard that the Runestaff might be found in a certain city – called, by some, Tanelorn. I sought Tanelorn. My investigations led me to a sorcerer in a city on the world where I found young Oladahn here. The sorcerer was a man made all of metal and he was able to direct my path to the next plane, where Oladahn and I lost each other. I found a gateway and entered it and here I am . . .'

'Then let's make haste back to your gateway,' said Hawkmoon eagerly.

Orland Fank shook his head. 'Nay, it's closed behind me. Besides, I've no wish to return to that strifing world. Is this not, then,

Tanelorn?'

'It is all the Tanelorns,' said Erekosë. 'Or so we think, Master Fank. Leastways, it is what remains of them. Was not the city we're in called Tanelorn?'

'Once,' said Fank. 'Or so a legend said. But men came who made selfish use of its properties and Tanelorn died, to be replaced by its opposite.'

'So Tanelorn can die?' Brut of Lashmar looked miserable. 'It is not invulnerable . . .'

'Only if those who dwell in it are men who have lost that particular kind of pride which destroys love – so I heard, at any rate.' Orland Fank looked embarrassed. 'And are therefore themselves invulnerable.'

'Any city would be preferable to this dumping ground of lost ideals,' said Emshon of Ariso, showing that while he had taken Orland Fank's point he was not particularly impressed by it. The dwarfish warrior tugged at his moustaches and grumbled on to himself for a while.

'So these would be all the "failures,"' said Erekosë. 'We stand amongst the ruins of Hope. A wasteland of broken faith.'

'So I would surmise,' Fank replied. 'But nonetheless there must be a way through to a Tanelorn which has not succumbed, where the borderline is narrow. And that is what we must seek for now.'

'But how do we know what to seek?' John ap-Rhyss asked reasonably.

'The answer lies within ourselves,' Brut said in a voice that was not really his. 'That is what I was once told. Look for Tanelorn within yourself – an old woman said that when I asked her where I might find that fabulous city and know peace. I dismissed the statement as being empty of any real meaning, merely a piece of philosophical obfuscation, but I begin to realize that she offered me practical advice. Hope is what we have lost, gentlemen, and Tanelorn will open her gates only to those who hope. Faith flees from us, but faith is required before we can see the Tanelorn we need.'

'I think you speak good sense, Brut of Lashmar,' said Erekosë. 'For all that, of late, I have come to adopt the soldier's armour of cynicism, I understand you. But how can mortals hope in a sphere dominated by bickering gods, by the warring of those they desire so much to respect?'

'When gods die, self-respect buds,' murmured Orland Fank. 'Gods and their examples are not needed by those who respect themselves and, consequently, respect others. Gods are for children, for little, fearful people, for those who would have no responsibility to themselves or their fellows.'

'Aye!' John ap-Rhyss's melancholy features were almost cheerful.

A mood was coming to them all. They laughed as they looked from face to face.

And then Hawkmoon was drawing out his sword and pointing it upward, towards the stagnant sun, and he cried:

'Here's Death for gods and Life for men! Let the Lords of Chaos and of Law destroy themselves in pointless conflict. Let the Cosmic Balance swing how it likes, it shall not affect our destinies.'

'It shall not!' shouted Erekosë, his own sword raised. 'It shall not!'

And John ap-Rhyss, and Emshon of Ariso, and Brut of Lashmar all drew their swords and echoed the cry.

Only Orland Fank seemed reluctant. He tugged at his clothing. He fingered his face.

And when they had done with their impetuous ceremony, the Orkneyman said:

'Then none of you will help me seek the Runestaff?'

And a voice from behind Orland Fank said:

'Father, you need seek no further.'

And there sat the child whom Hawkmoon had seen in Dnark, who had transformed himself into pure energy in order to inhabit the Runestaff when Shenegar Trott, Count of Sussex, had sought to steal it. The one who had been called the Spirit of the Runestaff, Jehamiah Cohnahlias. The boy's smile was radiant, his manner friendly.

'Greetings to you all,' he said. 'You summoned the Runestaff.'

'We did not summon it,' said Hawkmoon.

'Your hearts summoned it. And now, here is your Tanelorn.'

The boy spread his hands and it seemed as he spread them that the city became transformed. Rainbow light filled the sky. The sun shuddered and burned golden. Pinnacles, seeming slender as needles, raised themselves into the glowing air, and colours gleamed, pure and translucent, and a great stillness came upon that city, the stillness of tranquillity.

'Here is your Tanelorn.'

CHAPTER TWO

## In Tanelorn

'Come, I will show you some history,' said the child.

And he led the men through quiet streets where people greeted them with friendly gravity.

If the city shone, now, it shone with a light so subtle that it was impossible to identify its source. If it had one colour, it was a kind of whiteness which certain kinds of jade have, but as white contains all colours, the city was of all colours. It thrived; it was happy; it was at peace. Families lived here; artists and craftsmen worked here; books were written; it was vital. This was no pallid harmony – the false peace of those who deny the body its pleasures, the mind its stimuli. This was Tanelorn.

This, at last, was Tanelorn, perhaps the model for so many other Tanelorns.

'We are at the centre,' said the child, 'the still, unalterable centre of the multiverse.'

'What gods are worshipped here?' asked Brut of Lashmar, his voice and his face relaxed.

'No gods,' said the child. 'They are not required.'

'And is that why they are said to hate Tanelorn?' Hawkmoon stepped to one side to allow a very old woman to pass him.

'It could be,' said the child. 'For the proud cannot accept being ignored. They have a different sort of pride in Tanelorn – and that is a pride which prefers to be ignored.'

He took them past high towers and lovely battlements, through parks where excited children played.

'They play at war, then, even here?' said John ap-Rhyss. 'Even here!'

'It is how children learn,' said Jehamiah Cohnahlias. 'And if they learn properly, they learn enough to abjure warfare when they are grown.'

'But the gods play at war,' said Oladahn.

'They are children, then,' said the child.

Hawkmoon noticed that Orland Fank was weeping, but he did not seem to be sad.

They came to a cleared part of the city, a kind of amphitheatre, but its sides consisted of three ranks of statues, somewhat larger than life size. All the statues were of the same colouring as the city; all seemed to glow with something resembling life. All the first rank of statues were of warriors, the second rank was chiefly of warriors, too, and the third rank was of women. There seemed to be thousands of these statues, in a great circle, beneath a sun which hung above the centre, red and still, as it had been on the island – but the red was mellow, the sky a warm, faded blue. It was as if it were evening here, always.

'Behold,' said the child. 'Behold Hawkmoon, Erekosë. These are you.' And he lifted one of his arms in its heavy, golden sleeve, to point at the first rank of statues, and there was a dull, black staff in his hand which Hawkmoon recognized as the Runestaff. And he noticed, for the first time, that the runes carved on it were in a script not dissimilar to that which was carved into the sword which Elric had borne, the Black Sword, Stormbringer.

'Look on their faces,' said the child. 'Look Erekosë, look Hawkmoon, look Champion Eternal.'

Looking, Hawkmoon saw faces he recognized amongst the statues. He saw Corum and he saw Elric and he heard Erekosë murmur: 'John Daker, Urlik Skarsol, Asquiol, Aubec, Arflane, Valadek . . . They are all here . . . all, save Erekosë . . .'

'And Hawkmoon,' said Hawkmoon.

Orland Fank spoke. 'There are gaps in the ranks. Why so?'

'They wait to be filled,' said the child.

Hawkmoon shivered.

'They are all the manifestations of the Champion Eternal,' said Orland Fank. 'Their comrades, their consorts. All in one place. Why are we here, Jehamiah?'

'Because the Runestaff has summoned us.'

'I'll serve it no longer!' This was Hawkmoon. 'It has done me much harm.'

'You need not serve it, save in one way,' said the child mildly. 'It serves you. You summoned it.'

'I tell you that we did not.'

'And I told you that your hearts summoned it. You found the gateway to Tanelorn, you opened it, you allowed me to reach you.'

'This is mystical maundering of the most outrageous kind!' Emshon of Ariso bristled. He made to turn away.

'It is the truth, however,' said the child. 'Faith bloomed within you when you stood in those ruins. Not Faith in an ideal, or in gods, or

318

the fate of the world – but Faith in yourselves. It is a force to defeat every enemy. It was the only force which could summon the friend that I am to you.'

'But this is a business concerning heroes,' said Brut of Lashmar. 'I am not a hero, boy, not as these two are.'

'That is for you to decide, of course.'

'I'm a plain soldier, a man of many faults . . .' began John ap-Rhyss. He sighed. 'I sought only rest.'

'And you have found it. You have found Tanelorn. Do you not, however, wish to witness the outcome of your ordeal upon the island?'

John ap-Rhyss directed a quizzical glance at the child. He tugged at his nose. 'Well . . .'

'It is the least you deserve. No harm will come to you, warrior.'

John ap-Rhyss shrugged and his shrug was imitated by Emshon and Brut.

'That ordeal? Was it connected with our quest?' Hawkmoon was eager. 'Was there some other point to it?'

'It was the Eternal Champion's last great deed for humanity. It has come full circle, Erekosë. You understand my meaning?'

Erekosë bowed his head. 'I do.'

'And the time is coming,' said the child, 'for the last deed of all – the deed which will free you from your curse.'

'Free?'

'Freedom, Erekosë, for the Champion Eternal and all those he has served down the long ages.'

Erekosë's face filled with dawning hope.

'But it has still to be earned,' cautioned the Spirit of the Runestaff. 'Still.'

'How can I earn it?'

'That you will discover. Now – watch.'

The child motioned with his staff at the statue of Elric.

And they watched.

## CHAPTER THREE

## The Deaths of the Undying

They watched as one statue stepped down from its dais, face blank, limbs stiff – and slowly his features assumed the qualities of flesh (though bone-white flesh) and his armour turned black and a real person stood there; and though the face was animated he did not see them.

The scene around him had altered profoundly. Hawkmoon felt something in himself drawing him closer and closer to the one who had been a statue. It was as if their faces touched, and still the other was not aware of Hawkmoon's presence.

Then Hawkmoon was looking out of Elric's eyes. Hawkmoon was Elric. Erekosë was Elric.

*He was tugging the black sword from the body of his greatest friend. He was sobbing as he tugged. At last the sword was dragged from the corpse and flung aside, landing with a strange, muffled sound. He saw the sword move, approaching him. It stopped, but it watched.*

*He placed a large horn to his lips and he took a deep breath. He had the strength to blow the horn now, whereas earlier he had been weak. Another's strength filled him.*

*He blew a note upon the horn; one great blast. Then there was silence upon the plain of rock. Silence waited in the high and distant mountains.*

*In the sky a shadow began to materialize. It was a vast shadow and then it was not a shadow at all but an outline, and then details filled the outline. It was a gigantic hand and in the hand was a balance, its scales swinging erratically. Now, however, the scales became steadier until, at length, the balance righted itself.*

*The sight brought a certain easement of the grief he felt. He dropped the horn.*

*'There is something, at least,' he heard himself say, 'and if it's an illusion, then it's a reassuring one.'*

*But now, as he turned, he saw that the sword had risen into the air of its own volition. It menaced him.*

*'STORMBRINGER!'*

*The blade entered his body, entered his heart. The blade drank his soul. Tears fell from his eyes as the sword drank; he knew that part of him, now, would never have peace.*

*He died.*

*He fell away from his fallen body and he was Hawkmoon again. He was Erekosë again . . .*

*The two aspects of the same thing watched as the sword pulled itself free from the body of the last of the Bright Emperors. They watched as the sword began to change its shape, though a husk of the blade remained and became human in proportions, standing over the man it had conquered.*

*The being was the same Hawkmoon had seen on the Silver Bridge, the same he had seen on the island. It smiled.*

*'Farewell, friend,' said the being. 'I was a thousand times more evil than thou!'*

*It flung itself into the sky, laughing, malicious, without kindness. It mocked the Cosmic Balance, its ancient enemy.*

*And it was gone, and the scene was gone, and the statue of the Prince of Melniboné stood again upon its dais.*

Hawkmoon was gasping as if he had escaped drowning. His heart was beating horribly.

He saw that Oladahn's face twitched and that his eyes held shock; he saw Erekosë's frowning countenance, and he saw Orland Fank rubbing at his jaw. He saw the serene face of the child. He saw John ap-Rhyss, Emshon of Ariso and Brut of Lashmar, and he knew, when he looked at them, that they had witnessed nothing in the scene which had disturbed them. – 'So it is confirmed,' said Erekosë's deep voice. 'That thing and the sword are the same.'

'Often,' said the child. 'Sometimes its whole spirit does not inhabit the sword. Kanajana was not the whole sword.'

The child motioned. 'Watch again.'

'No,' said Hawkmoon.

'Watch again,' said the child.

Another tall statue stepped from its place.

The man was handsome and he had only one eye; only one hand. He had known love and he had known grief and the love had taught him how to bear the grief. His features were calm. Somewhere, the sea crashed. He had come home.

Again Hawkmoon felt himself absorbed and knew that Erekosë, too, was absorbed. Corum Jhaelen Irsei, Prince in the Scarlet Robe, Last of the Vadhagh, who had refused to fear beauty and who had fallen to it, who had refused to fear a brother and had been betrayed, who had refused to fear a harp and had been slain by it, who had been banished from a place where he did not belong, had come home.

He emerged from a forest and stood upon a seashore. The tide would be out soon and it would uncover the causeway leading to Moidel's Mount where he had been happy with a woman of the short-lived Mabden race, who had died and left him desolate (for children rarely came from such a union).

The memory of Medhbh was fading, but the memory of Rhalina, Margravine of the East, could not fade.

The causeway appeared and he began to walk across. The castle of Moidel's Mount was deserted now, that was plain. It showed neglect. A wind whispered through the towers, but it was a friendly wind.

On the other side of the causeway, standing in the entrance to the castle courtyard, he saw one he recognized – a nightmare creature, greenish blue in colour, with four squat legs, four brawny arms, a barbaric, noseless head with the nostrils set directly into the face, a wide, grinning mouth, full of sharp teeth, eyes that were faceted like a fly's. There were swords of strange design at its belt. It was the Lost God: Kwll.

'Greetings, Corum.'

'Greetings, Kwll, slayer of gods. Where is your brother?' He was pleased to see his old, reluctant, ally.

'At his own devices. We grow bored and ready to leave the multiverse. There is no place for us in it, as there is no place for you.'

'So I have been told.'

'We go on one of our journeys, at least until the time of the next Conjunction.' Kwll gestured at the sky. 'We must make haste.'

'Where do you go?'

'There is another place – a place deserted by those you destroyed here – a place where they still have use for gods. Would Corum come with us? The Champion must remain, but Corum can come.'

'Are they not the same?'

'They are the same. But that which is not the same, that which is Corum only, he can come with us. It is an adventure.'

'I weary of adventures, Kwll.'

The Lost God grinned. 'Consider. We need a mascot. We need the strength you have.'

'What strength is that?'

'The strength of Man.'

'All gods need that, do they not?'

'Aye,' Kwll agreed, somewhat reluctantly, 'but some need it more than others. Rhynn and Kwll have Kwll and Rhynn, but it would amuse us if you came.'

Corum shook his head.

'You understand that you cannot live after the Conjunction?'

'I understant that, Kwll.'

'And you know now, I suppose, that it was not I who actually destroyed the Lords of Law and Chaos?'

'I think so.'

'I merely finished the work you had begun, Corum.'

'You are kind.'

'I speak the truth. I am a boastful god, having no loyalties, save to Rhynn. But I am, by and large, a truthful god. Departing, I leave you with the truth.'

'Thank you, Kwll.'

'Farewell.' The barbaric figure vanished.

Corum walked through the courtyard, through the dusty halls and corridors of the castle, up to the high tower where he could look across the sea. And he knew that Lwym-an-Esh, that lovely land, was now drowned, that only a few fragments still stood above the waves. And he sighed, but he was not unhappy.

He saw a black figure come capering over the waves towards him, a grinning figure with an insinuating stare.

'Corum? Corum?'

'I know you,' said Corum.

'May I guest with you, Corum? There is much I can do for you. I will be your servant, Corum.'

'I need no servant.'

The figure stood upon the sea, swaying with the movement of the waves.

'Let me into your castle, Corum.'

'I require no guests.'

'I can bring your loved ones to you.'

'They are already with me.' And Corum stood upon the battlements, laughing down at the black figure, who glowered and sneered. And Corum jumped so that his body would strike the rocks at the foot of Moidel's Mount, so that his spirit would be free from it.

And the black figure bellowed with rage, with frustration and, finally, with fear . . .

'That is the last creature of Chaos, is it not?' said Erekosë when the scene had faded and the statue of Corum resumed its place.

'In that guise,' said the child, 'it is, poor thing.'

'I have known it so many times,' said Erekosë. 'It has sometimes worked for good . . .'

'Chaos is not wholly evil, surely?' said the child. 'And neither is Law wholly good. They are primitive divisions, at best – they represent only temperamental preferences in individual men and women. There are other elements . . .'

'You speak of the Cosmic Balance?' said Hawkmoon. 'Of the Runestaff?'

'Call that Conscience, eh?' said Orland Fank. 'But can you call it Tolerance?'

'All are primitive,' said the child.

'You would admit that?' Oladahn was surprised. 'Then what would replace them that would be better?'

The child smiled, but would not reply.

'Would you see more?' he asked Hawkmoon and Erekosë. They shook their heads.

'That black figure daunts us always,' said Hawkmoon. 'It plots our destruction.'

'It needs your souls,' said the child.

John ap-Rhyss said calmly, 'In Yel, in the villages, they have a legend of such a creature. Say-tunn, is that his name?'

The child shrugged. 'Give him any name and he grows in power. Refuse him a name and his power weakens. I call him Fear. Mankind's greatest enemy.'

'But a good friend to those who would use him,' said Emshon of Ariso.

Oladahn said: 'For a time.'

'A treacherous friend, even to those he helps most,' said the child. 'Oh, how he longs to be admitted to Tanelorn!'

'He cannot enter?'

'Only at this time, because he comes to barter.'

'In what does he trade?' Hawkmoon asked.

'In souls, as I said. In souls. Look, I will admit him.' And the child seemed perturbed as he motioned with his staff. 'He travels, now, from Limbo.'

## CHAPTER FOUR

Captives of the Sword

'I am the Sword,' said the black figure. He waved a hand airily at the massed statues all around them. 'These were mine once. I owned the multiverse.'

'You have been disinherited,' said the child.

'By you?' the black figure smiled.

'No,' said the child. 'We share a fate, as you well know.'

'You cannot give me back the things I must have,' said the figure. 'Where is it?' He looked about him. 'Where?'

'I have not yet summoned it. Where are . . . ?'

'My bartering goods? Those I shall summon when I know that you have what I need.' He grinned a greeting at Hawkmoon and Erekosë, saying carelessly, to nobody in particular, 'I gather that all the gods are dead.'

'Two have fled,' said the child. 'The rest are dead.'

'So only we remain.'

'Aye,' said the child. 'The sword and the staff.'

'Created at the beginning,' said Orland Fank, 'after the last Conjunction.'

'Few mortals know that,' said the black figure. 'My body was made to serve Chaos, his to serve the Balance, others to serve Law, but all those are gone now.'

'What replaces them?' said Erekosë.

'That remains to be decided,' said the black figure. 'I come to barter for that body of mine. Either manifestation will do; or both.'

'You are the Black Sword?'

The child motioned again with the staff. Jhary-a-Conel stood there, his hat at an angle, his cat on his shoulder. At Oladahn he stared with particular bemusement. 'Should we both be here?'

Oladahn said: 'I do not know you sir.'

'Then you do not know yourself, sir.' Jhary bowed to Hawkmoon. 'Greetings. I believe this is yours, Duke Dorian.' He held something in his hands and was moving forward to offer it to Hawkmoon when the child said:

'Stay! Show him.'

Jhary-a-Conel paused somewhat theatrically, eyeing the black figure. 'Show him? Must I? The mewler?'

'Show me,' whispered the black figure. 'Please, Jhary-a-Conel.'

Jhary-a-Conel rubbed at the head of the child, as an uncle might greet a favourite nephew. 'How fare you, cousin?'

'Show him,' said the child.

Jhary-a-Conel put one hand on the pommel of his sword, stuck out his leg, stuck out his elbow, looked thoughtfully at the black figure, then, with a sudden, conjurer's gesture, presented that which lay in his palm.

The black figure hissed. His eyes glowed.

'The Black Jewel!' gasped Hawkmoon. 'You have the Black Jewel.'

'The Jewel will do,' said the figure eagerly. 'Here . . .'

Two men, two women and two children appeared. Golden chains held them; links of golden silk.

'I treat them well,' said the one who called himself Sword.

One of the men, tall, slender, languid of manner, dandified of dress, held up his shackled wrists. 'Oh,' he said, 'this luxury of chains!'

All but one of them did Hawkmoon recognize. And he was full of cold anger now. 'Yisselda! Yarmila and Manfred! D'Averc! Bowgentle! How are you this creature's prisoners?'

'That tale's a long one . . .' began Huillam D'Averc, but his voice was drowned by Erekosë and Erekosë was shouting with joy:

'Ermizhad! My Ermizhad!'

The woman, whom Hawkmoon had not recognized, was of a race resembling Elric's and Corum's. In her own way, she was as beautiful as Yisselda. There was much in the two women's very different faces which provoked a sense of resemblance.

Bowgentle turned an apparently placid face this way and that. 'So we are in Tanelorn at last.'

The woman called Ermizhad was straining at her chains, trying to reach Erekosë.

'I thought you Kalan's prisoners,' said Hawkmoon through the confusion, addressing D'Averc.

'I thought so, too, but I believe this somewhat demented gentleman intercepted our journey through Limbo . . .' D'Averc made a pantomime of dismay as Erekosë glared at the black figure.

'You must release her!'

The being smiled. 'I will have the jewel first. She and the others for the jewel. It was the bargain we made.'

Jhary-a-Conel clenched his fingers around the jewel. 'Why do you not take it from me? You claim power?'

326

'Only a Hero may give it to him,' said the child. 'He knows that.'

'Then I will give it to him,' said Erekosë.

'No,' said Hawkmoon. 'If anyone has the right, I have it. Through the Black Jewel I was made a slave, Now, at least, I can use it to free those I love.'

The expression on the black being's face became eager.

'Not yet,' said the child.

Hawkmoon ignored him. 'Give me the Black Jewel, Jhary.'

Jhary-a-Conel looked first at the one he had addressed as 'cousin', then at Hawkmoon. He hesitated.

'That jewel,' said the child quietly, 'is one aspect of one of the two most powerful things at present existing in the multiverse.'

'And the other?' said Erekosë, looking yearningly at the woman he had sought for through eternity.

'The other is this, the Runestaff.'

'If the Black Jewel is Fear, then what is the Runestaff?' asked Hawkmoon.

'Justice,' said the child, 'the enemy of Fear.'

'If you both hold so much power,' Oladahn said reasonably, 'then why are we involved?'

'Because neither can exist without Man,' said Orland Fank. 'They go with Man wherever He goes.'

'That is why you are here,' said the child. 'We are your creations.'

'Yet you control our destinies.' Erekosë's eyes had never left Ermizhad's. 'How?'

'Because you let us,' the child told him.

'Well, then, "Justice," let me see you keep your word,' said the creature called Sword.

'My word was given that I would admit you to Tanelorn,' said the child. 'I can do no more. The bargain itself must be debated with Hawkmoon and Erekosë.'

'The Black Jewel for your captives? Is that the bargain?' Hawkmoon said. 'What will the jewel give you?'

'It will give him back some of the power he lost during the war between the gods,' said the child. 'And that power will enable him to bring more power for himself and pass easily into the new multiverse which will exist after the Conjunction.'

'Power which will serve you well,' said the black figure to Hawkmoon.

'Power we have never wished for,' said Erekosë.

'What do *we* lose if we agree?' Hawkmoon said.

'You lose my help, almost certainly.'

'Why is that?'

'I shall not say.'

'Mysteries!' said Hawkmoon. 'Discretion sadly misguided in my opinion, Jehamiah Cohnahlias.'

'I say nothing because I respect you,' said the child. 'But if the opportunity should come, then use the staff to smash the jewel.'

Hawkmoon took the Black Jewel from Jhary's hand. It was lifeless, without the familiar pulse, and he knew it was lifeless because that which inhabited it now stood before him in another guise.

'So,' said Hawkmoon, 'this is your home.'

He reached towards the creature, the Black Jewel upon the palm of his hand.

The chains of golden silk fell away from the limbs of the six captives.

Laughing, confident, his eyes glowing with evil triumph, the being took the Black Jewel from Hawkmoon's hand.

Hawkmoon embraced his children. He kissed his daughter. He kissed his son.

Erekosë held Ermizhad in his arms and he could not speak.

And the Spirit of the Black Jewel raised his prize to his lips.

And he swallowed the jewel.

'Take this,' said the child urgently to Hawkmoon. 'Quickly.' He handed Hawkmoon the Runestaff.

The black being shrieked his glee. 'I am myself again! I am more than myself again!'

Hawkmoon kissed Yisselda of Brass.

*'I am myself again!'*

When Hawkmoon looked up, the Spirit of the Black Jewel had vanished.

Hawkmoon turned with a smile to remark on this to the child, Jehamiah Cohnahlias. The child had his back to Hawkmoon at that moment, but his head was turning.

'I have won,' said the child.

His face had turned completely. Hawkmoon thought his heart would stop. He felt faint.

The face of the child was still its own, but it had changed. Now it glowed with a dark aura. Now it grinned with an unholy joy. It was the face of the creature which had swallowed the Black Jewel. It was the face of Sword.

'I have won!'

And the child began to giggle.

And then it began to grow.

It grew until it was the size of one of the statues surrounding the group. Its garments shredded and fell away and it was a man, dark and naked, with a red mouth full of fangs, with a yellow, glaring eye, with a presence which radiated immense and terrifying power.

'I HAVE WON!'

He cast about him, ignoring the party.

'Sword,' he said. 'Now, where is the sword?'

'It is here,' said a new voice. 'I have it here. Can you see me?'

## CHAPTER FIVE

## The Captain and the Steersman

'It was found on the South Ice, at sunrise, after you had but recently left that world, Erekosë. It had performed one action for humanity which was not directly to its benefit and so its spirit was driven from it.'

The Captain stood there, his blind eyes staring beyond them. Next to him was his twin, the steersman, with arms outstretched, the great black runesword held on the flats of both palms.

'It was the manifestation of the sword that we sought,' continued the Captain. 'It was a long quest for us and it lost us our ship.'

'But surely,' said Erekosë, 'so little time has passed since we left you?'

The Captain smiled ironically. 'There is no such thing as time,' he said, 'particularly in Tanelorn, particularly at the Conjunction of the Million Spheres. If time existed, as men consider it, then how can you and Hawkmoon exist here together?'

Erekosë made no reply; he hugged his Eldren princess closer to him.

The being roared. 'GIVE ME THE SWORD!'

'I cannot,' said the Captain, 'as you well know. And you cannot take it. You can only inhabit (or be inhabited by) one of the two manifestations, sword or jewel. Never both.'

The being snarled, but it made no movement towards the Black Sword.

Hawkmoon looked at the staff the child had given him and he saw that he had been right, the runes in the staff corresponded in some manner to those on the sword. He addressed the Captain.

'Who made these artifacts?'

'The smiths who forged this sword long ago, close to the beginning of the Great Cycle, required a spirit to inhabit it to give it power above all other weapons. They struck a bargain with this spirit (whom we shall not name).' The Captain turned his blind head so that it faced the black creature. 'You were glad to accept it, then. Two swords were forged and part of you went into each, but one of the swords was destroyed, so you inhabited wholly the remaining blade. The smiths who forged the swords were not human, but they worked for humanity. They sought to fight Chaos, at that time, for they were loyal to the Lords of Law. They thought they used Chaos to conquer Chaos. They learned the flaws in that belief . . .'

'They did!' The creature grinned. 'Oh, they did!'

'So they made the Runestaff and they sought the aid of your brother, who served Law. They did not realize that you and he are not really brothers at all, but aspects of the same single being, now united again, but infused with the power of the Black Jewel, with your own dark power magnified. A seeming paradox . . .'

'A paradox I find most useful,' said the black being.

The Captain ignored him, continuing: 'They made the jewel in an effort to trap you, to imprison you. It gave the jewel great power, it held the souls of others as well as your own, just as the sword did, but you could be released from the jewel just as sometimes you could be released from the sword . . .'

' "Banished" is a better word,' said the creature, 'for I love my body, the sword. There will always be men to bear me as a sword.'

'Not always,' said the Captain. 'The Cosmic Balance was the last great artifact created by these smiths before they returned to their own worlds – a symbol of Equilibrium between Law and Chaos, it had a power of its own, incorporated into the Runestaff – to produce Order between Law and Chaos. And it is that which checks even you, at this moment.'

'Not when I have the Black Sword!'

'You have tried for so long to assume complete domination of mankind, and sometimes, for a while, you have almost achieved it. The Conjunction takes place on many different worlds, in many different eras, the manifestations of the Champion Eternal perform their great deeds, to rid the multiverse of the gods their forebears' desires created. And, in a world free of gods, you can retain the power you have been greedy for through the ages. You slew Elric in one world; you slew the Silver Queen in another, you sought to slay Corum, you have slain more who thought you served them. But Elric's death set you free and the death of the Silver Queen brought life to the Earth when it was dying (your own interests were served, but the interest of mankind was, at last, served better). You could not get your "body" back. You felt your power waning. The experiments of two insane sorcerers on Hawkmoon's world induced a situation which you could exploit. You need the Champion Eternal, that is your fate, but he no longer needs you, so you had to gather captives and bargain with the Champion for those he loves. Now you have the power of the jewel and you have taken over the body of your brother, who was once Orland Fank's son. Now you would smash the Balance, but you know that in destroying the Balance you will be destroyed yourself. Unless you have a refuge – a new body into which your spirit can escape.'

The Captain turned his head so that his sightless eyes seemed to regard Hawkmoon and Erekosë.

'Moreover,' he said, 'the sword must be wielded by a manifestation of the Champion, and here are two such manifestations. How will you induce one of them to serve your purpose?'

Hawkmoon looked at Erekosë. He said: 'My loyalties were ever to the Runestaff, though I resented giving them, at times.'

'And if I had loyalties, they were to the Black Sword,' said Erekosë.

'Which one of you will bear the Black Sword, then?' said the creature eagerly.

'Neither has to bear it,' the Captain told them quickly.

'But I now have the power to destroy all here,' said the creature.

'All save the two aspects of the Champion Eternal,' said the Captain, 'and my brother and myself, you cannot harm us.'

'I will destroy Ermizhad, Yisselda, the children – these others. I will eat them. I will have their souls.' The black being opened his red mouth wide and he reached a hand of black radiance towards Yarmila. The girl stared bravely back, but she was shrinking from him.

'And what will happen to us after you have destroyed the Balance?' asked Hawkmoon.

'Nothing,' said the being. 'You can live out your lives in Tanelorn. Even I cannot destroy Tanelorn, thought the rest of the multiverse shall be mine.'

'It is true, what he says,' said the Captain. 'And he will keep his word.'

'But all humanity will suffer, save those in Tanelorn,' said Hawkmoon.

'Aye,' said the Captain, 'we shall all suffer, save you.'

'Then he must not be given the sword,' Hawkmoon said firmly, and he could not look at those he loved.

'Humanity suffers already,' Erekosë said. 'I have sought Ermizhad through eternity. I deserve this. I have served humanity through eternity, save once. I have suffered too long.'

'Would you repeat a crime?' asked the Captain quietly.

Erekosë ignored him, staring meaningfully at Hawkmoon. 'The power of the Black Sword and the power of the Balance are equal at

332

this moment, you say, Captain.'

'That's so.'

'And this being can inhabit either the sword or the jewel, not both?'

And Hawkmoon understood the implication of Erekosë's questions and kept his face expressionless.

'Hurry!' said the black being from behind them. 'Hurry. The Balance materializes!'

For an instant, Hawkmoon felt something of the experience that he had had when they had fought Agak and Gagak together, a oneness with Erekosë, sharing his emotions and his thoughts.

'Hurry, Erekosë,' said the being. 'Take the sword!'

Erekosë turned his back on Hawkmoon, staring up into the sky.

The Cosmic Balance hung, shining, in the sky, its scales in perfect equilibrium. It hung over that great concourse of statues, over every manifestation of the Eternal Champion there had ever been, over every woman he had ever loved, over every companion he had ever had. And, at that moment, it appeared to menace them all.

Erekosë took three paces until he stood before the steersman. There was no expression on the face of either man.

'Give me the Black Sword,' said the Eternal Champion.

## CHAPTER SIX

## The Sword and the Staff

Erekosë placed one large hand upon the hilt of the Black Sword and he placed the other under the blade, lifting it from the steersman's grasp.

'Ah!' cried the creature. 'We are united!'

And he flowed towards the Black Sword and he laughed as he entered it, and the sword began to pulse, to sing, to emanate black fire, and the creature was gone.

But, Hawkmoon noticed, the Black Jewel had returned. He saw Jhary-a-Conel stoop and pick it up.

Now Erekosë's face glowed with a light of its own – a light of violence, a battle joy. His voice was a vibrating roar, a snarl of triumph. His eyes were alive with blood lust as he held the sword in two hands over his head, staring up at its long blade.

'At last!' he shouted. 'Erekosë shall have revenge on that which has manipulated his fate for so long! I will destroy the Cosmic Balance. With the Black Sword I will make amends for all the agony I have suffered through all the long ages of the multiverse! No longer do I serve humanity. Now I serve only the sword. Thus I shall be released from the bondage of aeons!'

And the sword moaned and writhed and its black radiance fell upon Erekosë's warrior's face and was reflected in his battle-mad eyes.

*'Now, I destroy the Balance!'*

And the sword seemed to pull Erekosë from the ground, up into the sky, up towards where the Balance hung, serene, apparently invulnerable, and Erekosë, Champion Eternal, had become huge and the sword blotted the light from the land.

Hawkmoon continued to watch, but he said to Jhary-a-Conel, 'Jhary – the jewel – place it before me on the ground.'

And Erekosë drew back his two arms to strike his blow. And he struck once.

There came a sound as if ten million large bells rang at once, a shattering noise as if the very cosmos cracked apart, and the Black

Sword cut through the links holding one of the scales and it began to fall, the other scale rising higher, the beam swinging rapidly on its axis.

And the world shuddered.

The vast circle of statues trembled and threatened to tumble to the ground, and all who watched gasped.

And somewhere, something fell and broke into invisible fragments.

They heard laughter from the sky, but it was impossible to tell if the sword or the man who bore it was the source.

Erekosë, huge and dreadful, drew back his arms for the second stroke.

The sword swept through the sky and lightning flashed, thunder growled. It cut into the chains holding the other scale and that, too, fell.

And again the world shuddered.

And the Captain whispered: 'You have rid the worlds of gods, but now you rid it of order, too.'

'Only of Authority,' said Hawkmoon.

The steersman looked at him with intelligence, with interest.

Hawkmoon looked at the ground where the Black Jewel lay, dull, without life. Then he looked at the sky as Erekosë struck his third and final blow, struck at the central staff of the ruined Balance.

And light broke from the shattered remains and a strange, near-human howling reverberated through the world, and they were blinded and they were deafened.

But Hawkmoon heard the single word he waited for. He heard Erekosë's giant's voice call:

'NOW!'

And suddenly, the Runestaff was throbbing with life in Hawkmoon's right hand, and the Black Jewel began to pulse, and Hawkmoon raised his arm for a single, powerful blow, the only blow which would be allowed him.

And he brought the Runestaff down with all his might upon the pulsing jewel.

And the jewel shattered and it shouted and it moaned in outrage, and the staff shattered, too, in Hawkmoon's hand, and the dark light bursting from the one met with the golden light bursting from the other. There came a screaming, a wailing, a whimper, and finally the whimper died, and a ball of red stuff hung before them, glowing only faintly, for the power of the Runestaff had cancelled out the power of the Black Sword. Then the red globe began to rise into the sky, higher and higher, until it hung directly over their heads.

And Hawkmoon was reminded of the star which had followed the Dark Ship on its voyage through the Seas of Limbo.

And then the red globe was absorbed into the warmer red of the sun itself.

The Black Jewel was gone. The Runestaff was gone. Destroyed, too, were the Black Sword and the Cosmic Balance. For a moment, their substance had sought refuge respectively in the jewel and the staff and it had been at that moment, when one destroyed the other, that Hawkmoon could use the other to destroy the one. It was what Erekosë had been able to agree with him just before he accepted the Black Sword.

And now something fell at Hawkmoon's feet.

Weeping, Ermizhad kneeled beside the corpse. 'Erekosë! Erekosë!'

'He has paid at last,' said Orland Fank. 'And at last he rests. He found Tanelorn and he found you, Ermizhad – and, finding them, he died for them.'

But Ermizhad did not hear Orland Fank, for she was weeping; she was lost.

CHAPTER SEVEN

## Going Back to Castle Brass

'The time of the Conjunction is almost passed,' said the Captain, 'and the multiverse begins another cycle. Free of gods, free of what you, Hawkmoon, might term "cosmic authority". Perhaps it will never need heroes again.'

'Only examples,' said Jhary-a-Conel. He was walking towards the statues, towards an empty space in the ranks. 'Farewell all of you. Farewell, Champion Who is no longer Champion, and farewell to you, in particular, Oladahn.'

'Where do you go, friend?' asked the kin of the Mountain Giants, scratching at the red fur of his head.

Jhary stopped and removed the little black and white cat from his shoulder. He pointed at the empty space amongst the statues. 'I go to take my place there. You live. I live. Farewell to you, for the very last time.'

And he stepped amongst the statues, and instantly he was a statue, cocky, smiling, pleased with himself.

'Is there a place for me there, too?' said Hawkmoon, turning to Orland Fank.

'Not now,' said the Orkneyman, picking up Jhary-a-Conel's winged cat and stroking its back. It purred.

Ermizhad stood up and the tears were gone from her eyes. Saying nothing to the others, she, too, stepped into the ranks of the statues, finding another space. She raised her hand in a gesture of farewell, her flesh turned to the same pale colour of the surrounding statues and she stood frozen as they were frozen, and Hawkmoon saw that near her was another statue, the statue of Erekosë, who had sacrificed his life by taking up the Black Sword.

'Now,' said the Captain, 'would you and yours stay in Tanelorn, Hawkmoon? You have earned the right.'

Hawkmoon put his arms around the shoulders of his children. He saw that there was happiness in them and he became happy. Yisselda put her hand to his cheek and smiled at him.

'No,' said Hawkmoon, 'we go back, I think, to Castle Brass. It is enough for us to know that Tanelorn exists. What of you, D'Averc?

Oladahn? And you, Sir Bowgentle?'

'I have much to tell you, Hawkmoon, beside a good fire, with the good wine of the Kamarg in my hand, with good friends around me,' said Huillam D'Averc. 'At Castle Brass my tales would be of interest, but they would only bore the folk of Tanelorn. I'll come with you.'

'And I,' said Oladahn.

Bowgentle, alone, seemed a little reluctant. He looked thoughtfully at the statues and back at the towers of Tanelorn. 'An interesting place. What created it, I wonder?'

'We created it,' said the Captain, 'my brother and I.'

'You?' Bowgentle smiled. 'I see.'

'And what is your name, sir?' Hawkmoon asked. 'You and your brother, what are you called?'

'We have only one name,' said the Captain.

The steersman took his brother by the arm and began to lead him away from the circle of statues, back towards the city.

In silence, Hawkmoon, his family and his friends watched them go.

It was Orland Fank, clearing his throat, who broke the silence. 'I will stay, I think. My tasks are all completed. My quest is finished. I have seen my son come to peace of a kind. I will stay in Tanelorn.'

'Are there no gods left for you to serve?' asked Brut of Lashmar.

'Gods are but metaphors.' said Orland Fank. 'As metaphors they might be very acceptable – but they should never be allowed to become beings in their own right.' Again he cleared his throat, seeming embarrassed by his next remark, 'The wine of poetry turns to poison when it becomes politics, eh?'

'You three are welcome to come to Castle Brass with us,' said Hawkmoon to the warriors.

Emshon of Ariso fiddled with his moustache and looked inquiringly at John ap-Rhyss who looked, in turn, at Brut of Lashmar.

'Our journey is over,' said Brut.

'We are but ordinary soldiers,' said John ap-Rhyss. 'No history will count us heroes. I stay in Tanelorn.'

'I begin my life as a teacher in a school,' said Emshon of Ariso. 'It was never my dream to go warring. But there were indignities, inequalities, injustices and it seemed to me that only a sword could correct those things. I did my best. I have earned my peace. I, too, stay in Tanelorn. I would like to write a book, I think.'

Hawkmoon bowed his head in acknowledgement of their decision. 'I thank you, friends, for your help.'

'You would not stay with us?' said John ap-Rhyss. 'Have you not also earned the right to dwell here?'

'Perhaps, but I have a great liking for old Castle Brass, and I have left a friend there. Perhaps we can speak of what we know and show folk how to find Tanelorn within themselves.'

'Given the chance,' said Orland Fank, 'most find it. Only gods and the worship of fallacy, fear of their own humanity, blocks their path to Tanelorn.'

'Oh, I fear for my carefully manufactured personality!' laughed Huillam D'Averc. 'Is there anything duller than a reformed cynic?'

'Let Queen Flana decide that,' grinned Hawkmoon. 'Well, Orland Fank, we speak much of leaving – but how shall we leave now that there are no supernatural creatures to direct our destinies, now that the Champion is laid, at last, to rest?'

'I still have a little of my old power left,' said the Orkneyman, almost insulted. 'And it is easily used while the Spheres remain in Conjunction. And since it was partly my doing, and partly the doing of those seven you met in the unformed world of Limbo, it suits me to put you back upon your original journey.' His red face broke into a smile which was almost merry. 'Goodbye to ye all, Heroes of the Kamarg. Ye go to a world free of all authority. Be sure that the only authority you seek in future is the quiet authority which comes from self-respect.'

'You were ever a moralist, Orland Fank!' Bowgentle clapped his hand upon the Orkneyman's shoulder. 'But it is an art to make such simple morality work in a complicated world!'

'It is only the darkness of our own minds which makes for complications,' said Orland Fank. 'Good luck, too!' And he was laughing now, his bonnet bobbing on his head. 'Let us hope this is an end of tragedy.'

'And the beginning, perhaps, of comedy,' said Huillam D'Averc, smiling and shaking his head. 'Come – Count Brass awaits us!'

And they stood upon the Silver Bridge amongst the other travellers who moved to and fro upon that mighty highway, and the bright, winter sunshine shone down on them, making the sea sparkle with reflected silver.

'The world!' cried Huillam D'Averc in considerable relish. 'At last, at last, the world!'

Hawkmoon found D'Averc's joy infectious. 'Where do you go? To Londra or the Kamarg?'

'To Londra, of course, at once!' said D'Averc. 'After all, a kingdom awaits me.'

'You were never a cynic, Huillam D'Averc,' said Yisselda of Brass, 'and you cannot make us think you are one now. Give our greetings to Queen Flana. Tell her we shall visit her soon.'

Huillam D'Averc bowed with a flourish. 'And my greetings, in turn, to your father, Count Brass. Tell him I shall be sitting beside his fire before long and drinking his wine. Is the castle as draughty as it ever was?'

'We shall prepare a room suitable for one of your delicate health,' Yisselda told him. She took the hand of her son Manfred and the hand of her daughter Yarmila. For the first time, she noticed that Yarmila was holding something. It was Jhary-a-Conel's small black and white cat.

'Master Fank gave it to me, mother,' said the child.

'Treat it well, then,' said her father, 'for it is a rarity, that little beast.'

'Farewell for the moment, Huillam D'Averc,' said Bowgentle. 'I found most interesting the time we spent in Limbo.'

'I, too, Master Bowgentle. Though I still wish we had had that deck of cards.' Again, the dandy bowed. 'And good-bye, Oladahn, smallest of giants. I wish I could listen to your boastings when you return to the Kamarg.'

'They would be no match for yours, sir, I fear.' Oladahn stroked his whiskers, pleased with the retort. 'I look forward to your visit.'

Hawkmoon began to stride forward along the shining roadway, eager to begin the journey back to Castle Brass, where the children would meet their noble old grandfather.

'We'll purchase horses at Karlye,' he said. 'We have credit there.' He turned to his son. 'Tell me, Manfred, what do you remember of your adventures?' He tried to disguise a certain anxiety for his son. 'Do you remember a great deal?'

'No, father,' said Manfred kindly, 'I remember very little.' And he ran forward, and, taking his father's hand, led him towards the distant shore.

*This ends the Third and Last of the Chronicles of Castle Brass.*
*This ends the long story of the Eternal Champion.*